GODDESS OF ORIGIN

CHIARA FORESTIERI

For those who aspire to bring more love into the world... Our sole purpose and moral imperative.

1

Despite the frigid air, my bare skin burned beneath the sun. A violent shudder reverberated through my bones as hammer met crystal with each pounding blow. A deafening cacophony as hundreds of us laboured to harvest the precious crystal traded throughout the realm.

The crisp breeze was the only relief any of us found as it kissed and caressed our sweaty, dust and dirt-caked skin. The pealing of a bronze bell sounded, yanking my distant mind back into my aching body. I looked around at those near me, labourers and guards, to see if anyone was looking and as I began carrying the newly hewn crystal boulders to the quarry carts, I let a shard-like chunk fall off into my hand. I glanced down at its shimmering brilliance and stole a glance behind me- no one was looking. I raised my hand, feigning the need to wipe the dirt from my brow, and pocketed the chunk of luminous crystal in my mouth.

. . .

When my brother and I finished our work, we made our way to the bathing lake, where Queen Nuala's sentries patted us down to check for anyone who might be trying to steal aeternam crystals. Like me. I grinned up at the handsome sentry who took his time patting me down, praying to the gods he wouldn't ask me anything that would actually require a response. His eyes met mine, and my breathing stilled, on the cusp of panic, for the split second before he gave me a wink and moved on to the labourer beside me. I swallowed against the hidden chunk of crystal I held beneath my tongue as I clenched my jaw at the bite of the ice-cold water, thanking the gods I'd been fortunate enough to escape with some aeternam crystal today. Had I been caught, I'd have been publicly flogged. Again. I quickly ducked beneath the surface to cleanse my hair and rose from the icy water, pale clouds of beige swirling around my waist in the crystalline water as my skin quickly grew numb.

By the time we arrived back to the resident quarter of Pauperes Domos- the area of slum dwellings that Queen Nuala's poorest working class called home- I had been wind-whipped dry again. As my body found the firm but welcome bedroll of the top bunk of mine and my brother's home, I was mildly surprised by the question that rose within my mind. *Would I miss this place? My home?* Despite the fact that the quarry, that frigid lake, and our tiny home were all I had ever known, the answer was most certainly *no*. I was born in that crystal quarry. My mother died giving birth to me there. My father, who had been killed in an accident at the quarry nearly two years ago, had found himself here with my mother, among so many others after they'd lost the war almost two hundred years ago.

A war in which the Queen, who was said to also possess a *chimera* form, in her thirst for power, conquered the entire Realm of Aeternia- a world made up of two large continents and several archipelagos. Aerternus, the capital continent consisting of the four guards- North, South, East, and West- was where most of the realm's population resided. The other continent- Ferox- was an infamously wild place. As were most of the other Archipelagos. Aeternus also had the largest known deposit of this realms most precious resource: aeternam crystal. The crystal is what provided power to the entire realm and was also a form of currency only the most wealthy possessed. Prior to the war, Aeternia's former ruler, Emperor Orova, had been surveying Feroxian lands to find more aeternam deposits. All of that ended with Nuala.

My family had been wealthy before the war. Nobility, even. On the lower rungs of it, but nobility nonetheless. So they'd said. My father and mother were barons within the Western Guard. That would have made me a baroness by birth. Yet I had never been given a chance to experience anything other than the poverty I'd been born into.

The city of Pauperes Domos had been created to serve as the dwelling area for the former nobility and those of the *bayathus* class that had lost the war. The bayathus class or the bayathi referred to those that had once possessed substantial wealth and affluence, which had fought and conspired against Nuala and her militia before she won the war and dubbed herself Queen. And Pauperes Domos was now inhabited entirely by them; the ones who survived the war and their offspring. The majority of their wealth and fixed assets stripped from them to prevent them from rising against the Queen.

The city lay far outside of any of the realm's other towns and villages where the rest of the world dwelled. All that filled and surrounded Pauperes Domos were its slum dwellings, a crumbling central town, and agricultural and industrial sites such as the quarry where my brother, Mateus, and I worked. It was a bleak existence and the only one I'd ever known because now, people were born here, and they died here. We were all too poor to leave, forced to wear magic-suppressing palladium collars, and the only safe way out of the city was via train that required a permit that was nearly impossible to obtain. The train was almost solely used by the Queen's Royal Sentry. Pauperes Domos had become so riddled with crime that, while originally a self-governed populous, the Queen had to send her Royal Sentry to patrol the streets and enforce a curfew.

However, the biggest reason no one ever left Pauperes Domos was because of what surrounded it. The Sable Forest. Which was precisely where we were headed.

As my brother turned off the aeternam lanterns, casting the room in utter blackness, I laid there wide awake. My heart pounding for what felt like aeons, idly fiddling with my newest shard of aeternam crystal. Those of us who dared had each been stealing one at a time, as often as possible, to sell once we made the journey out of Pauperes Domos and the Sable Forest, if we survived, to help us settle in the outside world. Just a few would be enough to secure lodging and food for at least a month or so while we got our feet on the ground. The aeternam crystal provided the energy required to power homes, machinery, and the like across the realm. It was the best form of currency anyone in our realm could have and was coveted in realms even outside of Aeternus because we were the only known realm that possessed it as a natural resource.

I finally felt the grasp of a warm, calloused hand around my arm. Wordlessly, I sat up and silently climbed down from the top bunk, pulling the small *kitchen* knife out from
    underneath my pillow and sliding it into the makeshift sheath strapped to my thigh.

My head emerged from around the wooden door at the back of our tiny, terraced hut. The ice-cold wind slammed into my face as my brother's hand extended toward me. "Hurry," Mateus whispered. Even in the pale moonlight of the newly waxing moon, I could still see the warmth in his face.

As silently as possible, I practically held my breath the entire time Mateus and I ran through the winding maze of tiny, dilapidated homes on the city's outskirts. Thankfully, most of the Sentry's attention was usually focused on the more central part of city where most of the crime occurred. Few had ever dared to escape via the Sable Forest.

When we finally made our way beyond the hundreds of crumbling tenements, through the gate that always remained open, and found the realm's most unwelcoming welcome sign, I felt as though I could finally exhale the breath I'd been holding. We saw several shadows sneaking ahead of us in the distance where our group, either phenomenally brave, or fatally optimistic, souls had decided to rendezvous before making our escape together. Three months ago, I had spoken to my brother about escaping, who then began talking to others. And there we were, at last.

A dozen of us stood in the shadow of the 30-foot stone wall beside the welcome sign reading, 'Pauperes Domos - Enter at Own Risk - All Visitors Must Leave by Dusk - Resident Curfew Dusk til Dawn - Enforced by Penalty of Electrocution Until Cusp of Death'. I could taste the energy in the air. One of hope, anxiety, excitement, and fear. Once the moon reached its zenith, the last of us arrived, and we exchanged a few glances and nods, not wanting to risk speaking aloud and accidentally alerting the Sentry. The group of us turned towards the Sable Forest in unison and ran without a glance back.

Mateus flashed me his white teeth, lips parting in a galvanizing smile as we sprinted side by side towards the black tree line of the forest. Anxiety tightened in my chest as the sound of heavy breathing and the rushing whispers of our feet on the dense foliage that covered the forest floor filled my ears. I could feel the life within the forest watching us, running from us, in our manic race through the trees.

After what must have been more than an hour, the cold air in my lungs began to feel like lancing spears but as soon as I felt the foliage beneath our feet become rocky. A rush of relief and joy filled me as the sound of pounding water joined us. We emerged from the tree line to face another, across a rushing and turbulent river. I'd never seen one in real life. I'd only ever heard of them. It was so beautiful it made my heart ache. From what the elders had told us, upon reaching the river, we had reached the border of the Northern and Western Guards.

Several escapees were already down at the river's edge, forming a hand-to-hand chain to try and safely cross through the torrential waters. Mateus and I lowered ourselves towards the water, grappling down on an exposed tree
root. As I looked down to see him standing beneath me with open arms, waiting to catch me, something caught my eye. The gaze of another. Across the river, the iridescent glow of a nocturnal predator's eyes met mine- stealing the very breath from my lungs as it stepped into the moonlight.

.   .   .

Seven feet of a towering humanoid beast. Its body appeared to be missing the layers of skin that would typically cover the corded muscle beneath. The exposed strands of intertwining muscle tissue and ligaments were blacker than the midnight sky. Mateus' gaze followed mine. And like a row of dominoes, the escapees' gazes fell on it as it grinned. "*Bayathi.* How the tides have changed. What a gift the Gods and Goddesses have bestowed upon us. And though I see time has not been kind, and you are no longer fat and delicious as you once were, I will enjoy devouring you with equal fervor."

Even the glorious scent of the forest, the moist, dense earth beneath, and the river's crystalline water couldn't mask the palpable odor of our fear. Its bitter, oily taste slithered onto my tongue, forcing me to swallow.

Pair by pair, more nocturnal eyes appeared behind the tall creature and stepped out of the forest to join it. Creatures like it, and others. Like Lykanthirs, *wolf shifters,* who were double our height on hind legs. The escapees nearest the beasts were the first to scream and, as though those screams were a starting pistol, the lykanthirs and dark fae, if that's what they could be called, beside them charged towards us.

Horror tore through me. I had led them here. Mateus looked up at me, fear and panic searing his gaze. "Run," he breathed as he shoved me back over the edge into the forest. With the force of his push, I face-planted in the dirt and tree roots and leapt up to turn and help him climb over the edge. "Run, Aurelia!" He roared. "I'm not leaving you!" I screamed back as Mateus launched himself over the edge and turned to pull those nearest back up. "Aurelia, go!" For a fleeting moment, I watched the horror unfold around the river. The beasts tore our friends limb from limb with preternatural ease. My throat seemed to close as my heart pounded furiously against my ribcage. Mateus yelled over his shoulder, "I'm right behind you, just go!" as he yanked a female over the ledge.

I reached to help Rolam, an older fae male I'd known since we were children, climb over, but as he went to grip my arm, the root he was grabbing onto snapped, and before I could catch him, he fell back to the ground below. *"No!"* I screamed in horror, unheard over the screams and snapping of bones and sinew coming from the river. He didn't move for a painfully long second, and I looked up to find one of the monstrosities standing in the middle of the rushing river, gore dripping from its mouth, as it scanned the vicinity for new prey to tear.

As though feeling the heat of my gaze, its head snapped in my direction, and looked straight into my eyes. He tilted his head, studying me with what almost seemed like curiosity, a grin slowly carving his face, before his gaze flicked down at Rolam and leapt. A spear of terror lanced my heart as Mateus yanked me backwards by my collar. I jumped to my feet to follow Mateus and the others he'd managed to help up, but I couldn't see them in the darkness. Mateus gripped my arm as we sprinted through the dense forest but I could barely see more than a foot or two in front of me. Never in my life did I ever imagine I'd be praying to be back in Pauperes Domos.

My foot snagged on a root, and I went flying forward. My fingers yanked free from Mateus'. "Aurelia!" He shouted frantically as he turned to run back towards me but abruptly stopped in his tracks. I looked up at him as I scrambled back to my feet to see Mateus slowly stepping backward as a lykanthir appeared between the trees, growling menacingly. Mateus' eyes briefly met mine, a meaningful look that shattered my heart like nothing I'd ever experienced.

"*Don't-*" I shrieked as he turned and ran, bating the lykanthir after him, so I had a chance of escape.

The lykanthir snarled, leaping and bounding behind him into the darkness. The sound of twigs snapping behind me sent a new bayonet of fear up my spine, launching me into another run. Pure adrenaline and the sound of what could only be an apex predator closing in behind me were all that kept my frozen lungs from bursting and my burning limbs in forward motion.

After only a few brief moments, a heavy body slammed into me, barreling us into a tree trunk. I gaped like a fish trying to breathe out of water as my lungs fought for the air that had been knocked out of them. All while trying to scramble out from beneath my attacker. I lashed out, kicking my legs at the dark humanoid creature who'd spotted me by the river. His laugh was a raspy, wet scrape as he pinned me down. His teeth glistened with someone else's blood as he smiled down at me. "I'm going to savor you bit by-" His words were cut off in a gurgle as I plunged my small kitchen knife into the side of his neck and *twisted*. Blood sprayed onto my face as I ripped the blade free. He fell to my side, clutching at his throat. I plunged the knife into his chest, where his heart was, just in case the throat wound healed too fast. The snarling of a lykanthir only a few feet away had me scrambling to my feet. I gripped the blood-slicked knife in my hand, knowing my chances of outrunning him were nonexistent.

The wolf lunged for me and put me flat on my back. I braced its neck against my forearm, trying to keep its colossal maw away from my head. Bloody saliva dripped onto my already blood-splattered face. With my free arm, gripping the knife, I swung at its face and managed to stab its eye. It yelped and rolled off me, taking my weapon with it, shaking its head furiously, trying to paw the knife from it.

I took this opportunity to turn and run, only making it a dozen feet before being slammed to the ground again as its jaws clamped down on my leg. I kicked at its wounded, empty eye socket, only further infuriating it as its snarling maw went for my legs again, but before it could clamp down, the lykanthir was suddenly ripped away. It howled shrilly in pain, the cracking of its bones audible as it slammed into a nearby tree trunk.

Standing before me stood the silhouette of a tall, broad male whose face I couldn't make out in the darkness. His clothes were black. A palace sentry, I could only assume. He towered above the crying wolf and ripped it's throat out with a single swift, graceful movement. The figure panted, scanning the vicinity for more threats. A fiery throbbing sensation had my gaze falling to the spurting blood that poured out of the wound on my leg. *Too much blood.* The vicious bite had lacerated my flesh so deeply that the lips of the wound were already beginning to curl. I tried to clamp my hands over it to slow the bleeding but electrifying pain shot through me. My breathing became shallow, uneven, as my body numbed. The sentry made his way toward me as my vision began to blur.

A breath later, strong but gentle hands were on me, scooping me up, as consciousness fled me.

2

The bitter, oily smell of fear was heavy, and the pallid taste of despair was like a poison that filled my nostrils and coated my tongue. I opened my eyes to find myself in a dungeon cell. My hand carefully wandered to the wound on my leg... That had already healed. Thankfully, the cursed palladium collar around my neck at least allowed the wearer's innate healing magic to function, despite suppressing all other forms of magic. I knew not what mine even were. Still, I was surprised it'd healed so fast.

I laid there for several moments, shaking as the horrific memories returned to me. Soul-crushing grief and guilt now cracked open my chest. It had been my idea to escape, and my brother and our friends had met violent ends because of me. I prayed that Mateus and at least some of the others had also escaped. Perhaps they had been rescued by guards as well. The thought gave me a tiny blossom of hope. Maybe I'd be sent back to Pauperes Domos soon after receiving my punishment- I already knew it'd fall somewhere between flogging or some other form of torture and death.

. . .

At this point, after watching my bother run away from the lykanthir and knowing his chances of survival were next to nonexistent... I felt nothing but apathy towards death. Mateus was strong and fast but nothing compared to a lykanthir. The idea that I had led these people to their death, and returning to Pauperes Domos without my brother, made me wish for it myself.

In desperation and clinging to that tiny blossom of hope, I called out into the dungeon several times for Mateus, willing for him to be here. To have survived. Only to be met with silence. For what was most likely hours, I wept. Violently. Until my throat was so hoarse it could project no more sound and I laid there wishing I had died with them. At some point, I must have fallen asleep, but when I awoke, the night was still pitch black, save for the waxing moon and starlight shining upon the land outside the small, barred dungeon cell hole that failed to pretend it was a window.

I stared out of that hole in the wall, utterly motionless, for so long that I watched the stars and moon shift in the sky until I heard a *tap, tap, tap.* I held my breath as I strained my ears. *Tap, tap, tap.* The gentle tapping of a finger on glass. I picked my head up, looking around for the source of the sound and saw a large frame leaning against the wall of a darkened corner. The dungeon was nearly pitch black, save for the sliver of moonlight shining in through the barred hole that I hadn't noticed it. *Tap, tap, tap.* My throat worked on a swallow, and I shifted to sit up. *Tap, tap, tap, tap, tap.*

I rose to stand on weak legs, walked over to the frame, gripped the edges, and turned it around- no minor feat, considering how large it was. I leaned it against the opposite wall and stepped in front of it. Stars. Or the reflection of them from the window. And standing beside those stars was a swirling shadow through which peered a silver gaze. My whole being stilled. Despite its somewhat chilling, otherworldliness, all the fear had already been beaten out of me so I simply froze, watching it apathetically while it stared curiously from behind the pane of mirrored glass it stood behind.

"Aurelia Eleftheran." Its voice was deep and melodious in an ethereal way that made all my hairs stand on end. And although I made no attempt to move or speak, it must have recognized the acceleration of my heartbeat. "I wish you no harm," the moving shadow spoke soothingly.

I took a few steps away and laid back down on the ground, planting my face sideways on the grimy dirt floor to face the mirror. I searched my memory, trying to recall what type of being here could be incorporeal. And the fact it was trapped in a mirror gave me the most likely answer, causing my heart to thump a little louder in my chest. Less out of fear, more out of awe. *A Vagus.*

The parents in Pauperes Domos, my father included, used to tell us horror stories of a shadowy being from another dimension. No one knew exactly which one, only that it could travel through time and space, even between realms, as though it were walking from one door to another. It had access to the knowledge of all things past, present, and future potentialities and beyond. The terrifying part is that this creature had a thirst for not blood- but souls. It was said that if you were to come across one, it didn't even have to lift a finger to drain the very life force within you in seconds.

Supposedly, there was no way to kill one. The most you could do was trap it, which was only possible if it were in its incorporeal form- a rare sight. And to trap it, it needed to pass in front of a mirror warded from escape. I dared to ask it- him- a question., the words of which I nearly choked on as I croaked them out, "Is he alive?"

The Vagus stared at me, swathes of shadows billowing and whirling around him, occasionally revealing parts of his corporeal form- a shoulder, a mouth, a leg. Before he spoke, his silver eyes not breaking their gaze on me, I caught a glimpse of his mouth. He seemed to be frowning. As he hesitated to respond, I felt my heart cave in on itself, knowing the cause of his grave expression, and the tears once again resumed streaking down my filthy cheeks.

The Vagus gave a subtle shake of his head as he studied me with eyes that, shown with something like compassion, merely said, "They are no longer in this dimension." *So dead.* "Did anyone else from Pauperes Domos survive?" His eyes glowed brightly for a moment before responding. "They have found their peace." My lungs expelled a ragged breath as another sob racked through me. If I hadn't been so fucking ignorant and blithely optimistic... They'd still be alive with their families. *My brother* would still be alive. I wished with every ounce of my being I'd have died with them. It wasn't fair that I was the only one who survived, especially when I was responsible for planting the seed in their mind. Who had led them directly to their demise. Only hours ago, our hearts had been bursting with excitement and hope at finally making our escape. And I hadn't been able to do anything to save them or protect them.

Sensing my mental thread, he said, "It's not your fault, Aurelia. You may have been the first to take action, but they all already had the burning desire. And you couldn't control the outcome. You all knew death was a possibility. They knew, just as much as you, that some things are worth dying for." I shook my head, trying to speak through a sob. Nothing intelligible escaped my lips, but the vagus understood regardless. "I see what lies ahead of you, and I can assure you it was not your time."

His words failed to give me any sense of relief. "I can only hope that it will come soon." The vagus was silent for another moment. I glanced at him as he appeared to sit on the ground of whatever space the inside of that mirror provided and leaned against the frame looking over at me. "No, you won't leave this body for quite some time. I think you'll be glad of it soon enough." His words only left me feeling numb.

I looked over at him as he continued to study me with piercing eyes. His shadows dissipated to reveal his humanoid form. He looked young. Perhaps in his thirties. Although he was sitting, I could tell he was tall and had broad shoulders complimenting his powerful physique. It was alarming how human he looked. Not that I could judge, my parents were both fae, yet somehow, I'd been born with rounded ears. He was strikingly handsome: darkly tanned, bronze skin, his beautiful face held a piercing turquoise gaze that seemed to be every shade of blue and green with flecks of gold. His strong jaw featured curved lips and a straight nose. His hair was dark gold and slightly unkempt. And I swear I saw a few feathers peaking out around the hairline at his neck. He wore strange clothing in a style I'd never seen before. Reminding me that he was from another dimension altogether. The sleeves of a simple white shirt with buttons down the front were rolled up his muscular forearms to reveal tribal-looking tattoos with ancient symbols and designs, the most notable of which was the large feathered serpent, on his right hand, whose open maw ended at his fist.

He held my gaze for what seemed like a small eternity, and I felt myself drifting off to sleep. His eyes seemed to reflect whole galaxies and realms within. Thoughts of my present circumstances and the horror of the night drifted away. I felt myself floating, and I wondered if I was dying, and found myself completely at peace with the notion. His ethereal voice whispered in my mind. *"Sleep, Aurelia."*

When I awoke, the first rays of dawn were peaking through the window, illuminating half of The Vagus' mirror. Where he was silver last night, he was now gold and bronze. Golden wisps of shadow and magic swirled around him had dissipated to fully reveal his corporeal form. "Is that your true form?" He chuckled, walking to one corner of the mirror, up the side of it and on the top, upside down, as if defying gravity. His form again became dissolute whorls of vapor, incorporeal, before he shifted once again to stand in his corporeal form at the bottom centre of the mirror.

"The only true form anyone has cannot be perceived in this dimension." I sighed heavily, not even having the energy or desire to respond. He smiled softly at me with encouragement and compassion. "Perhaps you have questions you'd like me to answer for you? You won't be in here much longer." My eyes burned in anguish as I raised my voice, "I have no questions, and my only hope is that the Queen's punishment is death."

I could feel the glass separating us tremble as The Vagus' power pressed against the mirror. A deep frown carved his face. "How very short-sighted. And futile. There is no such thing as death. What you call death is nothing more than the equivalent of changing one's coat... Tell me why you left Pauperes Domos, Aurelia."

My salty tears burned the still healing cuts on my face as I tried to gather my breath at the memory, "Freedom, obviously." "Freedom for whom?" I baulked, ashamed to admit my ridiculous, lifelong aspiration. "I wanted freedom for us all. I wanted to bring freedom and peace not only to Aeternia but all the nine realms." At his silence and my shame, I continued. "I know it's absurd and grandiose, but ever since I was little and realized that there was more to life than indentured servitude, I, for some reason, felt like I might be able to do something to change it. I've no idea how or why I ever felt it was a remote possibility."

A soft smile danced across The Vagus' face. His eyes seemed to shimmer with that mysterious light emanating beneath the surface. "There is someone who can help you achieve this..." I stared at him, apathetically waiting for a response. "The Goddess of Origin," he grinned. I couldn't even be bothered to roll my eyes at this. "How long have you been stuck in there? She died in the war." The vagus hummed. "And what exactly have I been saying to you?" I rolled onto my back, growing increasingly restless with this conversation. "No such thing as death. Got it... And even if she was alive, I doubt she'd be much help. She's only the most evil being to ever walk the realm."

The mirror trapping the vagus shuddered again as he threw his head back in laughter. I sighed in exhaustion. What did he know. He was probably as evil as she was. His words were lighthearted with curiosity. "How fascinating. I wonder what led you to believe that."

The soul-deep anguish was the only thing my mind could process at the moment. Whatever he was trying to tell me about The Goddess of Origin and reminding me that there was no such thing as death, I had no idea. It was kind of him to try and console me with the notion that my brother was, in fact, still living but just in another form... and it did, in the very back of my mind, plant a seed that perhaps would blossom into something that would give me peace eventually.

However, at the moment, there was nothing that could give me peace. And why he suggested I find the spirit of some long since dead Goddess... Well, it was beyond me. Not to mention impossible. The nine realms were possible to travel through should someone be powerful enough. But to travel across dimensions... I'd never even heard of such a thing. Although... The vagus was right here in front of me. So perhaps not '*im*possible'. But definitely far beyond the capabilities of anyone I'd ever known or heard of.

The Goddess of Origin, from what I'd been taught in Pauperes Domos, was a Goddess primarily known for being capable of exerting her will over all life, including spirits. Meaning she could raise the dead or kill someone with a single thought by forcing their spirit to leave their body. That kind of power.... was unfathomable. Dangerous. Which is precisely what led to her death during the war. The retelling of it sounded like the nightmare of fairytales.

The Goddess, whatever her name was, I don't even remember if I'd even been told it, was who helped Queen Nuala win the war. The Goddess would arrive on the battlefield, and *thousands* would be killed in a single breath. The only thing I could recall about her death was that she was murdered in her sleep by separating her head from her body and removing her heart to then burn it to ashes. Supposedly, this was the only way to kill a God. Or at least their physical form, according to the vagus.

'*The Ones*' could have them reincarnated to return to the nine realms., or elsewhere. The Ones being the sole entity, and simultaneously many entities depending on how The One(s) chose to take form, was and is the only one in creation who controls reincarnation. *Had The Ones reincarnated the Goddess of Origin?* Gods forbid. I shuddered at the thought. Her soul was probably trapped somewhere in the seven circles of hell being tortured for aeons to come.

By whom the Goddess of Origin was killed, no one knew. Presumably they were trying to end the war and prevent Queen Nuala from winning but, as we well knew, it was too late. The very idea of this Goddess was terrifying, and I honestly couldn't fathom ever killing so many, regardless of it only being their physical bodies. Those people had loved ones who would mourn them for years to come, if not for the rest of their lives in the case of Nexus Mates. Husbands, wives, children... So many sentenced to such tremendous suffering. It was unforgivable.

I pushed the thought of the dead Goddess from my mind and closed my eyes, trying to shut out reality. A few moments passed and I looked back over at him, studying his watchful gaze. "How did you end up in here anyway?" The Vagus' eyes burned brightly, and a brilliant smile illuminated his otherworldly, handsome face as he began to laugh. "Well... Let's just say it isn't without good reason." "Go on a murdering spree, did ya? Insatiable hunger get the best of you?" The vagus gave a chuckle. "Not in the slightest." I shook my head sadly in frustration. "Well, as stimulating this conversation has been, I think I'm gonna just try and sleep some more until the Queen decides what time I should die." I rolled over in resignation.

His voice was nonchalant despite his words. "Did you know that the Queen was once a slave?" I slowly turned to look at him in disbelief. "What?" The vagus smirked in amusement. "Being realistic is merely a matter of perspective. Especially for you, Aurelia. Your aspirations aren't so far-fetched." The hairs on the back of my neck rose as he spoke my name.

. . .

I stared at him in shock, ignoring his enigmatic remarks. "Queen Nuala was a slave before she started the uprising? How is it even possible to enslave a chimera?" The vagus nodded, still boasting his serene grin. "She was part of the former Emperor's harem for 300 years. She was born in it. It was all she'd ever known. She had no idea she possessed a chimera form until The Night of Spilled Blood... When her palladium collar was removed." *The Night of Spilled Blood.* The night Queen Nuala murdered Emperor Orova. I sat up, shaking my head in disbelief. "Then she's even worse than I thought. How could someone who knows true suffering and escape it, ever force it upon others?" The vagus sighed deeply, "While Pauperes Domos is not an ideal solution to another uprising, believe me when I say there's more to the story than what you've been taught." I couldn't help but sneer at this. "Enlighten me." He shrugged nonchalantly. "It is not my story to tell. And I'm afraid we will soon run out of time."

I sighed heavily, no longer caring about whatever story he was referring to. Grief and hopelessness pressed upon me like a crushing anvil. "Aurelia, come closer..." My eyebrows furrowed. *"Why?"* I asked, my voice wary. He chuckled softly. "I think it would be beneficial to you if I simply showed you." My hackles rose in suspicion. "As handsome as you are, if it's your dick, I'll have to give that a hard pass," I said flatly. The vagus burst into a raucous laugh. "You are so loved. And it's so easy to see why," he hummed between his waning laughter, "Now quickly, place your palm on the glass so I can show you your brother before the dungeon twat arrives." My breathing stilled. "Wait, what?" I breathed in disbelief, sitting up. "30 seconds until he arrives." I scrambled, most ungracefully, and nearly toppled onto the mirror, slamming my palm on the glass. His face lit up with a smile so radiant I felt it in my soul and aligned his palm with mine.

At that moment, the glass disappeared as the vagus pulled my *soul* from my body. My being tensed, trying to pull itself back into my body, but his voice filled my being in a words-without-thoughts manner. *"Let go, Aurelia. There is nothing to fear."* I felt his hands gently but firmly take hold of my soul to finish pulling it from my body, and as soon as it came free, I felt something snap with a soft *pop*, and the entire world shifted into a tunnel of glowing golden fractal-like rings that rotated, spun, and folded in on themselves like some sort other-worldly machinery. The power radiating around us made every molecule of being shiver. It was so powerful that it was genuinely terrifying without being malevolent in any way. I couldn't help but recoil, and I felt like I was being sucked back into darkness. Back to my body. Which suddenly felt wrong. The vagus' words came to me as a soothing, loving wave. *"You are loved. There is nothing to fear. The only way forward is to let... Go."*

And so I did. We blasted out of the tunnel of fractals and were catapulted through a cosmic whirling cloud of... what at first glimpse looked like glowing clouds of space dust, but as my eyes focused, I saw that staring back at were eyes. Ever watching, sentient eyes. The gases around them swirled, and as the clouds of space dust shifted and parted, planets were revealed. The vagus gave me a knowing grin. *"Yes,"* he responded within me before the question of, *"Is this your home?",* had even formed as words in my mind.

The world, *the cosmos,* shifted and a tunnel formed solely of gargantuan beings made purely of divine flames that towered over us watched as we passed through a fiery gate they seemed to guard. I locked eyes with one of them and saw its eyes weren't eyes at all but galaxies. *Worlds.* We passed through the gate, and I turned my head to look back. The fiery beings no longer formed a tunnel but a wall in front of the gate and shifted to reduce in number until only one remained. It seamed to stare *into* me as its mouth opened and swallowed the gate whole. *Oh sweet gods.*

· · ·

As soon as I faced forward, I found the faces of a dozen others only inches away from me. *Sphynxes.* Their bodies were that of a jungle cat but their fur in patterns and colours I'd never seen. Their large feline torsos grew into humanoid ones with arms, hands, breasts, and all. Their beautiful human-esque faces had cat-like eyes that twinkled with mischief and power. Their lips parted in unison to reveal perfectly white teeth. And fangs. *"Hello,"* their voices echoed within me as one as they bowed their heads to me. I'd have screamed in terror if it hadn't been for the overwhelming sense of love and protection I felt radiating from them in waves that brought tears to my eyes.

The group of them parted to reveal double doors of silver with breathtakingly beautiful reliefs depicting the Sphynxes in battle against what I assumed were demons. The moment the doors opened it felt as though time slowed and the weight of gravity was pulling us in. As soon as we reached the threshold, the world around us changed quicker than I could have blinked. We stood in a green meadow, resplendent with flowers of all shades. A bubbling creek flowed to our left, and in the distance, I could see a waterfall that appeared to fall into... nothing.

I looked around in awe at the majesty of this world. A golden palace could be seen far in the distance. Birds sang and tittered happily in the trees. Bumbles bees bouncing from flower to flower. It wasn't just the beauty of this place that was overwhelming. It was also the *peace.* *"Where are we?"* I asked, startled by the sound of my own voice. I looked down to see I had a corporeal form again. Or so it seemed. When I received no answer, I whirled around looking for the vagus but instead came face-to-face with Mateus.

My breath caught, and a well of emotion within me burst. Mateus took me in his long, muscled arms and held me to his chest, and

I *sobbed.* Several minutes passed before my sobbing finally calmed, and I pulled back slightly, gazing into his deep brown eyes that always held *so* much love. He beamed down at me. "I love you, sis." The words had me breaking again. *"I love you,"* I sobbed into his chest, "And I'm *so* sorry. I should never have thought we could escape."

He kissed my head and pulled back to look into my eyes. "Aurelia... It is because you led us there that *so* many more will find their freedom." I shook my head in disbelief, not knowing how to interpret his words. "I can't do this without you." He pulled me to his chest again, kissing my head and caressing my hair as he spoke. "Yes, you can. And you will. And it will be so much more than we could've possibly imagined. I can promise you that, Aurelia." I pulled back again to look up at him as I laughed mirthlessly, wiping my eyes. "Ugh, I'm literally in some rank dungeon right now." Mateus laughed, shaking his head. "Not for much longer. Don't worry." My brows furrowed. "Is the Queen going to execute me or send me back to Pauperes Domos?" Mateus gave another chuckle. "You'll soon find out."

I looked around at our surroundings. "Are... Is everyone else here too?" Mateus grinned at something in the distance. I turned to follow his gaze and saw the group of familiar Pauperes Domosians watching us. Smiling, some waving. My breath caught again, tears renewed. Mateus gave a contented sigh, his eyes twinkling as though he held some wonderful secret I had yet to discover. "So is this Heaven?" Another chuckle. "Something like that." I arched an eyebrow, a small smile finally blossoming on my face. "What does that mean?" He shrugged, still grinning, casual as ever. "It's all so much more than words could ever describe. Then we could ever even begin to fathom. It'd be like trying to fit the cosmos in a mop bucket. Ya know?" I huffed a laugh. "No. I don't know." His grin only broadened. "You'll soon find out."

.   .   .

Another eyebrow arched in confusion. "Soooooo, I am gonna die?" Mateus laughed heartily as though it was the most absurd thing he'd ever heard. The sound soothed my soul and the tears brimming my eyes became ones of gratitude and awe at his joy. "What a ridiculous notion," he said, still giggling as he caressed my cheek with his thumb. I could still feel his calluses. "You know what I mean, turd," I said softly and without bite. He laughed at the crude endearment, humming as he tugged me into his chest again and squeezed. "Now is not your time to leave the nine realms, Aurelia." He pressed his lips to my forehead.

My heart caved as the meadow was suddenly replaced by the dungeon. *Well fuck.* I opened my eyes, to find the vagus staring at me. Smiling serenely. Knowingly. I was beyond words. All I could do was breathe and stare into his silver, twinkling eyes. After a moment of wordless but somehow-communicating-everything-staring he began to laugh softly. The heart-warming sound snapped me out of my daze and I realized my hand was still pressed against the glass.

The whining of rusted metal sounded as a guard swung open the cell door and spotted me, his eyes widening in fear at the sight of the now turned mirror and me touching it. *"Merciful Gods,"* the dungeon guard breathed, "Do you have a death wish?" I didn't bother responding. I let my hand fall from the glass, and it felt like I was leaving all those worlds, otherworldly beings, my brother, and now- the closest thing I currently had to a friend- the vagus, behind. My parted lips closed, and I licked them, realizing how dry they were. My mouth must have been hanging open this entire time. All 30 seconds of it which was mind-boggling to imagine. It *felt* like hours had passed. "Get over here, girl. Before that *thing* devours you," the guard growled.

.   .   .

I ignored him, knowing he wouldn't dare step in front of the mirror to retrieve me, and held the vagus' gaze. *"Thank you...,"* I breathed, realizing I didn't know his name. The vagus gave me a nod. *"See you soon,"* he smiled.

Rendered speechless, I stole a glance back over my shoulder to see the vagus concealing himself in shadows once more but for a fleeting moment they dissipated again to reveal his corporeal form, gilded and glowing. He offered me a gentle smile as the guard grew impatient and tried to yank me through the door.

The vagus' voice was like a soothing caress as he spoke within in my mind. *"The Freedom you seek is so much closer than you think, Aurelia."*

After everything he'd just shown me, nothing seemed so impossible anymore. I felt so many conflicting emotions- the weight of my brother's absence, the joy at seeing him- and everyone else who'd died because of my naivety- *so* much happier than they'd ever been here, the heartache that I was now alone here, and the new fragment of hope that perhaps I did have something beautiful ahead of me, however exhausting, as my brother had promised. And finally, some of the peace lingering within me that I'd experienced in 'Something-like-that-heaven'.

"Let's see," I replied with genuine calm. I caught the twinkle in the vagus' eyes as the guard slammed the cell door shut. And I sent a silent prayer up to The Ones that one day I'd be able to get him out of there.

3

The Vagus' words echoed in my mind. The inter-dimensional journey still making me reel. Obviously. Being here in this world, in this body, suddenly felt so... strange. Stranger than anything I'd experienced there. But I also felt a strange peace about being here. Unattached to any outcome. Whatever lingering fear of death I had was now gone entirely. And if things were meant to go beautifully- great. If not, the worst that could happen was death, right? Which seemed like just one of perhaps many beautiful options.

Two guards led me through the crystal palace hallway that sparkled in the light of day, adorned in gold fixtures, and crystal chandeliers. I felt no small amount of surprise that both of them were trolls. From what I'd been told, before Queen Nuala, trolls were never allowed to serve royalty. They had been condemned to living in the wilds due to their 'beastly' nature. These two, however, disgruntled towards me, seemed as tame as any fae.

. . .

I stared up slightly in awe, being reminded not only of the sphynxes' silver doors, as we reached a towering set of ornately carved pale blue and white crystal doors, but of the fact that my parents had almost certainly been among the laborers who mined the crystal for the very doors I was about to walk through. It made my heart ache. In that brief moment, I felt a seed of resolution plant itself within me, reminding me of what I'd always wanted to do.

Queen Nuala had the crystal palace built after she and her army of immortals and mortals alike won the war two hundred years ago, here in the North Guard. The surreal-ness of the fact that everyone I'd ever known and loved had hewn the very crystal I stood upon as I looked around, mouth slightly agape, whilst the massive crystal doors yawned open. It felt like some sort of omen. Like the moment I passed through them, nothing would ever be the same. And as I did, I took a fortifying breath and heard the Vagus' last words to me echo in my mind: "*The Freedom you seek is so much closer than you think, Aurelia.*"

When we were about 10 feet from the dais of the throne they shoved me to my knees. Instead of angering me, I felt nothing but pity for them. I stared at the empty, multicolored serpentine crystal throne. I knelt waiting, my gaze gradually drifting to the floor before I heard the padding of unhurried footsteps. So lost in my own thoughts, my mind still distant and wandering through my journey with the vagus, I hadn't even noticed the guards at my side or peppered around the throne room were also kneeling with me until her voice rang, clear as a bell.

"Rise." The guards rose as one, and as I tried to stand, the one on my right shoved me back to the ground. "Not you," he growled. My hands being bound behind me had me catching myself by nearly face planting on the crystal floor. There was a moment of silence in which I could feel the penetrative heat of her gaze on me. "This is the only one who survived?" She asked grimly.

"Yes, your majesty."

A pause.

"Give me a look at you."

The guards grabbed me by the back of my torn tunic and hauled me to my feet. I dared a glance at her. Her face was taught as she stared down at me. Her nostrils flared, jaw feathering. As I looked into her eyes, I saw a phantom of pain in her gaze. I'd never seen her before. She was pretty but not as breathtakingly beautiful as one might imagine a fae queen to be. A burnt umber chiffon gown clung to her slender body and pooled around her bare feet. As I studied her face, I realized that had it not been for her fae, pointed ears, I might have even mistook her for being human. Although her long auburn hair did hold that natural glow of the fae. Her features may have been warm had it not been for her severe expression. I struggled to imagine this deceivingly delicate-looking fae female as the infamous chimera she was rumored to be.

We studied one another for several moments. A great many emotions seemed to be welling beneath her surface, none of them discernible. Finally, a corner of her mouth twitched in amusement. "You're a brave thing, aren't you... Running into The Sable Forest in the middle of the night like that, palladium collar and all. It's been at least a century since we had anyone dare such a thing... Do you not realize why I don't bother to post guards *outside* of Pauperes Domos?"

I frowned, recalling what the vagus had mentioned... that the Queen was once a slave. "Do you no longer realize how worthy a risk death is for freedom?" I said softly. She peaked an eyebrow as she studied me. A small, sad smile tilting her lips. The soldier behind me raised his hand to me at my insolence, but she quickly cut him off. "Touch her and die," she said with lethal calm. The soldier lowered his hand and bowed. "Apologies, your majesty."

Her voice echoed through the cavernous throne room. "Leave us." She studied me, holding my gaze as she descended the dais, the soldiers all marching out of the room, only speaking again once they left. She stopped beside me and pulled me to my feet. Her hands were warm, her touch gentle, and the buzzing of her power radiated from beneath the surface. "There were people you loved who were killed?" She said, her words softened by compassion. My eyes swelled with tears at the fresh memory of their horrific ends. And the guilt that would haunt me. Having briefly experienced their 'post-death' reality for myself was all that kept me from breaking into a sob.

She stopped only when her face was mere inches from mine. The understanding and concern I saw in her eyes were mildly... unsettling, considering this female was supposed to be the embodiment of evil. Her crown, a simple pale blue crystal crescent moon on its side making it look more like horns than a moon, glimmered in the sunlight beaming into the room.

"I have... a proposal for you...," she said, sounding somewhat despondent, "Stay here... At the palace. However much aeternam crystal you managed to smuggle..." Her eyes darted to the pouch still tied to my hip. "... It's not nearly enough to protect you and give you the freedom you desire... Or to make your... *aspirations*... a reality. Even *if* no one stole it from you. You will find more freedom, safety, luxury, and resources here than the outside world would ever offer. And I can help you master your powers... Provide you with whatever you need to do whatever it is you want..."

. . .

I shook my head with confusion, brows knitting tightly. "Why?" I breathed dubiously. She looked me up and down, sadly. Perhaps seeing the poor, broken product of Pauperes Domos. Was she feeling guilty? She shrugged a shoulder. Her demeanor shifting to that of nonchalance, but I saw something else, something hidden beneath the surface. "I have grown weary of my solitude and... superficial encounters, I suppose."

My brows remained furrowed, wariness creeping in, but I couldn't find the words. I didn't know what to think. There must be some kind of ulterior motive. She lifted a finger, using a knuckle to gingerly wipe away a rogue tear that had escaped. "It would be wise to accept my offer willingly, Aurelia," she whispered in an alarmingly gentle tone. "... Or what? You'll kill me? If this is some kind of ultimatum, I'd honestly rather you just get it over with now." She didn't bother to mask her frown. "I'd sooner allow you to kill me...." She reached out and touched the collar at my throat. The palladium I'd had around my neck since I was a small child clattered to the floor, and a weight hit me- filled me- my blood began to tingle and the very fibers of my being seemed to dance with a cool fire in awakening. I gasped, swaying on my feet. She steadied me with a hand as her throat worked on a swallow before she called out. "Bring her to the thermal baths. Call Syan down take care of her." A guard rounded the corner behind the dais to follow her orders.

After being led through the breathtaking crystal palace that I'd only ever gazed at from afar, I found myself in a magnificently carved thermal spa. Steam whorled above the large heated bathing pool. I stood in the room alone and barefoot, waiting for Syan, having left a trail of black and brown footsteps behind me on the perspiring crystal floor.

· · ·

My body seemed to hum with energy, my magic. It was dizzying as though I'd been drugged, but I could feel my body gradually adjusting. I gazed at the magnificence of the spa around me, and it made me feel sick. How many of us- my family, friends, even past lovers- had bled for the crystal carved in this room. And how many had enjoyed it at our expense. Or rather who. This beguiling Queen and her... loyal subjects.

The sound of quickly approaching footsteps had my attention snapping to the door behind me to discover my grimy footsteps had disappeared, replaced by a petite female with delicately webbed fingers and feet walking towards me. A siren. Her long dark green hair swung in a single plait, grazing against the generous arch of her backside with each step. Her skin was the color of seaweed. A trait that had surely evolved to aid her ancient ancestors in hunting deep within the kelp forests. When they weren't singing to pirates and other seafarers, luring them to their watery graves, so I'd been told. Sirens were another immortal species that, prior to the war, also weren't allowed to work in places of repute. Much less among royalty. Their power was feared- the ability to control immortals and mortals alike with nothing more than the sound of their voice. She wore a single sheer gold chiffon sheet with a deep-v that was neatly cinched at the waist by a gold belt. The sheet did almost nothing to hide her womanly figure. She smiled at me, and despite her sharp needle-like teeth, it was warm and sincere.

"Lovely to have you with us," her melodic, alto voice at once reminded me of water, soft and smooth yet capable of wielding enormous power. I met her gaze, trying to reconcile everything I'd been told about sirens with the female before me.

. . .

"Thank you for your help," I managed. She studied me with saddened eyes. "Happy to... My name is Syan. You can call me 'Sy' if you like." She examined my clothes, frowning at them. If that's what my tattered tunic and trousers could be called. "Aurelia, is it?" I dipped my chin in confirmation. She continued studying me. "For your clothing, in terms of color and style... What is your preference?" I opened my mouth to respond, only to realize I didn't have one.

The only clothes I'd ever worn were what had been available in Pauperes Domos. None of which was particularly fashionable, elegant, or fine in quality. She shifted on her feet, studying my frame, "A dress or... do you prefer... trousers?" She stared at the rag that had become my trousers. "Oh... I mean... I've never worn anything else. Other than some variation of this," I gestured awkwardly towards my clothing. She sighed, raising her eyebrows at the notion as her throat worked on a swallow. "Well... That's pretty fucking heartbreaking to imagine." I couldn't help but chuckle at how true her words were. She flitted her eyes towards the bathing pool. "Let's clean you up first, shall we?" I stepped toward the pool, but she stopped me, gently grabbing one of my arms with a cool webbed hand.

"Not in that," she laughed. I paled. I'd never bathed naked before. We'd only ever been forced to do so fully clothed in the frigid lake. It had been *a while* since anyone had ever seen me naked. The only people who had ever seen me completely naked were the lovers I'd taken: two men and a handful of women that I'd slept with over the years in Pauperes Domos. Sensing my discomfort, she smirked and said, "Despite my webbed appendages, there's little difference between my body and yours." She shifted on her feet again, waiting, as I began pulling my clothes off.

. . .

"You've never used your gifts before, have you?" She asked, a slight frown tilting her mouth. I shook my head, pulling off the remnants of my shirt and the band of cloth I used as a brassiere. However, it was a small lie. I could taste lies and emotions. My father always warned me never to tell anyone so I could always discern those who are sincere. "Do you know what gifts your parents bore?" I shook my head again, another lie. From what I'd been told, both of my parents wielded power over energy and electricity. My mother was who I'd inherited my ability to taste lies and emotions from. Why the palladium collar failed to suppress it, I had no idea. My father was also gifted in telepathy.

Lying in general sickened me, but in the current circumstances, I felt the less they knew about me, the better. For now, at least. But I could feel my parent's magic and electricity flowing through me in waves of what I could only describe as a flowing sensation of cool and warm liquid energy cascading throughout my body, throughout every cell. It was as if each cell within me was a bud blossoming into a flower.

Syan opened her palm, and a basket appeared filled with loofahs, brushes, oils, and other various herbal liquids. She unbuckled her belt and shouldered off the chiffon sheet-like dress. It pooled onto the floor at her feet before she led me into the pool. A groan escaped me as I stepped into the warm water. I'd never felt anything so wonderful in my life- including sex, which had been a mostly underwhelming experience. Especially when it was with males. And having only ever experienced nearly thirty years of frigid lake water to bathe in, my jaw became unhinged at the sensation of this hot, liquid heaven that embraced me. I gulped as my eyes rolled into the back of my head. Not caring in the least about whether or not I looked ill as my muscles finally relaxed, and I'm pretty sure I became little more than a gelatinous mass.

· · ·

Syan, graciously, only grinned to herself, "A far cry from the lake, I suppose?" All I could muster was a groan. Shortly followed by the sinking sensation of guilt that promptly settled into me. Guilt at experiencing the pleasure of the pool after everyone I'd ever known and cared for had been slaughtered viciously. And everyone else who was still stuck in Pauperes Domos.

Syan handed me a body brush, "Here. Scrub in a clockwise direction. I'll start on your back." She grabbed the now half-drenched tendrils of my hair and draped them over my shoulder before grabbing another brush and scrubbing my back, starting at my shoulders. When we' finished, she led me towards a curve of marble that sat beneath the water for bathers to lay down on. I laid back, my head perched on the top curve, and Syan began gently pouring water over my hair. Her hands stilled as she stared down at me, and I looked up to meet her puzzled gaze. "Your ears... I assumed you were fae." I shrugged. "Full blooded. It's a deformity, I guess...Although my parents would have denied it, I always wondered if it was some distant human gene or some other mixed genetics expressing itself in me. Was the bane of my existence growing up." She tilted her head in curiosity. "How curious...," she murmured, resuming her ministrations once again.

Her touch was soothing, tender. She poured a viscous, shimmering substance into her palm and began massaging the liquid into my wet hair. Within a few moments, I couldn't help but close my eyes. Not out of exhaustion or pleasure but out of sorrow. The chasm that was now my heart thumped in pain, and with each stroke of Syan's fingers, it triggered an unending flow of tears that I could do nothing against breaching the dam of my shut eyelids.

. . .

Somehow, the compounded experience of something as simple as a warm bath and the gentle touch of another person was enough to break me. I'd never experienced either of these in this manner. Even on the rare occasion I'd taken a partner for the evening, it was only ever nothing more than a quick cure to an itch. As opposed to the tenderness found in love-making which I'd yet to experience. The closest Mateus and I ever got to experiencing a hot bath was sitting in a shin deep wash basin that left you shivering because all but your bum and thighs were exposed to the chill air of our slum dwelling. The same went for anyone in Pauperes Domos. At least since losing the war two hundred years ago.

Syan, to her credit, said nothing as she continued to soothingly massage and stroke my head. After a few minutes of silent, bountiful tears, she stepped around to face me and wrapped her arms around me. And that's all it took for me to burst into a violent sob. Only when my tears and shuddering sobs finally stilled did she resume her ministrations. I sighed in relief feeling like a weight had been lifted.

We didn't speak again until we entered a large room that I suppose was intended to be a closet. However, it was bigger than at least 3 of mine and Mateus' home. Fabric of every color and texture hung from the walls. The beauty of it lured me in and before the thought even crossed my mind, I found myself reaching out to touch the fabrics. My hand landed on lilac silk. The texture was glorious. Yet another first. Syan walked up beside me. "This is a favorite of mine as well. Would you like to wear it as a dress?" I shook my head in awe. "How do I even begin to decide? They're all so... magnificent," I breathed as my hand found its way toward another fabric. Dark emerald velvet. It was like fur yet not fur. I fell in love with it. She beamed with pleasure, "You don't have to decide anything, Aurelia. You can have as many as you like."

.   .   .

No sooner did the words leave her mouth than an invisible hand began to collect an assortment of fabrics, including the emerald and lilac I'd been drawn to, and sewed them together into various garments floating in the air above us. I watched in awe, feeling Syan's gaze on me, grinning in satisfaction. Within moments the articles of clothing were complete, and Syan walked over to where one of them hung in midair- an emerald silk that had been made into a gown- she plucked it down and handed it to me. "I guessed your measurements, so just let me know if you'd prefer something looser or tighter."

I removed the fluffy, blanket-like robe she'd given me after the bath before brushing and drying my hair and rubbing my skin in a divinely scented oil that smelled of tuberose. I slid the emerald gown over my body. The silk's caress made my hair stand on end. She grinned at me with delight and flicked a finger in the direction of a mirror. I turned to look, and the sight of my reflection took my breath away.

I didn't recognize the person staring back at me. My unremarkable brown hair, normally matted and dull from the years of working beneath the sun and layers of dust from the quarry, was luminous. Even the color was different. I'd always thought my hair was just a mud brown. But as I stared into the mirror, I saw subtle shades of auburn hidden in the darkest brown and umber strands that made up the tousled waves of my hair. My fair skin, also usually muted by grime, honeyed with color from working endlessly in the sun, was glowing and vibrant. My cheeks rosy. I'd never at all thought of myself as beautiful but looking in the mirror now, I recognized that my full lips, upturned blue and golden eyes, and high cheekbones were indeed something to be appreciated. The way the cowled neck-line of the halter neck gown draped over my full breasts and accentu-ated my hips was... stunning. "Do you like this style of nightgown?" Syan hummed in amusement. I snorted in disbelief. The most extravagant thing to have ever graced my body was simply a nightgown. I gaped at her through the mirror.

"Would you like to try on another?" She asked, leaping towards the other dresses excitedly. Before I could answer, she took another dress in her hand, made of the same sheer chiffon silk that she was wearing, but instead of gold, it was a color I'd only ever seen in the wild raspberries that grew during the summer near the Pauperes Domos tenements. I pulled the emerald gown off and traded with her. I baulked at what I saw. I could see my full breasts, along with everything else, beneath it.

Syan eyed me, grinning a little wickedly, pleased with her work, "Now *that* is flattering," she purred. My face instantly turned a rather alarming shade of crimson. "We can save that for another time... Whenever you're ready," she laughed, winking coolly as she handed me another dress. A black one of a similarly sheer but, thankfully, more opaque fabric that tied at the waist. The skirt of it reached the floor. Two slits rose high upon my thighs, exposing most of my long legs, toned from years of hard labor. Thankfully the sleeves were long and blousy, cuffed at the wrists helping me to feel not quite so naked.

Syan led me down another ornately decorated hallway to where another door opened as we approached. It was a bedroom. My breath caught at the sight of it, and I sent a silent prayer of gratitude to The Ones that the wooden four-post bed draped in white gossamer fabric, wasn't made of the crystal my family and I had spent our lives mining. "I thought you'd like to see your room before dinner," she said, watching me take in my surroundings. I turned to her, trying to smile, and nodded weakly. Dinner. Right. I took a hopeful breath.

"Do you think it would be possible to eat in here?... I don't feel very well." Syan nodded, offering me a compassionate smile before making her exit.

The pang of guilt returned as I stood alone in my new bedroom, looking around at its splendor. I felt helpless and frustrated to imagine that so few got to live in luxury all at the expense of the countless others living in poverty who mined the same crystal that made individuals such as Nuala so wealthy. I sighed heavily, trying to fathom how I could possibly create some kind of change, as I stepped out onto the balcony that overlooked the sprawling palace gardens along with it's beautiful lake. The setting sun casting everything in a coral and gold aura.

After a few minutes, the smell of *delicious* food wafted by on a breeze. I turned to find the balcony's dinette adorned in a large cooked bird, exotic fruits, an extensive variety of vegetables cooked and seasoned to perfection, breads and cheeses of all shapes, sizes, and colors. My mouth instantly flooded with saliva, and I gulped, staring at the food in wide-eyed desire.

As I filled my plate to heaping, a now newly familiar energy poured into the room. I turned to find Queen Nuala standing at the balcony doors. I felt her approach, stopping behind my chair. "Is everything to your liking?" she asked, stepping towards me. I studied her for a moment before responding. "The palace is even more beautiful than I'd ever imagined. And Syan is wonderful..."

Queen Nuala raised an eyebrow at me, sensing I had more on the tip of my tongue.
    "But..."

I sighed heavily, shaking my head as I spoke.

"Don't you ever feel guilty?"

The corners of her mouth curled downwards, understanding my train of thought.

"You are aware that I'm a former slave? From Emperor Orova's harem, no?"

"I'd recently heard something like that... vaguely," I nodded, hoping she would elaborate more than the vagus had.

The queen' jaw feathered as she took in a deep breath. "Imagine being raped on a near daily basis for three hundred years, watching everyone you've ever loved be forced into slavery. And then imagine fighting for 90 years against an oppressive class of people who live, much like this," she said, casually gesturing to our surroundings, "and treat you worse than cattle because you weren't born into their world of privilege. And when you simply ask them to remove their boot from your windpipe, you're met with hatred and lethal violence..." My throat worked on a swallow as she continued. "Would you feel guilty about subjecting those same people to a, might I add- much lesser, form of oppression?"

She studied me patiently for a moment as a sinking feeling settled in my stomach. My mind reeled at everything she'd just said, trying to reconcile everything I'd ever been taught in Pauperes Domos. That the Queen was blood thirsty, evil, greedy, and power hungry. What was the truth? Hers or my parents? My stomach churned with nausea at the idea that... my parents might have been... I steeled my heart against the idea. My father had been the most loving and selfless male I'd ever known, next to my brother. How could any of what she said be true? The vagus was her prisoner. Why would he lie about her being a harem slave? And also, I knew that the troll guard's and Syan, prior to the war would never have been able to work in the royal palace... Which seemed seemed so inherently wrong...

·   ·   ·

As if reading my mind, she added, "I imagine you've been taught an entirely different retelling of our realm's history..." Regardless of what was truth or fiction, the fact still remained that there were innocents-children, who had been born into the poverty of Pauperes Domos but had never oppressed anyone. "And what of their children? Who were and are innocent? Not to mention, it's been two hundred years."

"And how many generations, how many thousands of years have my people been oppressed?" I shook my head despairingly. "Why does it have to be one or the other? Why can't we all live in peace?" The Queen gave me a pitying frown. "Because for some, too much is never enough. And should I steal those children from their parents? Have them raised as orphans? Surely the moment I remove their palladium collars- theirs or their parents- they'll rise against us again."

I shook my head, trying to think of some alternative. "What if they swore a blood oath?" Queen Nuala threw her head back and laughed, shrugging her shoulder as she calmed. "Sure. If they swear blood oaths, by all means."

My eyebrows practically leapt off my forehead. "Seriously?" She nodded, giving me a look that wasn't entirely optimistic. "Absolutely... It would bring me great joy to remove the stain on Aeternia that is Pauperes Domos... I think your optimism is entirely misplaced but... If they're willing to swear a blood oath that they won't rise against us. Or try to take slaves. Or oppress others. Perhaps you're right, and they've had a change of heart after experiencing two hundred years of suffering." "Wouldn't you?" I countered, "Wouldn't you swear a blood oath to never retaliate against Emperor Orova after three hundred years in his harem if it was your only means of escape?" The Queen's smile withered. "Some things are worth enduring in order to bring about justice."

. . .

I nodded solemnly in understanding. If she hadn't endured those 300 years of suffering, Emperor Orova would still have his harem, and the 'lesser' immortals would still be oppressed if everything she claimed was true. "Let's hope your kin don't feel the same," she sighed. My gaze fell to the food. My excitement at the prospect of Pauperes Domos' residents being freed from the collars and the city... burned within me. So much so, that it almost took away my appetite. Almost.

I filled my plate and groaned with pleasure as I took my first bite. The corners of her mouth curled. "And what about the quarry? And all of the other industrial sites that have to be maintained?" She shrugged, unconcerned. "We'll hire people from the neighboring villages and towns and pay them fair wages." "When can we ask them to take the blood oath?" "I'll have my advisors drawer up the agreement tomorrow, and then my sentries can distribute them in the coming weeks." Excitement and hope blossomed in my chest. "Would you allow me to take a look at it... On their behalf...?" Her expression brightened further. "Perhaps... you would like to be my liaison... of sorts. My emissary." I gulped, barely looking up from my enormous plate of food. "And what exactly are the duties of an emissary?" I asked from around another mouthful of food. She studied me thoughtfully. "You would attend official and unofficial meetings with or without me to speak on my behalf and that of the realm, and gather information. To put it succinctly. You would be my right hand, essentially."

My chewing stilled, and my throat worked on a swallow, forcing a mouthful of half chewed food down. Between everything she had said, 'the truth' if that's what it in fact was, the prospect of freeing everyone in Pauperes Domos, now working with the Queen... It was a lot to process. "Can I think about it?" "Of course," she chirped without hesitation. I studied her, trying to detect any ulterior motives, but she revealed nothing. "Why me?" I asked, utterly confused. "Who better to work on my behalf than someone who has other's best interests in mind and has spent their entire lives on the bottom wrung of society? Living amongst the... enemy... for lack of a better word. It's that person who will not only have a vision for a better future for all but will have the necessary insight as to how we can make it happen... Not to mention, you have the desire. It clearly comes naturally to you." I nodded slowly. Pensively.

"Give yourself some time. I know it's a lot to process, and that you need time to recover. Just let me know if and when you're ready," Queen Nuala offered as she turned to leave. My heart skipped a beat as an idea formed in my mind. "May I...," I began, calling after her and she stopped in her tracks, "Make a suggestion?" Nuala turned slowly to face me. Her perfectly sculpted eyebrow arching. "I think there is someone I know who might also be of help to you..." She grinned in amusement. "Is that so?"

I chewed my cheek, wondering how best to present it. Perhaps I'd been too hasty and should have planned this better. But... "I know someone who can see all things past and present, and can see future potentialities..." Nuala's eyes narrowed to slits, amusement fading. "No," she said firmly. I heaved a breath in disappointment, my cheeks puffing out. "But the vagus was kind to me. Perhaps you could make him swear a blood oath?" She smirked. "A vagus has no blood by which to swear. And just because he was kind to you then does not mean he always will be. Or that that kindness will be extended to anyone else. The vagus is a dangerous creature, and you would be wise to remember it." I frowned my disappointment. Her expression softened. "You are kind, Aurelia. I admire that despite all that you have been through, it has not hardened your soft heart. Like it did mine." She turned on her heel and left.

. . .

As my eyes trailed her, I noticed a set of books piled on the desk facing the balcony. I padded over to the desk and picked the books up one by one to peruse the titles: *'Freedom's War'*, *'A Realm Freed'*, *'A Historical Extract on the 90 Year War for the Lesser's Freedom'*, *'Queen of Slaves'*. I stared heavily at the titles and began flipping through 'Freedom's War'. One of the first few pages read,

"... By 19444, the uprising of the lessers had barely begun and was already all but lost as Emperor Orova ordered all rebels to be given public executions. Millions of lesser beings, immortal and mortals alike, who were suspected of treasonous activity were brutally executed in public squares across the four guards; their bodies reduced to carrion for all to see...

"The turning point occurred when Morwen Sandara, Emperor Orova's most trusted seer, replaced the Emperor's favored harem slave's, Nuala Alkhimera's, palladium collar with one of silver, restoring magical power that she had never known, having been born into the royal harem. On what is now known as 'The Night of Spilled Blood', Alkhimera was called into Orova's bed chamber. The following morning when Orova's general, Olc Amhayn, entered the emperor's bed chamber all that remained of Orova were a few of his teeth and his blood which had been spilt across the entire room..."

I laid the book down slowly, barely breathing. My eyes stung, and I slid my back against the side of the bed, down to the floor. And wept.

4

Queen Nuala didn't send for me after that. I poured through the books on what I'd never realized was known as 'Freedom's War', or that she was known as 'Queen of Slaves'. I'd already thought things couldn't become any more surreal than they already were, but *The Ones* clearly wanted to prove me wrong.

Outside of bathing with Syan and an occasional walk in the gardens late at night when no one was around, I remained in my room, reading and grieving my bother and our friends, for a period of time that I was only able to count by the number of meals that had been silently brought to my door. Along with flowers. Fresh flowers and a new book- none of which were historical, thankfully- were delivered every few days around lunchtime. I was so grateful for those flowers and the books. I had no idea whether or not the flowers and books were picked by the Queen or one of her servants, but they seemed to have excellent taste. The bouquets were always a magnificent array of luscious blooms that I'd never seen before, and the books were mostly comedies or adventure novels that helped to heal my soul.

And I fully intended to personally thank whoever it was the keeping up with it over my weeks of isolation.

I thought of the vagus on a daily basis, and I felt tormented by the fact he was still trapped in that mirror, in the Queen' dungeon. And although my journey to the dimensions beyond with the vagus had given me peace at having seen Mateus so happy, I selfishly missed my brother. Only time, along with the joy and wisdom these books had to offer, genuinely helped me let go of the fact that my brother was no longer with me. Eventually, even I grew weary of grieving and isolation. Not to mention, I felt the pressure of a moral obligation weighing on me. I could do so much good as Nuala's emissary. Starting with freeing the residents of Pauperes Domos.

And as though the universe had aligned in perfect timing, one morning, along with my newest book, the contractual agreement for the blood oath for the residents of Pauperes Domos arrived. My breathing stilled as I stood in my bedroom doorway reading:

"All residents of Pauperes Domos are to have their palladium collars removed, permitted free passage via train, and one kilogram of aeternam crystal as severance pay in exchange for fealty sworn upon blood and magic to never:

1. Form a coup against Queen Nuala or her subjects and those that work on her/their behalf.
2. Participate (in any capacity) in the selling, purchasing, or employment of slaves or indentured servants.

As with any standard oath sworn upon blood and magic, this is a life-binding agreement, and any action taken that conflicts with the terms of this agreement are punishable by immediate death, as willed, by The Ones.

The blood oath rituals will begin in three days at dusk, individually, at the home of each resident…"

Tears of joy swelled, spilling down my cheeks, as I brought a trembling hand to my mouth. My brother's voice filled my mind… *"It is because you led us there that so many more will find their freedom."*

Dressed in nothing but my robe, I raced through the palace towards Queen Nuala's wing to run directly into the Queen herself just as she was exiting her strategy room. "Your Majesty!" I called from down the hall. She met my gaze with a grimace. "Please, don't call me that. Nuala will do." I didn't bother responding as I ran straight over to her and threw my arms around her in an embrace. The guards posted by the double doors behind her moved to separate us, but she raised a hand to wave them off and gradually brought her arms around me in a surprisingly firm and tender hug. "Are you alright?" She asked softly from over my shoulder. I nodded, stifling tears. "Thank you," I managed, without my voice cracking. She patted my back for a few moments. "I'm… I want things to be better for everyone too. I just… I don't want you to get your hopes up too much. I'm sure some will leave and have peaceful lives… But… I don't want you to be too heart-broken if things don't go exactly as you might hope."

I finally released her and stepped back, wiping my eyes. "Even if it's only one person… It's one life changed forever." "Let's hope for the best," she nodded, giving me a smile that didn't quite reach her eyes.

"I've thought about your offer, by the way...," I began, eye darting warily to her guards. Her smile broadened.

The following morning, I stood in the middle of a ballroom. A few string musicians tuned their instruments in a nearby corner. A door shut across the ballroom, and a male faun dressed elegantly in a silken tunic with floral designs clopped his way gracefully across the room. "Oh my Gods, I'll never forgive Syan for not making me that exact dress." I'd worn a conservative periwinkle version of my favoured black one. The faun bowed and took my hand in his, kissing the top of it. I blushed. "You look ravishing, my dear," he crooned, "My name is Evrin." "Aurelia," I grinned and traced a small curtsy- my first ever. Evrin burst into a short laugh, "I don't think anyone's ever curtsied for me before." My face flushed with embarrassment. "It was a first for me as well," I chuckled awkwardly. He quickly reassured, "Well, I'll tell everyone to blame you now that I'm going to insist that everyone curtsy in my presence." I couldn't help but give another laugh, shaking my head as I looked up into the faun's boyishly handsome face. "Sorry. I imagine that looked as awkward as it felt." Evrin raised a brow, grinning winsomely, "My dear, you needn't worry. With your exquisite beauty, you could make food poisoning sexy." I giggled as he quickly gave a short clap of his hands at the musicians to begin playing whilst offering them a magnanimous grin. I couldn't help but notice one of them, a handsome fae male holding a violin, grinned back at him and winked.

The musicians began playing a simple waltz, or so Evrin informed me. I'd never heard music like this before. He extended an upturned palm, leading me into the centre of the ballroom, and gently laid a hand at my hip and the other behind my shoulder. "Shoulder's back, head up, eye's on me, spine... erect." Evrin's lips twitched and that was all it took for the two of us to burst into laughter. "Now, now, naughty girl. Allow me," he chirped as he began leading me into a basic waltz. I thanked the Gods he had hooves and not feet, or I'm certain I would have been traipsing all over them. But after a few minutes of basic instruction and practice, I found my confidence and was able to dance with him in a fluid motion. He grinned down at me, "Oh, we're going to have so much fun."

I'd always loved dancing. But dancing with Evrin to a live quartet was the stuff of dreams. I felt like another part of me had awoken. I'd dance before, albeit rarely, usually just during the solstice celebrations in the summer and winter, but that was different. All drums and primal, for the most part, which I absolutely love, but this... How we wound and weaved our way across the room as if sailing... It was breathtaking. I could only hope that Queen Nuala's solstice celebrations included both.

After class, I was met by a servant who escorted me to the palace garden, which was in full bloom despite still being early spring, all thanks to magic. The servant sat me at a small table and made a gesture as if to part the very fabric of space, and pulled out a large tray of food and drink. "Her majesty has other commitments this afternoon. She shall return by sundown. Do you require anything else?" I shook my head. "No. Thank you so much." The servant gave a small bow in farewell and left the garden. As he disappeared inside the palace, I gazed up at the clear blue sky, feeling overwhelmed with joy that in three days, the residents of Pauperes Domos would be free to leave and with more wealth than they had ever dreamed of. At least since the end of the war.

My gaze dropped to the food before me, salivating at its mouth-watering seduction. My stomach growled angrily in protest quickly that I'd allowed the sky to steal my attention, however briefly. After a few minutes of thoroughly stuffing myself, I realized the quiet that suddenly filled the garden. Like the garden itself was holding its breath. And a strange tugging sensation pulled at my middle. Perhaps an intuitive warning. My heart began to pound as I felt a thrum of power pouring into the space around me. A dark cloud eclipsed the sun as I swallowed a mouthful of half-chewed food and turned in my seat to discover a male barely more than a foot behind me.

I let out a yelp in surprise and clutched my chest. I looked up at him as he stared down at me with a handsome, crooked grin, "Should I leave you two alone?" His bright amber gaze briefly flicked to my plate. "I'm not usually into ménage à trois," I managed. Barely. The male threw his head back and laughed, revealing his luminous teeth and the slightly, preternaturally elongated canines. *A vampire*, I realized. I'd never met one in real life. Pauperes Domos had never housed one. "Do you wanna sit?" I offered, surprised at the words that almost unconsciously spilt from my lips.

I couldn't help but stare as he sat down across from me, laying an ankle over a knee and leaning back in his chair. He took up so much space. He, and his magic, seemed to make the air hum in his presence. Not to mention how gorgeous he was. His short black hair had that perfectly imperfect coif- not overly styled but not messy- framed his face, complimenting his golden skin. He stood several inches over six feet, his shoulders broad. The perfectly tailored tunic and trousers did nothing to hide his powerful, muscular form beneath. His gaze met mine and his chest expanded, taking in a deep breath. His lips parted as if wanting to say something, but apparently he thought better of it, simply smiling instead. I saw him chew his cheek as if he were anxious.

.   .   .

His voice was deep, warm, and velvety. And I felt like the sound alone would undo me. "How're you finding the palace?" I raised my brows at the question. "You could have given me two sticks and a single sheet of toilet tissue to sleep under, and it'd have been cozier than Pauperes Domos." He laughed again, despite looking pained by my words. Something dark flickered in his eyes that seemed to glow like embers. "I can imagine...," he murmured sadly.

He began rolling his sleeves midway up his forearm, displaying the striations of the muscles in them as the sun returned. "Can you?" I asked, genuinely curious. His throat worked on a swallow as he gave me a sad smile. "More than you know." A sympathy pain formed in my chest. "Well, I am truly sorry to hear that then," I offered, massaging my sternum at the phantom pain and strange tugging sensation. His eyes dipped to where my hand rubbed briefly.

"Kyril," he offered, leaning forward, extending a large, long hand. My jaw nearly dropped. According to the history books, he was basically some kind of ultra-powerful and badass vampire-hybrid warrior. "Aurelia," I replied, reaching out to take his hand. As soon as our skin touched, I felt as if every molecule in my body hummed in response. "I'm happy you're here, Aurelia," he offered as our palms separated. The sound of his voice and my name on his lips made an energy coil up my spine, and my body instantly heated, making my cheeks flush. "Making big changes already, from what I hear," he continued. My throat worked on a swallow. "Let's see," I sighed, hopefully. "So, when shall we begin your lessons?" My brows knit together in confusion. "Come again?" He grinned, revealing the most dazzling smile I'd ever seen, and laughed to himself. "She didn't tell you, did she?" He sighed in amusement at my silence. "I'm to be your tutor."

. . .

I quirked an eyebrow. "Tutor for what, exactly? Nuala only mentioned dance lessons today and that I should start shadowing her soon." Kyril's eyes twinkled, and I swear I could see suns, moons, and stars- whole galaxies- in them. His head tilted, studying me with something I recognized as affection. My heart began kicking at my chest. It was only mildly unsettling, to say the least, to feel naked in front of this male. As though he gazed into the very depths of my soul. My throat worked on a swallow, something in my blood and spirit-stirring, like a sleeping beast peeking its eye open for the first time in aeons. "Well, for one, coming to know and master your powers. But we will go far beyond that. Most importantly, I suppose the purpose of our lessons can be summed up as learning how to live and find the freedom you seek," he hummed thoughtfully.

My breath caught. I swallowed nothing as my heart thudded loudly in my ears along with the vagus' words. *The Freedom you seek is so much closer than you think, Aurelia."*

Somehow, intuitively, I felt like Kyril, and the vagus meant so much more by the word "freedom" than I had ever imagined. I also felt nervous about working on my magic with him. I had no idea what potentially I, or it, had. What if my powers were next to nil? His brows drew together with concern before raising an eyebrow. He could probably hear the clamoring of my heart. I quickly cleared my throat." Good luck... I have no idea if I even really have any powers." Kyril chewed his cheek to stifle a grin, looking intensely smug. "Somehow, I'm not worried that'll be an issue." I sighed heavily, hoping for the best. "Where do we begin?"

Kyril's lips quirked in amusement as he watched me roughly cut a too-large hunk of meat and put it in my mouth. "While we're here, we may as well begin with etiquette... As much as I appreciate your ravenous appetite. My chewing slowed, and I barely managed to force down the hunk of meat. "Unfortunately, some people are only capable of seeing things skin deep and fixate on the superficial, and they will judge you on trite things such as this," Kyril said as he leaned in and a long, strong, capable hand stroked my own as he spoke gently to me. My gaze dropped to the hand touching my own, and I couldn't help but notice the scars that decorated his knuckles. The only way scars are formed on immortals is if when the wounds are made, the immortal is so weakened that their healing ability is stifled. "You're not in Pauperes Domos anymore..."

Every hair on my body rose, and my magic sang in response to his touch. My eyes met his, and I found pain there. I gave a tight nod trying to quell the emotion swelling in my chest, and tore my gaze from his, removing my hand from beneath his, a chill forming at the absence. "Right... No one likes a feral creature." A dimple appeared as a crooked grin graced his features. "Speak for yourself," he purred. Heat and need suddenly pooled low within me at his words, my eyes darting back up to his.

We spent the entirety of the day together as he ran through the basics of the various forms of etiquette, beginning with the only one he thought I might struggle with- eating etiquette. Apparently, he'd seen a Cerberus eat with more couth. I could only laugh at the truth of it. Years of near starvation will do that to you.

Hours later, the sun began to set as we strolled through the magnificent palace gardens. He offered me the crook of his muscular arm and led me through a maze-like, flower and shrub-lined path. He instructed me as to how I should properly align my body beside the male or female- which provided two different sets of guidelines. When and where my gaze should fall. How I should tilt my head and just much of my neck I should display towards them, and precisely what it would all suggest. I quickly came to realize how much body language was an utterly foreign language to me. The nuances and their subliminal, unconscious effect were staggering when he brought it all to my attention.

Kyril watched me heave a sigh as I stared out at the small lake at the bottom of the tall hill we stood upon and finally asked, "You ok?" he asked with a familiarity that existed only between family, friends, and lovers. I chewed my cheek, hesitating. "... Yeah... I just... This is all so surreal. Sometimes I feel like I'm going to wake up from this dream, and I'll be back in Pauperes Domos. Like the rug is going to be ripped out from underneath me as soon as I get comfortable. And... I also feel so conflicted. Everything I'd ever learned growing was... so, so *wrong*. It's painful to reconcile the people I knew and loved with people who once... owned and oppressed others. To say the least." Kyril frowned a little, watching me. "Ah. That... Do you want my advice? You're free to say no. I won't take it personally." I nodded almost desperately. "Please." He blew out a long breath before speaking. "Let go." My breath caught as my mind briefly returned to my journey with the vagus, *his words filling my being as he pulled my soul from my body. "Let go."*

My throat worked on a swallow, and Kyril's stare became concerned as he studied me. "You sure you're ok?" I shook my head, returning to this reality. "Yeah... Just... Déjà vu, I suppose..." He nodded slowly, watching me with those eyes that seemed to stem from the infinite cosmos as he rubbed soothing circles on my back. "Let go, Aurelia. We all play a role, whether it's preordained by The Ones is beyond my depth of knowledge, but I do know that you can't move forward if your focus is on the past and on things entirely beyond your control."

5

Syan was waiting for me as Kyril and I entered the palace. Her cheeks flushed, deepening in color at our approach. "Syan," Kyril hummed. Syan beamed up at him, "Lord Ronan. It's lovely to see you again." "Always a pleasure," he said, smiling warmly down at her. Syan gave a heavy sigh. Watching Syan's reaction, I bit my cheek so hard it drew blood to try and stifle my grin. His gaze snapped to mine, nostrils flaring. Something fiery flickered in his eyes, but he only gave that lover's smile, easy and seductive. "Aurelia," he purred. And then disappeared into thin air.

As Syan and I headed for the baths, she grinned at me excitedly, "I had a feeling you two would hit it off." I blushed, chewing my cheek. "Oh?" I tried to ask innocently. She gave me a knowing look, rolling her eyes, laughing. "I'm surprised you two didn't rip each other's close off." I couldn't help but laugh. "He's a good male," she continued, "And has been through a lot... I don't think he's been with anyone in... years." My breath hitched. "Why?" I asked, anxiety already rising. We entered the thermal baths, and she shut the door before she responded. "I actually don't know the whole story... I've only heard rumors because this all took place before I was born but... Apparently, his mate was killed in the war."

Syan removed her belt and sheer chiffon tunic to step into the bathing pool, waiting for me as I undressed to join her. By now, my nudity had become something I didn't think twice about around Syan. I felt a sharp stabbing pain in my chest, both in empathy for what he must have gone through and sadness that meant whatever bizarre sensations I'd experienced meeting him... Must be nothing more than... I don't didn't know what. But it meant that we couldn't be nexus mates. Shame filled me at the idea. How stupid I must be to be so wide-eyed and entranced by him. He probably experienced that everywhere he went. "His nexus mate?" I asked, seeking confirmation. She nodded solemnly.

My heart ached, trying to imagine the pain and suffering the loss of a nexus mate must cause. *Gods.* I couldn't even imagine. The few nexus mates I knew of in Pauperes Domos when one passed, the other quickly followed. It was a death sentence. Supposedly it was a mercy granted by The Ones to reunite nexus mates in the realms *beyond.* How he had survived it, I had no idea.

That evening I waited for Queen Nuala in the garden, sitting at the same table I'd dined with Kyril at, dressed in a berry-colored dress made of silk- *spider silk-* as Syan had informed me. Admittedly, it was divine. And one of the few truly opaque dresses I could wear to fully conceal my... assets. It had a deep v-neck that plummeted to my waistline but was narrow enough that it still covered my breasts, which had grown fuller thanks to the delicious food, and the weight I'd put on in the past several weeks. The dress hugged my newly developed curves- a bum and hips that I had never known I could possess whilst living in Pauperes Domos.

.   .   .

Aeternam light orbs were peppered around the area, floating. It was a romantic setting that had my thoughts returning to Kyril. I willed them away from him, trying to direct them anywhere but him, and by the grace of the gods, my thoughts were cut off by a now familiar current of electricity that snaked its way into the room. And even though I knew this person had once been my sworn enemy, I now felt a modicum of relief at her presence. I turned in my seat to see her striding in from the garden doors.

Her face lit up with a smile that somehow looked so familiar even though I barely knew her. I stood to greet her, and before she sat down, she wrapped her arms around me. "You're looking remarkably beautiful. Palace living looks good on you," she chirped as she sat. "Thank you. Syan's been taking exceptional care of me," I chortled.

An extraordinary array of food and drink magically appeared on the table, my glass of red wine already poured. "So, how was your trip?" I asked, surprised by the familiar air that we both seemed to settle into. She scoffed, rolling her eyes as she reached for her own glass of wine and took a lengthy swig.

"Boring. Which is a good problem to have. It means nothing bad has happened. So I shouldn't complain."

I smiled appreciatively. "I can hardly wait."

"You let me know when you're ready, your royal emissary," she winked, "... So... How do you like Kyril?"

I nearly choked on the gulp of wine I was swallowing. I couldn't suppress the smile his name drew, "He's... a lovely tutor."

Aurelia threw her head back with laughter. "Oh, gods... You two...," she giggled, shaking her head.

I couldn't help but laugh, albeit red-faced. "What?"

She took a deep breath, studying me all while grinning broadly. "I'm just happy that... you're getting along so well. You'll be working together a lot."

I narrowed my eyes at her suspiciously. Excitedly.

"Did he say something?"

"Loads," she hummed, grinning smugly.

"Care to share?"

"Pretty sure he'd murder me."

I found a tiny grin curling at the corner of my cheek at this.

"How'd you meet him?" I asked, not wanting to push any further.

Her lips quirked as she studied me, a look of nostalgia coming over her. "Through a mutual friend of ours, after I'd escaped the royal harem. He was the one who helped me hide whilst the rebels regained their strength and forces," she said from around a large bite of food.

None of this had been written in the books, and I found myself eager to find out what other details were missing from them.

"Is he... a good male, do you think?"

Her eyebrows practically leapt up to her hairline. "He's the bravest, most selfless male I've ever known. And he was monumental in helping me win the war, as you may have read."

I heaved a sigh at her impressive words. Chewing my cheek as my mind began to wander...

"Did you two ever...?"

She threw her head back and laughed. "Not at all."

"So... it wouldn't be a problem if... ya know."

She huffed a laugh. "Aurelia, he may as well have tattooed your name on his face. And vice versa, from the looks of it. You two belong to each other."

Surprise fluttered my expression as my heart swelled at her affirmation. Nuala rolled her eyes as she grinned.

She chuckled, shaking her head, "We'll find out soon now won't we."

.   .   .

I took a bite of food, deliberating whether or not to ask about his nexus mate. If that's what she was. "I heard his mate was killed in the war." Nuala's breath caught, her throat working on a swallow. "I... I think that's a subject perhaps best left to Kyril to discuss. I'm sorry you learned about it from someone else." I blew out a heavy breath, shaking my head. "Why would you be sorry? Honestly, I'm ashamed I even asked. I know it's not my place. I barely even know him. *I'm* sorry." I took a gulp of wine to try and quell my embarrassment. Nuala leaned forward, reaching for my hand. "Aurelia, it's fine... I just know that Kyril would rather talk to you about it himself because it's... It's all rather complicated. And I don't want to misinform you."

Nuala leaned back in her chair and gifted me with the change of subject. "How are you finding the others? I see Syan has made you some beautiful garments," she nodded towards my dress, smiling again. I couldn't help but grin at the thought of Syan. "Syan is... an angel... really. No one has ever seen me cry as much as she has, nor been near as patient with me." Nuala nodded in understanding. "She has a healing touch, doesn't she?... And Evrin?"

I smirked. "He's a charmer... Also a relative?" I asked jokingly. "*So charming*. I know. Evrin could charm the pants off a nun," she hummed.

"Is he from here?"

She shook her head, her expression dimming again.

"He's from the South Guard. His parents died in the war. But... He and others who lost their family were brought here to be taken care of." My chest ached in dismay at hearing this. I'd read about it in the history books she'd given me. "I have to say... When I read that in those books... I cried. My father told me I had cousins who had survived, children, who you'd taken. I'd assumed they were killed... And I know this sounds weird but thank you... I can't imagine there being any other ruler who would do such a thing." She smiled appreciatively at me. Although sadly. "I'm just so grateful that I was actually able to. That things worked out. Do you happen to know any of their names?"

I sighed, shaking my head. "It was so long ago... But I imagine some of them would have my last name. Eleftheran." Nuala's expression grew thoughtful. "There were so many... And except for the children I worked closely with, I rarely came to learn their surnames. But most of the people who worked with them are still alive. We could try asking Evrin if he knew any other children by that surname. And Kyril, he worked closely with so many of them, helping them to master their powers, etc." I couldn't help the heart-fluttering reaction I had at the mention of Kyril and the idea of him helping children as Nuala continued to speak. "I would be happy to connect you with them and help you find them... As my emissary, you'll be working alongside one of them anyway- Like Lord Batlaan of the Eastern Guard and his Mother Morwen. You'll meet them soon enough, I'm sure."

My breath caught at the idea that I could potentially be reunited with family... My eyes watered, and I chewed my cheek to stifle the tears. "That would be a dream come true... Thank you." Nuala nodded and reached out to rub my hand soothingly. I gasped, remembering something I'd meant to ask her. "By the way, was that you who left the other books and flowers for me with my breakfast every day?" Nuala's eyebrows furrowed in surprise briefly before smiling knowingly. She chuckled to herself, closing her eyes for a moment. "No. It wasn't..."

When I laid in bed that night I could find no sleep. My mind writhed with questions. Most of all, *how was it conceivable that everyone I loved- specifically, my parents- had been on the wrong side of the war?* And other things like why the vagus wanted me to find the Goddess of Origin. Although, eventually, my mind drifted back to Kyril. Despite my best efforts. I swung my legs over the edge of the bed, finally giving up on any designs I had on getting any sleep when the moon had reached its zenith. Dressed in a robe and one of the many too-see-through nightgowns that Syan had given me. I silently turned the handle of the bedroom door and crept into the hallway, carefully closing it behind me.

In the near two months I'd been here, I still hadn't explored the whole palace. As I crept through the bejeweled hallway beneath the 25-foot ceilings and crystal chandeliers, I figured there was no better time to do so than in the middle of the night, free from prying eyes. I followed the hallway down and around until it opened up to one of the several central sets of red-carpeted, white crystal stairs that branched off in different directions- some up, some down, some east, some west, north, and south. It almost made me dizzy just looking at it. I decided on taking the one hewn in the direction of the Western Guard.

As I walked, I made mental notes of various pieces of artwork and other distinguishable differences that marked each corner and wall so I could find my way back. I paused in front of various smaller doors for fear it was someone's bedroom, but when I came upon a pair of gargantuan double doors, I couldn't resist my temptation and cracked one of them open. The large windows at one end of the room illuminated the space with enough moonlight that I could make out the towering bookcases. Rows and rows of them. A library. It was breathtaking. I'd never even heard of such a thing. I closed the door behind me, and as I walked further into the room, an aeternam lantern flickered on at the end of the bookcase I now stood beside. The bookcases nearly reached the ceiling. I looked around but found no ladder. Magic. Right. Why would they need a ladder when they could just float up to the shelf or call the book down? And I still had no idea how to access any of my own magic. But perhaps this was a good place to start. I scanned the titles of the books, many of which were in languages or characters I didn't recognize.

I wound my way down and around towards another bookcase, another aeternam light twinkling on. I was looking for anything regarding The Goddess of Origin or something that I hoped would plainly be called, 'How to Access Your Magic'. I had no such luck. After several minutes, I completed scanning the titles of the books on shelves at or below eye level to me in the row I stood and sighed heavily, looking down towards the very end of the library. A considerable distance.

As I continued down the isles, I began to realize that the books and their shelves all looked identical. I turned 360 degrees, feeling doubly confused. I pulled a book off the shelf and looked down at the title. "'Please Wait for Assistance'," I murmured aloud. *What the hell?* I glanced around, half expecting to see someone playing a joke on me. I slid the book back on the shelf and grabbed another. The title read, "It's 3 o'clock in the morning. Why are you awake?'" My jaw dropped, and I couldn't help but chuckle to myself. "Anxiety and insomnia. You?" I answered aloud, suddenly feeling very foolish. I looked around again, still seeing no one. I sighed, quickly returning the book to its spot and pulled out one last book. The title read, "Wanking Yourself to Sleep: A Beginner's Guide" I burst into laughter, still a little in disbelief, and dared to open the book. Just out of curiosity. Obviously. I gave a soft gasp as my eyes beheld the *illustrations. Explicit ones.* My eyes widened even my eyebrows tried to hide in my hairline. My core began to tingle, and I slammed the book shut. *Brilliant. A bewitched library with a dirty sense of humor.*

.   .   .

I returned the book and leaned my head on the shelf, blowing out a heavy breath. After a few moments, I turned to leave but felt something... somewhere in the distance within that pitch-blackness beyond the shelves, something beckoned. *Come closer.* I felt my heart begin to beat heavily in my chest, unable to do anything other than acquiesce to the pulling sensation drawing me deeper into the darkness. Thankfully, with each step towards another row, an aeternam light would flitter on in front of me. Although, the one behind me would turn off. After walking past at least a dozen rows, I looked back in the direction I'd come. Only the moonlight illuminated the doors. But then I noticed something. The door was open. I could have sworn I closed it. *Did I close it?* The hammering in my chest intensified at the thought that followed. *Closer,* it whispered in my mind. I tried to shake off my fear and turned back around to face the darkness looming in the distance.

I let out a shrill scream, and a bolt of lightning struck the floor behind the tall luminous figure that floated before me, the bookcase behind her visible through her translucent form. She yelped in shock, eyes widening. I clutched my chest in relief as she burst into a laugh. "I'm so sorry, that wasn't deliberate. I swear," she said as her mouth pressed into something like a stifled grin, contradicting her brow that was scrunched up with concern. Her pretty, heart-shaped face had full features: large doe eyes, a broad nose, and full lips. She was at least six feet tall, and her voluptuous curves put mine to shame. I lowered my hand, my heart finally catching my breath, laughing at how much she'd terrified me. "It's ok... I'm sorry about the...," I said, finding myself at a loss for words as I peaked around her at the burnt hole in the floor. That was *new*. She chuckled, "Don't be. I'm just glad you missed."

"Well, it's actually the first time I've ever used my... gifts. Albeit unintentionally."

"I can help you with that. We've got loads of books on mastering your magic," she grinned excitedly, turning back towards the rear of the library, "Follow me."

An orb of aeternam light appeared in her palm, purely for my benefit, I imagine, as she led me past what must have been at least a hundred rows of bookshelves. The deeper we walked into the library the stronger the scent of ancient papyrus, paper, leather, and ink became. There were no windows at this end of the library. An attempt in better preserving them. "Are you the... librarian?" She offered me me her hand. "Penelope," she grinned, "And think less librarian, more guardian."

"Aurelia," I beamed back, surprised to feel how warm and firm her hand was. Corporeal. "And what do you mean by guardian?" Her gaze roved over the towering shelves of books lovingly. "My life is bound to protecting these books. I'm to protect them and the knowledge within at all costs. I also preserve them with my magic. And yes, I also keep things orderly and organized. Particularly when curious creatures like you come sniffing around." She turned her head briefly, giving me a wink. "Although, we rarely have visitors, so..." As we continued strolling, I realized it felt like we'd been walking for ages but the end of the library didn't appear to be any closer still. "How deep does this library go?" She raised an eyebrow, "Have you never been to a library before?"

Her mouth formed an 'O' in realization. Right. Why would Pauperes Domos have libraries? "I am *so* sorry... I wasn't thinking. That was very rude of me...," she said, shaking her head at herself and making the tight curls of her hair bounce, "But in that case, allow me to explain. One of the many ways employed to protect the books, especially ones as rare and priceless as those found here, you won't ever find what you're looking for unless I personally lead you to it. The library doesn't have an end for you. Only for me because I'm it's guardian. Not even for Her Majesty." My face scrunched up, "You mean even the Queen can't access her own books without you?"

"Merely a precaution in case she were to...," the wraith's eyes seemed to flicker with a shadow, "... be compromised in some capacity." She smiled again, quickly changing the subject. "So, what sort of things are you looking to study?"

"Well, as you mentioned earlier... Perhaps some books on accessing my magic. For beginners... And any other books on the history of our realm, or the war," I'd added. She crooked a finger at a petite book, "Come here ya wee thing," she demanded sweetly. The book promptly jumped into her hand. "There, start with this one."

She began reaching towards other various books, all of them happily plopping themselves into her open arms before turning to me with the large stack, "And then, you can dive into these... Let me know if you'd like me to go over anything with you." I let out a small grunt as she passed me the small tower of books.

By the time I approached my bedroom door, I could see the reddish glow of the sun's ascent nearing the horizon. I set the books down and peaked out of the window. It was a magnificent view. I could see the garden beneath, expanding far and wide, peppered with lakes and fountains. And beyond that I could see the very edge of the Sable Forest. I felt an anchor drop in the pit of my stomach at the sight of it.

6

I t was pouring rain. Kyril stood beside me, an invisible canopy of his making raised above us, in the middle of a field beyond the gardens. I could see sheep being herded in the distance. We were both dressed to match- entirely in black, the material of our form-fitting clothing made from thick spider silk embossed with a swirling design and characters I didn't recognize but knew must be the runes Syan had explained were meant to protect the wearer from magical and physical assault. And apparently, spider silk fabric was not only light and flexible, but it was near impenetrable- making it ideal in combat and far superior to the traditional fighting leathers found elsewhere. Syan had even mentioned the use of it on Midgard- that the warriors there made thick vests out of it to protect them during battle.

"Close your eyes," he said, turning to me as we remained huddled together beneath the canopy. Nervous, I hesitated for a moment before following his orders. "Lay your attention on your breath. The rain. The sensation of the wind on your skin. My voice," he purred hypnotically, "Your heartbeat... My heartbeat." I listened to the rainwater cascading off the invisible corners, slapping the grass and mud as it fell. The hushing sound of the rain beating upon the invisible shield above us. I listened deeper and could hear Kyril's heart beating. A little faster and harder than I expected. I focused on my breath, and as I did, I could hear my own heartbeat beating in unison with his. I opened my eyes to find him watching me. Grinning knowingly. "No peaking, my fire," he purred. My heart trilled at the endearment, and his grin widened, gifting me with two dimples. I closed my eyes and took a deep breath, trying to soothe my nerves and direct my focus. "Well done...," Kyril's voice was like a deep caress, "Now draw your attention to your core... *Lower.*" I peeked open an eye at him, and his grin became rogue. "*Lower...,*" he urged smoothly. I closed my eye and did so. "What do you feel?" I searched for the words. "... I feel... energy. Dense coiling of energy." I could feel him smiling. "See this energy. With color and texture... And watch it flowing through you. Rising out of the top of your head. See it branching out of your body, your limbs, like the branches of a tree or in tendrils.... See it filling the spaces between and radiating from you..."

I saw it so clearly, in my mind's eye. It was brilliant and thrumming, pulsating to the rhythm of my heart. And his, apparently. I saw webs of energy branching out rapidly, filling every crevice of dark space around me, several feet in every direction, like lightning. Lightening that emitted every element. As I watched it grow, unfurling around me, I felt my skin begin to hum. Humming a single note that resonated within the verses. It tingled. The tingling grew powerfully until I felt tendrils of electricity forming on my fingertips, wrapping around my hands. My lungs seemed to fill with something new. More than air. Ether. My eyes fluttered open, and my heart began to pound wildly. Blue white light, like what I'd seen in my mind, roiled around my body.

. . .

"What was it you were saying the other day? Something about potentially not having any powers?" Kyril teased, beaming with pleasure. I laughed excitedly, and the tendrils of electricity glowing around me lengthened and thickened, reaching for him. He reached up and touched one of the white glowing tendrils with his fingertip, and it, along with several other tendrils, entwined themselves around his fingers and hand. He grinned so broadly in response I could see the tips of his fangs. "Someone's eager," he breathed before meeting my gaze. The tendrils of energy grew brighter and broader to the point where they reached Kyril's invisible barrier shielding us from the rain. The barrier broke with a soft *'pop'*, and the rain immediately fell upon us in sheets.

Kyril burst into a laugh, and I couldn't help but join him. The tendrils of my power, my energy seemed to return to my body at my losing focus. He stepped in closer to me and took my face in his hands, scanning my features as if trying to memorize them. Our hearts thundering as loudly as the rain. "Put it back," he shouted above the monsoon, "If you want." His grin widened again as if it were a dare. My eyebrows scrunched in confusion. "How?" He lifted a shoulder as if it were as easy as that. "*See* it in your mind as though it's already there. Feel it because you *know* it's there. You don't even have to force it." His thumbs caressed my cheeks. I closed my eyes to visualize the same transparent barrier Kyril had created. And nothing happened. "It's not working," feeling a pang of disappointment. "You have to do more than just see it. You're just forgetting to feel it's existence. All the energy and matter necessary to create it is already there. Just acknowledge it. Why do you need to force something that's already there?"

Kyril tucked the strands of my hair behind my ears before taking my hands in his and pressing one of my hands against his cheek. My breathing slowed as we held each other's gaze. I forced my mind to focus on willing the matter and energy to come together and create a barrier but... "Perhaps this would be easier if you'd stop deliberately distracting me," I said half-heartedly, inwardly hoping my hand would be stuck to his cheek forever.

He leaned down and spoke gently, his lips grazing the shell of my ear. "There will always be distractions, Aurelia." He closed the distance between us and rested his face in the crook of my neck, still holding my hands. My breathing hitched at the closeness, but I fortified my determination and let go of the distractions instead of mentally fighting them. I let my body press and lean against his as I drew my hands to his chest, letting my face rest between them. Focused on the feeling and sound of his heart pounding in time with mine as he wrapped his arms around me. Never in my life had I felt so whole. I let go of trying to *force* the barrier there and instead felt a sudden sense of gratitude that it was there.

I felt the apple of Kyril's cheek press against my neck as he smiled at the rain no longer pouring onto us. However, the wind still whipping away at us sent a shiver through me. He pulled back to look at me, his face tensing with concern. Before I could even open my mouth to complain, darkness and stars exploded into the horizon around me. And as quickly as it appeared, it was gone. Replaced by my bathroom. Strategically, right beside the toilet. Knew what was coming, and a bucket appeared in her hands. He pulled my wet hair back as I wretched, hurling up my breakfast.

When I finished heaving, wiped my mouth off with toilet paper, and flushed away the evidence of my shame, I looked up at him in shock, "What... the fu-," but was cut off as I suddenly realized I was dry again. Even my hair. My jaw dropped, examining my now dry clothes. "How?" I breathed. The shower behind him, by some invisible hand, turned on. Steam curling in its wake. "Ok, show off." Kyril laughed. "Oh, don't get too excited. That's literally the extent of my powers," he joked, "If you're ever caught in the rain or have some clothes that need drying. Or a handle that needs turning, I'm your guy. Other than that, I'm pretty useless."

I huffed a laugh rolling my eyes as he wrapped me in his arms again for warmth. "Thank you," I murmured softly into his chest. He nuzzled his nose in my hair. "You did incredibly well today. I've helped others like you before. During and after the war... Slaves who had never known their magic either. It usually takes much longer to tap into and control their power like that."

Kyril had waited for me in the garden to join him for lunch after my shower. Or for him to watch me eat lunch anyway. He grinned, watching me as I took a *medium-sized* bite of my food. "I think I already miss ravenous you." I chuckled, sighing with pleasure at the delicious food. And company. "So... How often do you need to eat, by the way?" I asked, immediately regretting having asked. "Sorry, I just... there were no vampires in Pauperes Domos. You're the first one I've ever met." Something like sadness fluttered behind his eyes. "No, you wouldn't have. There weren't that many left after the war."

I swallowed thickly. "Oh, gods... I'm so sorry."

A corner of his mouth curved. "Thankfully, procreation is something that comes quite naturally to us," he winked, "Our populations have quadrupled in the last hundred years."

My interest was piqued. "Quadrupled through bite or birth?"

He huffed a laugh. The perennial grin on his face never faltered. "Both, I suppose."

I bit my cheek. "And have you... procreated?"

.   .   .

He erupted with laughter. My cheeks flushed. After a few moments, he calmed, studying my face in the same way he did every time I was with him. "You look so beautiful when you blush. You're lucky I have a full belly." To my own shame, my heart kicked at the idea and a bolt of lust coursed through me. He leaned forward, nostrils flaring. I crossed my legs, leaning back in my chair. It was all I could do to try and mask the pheromones my body was now undoubtedly producing. He gave me a knowing, devilish grin. The warm, almost sweet smell of balsam and burning firewood filled my nose. *His smell. Yum.* My nipples peaked in response. I could hear my heart thundering in my chest. I'm sure he could too. *How did we get here?* Never had I had such a reaction to someone. I'd taken several lovers and never had they inspired this... need. If I hadn't known that he'd already met his mate, long ago, before I was even born, I'd think he must be my nexus, but...

Now that my arousal was thoroughly dampened, I tried to change the subject. His grin dimmed as though he'd noticed. It was almost as though I felt it dim. I internally shook my head, trying to liberate myself from my train of thought. "You didn't answer my question." He leaned back in his chair again as if the question had grounded him. "Once. By bite." His expression became neutral.

After I finished eating, we walked in comfortable silence together. I wondered if perhaps I'd drug up long-buried memories when I'd asked about his... *procreation* efforts. Or the lack there of, it seemed, with the exception of one. He seemed to read my mind just as I felt the urge to ask.

"It was a hundred years ago. Her name was Siaorse. She was human...," he began. *A hundred years ago.* So not his nexus which had been killed in the war. "She lives somewhere in the Eastern Guard still, I believe. I haven't spoken to her in perhaps 98 years. She worked for a lykanthir friend of mine." *Lykanthir.* A wolf shifter. "She became ill, and Batlaan asked me to help her..." He met my gaze as if anticipating my next question. "You became close?" He nodded. "We were lovers for a brief period of time..."

I chewed my cheek to try and mask the grimace that was trying to tighten my features at the unrighteous jealousy I found springing up within me. "Do you miss her?" *Siaorse or your nexus,* I wanted to ask but thankfully stopped myself as the words unintentionally spilt from me and my face heated. A broad grin filled his handsome face. "There's no reason to be jealous, my fire." My jaw dropped. "I- I'm not jealous!" I sputtered. His grin widened even further as he stepped closer to me. His face only inches from mine as he cupped my cheeks and pulled my gaze back up to his. He offered me an appreciative smile. "We were simply two people with kindred spirits keeping the darkness of loneliness at bay. Nothing more than friends that cared for one another in a way that is purely platonic..." He leaned in closer, caressing his cheek against mine. As he spoke, his lips brushed against my cheek, making my breath hitch. "And could never hold a candle to my nexus..."

My heart pounded its unrighteous protest, gut-twisting despite barely knowing this person. I felt so... stupid and irrational. Kyril, clearly having felt my change in mood, pulled back to meet my stare. "Aurelia...," he studied my gaze, reading me like a book. The pupils of his eyes that normally seemed to hold whole galaxies in them darkened. His jaw feathering, he shook his head. My heart splintered. So it was true. "Why?" I asked, incensed. "Why mislead me? Is that what you do to females? Make them think they're your nexus? For what? Surely, they'd be willing to sleep with you regardless."

· · ·

His face slackened in shock."Oh, Aurelia... That's not-." I stepped away from him, shoving his hands away as he tried to hold onto me. "Don't." I turned and stormed back towards the palace. A few breaths later, Kyril appeared beside me out of thin air, keeping in step. If I hadn't been so angry, it'd have startled me, but I was too upset to care. "Aurelia, please... I promise you it's not what you think." I whirled to face him. "Just what exactly did you mean then? Why would you even say something like that when you know I can't possibly be *that*?" Kyril's expression became pained. So very, very pained. "There is so much that I want to tell you. Need to tell you... But I just... Can't right now." I shook my head in dismay. "Who was she?"

Kyril's eyes seemed to glisten, his jaw working. "One day, Aurelia, I will be able to tell you everything." I shook my head at him, feeling so incredibly stupid at being heartbroken over someone I'd known for a couple of days. I steeled myself as I looked up into his stricken face. "I know we have to work together, but that's all that this is and will ever be. So let's forget about whatever this was. Things don't need to be awkward or difficult between us. Let's just maintain a healthy boundary of respect and professionalism."

7

Evrin caught me in the hallway on my way back to my room, feeling on the verge of implosion. The tension in my chest was so tight I felt as though my sternum would crack. Evrin and all his loveliness were a welcome distraction. His face furrowed with concern as he took me in. "Darling, you're wearing the look of a thoroughly scorned lover. Give me their names, and I will remove their genitalia and feed it to them. Discretely." My jaw dropped, breathing a laugh, and he waved away my horror. "Don't worry. It'll grow back eventually. In case you ever change your mind. Unless they're human, in which case, I can utilize other methods of torture."

"You're such an angel," I sighed jokingly as I wove my arm into the muscled crook of the elbow he offered. The laugh I gave was a welcome release, a modicum of tension in my chest easing. "Seriously, though. Just say the word, my beauty. Don't be fooled by this winsome exterior," he said, gesturing towards his aesthetic perfection, "I have no qualms with serving justice..." My eyebrows leapt up, and I eyed Evrin up and down, trying to see beyond all the saccharine charm. His smile turned wicked, and I could easily see it. "Oh," I whispered, almost in awe- equal parts impressed and warned. He winked at me and wrapped an arm around my shoulder, tucking me into his side as he kissed my temple. "You're so wonderful," I said as much to him as I did to myself, feeling so grateful to have him as a friend. And dance tutor.

That is until he had me put on a pair of pale pink shoes with soles that felt as though they were made of wood. And expected me to dance on my toes in them. "Is sadist another one of those traits hidden beneath your mask of disarming charisma?" He tossed his head back with laughter as he handed me a bag full of cotton balls. "You'll thank me soon enough, darling. Just jam those in there before your feet."

Evrin helped me fix my posture, which according to him was the equivalent of a "heavily pregnant "orangutang", he had me practice a series of elegant, stationary moves. Once the quartet with Evrin's lover arrived, the real fun, and pain, began. He held my hand to help me balance as I practiced what he called 'pirouettes' and 'arabesques' across the ballroom. Within a few minutes, my toes were literally howling in pain. But even so, it couldn't eclipse the joy and freedom I felt dancing across the room with him. Gratitude swelled in my chest. Not only had I escaped Pauperes Domos, but tonight, at dusk, so many others would be free to experience this joy as well.

After I showered post-dance lesson, I walked to Nuala's wing. Stopped, as usual, by her guards. Today two females, one fae, and one lykanthir stood at the staircase landing. The lykanthir's gaze became distant for a moment before she silently stepped aside to let me through. There were several sets of doors, none of which revealed which belonged to her bedroom, until her head popped out of one towards the end. "Would you like to join the guards in Pauperes Domos?" She asked as I approached. My breath caught. I'd thought about it... but I had mixed emotions. So many of the friends and family of those I'd tried to escape with would be asking where they were if they'd made it. She studied me and nodded in silent understanding, her expression solemn. "My guards notified me who had gone missing. I had them notify their relatives." Relief whooshed out of me in a heavy breath.

Apprehension still filled me at the idea of stepping foot in Pauperes Domos ever again. I never wanted to go back. Not only because it was a place that had been filled with so much suffering, but the fact that it was the last place I'd been with my brother before he was killed in The Sable Forest. Nuala led me over to the edge of her enormous bed that sat on a raised dais in the back of the room that gazed out at the balcony, framed by sheer silken drapes blowing in the breeze that housed the swimming pool that seemed to flow directly into the horizon. Its invisible end spilt over the edge in a waterfall that led to another pool and finally a hot tub.

Nuala sat me down next to her. "You don't ever have to go back, Aurelia." Her gaze met mine, compassion simmering there. "Thank you," I managed, throat closing and working on a rough swallow, "I feel like... Like I need to. Like I owe it to them." Her brow scrunched in concern. "Why?" I took a deep breath, trying to quell the tears that threatened to erupt. "Because... Escaping Pauperes Domos was my idea." Nuala's mouth carved a frown. "That doesn't put their blood on your hands, Aurelia... And just imagine if you hadn't. No one would be freed tonight." Tears spilt down my cheeks, and Aurelia pulled me into her arms as a sob escaped me.

. . .

She held me and rubbed soothing circles on my back until my crying calmed. "Want me to call Kyril over?" That only renewed my sobbing. She pulled back to look at me. "What happened?" I shook my head, feeling wholly ashamed by my idiocy.

"Nothing you need to worry about. I just think it's better Kyril and I keep things professional."

She laughed, shaking her head in disbelief.

"I'm sorry... What?"

I exhaled heavily. "I don't know what he was expecting, or what his intentions were... but.... I think I wanted more than what he could offer. I don't know why. I've never felt so powerfully pulled towards someone."

She studied me as confusion settled on her face. "And why do you think you wanted more than what he could offer?"

I chewed my cheek, willing myself not to burst into another sob. "Because I feel this...," I gestured helplessly towards my chest, "thing! And I know it must all be in my head for some reason because he already found his nexus. Who was killed in the war!" Her jaw dropped, expression slackening in shock- exactly as Kyril's had. Her gaze fell to the floor for a moment. "All I can say is that you've been misinformed."

My brows furrowed, hope flickering. "So... The female he was with during the war... who was killed... wasn't his nexus mate?"

She heaved a sigh rubbing at her temples with her thumb and forefinger. "She was."

My heart shattered all over again.

"But that doesn't mean that you're not either."

I reared back. "What?"

Nuala's gaze met mine again. "She died two hundred years ago, Aurelia. Who's to say The Ones haven't woven another nexus into the thread of his fate? They're known to show mercy."

My jaw hung ajar. "I've never heard of such a thing...," I breathed.

She took my hand and gave it a squeeze. "Nothing is beyond the realm of possibility." We sat in thoughtful silence for a moment, our gazes drawn to the horizon beyond the balcony. Dusk was approaching.

"Are you sure you want to go?" Nuala asked.

"I think... I need to. I know that their families will resent me if they find out I'm alive... but... perhaps it will give them some form of catharsis. Even if it's by doing nothing more than spewing righteous vitriol."

She heaved a sigh, pulling on her darkest red fighting silks.

My brow furrowed with concern. "Are you expecting there to be bloodshed?" Her expression matched my own. "I fear that my sentries will be attacked as soon as they remove the palladium collars. I will not ask them to do my bidding while they suffer the consequences."

Admiration and appreciation for her filled me. It was jarring how much had changed between us, or at least in my perception of her, in such a short period of time. "Not to mention, it's Pauperes Domos. When is there not bloodshed?" Fair point. "Well, hopefully, they will also realise that if they attack your sentries, they will sabotage the freedom of their compatriots. Who will then retaliate, I'm sure. Also, I imagine your sentries won't allow them to make it as far as the train if they do." She shrugged casually, blowing out a breath that puffed out her cheeks.

"Let's hope for the best. Peace," she chirped, handing me a dagger and it's thigh holster, "Here... Just point it away from you," she teased. I huffed a laugh as I examined it. It was a dagger fit for an queen for sure. The hilt was asymmetrical- the grip was crafted of pale blue angelite stone that fit perfectly into the groves of my slender fingers.

Its pommel was a perfectly polished silver engraved with intricate whorling embellishments.

I withdrew the blade from its worn black leather sheath that was tipped with matching engraved silver to reveal a gleaming titanium blade welded into the shape of a wing. It seemed not merely to reflect light but emanate it, as if from within. My breath caught at the sight of it, and I swore I could hear its song like the pealing of a distant bell. Energy, so powerful, yet so familiar it felt like an extension of my own, poured into me. My hands and arms tingling as it did.

Nuala's voice snapped me back to reality. "Her name is Thea. Breathtaking isn't she?..." She said softly, smiling over my shoulder.

"Oh, Nuala..."

"I was told that any who die by this blade experience not only a physical death but an ego death, and are swiftly brought to the karmic destiny necessary for them to become beings of selfless devotion."

My jaw dropped trying to process that.

"Holy ... shit."

"Holy shit, indeed."

I grinned, "So you're telling me that if I kill someone with this blade, I'm basically doing them a favour."

Nuala tipped her head back and laughed.

"If anything, they should be thanking you and *throwing* themselves on your blade."

We both cackled a little wickedly.

"It's yours," she beamed.

My laughter stilled, brows furrowing. I shook my head speechlessly, trying to place Thea back into her hands. "What? No... I can't... It's..."

Nuala smirked, pushing the dagger away.

"As I said, it's yours. Take it."

My throat worked on a swallow.

"But I don't know how I can ever repay you-"

"Umm... Use it. Not on me. And don't die."

I rolled my eyes, laughing, still in shock. My eyes were drawn back to it. "It must be priceless..."

"I wouldn't know. I wasn't the one who bought it. "

She gave me a smug shrug before turning on her heel to walk away.

8

We stepped onto the train, admiring the wood and brass details. The emerald velvet seats. If the Pauperes Domosians made it to the train, it would be the nicest thing they'd seen in two hundred years. Several dozen of Nuala's sentries filed into the train. Nuala and I settled in at the rear of the luxurious carriage. As the last of her sentries piled in, the hairs on my arms rose as a familiar energy caressed me, and Kyril appeared in the doorway. His gaze met mine, and my breath caught. That knot in my chest, twisting like a knife inside of me. "Yikes," Nuala said quietly as she stood to join her sentries on the other side of the carriage, "I'll give you two some privacy."

Kyril's gaze didn't leave mine as he passed Nuala on his way to me. Kyril sat down beside me. I could hear his heart thumping as heavily as mine. In time with mine. Perhaps Nuala was right, that The Ones were not beyond mercy. My throat squeezed, and my energy hummed in his presence, swelling to bursting. My gaze fell to my lap as tiny tendrils of pale blue and white electricity stretched from my finger-tips and appeared to me, sneaking their way towards him. I curled my hands into fists and turned to look out of the window. Dark tendrils of fiery golden sparks so warm they were almost hot curled around my hands. My palms opened of their volition, and I saw my energy seep from my palms and twine with his, blending until they became a deep gold, and I couldn't tell where his energy began, and mine ended.

I felt the heat of his stare, and I drew my eyes up to meet his. I swore I saw burning suns and stars in his eyes. The depths of the cosmos. The verses. And a deep well of sadness. "Aurelia, please forgive me...," he said softly. His words seemed to reverberate around us, and I looked to find a translucent bubble around us to give us privacy. I twisted in my seat towards him. I shook my head, feeling a pang of guilt. "I'm sorry for... assuming that you were being dishonorable."

The train hummed to life and began a smooth acceleration. Anxiety flooded my veins at having to face the pain and suffering I'd caused people I'd known for most of my life. Had worked and lived alongside for decades. And although I wasn't close with them because Pauperes Domos was a ruthless place, and my life there hadn't allowed for much beyond basic survival, I still felt the need to be loyal to them. And soul-crushing guilt.

Kyril wove his fingers with mine, and I instantly felt some of my anxiety dissipate. "I will not leave your side," he vowed.

The train arrived just as the sun began to dip below the horizon. We poured out of the train's carriages and silently made our way to the perennially open gates of Pauperes Domos. The massive stonewall and foreboding welcome sign loomed above, and I forced my gaze away from it, feeling my heart tearing in half at the remembrance of the last time I was here. With my brother. The words, "Enter At Own Risk," now seemed particularly ominous. Kyril's hand didn't leave mine, his thumb caressing the back of it as my heart beat a frantic staccato rhythm. "If at any point you want to leave, just say the word." I took a deep breath, trying to calm my nerves, nodding my gratitude. "If I don't face them... I'll never forgive myself."

Sentries, in groups of four, made their way to the various residential alleyways that encircled the city centre. Nuala stepped in front of us, a sentry tailing her as her eyes begged the question, *'you're sure?'* I nodded. The four of us walked to the final alleyway. The one on the edge of the city centre. I could feel the sentry's gaze periodically flitting towards me. "Aurelia," I offered, extending my hand. He nodded a little nervously. "I know... s," he replied, taking my hand in his sweaty palm. His face was boyish, his body tall and lanky, as if he had only just escaped puberty. His scent, which I'd only recently come to recognize, told me he was a lykanthir.

The empty alleyway stank of garbage, cheap ale, and charred meat. The all too familiar smell that I'd so recently been accustomed to was now cloying and made my stomach turn. Utrev knocked on the first door. A large fae male opened the door, his small family standing behind him. Their bags were already packed. Hope and excitement flooded the air around me, and much of my tension left my body. *Thank the gods.* The family all quickly made their blood oath, their palladium collars clattering onto the worn wood floors. "Make your way directly to the train. The first one leaves in an hour. You'll be given payment after departure," Utrev advised. The fae male nodded, hesitating briefly as his family left ahead of him. He swallowed thickly before turning and leaving without saying a word. The four of us exchanged a wary glance. "Let's hope they all go as easily,"

Kyril murmured as we exited the first home. I halted, gazing down the throughway that led to the gates. Dozens of fae, some carrying bags, some carrying nothing at all, rushed for the train. Cries and howls of joy rent the air as some of them even danced and pranced their way to the train. Tears of joy filled my eyes as I watched. Yet again, hearing my brother's voice echo in my head. Kyril draped an arm over my shoulders and kissed the top of my head. My chest filled to bursting.

Utrev knocked on the next door for it to immediately swing open as if the person on the other side had been waiting. And as their eyes landed on me, all the joy I'd felt dissolved at the guilt and anguish that replaced it. In the doorway stood Mateus' former lover, Dahlia. We'd never gotten along. She'd never treated Mateus the way he had deserved. And she hadn't wanted to leave her family behind when we tried to escape. *"You,"* she seethed, "I'd heard you'd survived somehow. And that you'd become thick as thieves with these ones." She spat at our feet. Utrev stepped forward, grasping the hilt of his sword but not drawing it. "You will respect Her Majesty and her royal subjects." I cringed at the words. *Royal subjects.* Dahlia threw her head back with laughter. "The only royal thing about you is your fancy new clothes. You're a traitor. And it's because of your arrogance that Mateus is dead. It should have been you that died. Not him."

My jaw flexed, trying desperately to hold back my tears. As if being of one mind, Kyril and Nuala stepped in closer to me for support. The gesture helped me steel myself, keeping the tears at bay. I was also grateful they remained silent, allowing me to fight my own battles. Even if it was silently. There was nothing I could say. Dahlia wasn't wrong. She just shook her head at me, sneering, as her gaze moved to Utrev. "Well? How do I make this blood oath?" Utrev looked to Nuala, who looked to me. I nodded, urging them on. Dahlia sniffed with disgust but said nothing more.

· · ·

I heaved a sigh of relief as we finally turned away from Dahlia's to move on. The smell of smoke drifted on the wind. The four of us looked to the horizon, stopping short at the city centre below. It was on fire. And admittedly, a part of me was glad for it. "Your Majesty," Utrev urged, "You should return to the palace." "Absolutely not," she said calmly, watching the city burn. "It's been a while since I've had a good bonfire."

We managed to free over a dozen more families before twilight arrived and I saw another familiar face. Tabitha, the sister of Rolam. The older male who'd slipped from my grasp to be attacked by the skinless beast in The Sable Forest. *"Aurelia...,"* she breathed. Her pretty, delicate face paled at the sight of me. I'd known this woman my entire life. She shook her head in disbelief. "I'd heard you survived." She stepped towards me and took me in her slender arms. "I'm so glad you're ok." Emotional exhaustion and relief had me nearly sagging in her arms. "Tabitha," I managed with a wobbly voice, "I'm *so* sorry." She pulled back to look at me, tears in her eyes, shaking her head. "Oh my sweet girl... Don't you dare blame yourself. Rolam had always dreamed of escaping. He knew the risks. They all did. What happened was beyond your control."

My throat worked on a swallow, tears spilling. She pulled me to her chest again, rubbing my back. "We all know that, Aurelia. No one blames you," she said firmly. My memory of her brother in... whatever that paradise was that the vagus had taken me to filled my mind. And as crazy as it would sound, I knew I was obligated to tell her. "I saw him," I whispered, "In one of the realms beyond... A vagus took me there." Her face slackened in terror. "A vagus?" I shook my head, dispelling her fear. "He was kind. And he took me to Mateus... They were all there. Happy, and at peace. More so than ever possible in this realm." Her chin quivered, tears spilling down her cheeks.

By the time we finished, it was dark. And a massive crowd of fae stood, like a herd of cattle, all gradually making their way through the gate waiting to board the train. I stood in awe as fae stood celebrating as they waited. Many of them playing and experimenting with their gifts. My chest filled with joy and gratitude again. I turned to Nuala who grinned watching everyone celebrate. "Thank you, Nuala..." She nodded her appreciation to me and opened her mouth to speak but instead, blood sprayed across my face as a dagger speared through her mouth from the back of her neck.

"No!" I screamed, catching her as she fell into my arms and we both tumbled to the ground. Utrev drew his sword to cut down the masked fae male who stabbed Nuala but his blade only met air as the fae disappeared into thin air. Kyril dove in front of us as another masked fae appeared, dagger in hand, and lunged for us. Kyril drove his sword up into the gut of the male, impaling him in midair.

Nuala clutched my arms, making choked, gurgling sounds as blood poured out of her. I reached for the hilt of the dagger and squeezed her hand, pulling the weapon free from her throat. As I did, she vomited blood and bile onto my front and the ground. I looked up to see a circle of masked fae, several people deep, surrounding us. Beyond them, I could see Nuala's sentries all fighting to reach us. "The False Queen," a fae male growled before his gaze fell to me as I reached for the hilt of the dagger Nuala had given me, "And the traitor." The male spat at our feet. I couldn't tell who he was by voice alone. The fae male stepped towards us, wagging a flaming finger at me in warning. "Ah, ah, ah." My magic swelled angrily inside me and began to crackle at my fingertips. If only I knew what do with it. Kyril stepped in front of me, taking a wide stance, blade dripping with flood beside him. Nuala gasped for air, kneeling on all fours beside me as the hole in her neck gradually healed.

Due to the stillness and silence alone, I tore my gaze from Nuala to Kyril, who stood staring down the fae male who had spat at us- and was now frozen in place before us as were every single one of his accomplices. Even from beneath their masks, I could see the pain contorting their faces. The crinkling around their eyes, the clenched jaws and gnashing teeth. They all seemed to clutch at their chests and stomachs at the same time and dropped to their knees. That's when *the smell* was carried to me on a smokey breeze. The smell of charred, burning flesh. Blood-curdling screams tore from their lips until, one by one, their screams were cut off as their throats *burned* away. All that remained were curls and wisps of smoke and burning embers. Black veins streaked across the visible skin of their hands, necks, and the lower half of their faces as if those too had been charred and blackened.

There were thousands of Pauperes Domosians still fighting with Nuala's sentries in the nearby distance but many of those nearest us had stopped, to watch in horror. Many of them masked fae. Some turned and ran directly into the melee, ripping off their masks to blend with the crowd. Others dared not move. Their weapons were raised already in defense. Though little good it would do them. The original group of masked fae were now nearly nothing but ash that had begun to blow away in the wind, coating us all in their remains.

Kyril still holding his ground, reached for my hand as his voice filled my mind. "Aurelia, grab Nuala and take my hand." Surprise stilled me. "What about Utrev and the others?" "I will come back for them." "Without me? The fuck you will." Kyril growled his displeasure.

. . .

Nuala's neck wound finally closed, and she coughed, blood splattering everywhere, as she rose to stand. Another of the masked fae took that as their cue, a crossbow appearing in his hands, and as it loosed an arrow, a jolt of energy rained down on him from above, leaving nothing but ash behind. But the bolt found its home in Kyril's chest. An unholy roar left me and I leapt to my feet. Lightning struck, from a cloudless night sky, several more of the masked fae around us. Several more that my magic had missed, turned and ran.

Nuala's body glowed red and gold as bones snapped and grew, transforming her into the three-headed beast I'd only ever heard horror stories about, towering above us all. Saliva dripped from the maw of a lions head, and from it's mane, the head of a horned beast. In place of its tail a seven foot long snake reared back, hissing, readying to strike. *The chimera.* They were creatures of lore. I gaped up at her in all her glory. She tilted her lions head to the sky and roared so loudly I felt the ground beneath my feet rumble. She leapt into the fray with her sentries and began tearing the rebelling fae limb from limb.

Kyril, unfazed by Nuala's transformation, looked to the centre of his chest, and ripped the bolt free before disappearing, only to reappear less than a breath later behind another of the masked fae to sever his head from his neck. Before the fae's head fell to the ground, Kyril vanished again, reappearing behind another. Kyril's blade plunged into the fae's solar plexus. Kyril repeated this over and over, the remainder of the masked fae whirling frantically to defend themselves. Their efforts were an exercise in futility. I watched in equal parts awe and horror at the violence he wrought so swiftly until all of the masked fae laid in pieces around us. Kyril's chest heaved heavy, rapid breaths as he stood, sword in hand, dripping in blood like some kind of dark, vengeful god.

Beyond him, Nuala, still in her chimera form, scanned the vicinity for any remaining threats. The remaining fae, those who were still waiting to leave peacefully, were either hiding on the train or running along the train tracks. Utrev was no where to be seen. I said silent prayer of thanks that he wasn't amongst the dead whose bodies littered the ground around us. The road leading to the gate was covered in blood and heavily peppered with limbs and dead bodies- sentries and masked fae alike. The city centre was now completely engulfed in flames and had begun to spread to the surrounding slums. I prayed that the towering stonewall encompassing all of Pauperes Domos would keep it contained.

Kyril examined me from head to toe for wounds. I shook my head, "I'm fine," I breathed, stepping towards him as Nuala shifted back to her fae form. I brought my hands to Kyril's chest, checking to make sure he had fully healed. I opened the tear in his fighting silks to find the skin there closed but still red and angry from the wound. My eyes, desperate for reassurance that he was ok, met his in question. "I'm fine," he said through gritted teeth. I buried my face in his chest, breathing in the scent and feel of him in an attempt to reassure myself that he was here with me, alive and safe.

"*How?*" Nuala seethed, pacing in her war room. Kyril and I stood opposite her. "I trust my sentries with my life. They wouldn't have removed the palladium collars without making them swear the blood oath first." Kyril's hand found mine and grasped it tightly, shaking his head as he spoke. "They must have planned this. We shouldn't have given them three days to prepare. One of them must have been a mage, and once their collar was removed, they were then able to remove the collars from the others..."

A feeling all too familiar burned inside me. Guilt. Again, so many met their demise all because of my naivety and arrogance. My fatal optimism. "Nuala," I began, feeling hopeless, "I... I don't know what to say. What I could possibly say to make any of this better." She stepped toward me. "Don't," she ground out, "Don't you dare try to blame yourself. Despite today's massacre, thousands were freed because of you..." I swallowed thickly. "Yeah, and you and Kyril nearly died because of me. Your sentries...," I said, forcing the words out. Steeling my voice. Frustration and grief tightened my vocal cords to the cusp of cracking.

She shook her head at me, her eyes filled with grief and rage. "Those who died did so out of selflessness in protecting the freedom and wellbeing of others. There is no greater honour. And now they will rest peacefully in the realms beyond. That is not something to feel guilty about." I took a deep breath and nodded slowly. "Some of the masked fae escaped. Amongst the others." Kyril's voice beside me was a low growl. "We will find them and end them."

A plan revealed itself in my mind. A solution to a problem that had been plaguing me since that fateful night in The Sable Forest. My voice found its steel. "I have an idea."

9

"No," is all Nuala had said when I suggested we free the vagus to help us find the masked fae who'd escaped. "And how else do you plan on finding them?" I countered. Nuala's gaze could have burned holes through me as she seemed to think over my words. I was mildly surprised that Kyril didn't vocalize any concern either. "Fine," Nuala had said reluctantly, "I'm going to have to travel to the other Guards to warn them so they can be hyper-vigilant against any potential threats. I'll be back in two days for the Summer Solstice celebration. In the meantime, work on controlling your magic with Kyril. When I return, if you can get him to make The Creator's Promise- it makes no difference to me which of us it is that he binds himself to- you can free him from the mirror."

The Creator's Promise, as far as I knew - which was very little due to my limited experience and education in Pauperes Domos- was something that had to be given freely, could not be forced or made under duress if it wasn't something that both parties truly desired. And it bound the soul of the one making the promise to the soul of the other, and their will. As you might imagine, The Creator's Promise was something very few ever utilized. To whom would he be binding his soul to? I suppose that was up to the vagus... If he would even be willing.

Sometime later, Kyril walked me back to my room. As we arrived at my door, Kyril stared down at me, still covered in blood splatter. And me with Nuala's blood *and* bile. His face pale, and his expression exhausted. "Aurelia... I... After what happened today, I genuinely can't bare to have you out of my sight or my arms right now. If something had happened to you today... I...," Kyril's voice trailed off, his throat working roughly on a swallow as his eyes glistened. I nodded in understanding. The image of him being bolted through the chest would haunt me indefinitely. "I feel the same, Kyril."

I pulled him by the hand into my room and shut the door behind us. The only light came from the waxing moon that shone in from the balcony. I reached up and wiped uselessly at a speck of someone else's blood on his cheek. "We need to bathe," I murmured. He nodded solemnly, studying my face as he so frequently did. As though he were committing every detail to memory.

I led him into my bathing room, a single aeternam orb flickering on and casting the room in a soft amber glow. We reached the shower, again, as if by an invisible hand, the shower turned on. I couldn't help but grin softly, a tiny bit of the tension leaving my body. "Show off," I said, huffing a soft laugh with what little energy I had left. He couldn't help but smile either, albeit weakly. "For you? Always." I chuckled softly, reaching for the hem of his shirt and pulling it over his head before tossing it on the floor. He reached for the hem of mine, hesitating as he met my gaze as if asking for my permission. I nodded, and he pulled the top over my head. We took turns peeling off the rest of our filthy clothes and boots until all that remained were my

bra and panties and his form-fitting undergarment through which I
could see a very long, thick outline. That was hardening. Wetness
seeped from my core, and a moment later Kyril growled low in his
throat.

My heart fluttered in anticipation, unsure if I was ready for this. I
stepped backwards under the heavy stream of the shower and turned
around to remove my bra and panties. After a moment, Kyril pressed
behind me to fit beneath the stream of water. I could feel the massive,
hard length of him. My breath caught. I turned to face him, my throat
working on a nervous swallow. He shook his head. "That's not why I
came in here. All I want is to be near you. Feel you here with me.
Nothing more, Aurelia... I'm sorry if I...," his gaze dropped momentarily before meeting mine again, " Unintentionally, I'm giving you
another impression." He reached for the hair wash sitting on the
ledge behind me. His voice was a soothing balm to my frayed nerves
and exhausted body. "Turn back around for me." I did as he asked,
and he gently pulled me against him before squirting the floral-
scented hair wash into his palm and began massaging it into my hair.
I leaned into him, my head resting on his chest and let my eyes slip
shut. Relishing the feel of him. Including what was pinned between
us, against my lower- and mid-back.

I felt something so powerful blossoming in my chest it caused my
eyes to burn. Something I'd never experienced before and was terrified of acknowledging. The overwhelming gratitude I felt for him,
and to be here with him. Alive. It had me biting my cheek to stifle
tears. I took a few deep breaths as he continued to massage my head
and neck- another new experience. After a few minutes, I rinsed my
hair as he reached for the giant sea sponge hanging behind me and
another glass bottle of cleanser before he proceeded to scrub every
inch of my body with a level of tenderness and care that had whatever this thing was between us... aching with that terrifying sensa-

tion. His hands stilled as he reached the scars on my back. Scars from being flogged whenever I'd been caught stealing aeternum crystal out of desperation. He lifted my arms and found a scar near my ribs from when someone had tried to take my stolen aerternum crystal from me. They'd failed. Though there had been times when others had succeeded.

"Never again," Kyril ground out as he wrapped his arms around me. "Never again," he swore again softly. After rinsing off, I eagerly returned his tender gestures, slowly massaging his head and neck as I washed his hair before stroking and massaging the large, corded muscles of his body. When I reached the scars that decorating his skin, I took my time kissing every single one of them.

When we crawled in bed together, Kyril held me tightly against him with one arm while the other's bicep served as a pillow for my head. My face nuzzled against his chest, one hand pressed beside it, and my other hand caressed his back. Our legs twined together, and even though we were naked and I could still feel the hardness of him pressed against my stomach, and I was certain he could feel and smell my wetness lubricating the top of his thigh... We simply basked in one another's embrace, and despite the horrors the day wrought, I slept more deeply and peacefully than ever before.

I woke the following morning to the feel of Kyril tucking my body back against his warm, firm body. A deep-seated satisfaction and joy bloomed in my chest despite still being half asleep. I wriggled my hips and bum further back against that long, thick, hard length of him. He growled softly, a hand clamping down on my hips to still them. A soft moan escaped me as he nipped my shoulder before he licked and kissed away the hurt, his grip on my hips tightening. "My fire... don't test my self-control. It is rapidly waning." I chuckled, rubbing against him just a little more. "But I can't help it...," I purred in a voice I barely recognized as my own. His body tensed, and he pulled me against him so tightly, I had no more wiggle room. His voice grew husky, and his lips grazed my shoulder as he spoke. "Behave yourself, Aurelia. Before you force me to teach you a lesson." My breath caught, wetness blooming anew betwixt my thighs, but I stilled. Even if I was grinning to myself at the idea of one day learning what that lesson would be.

Kyril sweetly rubbed calming circles on my back and held my hair away from my face as I heaved. "Is this payback for teasing you earlier?" He chuckled. "I'd never make you pay in pain...," he promised, his tone suggestive. Thankfully, I managed not to vomit this time after he winked us out of the palace and onto the balcony of his home. "How do you do that?" I asked after I stopped dry heaving. The nausea it caused was notably less intense than the first time. He gingerly tucked my hair behind my ear and passed me his handkerchief as I straightened. "Hmmm... Well, it's called folding. We are literally causing a fleeting, minute fold in the fabric of space, time, and gravity, like folding one end of a napkin towards the other and stepping through the space between the two. I'm certain you'll be able to fold space on your own eventually after you get better control of your powers. And it won't always make you sick, don't worry." I stared at him, trying to fathom the feat. Such a fascinating world, magic, that I was only just being introduced.

The wind whipped at my hair, and now that the waves of nausea had passed, the sound of crashing waves had me turning away from Kyril. This was the first time I'd been outside Pauperes Domos or the palace. And I'd certainly never seen the sea. Seemingly sensing my train of thought, Kyril stepped in closer to me and wrapped his arms around me, pulling me into his chest. My heart trilled. "It stole my breath the first time too. Still does."

Emotion welled up within me. I'd never witnessed such majestic beauty. The crystalline water stretched out into infinite palettes of green and blue, all in varying shades I'd never even seen in the natural world. The sand was fair and soft, a stunning contrast to the brutality of the jagged cliffs winding into the distance as far as I could see. I bit down on my cheek, trying to stifle the swelling tears. "I can't believe it's taken thirty years for me to experience this." Kyril kissed my temple, making my heart squeeze even more.

"If it makes you feel any better, I didn't get to see the sea until I was twice your age." I looked up and over my shoulder, my gaze snapping to his.

"Why?" I asked in disbelief. A mournful smile appeared, and he leaned forward to kiss my forehead. Another heart squeeze. With all this tenderness, I was sure I'd be putty by the end of the day.

"That, my fire, is a question I'll be happy to answer another time. Lest I ruin your first experience... Would you like to go down to the beach?"

"Yes, please." A broad, brilliant grin parted his lips. "Excellent. I'll just change and grab a few things to bring down with us. Would you like to come with me? I can give you a tour." I looked back out to the sea and decided I couldn't bare parting with it just yet. I shook my head. "You're sure you don't mind? I imagine you're burned out on the beach by now... Between that and the training... I don't wanna be an inconvenience."

I pulled my gaze away from the beach to see his response. Kyril's eyes held mine as he leaned in closer. "I would describe you as many things, Aurelia, and an inconvenience isn't one of them. There isn't anything this world has to offer that I'd rather do than be by your side." Did I say I'd be putty by the end of the day? No, no. That transformation had now occurred. His expression was soft. Sincere. And I could see a genuine longing in those fathomless eyes. It stole my breath, and I felt the urge to bring my hand to his cheek. Instead, I bit down on my own cheek and nodded. "Thank you."

After a few minutes of my solitary sea-gazing, a door clicked shut behind me, and I turned to find Kyril striding towards me. My lips parted at the sight of him. He was only half dressed in a pair of loose-fitting trousers that hung low on his narrow, chiselled waist; linen towels hung over his shoulder. Ready for a swim. My eyes flitted over his body which had seemingly been carved from golden granite. He gave me a knowing, feral grin. I could hear my heart beginning to thunder in my chest but quickly managed to recover. I arched an eyebrow, grinning with amusement. "Between this display, your gifts at turning on showers, and drying things instantly, I'm beginning to suspect you're something of a show off." He tipped his head back, giving me one of his generous, core-warming laughs. "For you? Always," he promised once again.

He spared me the ensuing nausea of *folding*, thank the gods, and we walked down a narrow, winding set of stairs carved into the cliff and led directly to a private beach cove. He held my hand the entire way as there were no railings, and tumbling to my death seemed like a real possibility. When we reached the sand, he slipped off his sandals, beaming with excitement. "I wouldn't recommend swimming in fighting silks. The chaffing is unbearable," he offered casually. "Smooth. Real smooth," I laughed. He chuckled in a way that gave me a tingling sensation in... places. Or one very specific place. Kyril undid the tie at his waist before slipping off his trousers, a thin ivory undergarment all that remained. I could nearly feel my eyes twitching at the sheer force of will it took *not* to look down.

. . .

Kyril grinned knowingly with amusement. My throat suddenly felt parched, and my heart was bursting with excitement. His eyes seemed to burn as he watched me quickly pull off the spider silk trousers, followed by my top, leaving nothing more than my bra and panties to cover me. Before I could think better of it, I went bounding into the crashing waves of the sea, squealing the whole way. He barked a laugh and ran in after me.

I sucked in a harsh breath as the chilling waves crashed against my bare skin. I dove in and swam out until my lungs screamed for air. I popped up above the water, expecting to find Kyril just behind me, but he was not. My joy and excitement quickly became replaced by fear of whatever creatures I may not be able to see lurking nearby at this depth. I began to swim closer to shore just as a hand gripped my ankle from below. I let out a shrill scream as Kyril burst up from beneath the water. He was shaking with laughter. I couldn't help but laugh begrudgingly and splashed him with the salty water.

"I'm gonna get you for that." Kyril beamed all the brighter. "I certainly hope so." I panted, trying to catch my breath after that scare. Kyril watched me, still grinning. "Don't worry. Nothing dangerous will swim into this cove. I made sure of it. I swim in here nearly every day. Sometimes morning and night." I peered at him through my lashes, dripping with the salty seawater. "Would you say reading minds is a bad habit of yours?"

He smirked. "For one, did you ever consider another reason that might enable me to read you? For us to read each other?" I chewed my cheek to try to cover up that fact that what he was insinuating stole my breath. "And furthermore, I don't need to. You usually have whatever's going on inside your head written all over your face. And despite whatever unsavoury habits you may assume I have, I do my best not to pry into anyone else's mind. Tempting as it may be at times," he winked, "Although you certainly could do with some mental palisades. Especially now that you're going to be Nuala's emissary... Painfully few of the mind seers I know of possess such discretion." I studied his face for a few moments. "Where did you get your gift from?"

He smiled wistfully. My mother. She gave me the predisposition for it. But it's something I had to practice. Along with mind speaking." He gave a knowing grin as he continued. "You could also glean the ability, I'm sure."

I grinned, waiting for the offer. He sighed a smile, waving a hand out of the sloshing water.

"Yes, yes. Add it to our to-do list."

I took in a mouthful of salty water, squirting a neat stream of it into his face that he didn't bother trying to evade. Splitting a wild grin, the gleam in his eyes suddenly became feral. "You're gonna pay for that," he growled in a seductive voice that I could feel in my core. I let out a jubilant squeal as he dove beneath the water and picked me up over his shoulder. His strong, callused hands braced me by the backs of my thighs. I let out a rather uncouth sound that reminded me of a small undomesticated animal and kicked in protest, nails biting into the skin of his muscled back.

This only seemed to encourage him. The side of my bum was pressed against his cheek, apparently too much temptation for him to resist. He turned his head and gently sank his teeth into me without breaking the skin. I felt a powerful energy rise from the depths of my core, causing my core to clench longingly against nothing. "*Ow!*" I screamed. "Naughty, naughty," he taunted deliciously. "That hurt," I exaggerated. Slightly. Hoping he couldn't detect my tiny, almost lie. Or my arousal. I felt the apple of his cheek rising in a smile, still pressed to the side of my bum. A low growl rumbled in his chest. *That would be a yes.* I was instantly grateful he couldn't see my face reddening with embarrassment. He nuzzled the spot where he'd bitten and hummed. "Can you ever forgive me?" He purred before kissing my feigned wound tenderly. I felt my breath leave my body as my hair rose. I knew he sensed it. He carefully slid me down from his shoulder to face him. I savored the sensation of the hard span of his muscled chest pressed against my now aching breasts and peaked nipples as my toes gradually reached the soft, sandy sea floor.

Our eyes met, and we both seemed to be holding our breath. I felt that tingling pulsation between my legs and was grateful my lower half was beneath the water, lest he scent the growing wetness now lining me that had nothing to do with the sea. His scent of balsam and wood-burning embers filled my nose, and a brief flare of his nostrils told me the water did nothing to mask the scent of my growing arousal either. But his perennial smile eluded us. He just stared down into my eyes, his own filling with that familiar longing. And I swore I glimpsed the undulating flames of a burning star deep within them. His lips parted slightly, and I felt my back arching in response to bring my chest closer to his. Slowly, as if giving me the moment to stop him, he drew a hand from beneath the water and cupped my cheek, caressing it tenderly with his thumbs. My eyes slipped shut as I pressed my cheek further into the warmth of his palm. A soft humming growl left him, and my eyes flicked open to see him staring down at me as if I were the centre of his universe. "Aurelia...," he breathed.

My lips parted, half in awe of... whatever this was, half in anticipation as my heart fluttered like the wings of a bird. Kyril bowed his head to lay a heartbreakingly tender kiss upon my forehead. My eyes closed again at the sheer ecstasy that filled my veins at his touch, and he kissed each of my eyelids. My hands skated up peaks and valleys of his defined stomach, the broad plain of his muscled chest, and up the back of his neck to weave my fingers through the wet, silken strands of his hair. He hummed his pleasure and pulled me tightly against him. His nose nuzzling mine in a way that sent my heart soaring before at last, our lips met.

And in that moment, all the world faded away. Though my eyes were closed, I swore I could see the twinkling and burning of the cosmos surrounding us. All that remained was the union of two spirits. The caress of our lips and tongues it's own language. One of love. His hands drifted from my waist to cradle my head in his hands and a soft moan escaped me. A soft growl of pleasure was his response, and I sucked his bottom lip before nipping at it and licking away the tender pain in reply.

Kyril groaned, sweeping me up by the backs of my thighs. I wove my legs around his waist, my arms around his neck. My breasts became heavy, nipples peaking, pressing against chest as if to demand his attention. And he heard their silent cry, one of the arms bracing my back moved to pull the now nearly transparent white fabric of my bra aside. His lips left mine and his gaze dropped to my heavy breasts. My dusky nipples hardened nearly to the point of pain, desperate for the tender ministrations of his oh-so-gifted tongue. *"My fire... You are perfection...,"* Kyril breathed. He cupped my breasts and drew his mouth to them, raining open mouthed kisses to my soft flesh until he reached their pebbled tips to nip, lick, and *suck*. A high-pitched moan escaped me, and my core clenched with need. The grip he held on my bum tightened and he groaned, tongue flicking gingerly against my peaked nipple. I moaned his name, and my hips, now possessing a mind of their own, writhed against that enormous hard, thick length of his.

Kyril paused, growling. "Aurelia...," he breathed, "I don't want the first time we do this to be hindered by seawater, and gravity." I husked a laugh in agreement as I kissed and licked my way up his neck. As I reached his ear, I nipped and sucked at the lobe before licking up it's shell as I unwound my legs from around his waist and slid back down his body.

I stepped away from him, I nearly cried aloud in protest as the cool water was now ice against my skin in the absence of his body pressing against mine. Somehow I managed to turn and walk away from him back towards the shore. I shivered against the cool breeze as I reached to sand and a breath later he was there, sweeping me up into his arms. An excited laugh bubbled out of me, followed promptly by a gasp as my wet, chilled body suddenly grew dry and warm, and covered by the linen towels he'd retrieved. Our gazes met, and we laughed wordlessly at the ongoing joke only we understood.

Kyril began to ascend the steps of the cliff, still carrying me bridal style, and I wriggled for him to let me down so he didn't have to carry my 'dead' weight but his grip on me only tightened. "That's a long steep, set of stairs. Just fold us." Kyril's eyebrows furrowed as he huffed a laugh, "So you can puke?" I gently swatted his chest. "I didn't puke last time!" He chuckled and kissed my temple. "As much as I love fisting your hair, I think I prefer you to be nausea-free."

My toes curled at the mention of him fisting my hair, and all the other images it conjured along with it. It had me biting my cheek and the tang of blood blossomed in my mouth. Kyril's gaze snapped to mine. He shook his head at me, his voice low and rough. "Careful, my filthy-minded fire. Before the last of my restraint dissolves, and I have my way with you on these stairs." A devilish grin parted my lips. "If that's supposed to detour me, you don't know me nearly as well as I thought you did," I murmured into his neck before sinking my teeth in and sucking. He growled in approval.

By the time we reached the top of the cliff steps our bodies had both calmed down, thankfully. He lead me inside the manor, which was wholly different to Nuala's crystal palace. Huge stone walls- likely stone hewn from the very cliff on which the manor stood- led up to huge sweeping wooden beams. Tremendous fireplaces adorned every room. Sprawling fur carpets laid atop polished dark wood floors. The furniture huge and magnanimously cushioned. It looked like it was actually meant for lounging. Unlike so much of the furniture in the palace that I assumed was more decoration than comfort. Many-tiered, beautifully wrought iron chandeliers hung from the ceiling with dozens of candles- candles with real flames instead of aeternam crystal-powered orbs. Towering floor-to-ceiling windows lined every room facing the breathtaking view of the sea.

As we entered, an older fae female dressed in fine linen trousers and a tunic bowed slightly. "Aurelia, this is Leonith. She's a family friend and one of the people that help take care of the estate," Kyril announced, "She's already gotten more than one earful about you, so I'll spare you both the formality." Leonith bowed, smiling warmly. She was petite and ultra slender, a necessary trait for fae like her who were gifted with wings like that of a butterfly. One of the 'lesser' fae that I'd never seen in Pauperes Domos. They'd been slaves before the war. "It's truly a pleasure. Kyril speaks very highly of you," she said in a voice that reminded me of wind chimes. I offered my hand to her. "Always a pleasure to meet a friend of Kyril's." She beamed appreciatively at me and took my hand in hers. "I've drawn a hot bath for you if you'd like to follow me."

The bathtub was big enough to fit more than one person and provided a glorious view of the sun approaching the horizon. I closed my eyes in an attempt to do the power-summoning exercises that Kyril had taught me but my mind, and body, could conjure nothing but the persist tingling, aching need for him instead. My nipples tightened beneath the water and bubbles. My fingers found there way between my thighs as I spread my legs, pretending it was Kyril's perfect mouth. My core clenched, and my back arched against the porcelain tub in response. My breasts ached for his touch, his mouth again, and I recalled the breathtaking image of him slowly kissing, tonguing, and biting them. I couldn't help but wonder if Kyril was doing the same thing at that moment. Having felt that deliciously magnanimous length and girth of his, I couldn't help but imagine that too- filling me, stretching me, pounding me as he held me in his arms and bit me, finding his release deep inside me to the point that it spilled out of me.

When I finally emerged, feeling only slightly relieved, I caught him exiting his bedroom down the hall at the same time. My breath caught as I laid eyes on him, feeling as if he could see it drawn all over me. My cheeks flushed as he gave me a knowing, wicked smile and strode over to me. "Hungry?" he asked coolly. I hummed a chuckle. "Starved." Which was absolutely true. I hadn't eaten since breakfast, and my stomach had begun groaning in protest.

He sat across from me at a table on the balcony, drinking from a goblet filled with blood. Who's blood I wondered as my eyes flicked to his goblet. He gave a smirk. *"My enemies."* I blanched. He laughed at my reaction. "I get it from the butcher in the village. He seasons it for me."

I huffed a laugh. I asked in disbelief, "Really?"

"My fire, unless it's... straight from the source- which is by far the best- it's not terribly satisfying to the palate. Would you want to eat unseasoned meat?"

I tilted my head in consideration. "Well, I don't really like meat that much...," I sighed distantly, "but I suppose I wouldn't, no... And how often do you... drink it straight from the source?" I asked, feeling a swell of trepidation.

"Not since the war."

"Oh wow... Is it hard not to?"

"Occasionally. Yes. But it's a side of me I prefer to keep at bay unless it's... with the right person."

I arched an eyebrow at him, and he grinned from around his goblet and gave me a wink.

"Do you think you'll have the energy to do any magic or self-defense training after we eat?" I sighed, feeling thoroughly exhausted after not only yesterday but now, sun and sea. And post-self-induced-orgasm. But I knew that not training, was not an option. "Definitely. Do you think I could take a short nap beforehand? I'm feeling a little drained physically. And mentally. After everything that's been happening. But only for twenty minutes or so."

Kyril grinned. "Perfect. I have a few things I need to take care of anyway. How about you nap for an hour or so? It'd be advantageous for you to train at night as well."

10

Kyril led me down the hallway toward the various bedrooms of his villa and stopped in front of the guest room that Leonith had chosen for me to bathe. Kyril took my head in his hands and kissed my cheeks before settling on my mouth. "I told Leonith to prepare my bed for you but she insisted that I should give you your own room to sleep in lest you be given the wrong impression." I hummed my appreciation. "I would have preferred she not even change your sheets," I murmured against his lips, "But I am grateful for the gesture." I reached behind me and turned the door knob. "Good luck with your work."

As soon as my head hit the fluffiest pillow I'd ever encountered, I fell into a deep sleep plagued with visions of violence from the previous day at Pauperes Domos. It began with Kyril being bolted in the chest, Nuala being impaled through the neck and mouth, and me being showered in their blood. The horror only increased as the nightmare transformed, battle scenes unfolding that I'd never partaken in but seemed so intrinsically real and as though I had already lived through them. Throughout the dream, dread filled and sickened me as the violence ensued, and I knew exactly how it would all end.

I awoke from the nightmare to find myself in a bed made of various animal furs, the embers of a dying fire burned in the centre of the room. Or tent. Relief filled me at the realization that Kyril's warm body was safely curled beside mine. He tugged me into his body, and despite how foreign this place was, I was swiftly pulled back to sleep. But sometime later, the sound of metal singing through the air awakened me. My eyelids flew open just as a sword arched above my head. And before I could react, the stranger- all I could make out was the silhouette of a tall, powerfully built male- brought his gleaming, golden sword down on my neck, and everything went black.

I jerked awake, fisting the wonderfully familiar sheets and pillows of Kyril's guest chamber bed as I caught my breath. The realness of it calmed me, my eyes adjusting to the dark room, and I reached for my *intact* throat. I laid back against the mountain of pillows trying to push away the scenes my mind kept replaying from the nightmare. The sound of my heart kicking wildly at my chest as if it were trying to escape finally eased, and I could just barely make out the sounds of male voices. Arguing in hushed tones, it seemed. I tried my best not to listen, but as the hairs on my arms pricked, I found my ears straining but could still only pick up a peppering of words.

"... peace... realms, and beyond.... I could ensure.... but you... the bargain...," a strange voice growled.

I could make out Kyril's low, mirthless chuckle.

"If you think... taken from me... Nothing will be able... I no longer care...," he said in a tone I'd never heard him use before.

. . .

I silently rose from the bed and tiptoed, feeling a pang of guilt but compelled nonetheless towards the bedroom door. The scent of rain before a thunderstorm, *ozone*, seemed to drift in from beneath the door.

"Everything I do... No qualms with bringing...," Kyril continued.

"... Reckless... That golden-haired fop... Single-minded... And his wife...," the stranger seemed to counter.

As the scent of ozone continued to fill my nostrils, it also seemed to curl over my body, and something about it called to me, and I found my hand drifting to the bronze, curved door handle, and my heart began to beat a heavier rhythm. And their voices stilled.

"Perhaps we should add spymaster to your training list?" Kyril purred from behind me. I let out a shriek, whirling as I grasped my chest. "*Sweet gods*, Kyril," I breathed. Kyril chuckled, pulling me into his arms. "How'd you sleep?" He asked in a tone that told me he already knew. His nose nuzzled its way into my neck, inhaling my scent, and he hummed his pleasure. My nipples seemed to salute their reply. "Fitfully," I murmured, "How's your work stuff? Sounds like it was getting kind of heated..." He huffed a laugh. "It's only my uncle... I've been trying to help him with something. Would you like to meet him?"

"Oh, wow... I'd love to... I feel like I look kind of... unacceptable, though," I laughed a little self-consciously, gesturing towards my messy hair and the conservative but elegant, floor-length silk nightgown Leonith had left for me on the bed. The aeternam lantern beside the bed flickered on. Kyril's grin widened, gifting me with a dimple as he took me in. He braced his arms on either side of my head, pinning me against the door. "I think you're right. The sight of you being sleep mussed is far too delicious and has now given me far better ideas. None of which involve my uncle." I reached my hands beneath his shirt and caressed his sides, his ribs. "Perhaps after we meet your uncle? I'd really love to meet your family." His heavy-lidded gaze softened, turning appreciative. "He can be a bit of an asshole, just as fair warning, but is charming when he wants to be."

"Oh? That sounds oddly familiar," I teased as I slipped out from between Kyril's arms. We entered the hallway and strode down the hallway to Kyril's office- a massive study with towering bookcases overflowing with books. A gigantic, darkest blue velvet couch that looked as cushy and cosy as a bed sat in front of a 5-foot-tall fireplace with a whirling stone mantle that was sculpted to look like crashing waves that spilled onto the floor. Stacks of books and papers sat on top of a large mahogany desk that faced the ocean view across the room. Facing the ocean view stood a man with long, flowing tendrils of white hair, pulled halfway back. He was dressed in strange cloth-ing. Similar to that of Quetz when he'd still been trapped in the mirror. He'd said he projected the clothing style from what he'd seen in his visits to the Terrenean realm.

Kyril cleared his throat. "Uncle, there's someone very dear to me I'd like you to meet." Before turning around, his uncle hesitated for a few moments as if lost in reverie at the ocean view. The man who turned to face me bared a striking resemblance to Kyril. It was almost as star-tling as it was unsettling.

He appeared nearly the same age, although I knew that couldn't be the case. Other than the hair, the most significant difference was the sleeves of tattooed runes, faces, and creatures that I didn't recognize, revealed beneath the rolled-up sleeves of his dressy, black long sleeve shirt with a long set of buttons from the open collar to the bottom hem. A broad grin that didn't quite meet his eyes parted his lips, revealing his too-white teeth and canines that were a little more human looking than Kyril's. Although the energy and power he radiated was as far from human as you could get. "Aurelia."

"This is my uncle. Caelus," Kyril said as he rested a hand on my lower back. I stepped forward, offering my hand. "It's a pleasure to meet you, Caelus." His uncle chuckled. "My nephew speaks the world of you. And since... he met you, I haven't seen him this happy." My face flushed, and I chewed my cheek to try and prevent my grin from becoming *too* wide. "That's kind of you to say." Caelus studied Kyril and me for a moment. "It is not kindness but merely truth. I'm afraid I'll have to make my leave shortly. I have some rather urgent matters to attend... But I do hope to see you again soon, Aurelia."

I couldn't help as my eyes were drawn to Caelus'. Instead of being the blazing amber that were Kyril's that seemed to be fathomless... Caelus' were silvery... And chilling. And while they held a similar fathomlessness... They held none of the warmth. He looked down at me, catching my stare. My gaze. He studied me for a moment, and the hairs on the back of my neck rose. He flashed me another blinding grin. "Always a pleasure," he beamed. And then disappeared in a wink of silvery energy.

I couldn't help the sigh that left my body in a whoosh now that he'd left the room. Kyril looked down at me with concern, eyebrows furrowed. "You ok?" I forced a smile, not wanting to offend him. "Yeah... He seems... Lovely," I managed to finish on a gulp. Kyril gave a me disbelieving look before bursting into a short laugh. "He's kind of strange, isn't he? It's ok. You can admit it. I'm not offended." I couldn't help but laugh a little in relief. "... He just... He looks so much like you, but... also doesn't at the same time. I think maybe that's why I was so unsettled..."

Kyril pulled me into his arms and laid a kiss atop my head. "He'll grow on you. Don't worry. And even if he doesn't, he rarely shows up. So it's not like you'll have to see him often. He just... kind of turns up whenever he wants. Unannounced and at the most inconvenient moments. And I've grown certain it's deliberate."

I turned, laying my hands on his chest. "That's ok... He's family." Kyril's frown deepened at that, reading my train of thought. "Do you know if you have any surviving family?" I gasped, finally recalling what I'd meant to ask him ages ago. "Oh, that reminds me! Nuala mentioned something about you having worked with some of the children that had been orphaned by the war... My father told me I had some relatives who had been taken by her. I'd previously assumed they were dead, but as you know..." Kyril's eyes widened at the possibility.

"Maybe I know them... I helped train so many of those kids."
      I grinned smugly.
      "I know. You perfect specimen, you."
      Kyril revealed both dimples before he leaned in to kiss and nuzzle my cheek and neck.
      "Far from it, and you'd do well to remember it, my fire."

A feline grin arched across my face as I cradled the back of his head with my hands and sniffed at his pulse point before biting and licking it, his body pressing against mine, making him hum. I could feel that glorious length of his hardening. "Care to enlighten me and demonstrate?"

· · ·

Kyril chuckled, growling with pleasure, as he lifted the skirt of my nightgown and scooped me up off the ground by the backs of my thighs. I hummed in delight as I wove my arms and legs around him. "You have no idea how desperate I am to do just that," he purred, "And I would be honoured to do so *after* I show you how to effectively part your enemies from their lives and limbs so that you may outlive them." He buried his face in my neck again. "And continue to bless this realm- and my life, if you'll have me- with your divine presence," he added softly with a tender kiss, making my heart swell.

We spent the entirety of the evening training, with and without magic, and wielding Thea properly. And never have I ever felt so absurdly inadequate. While I managed to *barely* hold my own in terms of controlling my magic, Kyril endowed me with a thorough ass-beating by doing nothing more than blocking my attacks. He'd taken hours to teach me how to punch properly, kick, throw and slice with knees and elbows, and incorporate them all in a flurry of strikes that I imagine was supposed to incapacitate my opponent, but I was pretty sure if attempted to utilize them the only real chance I had of incapacitating them was if they laughed themselves to death.

He finished off our training session by telling me, "Land one blow- and we can stop for tonight." I clicked my tongue, scoffing in disbelief, whilst I panted my ass off. "How is that fair? You're a battle-hardened warrior. How in the seven circles of hell am I supposed to land a blow?" Kyril, who had barely broken a sweat, only offered me a smug grin. "*Surprise* me," he suggested pointedly. I groaned loudly, rolling my eyes. "Fine. Don't blame me if we both die of old age before it happens." He chuckled and taunted me forward with one hand. "You can thank me later."

· · ·

I took my time catching my breath before I moved for him. I wish I'd taken longer. Every time I struck, regardless of what extremity I unleashed- he'd block it and manipulate what momentum I'd used to try and kick, knee, punch, or elbow him and instead, I'd end up taking myself down. Every. Single. Time. I'd land flat on my ass. Or face. Or back.

Dawn was approaching, and still I hadn't managed to land a single blow. And finally, I couldn't take it anymore. At least for the night. He'd told me no magic, just hand-to-hand, but I decided he'd knocked me on my ass for the last time and we both desperately needed rest. Kyril stood above me, waiting for me to climb back to my feet, *yawning*. I rose and strode a few feet in the other direction before turning around to face him. He quirked an eyebrow at me as he yawned *again*. "You are *such* a turd." He only chuckled and smiled patiently. "You're doing beautifully, I swear."

It was my turn to laugh. I shook out my limbs, trying to liberate them of the lactic acid that I could feel burning my muscles. And then launched myself at him, probably looking like some feral and highly uncoordinated creature, and feinted right, sent a bolt of lightening streaking down directly to his left. As he leapt backwards- to his right- he jumped directly into the path of my shin and foot that I'd sent sailing straight towards his breathtakingly beautiful face in an arching roundhouse kick.

The kick landed with a sickening crunch. And *oh my fucks* it hurt. Kyril stumbled backwards and clutched his bleeding nose as I collapsed on the ground, clutching my shin, howling in pain though equally concerned about him. "Oh, my gods! I'm so sorry!" I yelled, cradling my leg.

. . .

He rushed for me, and I let out a scream as he swept me up off the ground and swung me around, howling with laughter. "I think your face broke my shin," I whined, only encouraging his laughter. He looked like some kind of crazed god, laughing so joyously with blood actively trickling from his nose, down his face, and over his perfect teeth. He tipped me up, so I was closer to his face and planted a juicy, bloody kiss on my mouth. Perhaps I should have found his blood off-putting, but it only increased my desire for him. And the throbbing pain in my shin seemed to dissolve.

"Is your nose ok? Is it broken?" I asked through our blood-smeared kiss.

"It's absolutely fine," he hummed delightedly.

I huffed a laugh.

"You are literally bleeding into my mouth," I said, emphasizing by licking some of his blood off his bottom lip.

"Gods, you're so fucking perfect," he husked.

"Perfectly clumsy...," I scoffed, kissing and nuzzling his cheeks.

"I'm so proud of you, Aurelia..."

I pulled back to look him in his eyes, feeling my heart knotting with a sweet sort of pain at his loving words. Kyril's grip on me tightened, eyes growing heavy-lidded. "Seeing my blood on your face is..."

Without even consciously doing so, my tongue slid across my bloody lips.

He groaned as if in pain.

"What's the matter?" I asked, my brow furrowing with concern.

"I'm going to have to put you down now."

"Why? What's wrong?" Worry knotted my stomach.

"Because Leonith is *definitely* awake by now, and I don't want to frighten her by walking back inside sporting an erection."

.   .   .

He set me down carefully, my body squishing the aforementioned erection in the process, before he re-situated himself, pinning his length between his stomach and the tightened waistband of his trousers. "How's that?" He asked confidently. My eyebrows climbed my forehead at the sight of the tent that had moved from his groin to the middle of his stomach. "Pretty incredible, in my opinion. But Leonith might not share my opinion."

I convinced Kyril to fold me back into the house with him, insisting I needed to hurry up and adjust so that I could eventually do it myself without being impaired by nausea. Only for Leonith to knock on the door just as we arrived. "My Lord?" She asked from the other side of the door. "Yes, my lady?" He teased. I could hear her tinkle of laughter. "I've received word from Master Hueghan that he'll be arriving shortly to tailor your garments for the Solstice celebrations."

Kyril heaved a sigh, dragging a hand down his face. "Thank you, Leonith."

"Oh, Master Kyril?"

"Yes, Mistress Leonith?"

"Shall I serve breakfast in your bed chamber?" Kyril gave me a look and before the words even left his mouth, my stomach growled its response. He grinned down at me, calling back to Leonith.

"Yes, please."

"Thank you, Leonith!" I called out.

A muffled tinkle of laughter.

"You're more than welcome, my lady."

After the sound of Leonith's footsteps, in one fluid motion, Kyril gathered me in his arms and carried me into his bathing room. The bathtub was already full, steam billowing from the water's surface carrying the scent of frangipani, rose, and other delicious blossoms.

A cold, perspiring carafe of water sat nearby. I arched an eyebrow at him. "Is this yours or Leonith's handiwork?"

He gave me a feline grin as he set me down. "Mine, of course. How am I doing?" I sighed, gazing at what he'd so beautifully prepared for me. My heart swelled again, realising how incredibly fortunate I was to be blessed- even if it were to last these few days- with someone so selfless and considerate towards me. I'd never been treated with so much love, reverence, and consideration despite having only known Kyril for such a brief period of time. They'd been the best days of my life. Despite the violence and madness we'd experienced in Pauperes Domos yesterday.

My eyes became pregnant with gratitude as my heart squeezed to the point of pain. I bit my lip to try and stop it from quivering. "Thank you," I wobbled. Kyril pulled me into him and slipped his forefinger under my chin to lift my gaze to his. I resisted, not wanting him to see me cry. "Aurelia," he breathed, dropping to a knee so he could peer into my face. And sure enough, just as he did, the first of my tears spilled down my cheeks.

"My fire," Kyril said, searching my face frantically, "What's wrong?" My bottom lip rebelled and began to tremble, and I bit down on it again. I took a deep, shuddering breath to calm myself before speaking. "I know it's only been a few days... which is ridiculous because it feels like it's already been a lifetime... but I've never felt so... cared for and cherished." *So loved,* I hadn't dared to say.

I caught a glance of myself in the mirror, and my jaw dropped. Kyril's, now dried, blood was still smeared all over my face. "*Oh my gods,* I look like some horrific clown," I sighed, wiping away my tears and his blood. Kyril grabbed my hands and turned me to face him. "Well, if that's true, then I have a crippling fetish for horrific clowns." I burst into a soft, sad laugh. Kyril pulled me back into him, and he bowed his head to kiss my cheeks, liberating me of my tears as he gingerly pressed his lips to my cheeks.

"Aurelia, you..." Kyril paused, slowly shaking his head as he stared into my eyes, and as I gazed into his, I saw a galaxy burning within them. "I have never met anyone so worthy of being cared for and cherished as you. And ever since that moment you stepped into my life, I have wanted to do nothing more than exactly that."

Tears poured down my cheeks as my throat worked on a swallow. "How's your nose?" I asked. His brows furrowed as he reached to touch it. "Healed now, I think. Why?" I didn't bother responding with words. I pressed my lips to his, still careful of his nose just in case, and wove my arms around his neck. Kyril groaned and wrapped his arms around me. I tugged gently at his shirt, and he let me pull it over his head, but as I reached for the waistband of his undergarment, he grabbed my hand and spoke against my mouth as he held my head in his hands.

"Aurelia, as desperately as I want to do this- *need*- to do this... I wanna to take my time with you. And... my fucking...," he shook his head in frustration and ground out the rest of the words, "wonderful, kind, generous, and *punctual* tailor is about to arrive."

"I just need to feel you against me," I murmured against his lips as I pulled my shirt off. He growled his approval. I promptly went to remove my trousers but he swatted my hands away and knelt to pull them off himself, along with my panties. His gaze, and breath, caught as he took me in- the apex of my core. "*Gods,* I can't wait to devour you," he breathed against me and pressed a kiss to her before standing.

As he rose, now that my face wasn't pressed against his, or we weren't standing in the dark, or covered by blankets... my eyes greedily took him in, and he literally stole my breath. I could hear the pounding of his heart beating in time with mine. My lips parted as my eyes fell to the length of him that stood, fully erect and nearly the length of my forearm. His girth alone eclipsed my wrist. And I gulped. I forced my eyes back to his hungry gaze. A gaze laden with something so much *more.* Something that I was too terrified to acknowledge or admit as I stepped into the large, freestanding copper bathtub.

He followed me in and sat down, dipping beneath the water briefly to rinse his hair and cleanse his face from the dried blood and ash before pulling me into his lap to sit between his legs. I quickly rinsed the blood and ash from my face and leaned back against his chest, my body curving perfectly into the groove of his, and nothing had yet to ever feel so right as his arms came around me, tucking me even closer against him.

The thick length of him was pinned between his stomach and my back, a toe-curling reminder of how desperately I needed him to fill me. To feel him. To come together. I couldn't help but writhe with need. His arms tightened, and he growled. "You have no idea how little it would take to make me burst right now." I chuckled, writhing still. "You and me both," I replied breathily. He hummed as though thoughtful, and one of his hands drifted to my full, aching breasts that were now pebbled with tingling desire and peaking above the water. He cupped my breast and gently caressed its tip in a back and forth motion that drew a soft cry from my throat and had my back arching against him. His other hand drifted between my thighs to slide his middle finger down my slit, directly to my clit, and he began to massage in slow, gentle circles. Occasionally dipping to my core to tease my sensitive, wet folds before retreating and returning to my clit.

I cried out in a soft, high-pitched, breathy moan- a sound I was absolutely certain I had never made before. "Oh gods, Aurelia... I can't wait to hear you cry out like that as I slide my cock inside you," he husked against my neck, licking , nipping, and kissing. His fingertips continued simultaneously teasing my nipple. *Gods, this gloriously ambidextrous and coordinated male.*

After only a few moments, my core began to clench, and I came undone. My nails dug into the hard flesh of his thighs as my parted legs widened even further. Back arching, my head tipped back against his chest and shoulder, further exposing my throat to him as I cried out his name in ecstasy. Kyril increased the pace and pressure of his fingers as he continued to milk my core-clenching orgasm with his divine ministrations. I could feel the sharp points of his canines grazing my neck as he bit down gently, careful not to break the skin, before licking and kissing the rest of the way up my neck.

As my climax gradually resceded, I rotated to face him in the water and climbed to a straddling position on his lap. I brought my mouth down on his, sucking his lip into my mouth before biting it and licking the pain away. I reached between us and took that massive length of his in my hand. I nearly gasped as I realised I couldn't even fully close my hand around him.

·   ·   ·

At the first stroke, his hips bucked, and he groaned, biting down on my lip. I couldn't help but grin as he released me, working him in smooth, gentle strokes, gradually tightening my grip. He growled, taking my breasts, already aching with need again, into his mouth. I alternated my stroke and began focusing the now teasing caress of my closed hand on the broad head of him causing every muscle in his body to tense. "*Fuck... Aurelia,*" he ground out.

My breath hitched at the words as a knock sounded beyond the bathing room- at the bedroom door. "Master Hueghan has arrived, my lord." "Just a minute!" We both called out in unison, and shared a grin, neither of us pausing.

Kyril's hips began moving in counter to my ministrations, and I returned to the long, deep strokes I'd begun with but quickened my pace. I kissed and nipped my way across his throat and neck, licked the shell of his ear, sucking the lobe into my mouth. My words were breathy with need for him.

"I imagined you stretching me, Kyril. Filling me and cumming deep inside me as you made me cum with your fingers." Kyril's muscles tensed, and his hips thrust upwards while I continued to pump him, now using both hands. I pulled back to look into his eyes, at the undulating flames of the sun that burned within him as he came. The bathwater splashing softly as I gently drew out his climax. His lips were parted in ecstasy as he groaned. *"You make everything worth it, Aurelia."*

11

Kyril held my hair back and caressed my back as I braced myself against the prison's exterior while I tried to suppress my retching. "Just take deep breaths, my fire. In through your nose and out through your mouth. Focus on the sensation of my hand on your back." This time, it'd been only half as bad as the last. I finally made myself upright and leaned against his chest, soothed by the steady rhythm of his heartbeat, mine gradually slowing again to meet his, as he wrapped his arm around me and kissed my head.

It was getting close to dark already. After I'd finished bathing and at the breakfast Leonith had left for me in Kyril's bed chamber, I fell into another deep, dreamless sleep whilst he'd been with his tailor. I'd been woken up by the feel of Kyril's body curling up against my and tugging me into front. We slept until nearly dusk, and by the time we reached the palace dungeons, the moon was nearing its zenith in the Aeternian sky.

. . .

A guard led us down the dungeon's cave-like corridor until we arrived at my former cell. My stomach churned at the memories and emotions it triggered. I gulped and instantly found Kyril's strong, long, warm fingers lacing themselves with my mine. I squeezed his hand in gratitude as his thumb caressed the top of my hand. His voice sounded in my mind.

"Never again, my fire. I will never allow something like that to come to pass ever again. And not even death would keep me from protecting you. No matter what happens." My heart squeezed as I felt no small amount of awe at his promise. *"I hope to soon have the ability to keep a promise like that to you too."* He tugged at my hand, drawing my gaze to his. *"You already do, Aurelia. You just need to harness it. And I'm going to make sure you can, not so that you can protect me, but so that you know how to protect yourself."* Gods, what had I ever done to deserve this male?

The cell door whined as the guard swung it open, the large mirror still facing away from it. We stepped inside, and Kyril nodded to the guard granting him permission to leave. The vagus stood in the mirror, hands stuffed into the pockets of his very modern and foreign-looking trousers, as his lips parted and he gifted me with a joyous smile. His slightly unnerving and otherworldly voice filled the room. "Palace life has been kind to you, I see. Your beauty shines like the sun," the vagus hummed, "Although, I suppose it is more so the noble warrior beside you we should credit. How long has it been, Lord of the Northern Guard?"

The vagus gave a feline grin that seemed to say something more, but what precisely, I had no idea. Kyril only held his gaze and gave him a smile that seemed appreciative, even apologetic, and it made my mind wonder as to how these two met. "We've come to make a bargain."

.   .   .

The vagus erupted into laughter and clapped his hands together as if he knew the punchline to some cosmic joke we hadn't been let in on yet. Kyril and I exchanged a grinning but wary glance. "Yes, yes. The Creator's Promise, no? So you can rest assured I won't go on a killing spree or whatever else it is the creatures of this realm assume we do out of pleasure and not self-defense." I offered an awkward, apologetic smile.

The vagus merely chuckled, shaking his head as he slid his hands in his pockets. Looking jarringly unassuming and casual. Remarkably beautiful and ethereal, but there was something so down-to-earth about his mannerisms. "... I have to say... Out of all the potentialities I've visited, I think this one is my favorite," he added with no small amount mirth. I smirked, arching an eyebrow at him. "Care to enlighten us?" The vagus' grin widened with excitement, his form shifting again in and out of corporeality to those whorls of... aether?

"And spoil the surprise?! Now where, my darling Aurelia, would be the fun in that?" The vagus asked, lips parting in a beguiling grin. Kyril chuckled, heaving a sigh, rubbing a palm down his face. "Somehow, I have a feeling we have two very different ideas of fun... I take it you've already had time to decide which of us you'll be shackling yourself to?"

This only encouraged more laughter from the vagus. "Indeed I have," the vagus said, buzzing with excitement, peering down at a nonexistent watch on his wrist. "We haven't a moment to lose, and I've grown weary of my astral travels. Now, how does the song go again?" The vagus began to ping pong his head side to side in a staccato rhythm, reciting the words of the creator's promise on a sigh as if it were the most boring lyrics ever written.

"By the power of the creators, the many and the one: The Ones, all things benevolent to which all paths lead, including the teachers of suffering and all that is deemed malicious; that holds all the nine realms and beyond in balance with the infinite divine, the unifying source that is beyond mortal and immortal comprehension, all for the evolution and betterment of all creation...," with each passing word the vagus spoke he began to glow and radiate a brilliant golden light that had my eyes squinting and watering as if I were trying to stare directly into the sun, "that I, *Quetzacoatl*, the creator god, and eternal guardian of time, wind and rain, the arts, and all good things; I am the feathered-serpent; One of the four sons of Ometeotl the god of life and duality, bind my soul to the will of Aurelia Eleftheran and her eternal form until she wills an end to my solemn vow."

Wind, from Gods knew what current, rushed around us, causing my hair to whip around my head. The light became so blinding Kyril and I had to shield our eyes. He clutched me to his chest and bent to bury his face in my neck. *Quetzacoatl* began to speak in an ancient tongue that I didn't understand, but his voice transformed into something deep and ancient, sounding like one and many, making the hairs on my neck and arms stand on end. My body began to tremble, my magic seemingly rising to the blinding light that Quetzacoatl emanated and was now pouring from my chest. I felt an intangible cord forming between Quetzacoatl and myself. My magic, in tendrils of blue and white electricity, began to stream out of me, and I tried to push Kyril away to prevent him from being electrocuted or burned, but he held me firm.

· · ·

The winds continued to whip at our hair, and I hear thunder crack beyond the dungeon window, in time with the shattering of glass. The light radiating from my body dimmed as Quetzacoatl grew silent, and I looked up from Kyril's chest to see darkness and clouds, the type of clouds I'd only ever seen in the form of nebulas, pouring out of the shattered mirror's frame. Or at least where it once stood. In the whorls of darkness, I saw distant stars, and closer than that, eyes. Like the eyes I'd seen that seemingly floated in the cosmos as the vagus, who, apparently, was something so much more than I'd ever imagined, when he'd taken me on that inter-dimensional journey.

The power that now emanated through the room was enough to make me drop to my knees. I clutched at my chest and solar plexus to see dark wisps of color and shadow pouring into my chest, seemingly being pulled and drawn inside me by my white and pale blue energy until it looked as though it'd all been sucked in and disappeared. Kyril dropped in front of me, kneeling knee to knee with me. "Aurelia!" He breathed, grabbing me by the shoulders. "I'm fine...," I shuddered.

Kyril pulled me to my feet, Quetzacoatl watching us with an exuberant smile on his face as he gradually shifted into his corporeal form. In the moonlight streaming in through the window, he radiated silver along with the blues and purples found on a raven's wing. The darkness and nebula clouds condensed into the familiar humanoid shape I'd missed and longed to free since he'd shown me compassion in my darkest hour: soothed my soul and reunited me with my brother. The one I'd then considered to be my only friend perhaps.

And a now very *naked* friend. Whose body was apparently built like the god of war. Not knowledge and the arts or the wind and rain. His heavily muscled form was covered almost entirely in tattoos. A feathered serpent whose open maw began at his right hand was loosely coiled up the corded muscles of his arm across his back, down his left arm, ending in a feathered and scaled tail that wound around his wrist. Tribal and geometric patterns that intertwined with various words written in characters I didn't understand caged his ribs. In the centre of his ribs, on his solar plexus, a pointed spear aimed for his neck, and wings fanned across his chest on either side of it. From what I could see, the only parts of his body- outside of the deliberate gaps between designs- that weren't tattooed were his face, ears, and... dick. Which was, shockingly- or perhaps not so shockingly- comparable in size to Kyril's. It hung, even flaccid, halfway down his thigh, thick and smooth, with a broad head. My throat worked on a swallow at the sight of... everything. *Not just his dick. Thank you very much.* There was something strange about the way he looked despite being breathtakingly handsome. His ethereal beauty was unnerving. And the power that rippled off him made the air crackle and become still all at once, as if the very air and energy around him grew tense and restless.

"Do you have any clothes I could... have?" Quetzacoatl asked a little sheepishly. "What happened to what you were wearing earlier?" Kyril drawled, practically burning a hole in my face with his stare. I cleared my throat, my face flushing an unflattering shade of crimson, as I met his gaze to see him wearing a mildly amused smirk.

Quetzacoatl, bless him, pretended not to notice as he drew his eyebrows together. "In the mirror? It was merely a projection of what I'd found on my astral travels. And when... I was *captured,*" he seemed to say pointedly, "I was in my incorporeal form. Obviously. The only clothes I still have are these." A massive plume of turquoise, red, green, blue, and gold feathers suddenly crowned Quetzacoatl's head. Large, geometrically shaped gold and lapis lazuli jewelry adorned his neck, wrists, biceps, and ankles. More blue, green, and gold feathers cuffed his calves. A dark blue-green skirt, belted in solid gold, tied around his waist. Although it was short enough that I'm pretty sure I could still see the tip of his dick. He casually held a spear that was even taller than he was- several inches over six feet- its blade identical to the one on his chest.

"But I thought this," he said gesturing towards his plumage and other amazing accoutrements, "Might be a little much." My eyebrows leapt towards my hairline and I huffed a laugh. "Too much? *Or just enough?*" I joked, staring at his *ensemble* in awe. Quetzacoatl beamed at me appreciatively as Kyril cleared his throat, chuckling. A pile of folded clothes appeared in Kyril's hands, and he handed them to Quetzacoatl whose phenomenal outfit disappeared again.

We approached the palace entrance to find Nuala returning, hopping down from an enormous black horse with long fur draping its hooves, her sentries with her. She did a double take at the sight of us- her gaze lingering on Quetzacoatl as we approached.

"Vagus?"

"Yes, your majesty?" Quetzacoatl asked, grinning broadly as he bowed at the waist.

Nuala examined him thoroughly.

"His name is Quetzacoatl," I clarified, deciding I'd explain *what* he was more in-depth later as I eyed her sentries.

"You can call me Quetz. If you like," he shrugged casually.

Nuala quirked an eyebrow at him. "That's a name I haven't heard in... many centuries... You're not at all what I expected..."

Quetzacoatl grinned, his gaze becoming heavy-lidded as he stared down at her. At least a foot taller.

"Is that so?... You're precisely what I imagined," he husked. Nuala's throat worked on a swallow, and I saw her fair cheeks and chest flush, still holding his gaze. A small, coy smile curving along one side of her pretty face. The energy in the air grew heavy. My eyebrows sought, and failed, to find shelter in my hairline from the sexual tension blossoming in the air.

I took Kyril's hand, clearing my throat as he watched them with a mixture of horror and amusement. My words were short, quick, and attempted nonchalance as I began to pull Kyril towards the palace doors. "Welp, I suppose you two have a lot to discuss. And on that note, I think Kyril and I will bid you a-."

"Wait," Nuala chimed, prying her gaze from Quetzacoatl, "I have some wildly unfortunate and troublesome news... But... I suppose it can wait for...," her gaze briefly returning to Quetzacoatl, "an hour... or three. We'll meet you in the strategy room at midnight. And go see Syan. You'll need something to wear for the Summer Solstice... I think we should all try our best to celebrate still and enjoy it." *It may be our last,* is what her eyes seems to say.

Through a collaborative effort, Syan and I designed the most spectacular gown I could have ever imagined. Syan clasped her hands excitedly as I tried on the dresses, gaping as I reappeared from behind a screen. She had insisted that Kyril leave so that the dress could be a solstice surprise. The dark emerald silk dress was backless and cowled at just above the somewhat ample curvature of my bum. It hung elegantly, clinging to the shape of my hips and pooled at my feet. The front also was also cowled, low between my breasts- a delicious drop from the straps draped on my shoulders.

As I stepped in front of the three-panelled mirror, my jaw became unhinged. It was truly divine. My heart skipped a beat, and I felt a pang of nervosity as I tried to imagine Kyril's reaction. Although, I wouldn't have to wait much longer to find out. The Solstice was tomorrow. Syan stepped behind me, grinning at me in the mirror as she held up a gift box. My jaw dropped again, and I whirled to face her.

"Oh, Syan... What's this?"

"A dress. For tomorrow."

I furrowed my brows in concern.

"What do you mean? We just made a dress."

"No, no. I mean the dress for... the night's celebration."

"I'm sorry?"

Syan rolled her eyes playfully, as if she were having to explain this to a child.

"There's the celebration during the day, and as the sun sets there's a celebration that continues into the night. Like an 'after-party'.

My face scrunched up in confusion.

"And is there a particular reason why I shouldn't wear this exquisite work of art?" I asked, gesturing towards the magnificence we'd created.

Syan hummed a laugh. "That dress is much too formal for the second half of the celebration. The are two intentions behind the second celebration: one is for us to forsake all our 'modernised', uptight, 'civilised' ways of being that are restrictive to our intrinsic nature, and we're just supposed to let go of it all for the evening. The other, perhaps more importantly, is about re-connecting. Reconnecting with the earth, the cosmic forces like the sun and moon, and with our roots...as tribal... animals. Immortal or mortal." Impressive. "Wow. Sounds amazing. We never did anything like that in Pauperes Domos. I think the sole intention for most people there was just to get as drunk as possible and forget about their problems.

·   ·   ·

Syan shrugged in understanding. "That too. There'll be plenty of drinking... among other *activities,*" she winked.

She handed me the box only to snatch it away.

"No peaking until Solstice. It's a surprise. You'll see," she promised, letting me take the box.

"Do the men change too?"

Syan's smile was broader than I'd ever seen it before. It was borderline wicked.

"So what's this whole second celebration thing like at Solstice?" I asked Kyril as we walked through the palace to Nuala's war room, now that midnight had arrived. Kyril gave me a devilish grin.

"Oh boy...," I sighed.

Kyril tossed his head back with laughter.

"What'd Syan say?"

I chuckled helplessly, shaking my head.

"Nothing. Just something about reconnecting to our primitive roots and unburdening ourselves with civility or something."

Kyril laughed smugly.

"That's... the idea," he offered uselessly.

I scoffed, rolling my eyes. "Care to elaborate? At *all?*"

Kyril threw his arm around me and tucked me into his side, laying a kiss on my head. "Nope."

The guards posted beside the entrance to the closed doors of Nuala's strategy room knocked for us as we approached. "Enter!" I heard Nuala shout from the other side of the room. The guards opened the double doors and promptly shut them behind us. Quetzacoatl, or *Quetz,* stood beside Nuala, still dressed in Kyril's clothes. Other than the pair of fluffy slippers, I couldn't help but notice he was wearing. He rose the crystal glass that was filled with amber liquid at us, a broad smile on his face, as he lifted his gaze from a map Nuala hadn't bothered to look up from.

· · ·

"Fancy a cocktail?" He purred delightedly. I imagine it was the first drink he'd had since... since whenever he'd been trapped in that mirror. My heart squeezed with empathy. Although I had no idea what a cocktail was but if I went by context clues... My brows furrowed. "Does it involve a cock with a tail? Because I have no idea what that is, but if so- you've definitely piqued my interest."

Quetzacoatl bellowed with laughter, shaking his head. "Not at all... I just meant a drink. They call them cocktails for some reason on Terrenea. I've no idea why, actually... but I clearly have spent way too much time there. Humans are weird fucking creatures... Brilliant when they wanna be. But crazy weird..." Quetz's words seemed to trail off as he suddenly grew thoughtful.

Nuala finally lifted her head from the map and straightened. "The Sigillum Terra's been stolen," she said flatly. Quetzacoatl sniffed at his amber liquid, looking as though Nuala's announcement wasn't news at all. Or terrifying.

The Sigillum Terra, just one of seven sigilla, or seals, that had been born in another dimension, given to us by one of it's creators- an entity of some kind- as a gift to the first emperess of the nine realms: a female who was descended from one of the inter-dimensional enti-ties *and* one of the fae from Aeternia, half an eon ago. All I could call to memory was that each of the seven seals was hewn from metal and other materials that could not be found anywhere in any of the nine realms. The seals, when put together and 'activated', were said to reopen the 'doorway' between the two dimensions. Where that was exactly, I had no idea. No one did. Except for perhaps Quetzacoatl.

·   ·   ·

"Based on what Lady Hadiya claims, she has *zero* leads as to how it could possibly have happened. It had been hidden, warded, and heavily guarded by her Seraphim and Nephilim warriors... How they managed to get passed them is... beyond me," Nuala continued.

Kyril's eyebrows narrowed. "That narrows it down significantly," he said with no hint of sarcasm, "Either it was her, one of her guards, or a being capable of either shielding itself from being seen or... perhaps taking on another form entirely... Like-." "A mute," Quetz chimed in. Kyril quirked an eyebrow, his lips drawing into a smirk. Quetz raised a shoulder innocently.

Before the question of what a mute was even had the chance to form in my mind Quetzacoatl answered it without words and an image appeared in my minds eye. It was... A man... An ordinary looking one. And mortal. Again, before the question formed in my mind, a sudden knowing filled my mind. I saw emptiness, A void of nothing. The mute took the form of a crow. And then a woman. A wolf. And finally, a petite woman with a feline curve to her dark monolid eyes and a gorgeous plait of straight black hair. There was also a fresh, pink scar on the side of her neck. She was young and seemed to be... a barmaid. This information passed to me from Quetz in a fraction of a second.

My brow furrowed. "Why a barmaid?"

Kyril and Nuala snapped their gazes to me.

"And why does it want to open the path between realms?" Kyril asked, features tightening with concern.

Quetz raised an incredulous eyebrow at her.

"Your Highness, I may have *many* gifts... Telepathy, however, is not one of them."

· · ·

Nuala blew out a breath. "I suppose the reasoning doesn't matter anyway. It'll all end the same if that doorway is opened. The entities on the other side are far too powerful for this not to end in blood-shed. And worse." Quetz stared. His brilliant turquoise eyes glowed a bit brighter for a few moments as he, seemingly, scanned through time and space as though it were a file cabinet. "She doesn't work alone... Although I can't see with whom. They will blindness to those who look."

"Where is she?" I asked, trying to push away the images of our potential dooms: war, death, poverty... another Pauperes Domos. Kyril's arm wound around my shoulders and pulled me into his side. *"Never again,"* he said within my mind. My heart squeezed, but I couldn't help but feel the futility of his words. If that 'doorway' was opened, beings as powerful, or even more so, would flood the nine realms. There were maybe only a few dozen here who could match them in power... We wouldn't stand a chance.

Quetz's gaze was distant, glowing brightly again.

"She's in the South Guard."

"Do you know where exactly?" Kyril asked.

The Vagus' eyes glowed brighter, ever so slightly, for a brief moment. "It's difficult to see. Her powers, or whoever it is that she's working with, obscure it. But I hear... voices. And... water. The sea... And..." Quetz's nostrils flared slightly, and his face contorted in repulsion. "Fish, beer, and... urine. I can smell it." I couldn't help the sneer of disgust that twisted my face.

Nuala's jaw tightened. "Great... There have to be at least a hundred different taverns on the Southern Guard's coast."

"It's possible, yes... Or a ship... Let's hope it's the former. I can hear music faintly in the background."

Nuala rolled her eyes.

"We could bring the seal here."

The Sigillum Terra. One of two seals here in Aeternia. The rest were peppered around several of the other realms. Deliberately. So that it would be that much more difficult for the doorway between realms to be opened. For good reason. Nuala and Kyril met one another's gaze.

"How agreeable do you think Batlaan will be about letting us take it?" Nuala asked, chewing her cheek.

Kyril sighed thoughtfully. "He's a reasonable male..."

Nuala only gave a harsh laugh.

"We could invite him for Solstice? Butter him a bit? Ply him with a few drinks...," Quetz grinned.

Kyril chuckled. "It'd take more than a few."

Nuala chewed her cheek, looking uneasy. "Yeah. And he's been a right fucking stick in the mud since his mate was kidnapped. Understandably so. Not to mention, we need that seal now. What if the mute tries to take it tonight?"

Quetz's eyes glowed again, perhaps flitting through the different future potentialities.

"He'll agree. Just tell him I've found his nexus mate."

Kyril's jaw dropped, his face paling.

"You found Eleni?" Nuala breathed.

Quetz's mouth curved upwards in a smug, feline manner. "As I said, your majesty. *Many* gifts."

Nuala grinned. "Don't I know it," she murmured softly, eyeing him with genuine admiration.

I gulped, forcing my eyes away.

"Can you see how many seals have been stolen already?" Kyril said, cutting through the tension.

"Only the one," Quetz reassured.

Nuala heaved a heavy sigh of relief.

"Thank the gods...," She said, turning to Kyril, "I'll let you go fetch him. Make sure he brings Morwen."

. . .

Kyril gave her a sharp nod before he turned to me and took my head in his hands and gazed into my eyes as though we were the only two people in this room. My throat worked on a swallow at the intensity there. The gravitas of it. The emotion behind those amber eyes that literally burned like the sun. He opened his mouth to say something but seemed to think better of it, hesitating for a few moments. "If you need anything at all, simply call to me from your mind, and I'll fold back to you in an instant." I nodded, heart squeezing. "I'll be fine...," I whispered. Kyril pressed his lips to mine in a way that was firm yet tender and had my toes curling in my boots.

"I'll be curling up in bed beside you before you know it," he added. I smiled softly, whispering, "I'm gonna spoon the fuck out of you when you do." Kyril's lips parted with glee, and his eyes became heavy-lidded as he held my gaze, as though making a silent promise. And then disappeared.

I now felt very alone left standing with Quetz and Nuala, both of whom were staring at me with raised eyebrows. My cheeks flushed. "What does it mean exactly to 'spoon the fuck out of' someone?" Quetz asked with no small amount of pleasure. Nuala and I burst into laughter as my face reddened further. "I have several ideas, though none of them actually involve spoons," he added. "Care for me to demonstrate?" I challenged. Quetz beamed his laughter. "That would be *delightful,*" he purred.

Nuala sighed, grinning to herself at our banter. "As much as I would *love* to see that, I'm afraid we have other matters to contend with." My stomach lurched. The masked fae. Quetz quirked an eyebrow. "Is it regarding the slums burning down?" My throat worked on a swallow as guilt sunk it's talons into me. Nuala's expression softened. "Still not your fault," she said firmly. I looked to Quetz, whose gaze had gone distant again, eyes glittering like a crystalline sea beneath the sun. He hummed after a few moments. "Well... As I said,

I'm no mind reader... However, I do see a few potentialities popping up... It all kind of depends."

Nuala frowned at all the uncertainty. "On what exactly?" Quetz huffed a laugh. "That's like trying to ask how you came to be born before your parents had even been born. All the infinite things that had to take place for their parents to be born, and meet, and have your parents, and then for them to survive, for your parents to meet, for them to come together, for that one sperm to meet make it to that specific egg...," he shook his head in awe, distantly staring off again, "I do however see meetings taking place. That is a certainty."

The beginnings of a revolt. An uprising and rebellion. All the violence that could ensue. Even another war, gods forbid. More stabbing guilt lanced me. And I began to wonder... Mercifully, Quetz's voice cut off my train of thought.

"There are only a few places where the first one might take place... All of which are here in the Northern Guard. And it seems we have some time. None of them will take place until Lunasa." The summer harvest celebration. I exhaled my relief... That gave us more than a month. More than a month to prevent... the end of the world as we know it... I didn't dare ask if we'd even still be alive by Lunasa, which was a valid question considering what could happen if that doorway between dimensions was opened.

12

By the time Kyril had returned from retrieving Lord Batlaan and his mother, Morwen, I'd been fast asleep and had only been mildly haunted by nightmares. I woke up the following morning in a puddle of drool to a note laid on the pillow beside me and the sound of music playing in the distance. Kyril's side of the bed had been remade, but I could smell his balsam and embers scent lingering on the blankets and pillows, making my heart swell and flutter.

The note was written in an elegant cursive.

"You look so beautiful when you drool. I couldn't bare to disturb you..."

My jaw dropped, and I couldn't help but laugh despite my mortification. *"You are* such *a turd,"* I exclaimed from the confines of my mind. Another note appeared on the paper.

"A turd that doesn't drool or snore and sleeps with its mouth closed."

I laughed. *"And has a* huge ...."

Three dots appeared on the paper.

"Ego," I finished, projecting the word to him in a more deliberate and intuitive way that I thought might reach him. Kyril's laughter bellowed in my mind. *"See you at dusk, my fire...,"* he replied in my mind.

"Wait- did you manage to convince Lord Batlaan to give us the Sigillum Aqua?" I asked.

"Yes. Just as Quetzacoatl said. He didn't even ask questions."

"Wow... That's mildly alarming."

"It's what anyone would do for their mate."

I didn't even allow my thoughts to linger on the things I would do for Kyril. And I didn't even know if he was my mate. Excitement swelled within me, and I rose to peek out of my bedroom window that over-looked the garden to discover hundreds of the palace's servants deco-rating newly erected wooden towers adorned with flowers and streamers. Musicians were practicing alongside other performers. Huge wooden pyres stood at least twenty feet tall, waiting to be set alight.

I spent the day filled with a simmering excitement at seeing Kyril again *in my dress.* Although there was a lingering anxiety every time I reminded myself that he'd already found his nexus. And had died. There was no way I'd ever compare to her. She would always have his heart, even if she wasn't here. What if Nuala was wrong... And The Ones hadn't given him another mate... I'd never in my life heard of such a thing. But that didn't mean he didn't deserve to find love again...

My chest tightened at the possibility this was all only perhaps something less than what I felt. I hadn't ever felt anything near this with either of the two males or the handful of women I'd been with. I also felt terrified at the fact that, in reality- I was little more than a freed Puaperes Domosian, while Kyril was Lord of the Northern Guard. Would I be expendable to him when he saw how different we were? I shook my head at the thought. Kyril's actions weren't ones of lust. This was something more, I willed myself to remember.

I took a deep breath, trying to let it go. The anxiety. And decided that whatever this was between us, I was grateful to experience it. Kyril was a *good* male. A fucking wonderful one. And I felt so wildly fortunate that we'd been given this time together. However brief it may be... I'd never been treated so well and felt so cherished. And he had now raised the bar impossibly high for anyone else if things between us didn't work out. *Oh, well.* I sighed, feeling slightly more at ease, feeling determined to enjoy myself.

I busied myself the rest of the afternoon helping the palace staff set up decorations, much to their dismay, out of fear of Nuala's wrath should she see me working amongst them, but I'd insisted and reassured them that *I* would deal with her should she say anything.

Nuala arrived shortly afterwards, folding into the space in front of me as I worked, dressed in nothing but a short silk dressing gown. The servants around me suddenly found themselves *very* busy elsewhere. "Syan is off work for the next few days for the celebrations. Come, and we can help each other get ready," she grinned, looking a little sheepish and grinning in a way I'd never seen on her before. She seemed... almost shy. I couldn't help the broad smile that blossomed on my face.

I'd never really had any close girlfriends in Pauperes Domos. I'd always longed to have a sister, a group of close girlfriends, or at least just one girlfriend. My brother had been my best friend. The curfews, though necessary, were obviously the biggest hindrance in everyone's social life.

.   .   .

Which meant if you didn't live with that person or weren't willing to risk being electrocuted to the cusp of death... Well, you'd basically never have the chance to develop much of a friendship. The only exception was if you slept at someone else's house, which meant sharing a tiny bed. And if you weren't having sex with that person well... No one had the energy to waste what little comfort and sleep had to offer on staying at a cramped stranger's home. That was also usually filled with most, if not all, of their family members. Even for sex it was rare.

"I... have no idea what to do here...," I said, taking a small sip of the fae wine she'd procured out of thin air for us. Nuala sat in front of a three-panelled mirror that had a thousand different types of make-up and hair stuff I had never seen or heard of before. She demonstrated with a thick metal rod that glowed menacingly, threatening to burn your skin off, and wrapped a thick tendril of hair around it for a few seconds before she released it and the tendril of hair held a coiled shape. She passed the rod to me. "Please try not to burn me. Or yourself. I'll do yours afterwards."

I furrowed my eyebrows in confusion and stared at the burning rod with no small amount of apprehension. "But Syan always just uses her magic. And those oils and stuff." Nuala rolled her eyes. "Syan has magical gifts most of us don't have. So here we are. With antiquated beauty tools that even magically-disadvantaged humans are reduced to using. But that also means, 'girl-time'," she winked, pushing the scalding rode closer to me.

I took a deep breath, relieving her of the curling wand, and pulled away a thick tendril of hair to wind around it. "Please don't go all chimera on me if I accidentally burn you." Nuala cackled a mirthful laugh. "I'm sure she'd appreciate having her manes done sometime."

I couldn't help but share her laughter as the vision of her massive, powerful chimera beast form with a perfectly curled main adorned in tiny pink bows. "That would be... absolutely breathtaking." We both howled our laughter as I very carefully continued to curl her hair. "So... How're things with Kyril?" I bit my cheek trying to suppress the guilty look that lit up my face. Her grin widened, knowingly, in response. 'That good, huh?"

"He's... an extraordinary male," I replied. My heart swelled and fluttered at the thought of him, and I felt that now familiar tugging sensation in my chest. "What about you and Quetz?" A wicked grin leapt across her face.

"Ten."

I arched an eyebrow at her, grinning at what I thought she might me implying as I reached for my wine glass. "As in ten out of ten? Orrrrr....?"

She laughed indulgently. "Oh, ten out of ten does not do this male justice..."

I chuckled, daring to ask. "Ten what then?"

Nuala gave another laugh. "Hmmmm... Where shall I begin? With the thick ten inches that he's endowed with?"

The mouthful of fae wine sprayed from my mouth onto the crystal floor beside us, and Nuala howled with laughter, the wine disappearing from the floor a moment later.

"With the fact that I have to use all ten of my fingers to work his length."

I coughed, choking on the single droplet of wine I'd had left to swallow. This only encouraged her of course.

"Or the ten different positions in which he *thoroughly* fucked me."

My coughing morphed into wheezing laughter.

"Or perhaps with the ten orgasms he gifted me this morning.... Or the ten last night."

.   .   .

You could practically hear my jaw hit the floor. *"The God of All Good Things", indeed.* I shook my head in awe feeling slightly envious due to the fact Kyril and I had yet to have sex. Despite the number of times I'd fantasized about it. I suddenly felt determined to change that.

"Wow. Let's hope you just don't end up pregnant with ten children. All at once." She gasped. "Would you believe he can control things like that? Will them to happen or... not happen." My eyebrows shot up. "And how do you feel about all that?" Her eyes widened, and she shook her head, taking a rather large gulp of wine at the idea. "I'm relieved that we don't have to worry about an unexpected pregnancy. I can't imagine bringing any more children into this world, considering everything that's at stake. Not to mention all of the children that are in need of adoption... But perhaps one day." I couldn't disagree with her. I felt the same. "And how do you feel about him? Despite having only just met..."

"Well... For one, I don't think I've ever been fucked so well in all my 400 years... And while there's definitely more than that... I don't think he's my nexus or anything. But who knows... We've only just met. And he does make it awfully hard not to adore him. Which... By the way, I do feel obligated to say that I feel no small amount of gratitude towards you for convincing me to free him."

I couldn't help but grin with pleasure for her. At her happiness. Even if it were to only last for 24 hours. It was still a beautiful experience. A question I'd been meaning to ask rose in my mind. "How long was he stuck in there for anyway?" She met my gaze in the mirror, her grin fading as she sighed looking mournful. "Thirty-one years..." My eyes widened, lips parting in shock. "Oh gods...," I breathed. Nuala gulped looking deeply guilty. "I know..." A voice seemed to whisper in my head that he had been in there as long as I'd been alive. As though there was some significance to that but I couldn't put together how.

So I allowed other questions to come to the forefront of my mind. "Has he expressed that he's upset with you in any capacity?" She sighed, shrugging. "I tried to apologise last night after we'd first... come together. He only grinned and said, 'All is as it should be.' And then he kissed me, and we continued to... *cum* together," she winked, giggling. And I couldn't help but join her. "Are you or is he holding onto the Sigillum Aqua?" Nuala sighed heavily at being brought back to reality. "I am." I nodded slowly... concern tightening my features.

"And I guess all can do is just wait for the mute to show up and rain on our parade?"

"Pretty much," she replied, bored and tired of this dialogue already.

"And what if she shows up in the middle of the celebration?"

"Then clearly she's a massive fucking party pooper... But just in case, I've warned all my sentries. Everyone is on high alert."

I shook my head absent-mindedly as images of potentialities came up. Violent ones. But I didn't have Quetz's gift, so it was all conjecture.

"Did Quetz say whether or not she would show up tonight?"

"Nope. Can we go back to talking about Quetz's dick now?"

I sighed a sad chuckle. "Yes. Please... Sorry for being a boner killer. I just... didn't know if I should really be 'relaxing' or not."

"I think we should cherish every single fucking moment. Especially right now. It's all we ever actually have anyway..."

Nuala and I spent the entire afternoon getting ready for the solstice celebrations. Now that dusk was approaching, and butterflies had begun to flutter in my stomach in anticipation of seeing Kyril, we finally pulled on our dresses. I found myself gaping at how beautiful Nuala looked. The plunge of her dress' neckline dropped nearly to her belly button. The dark, blood-red plaits of silk fabric over her breasts were cinched by a silk sash at her waist that was woven with jewels. The dress clung loosely to the seductive curve of her hips. She raised an eyebrow at me as I gawked at her.

"You look incredible," I breathed, slightly in awe. A faint smile tugged at the corner of her mouth in response. "You think Quetz'll like it?" I raised my eyebrows at the ridiculous question. "For sure, he's gonna explode in his pants the second he lays eyes on you," I huffed. Nuala beamed excitedly through her own bubble of laughter. I'd yet to see her so happy, and my own heart swelled with excitement for her.

I took one last look in the mirror before we headed down for the festivities, which we could hear beginning in the distance from her balcony. She'd curled my hair into long flowing waves and carefully adorned my strands in gold and emeralds, pearls, and crystals that glittered like diamonds. She'd added a blush to my lips, a dark green and olive powder to my eyelids, and elongated my dark lashes with some kind of paste. The dark emerald dress backless and low-cut dress I wore was the most revealing thing I'd ever worn, but I felt more confident than I ever had in my entire life. The electricity growing in my veins in anticipation of seeing Kyril was set to burst by the time we reached the stair landing.

The palace staff buzzed around us, all in fancy dress or costumes, as we approached the palace entrance. My heart leapt into my throat as I heard a familiar deep growl behind me. *"There you are..."* A feline grin parted my lips as Nuala met my gaze and nodded in understanding, disappearing into the crowd to, presumably, find Quetzcoatl.

As I turned, I could feel my magic crackling at my fingertips. A weight pressed- or rather tugged- at my chest as I took in the sight of him. He was dressed in a finely tailored black coarse silk jacket with matching trousers and a silky smokey white-grey shirt that parted at the chest to reveal the tanned, muscled chest beneath. It was tailored to perfection, accentuating his broad muscles. His hair was neatly combed in a diagonal swoop across the top of his head. His golden skin seemed to glow as if the very core of him were a fiery ember.

I could hear his heart thundering in time with mine as he slowly looked me up and down. A deliciously wicked grin unfurled upon his sensual lips as his eyes flickered with light and embers. He shook his head lightly as he looked me up and down. *"All the stars in all the realms couldn't hold a light to your beauty,"* his deep, velvety voice resonated in my mind like a roll of thunder that made me tremble.

The world around us seemed to disappear as he strode up to me, graceful and silent, and predatory like a panther in the night. And all that remained were the two of us. He stopped a few inches from my face and drew his hands up to caress my cheeks. "I missed you," he said softly as he studied my face as though he were memorising it, as always. And I found myself doing the same. "I missed you too," I whispered, bringing my lips closer to his. He closed that tiny distance between us, and as his lips caressed mine, I could have sworn electricity sparked between us.

My tongue licked the seem of his lips, and he opened for me as he growled his pleasure and gently bit my bottom lip. "If you keep kissing me like this, I'm not going to be able to face anyone." He leaned further into me and I could feel the hard length of him straining against the left pant leg of his trousers. I husked a soft laugh. "And I'm on the cusp of suggesting we celebrate Solstice in private." He hummed his pleasure and nuzzled my neck, inhaling. "Just say the word."

We, with no small amount of reluctance, stepped through the front doors of the palace into the blush of the setting sun. I gaped at the ethereal majesty of the live vines and flowers, all in varying enormity that I'd never seen before, trailed in every direction. Aeternam orbs twinkled from above, illuminating the unearthly glow of the flowers lining the pathways. Massive fountains peppered the grounds, and it was only the smell as we approached one of them as to what was in them. Pale effervescent wine. The guests drinking and laughing as they swayed lissomely to the live music.

"Care for a glass?" Kyril purred beside me, already pouring one. He passed me the glass, and before I even took a sip, I felt a sudden, overwhelming swell of gratitude at being able to witness and experience such beauty and joy.

I pushed away the memories of crude bonfires beneath the stars while dancing to tribal drums, drunk on summer berry wine trying to will away the memories of my last Summer Solstice. With my brother. The Solstice celebrations had been the sole respite for Pauperes Domos residents, and the only two nights a year the curfew was lifted.

Until now, those days and nights had been the most joy I'd ever experienced. My heart ached that Matteus wasn't here to share this experience with me, but my grief was soothed by the fact that thanks to Quetz, I actually knew he now had so much more peace and joy than Aeternia could ever offer. Despite its beauty. It only took a breath before Kyril was drawing my hand to his lips. "Stay here with me, my fire," he murmured against my hand knowingly. My heart squeezed so hard for this male.

The crowd parted for us as we made our way toward the centre of the music, where couples danced and twirled. My grin widened as I noticed Evrin, dressed fabulously as always, dancing with the male from the quartet who always played during our dance lessons.

My gaze drifted, and I saw Nuala, remarkably lithe and free with Quetz, who danced with an envious level of skill. They were laughing as they danced. Graceful as one. This was more than a dance. There was something tangible between them. My heart swelled with gratitude, even though I'd barely known either of them for more than a handful of days, that they had each other and this moment.

However, enduring or fleeting it may be. I felt Kyril's gaze on me and a tug in my chest that had me turning to Kyril, who sketched an elegant bow and extended his hand. I couldn't help the gulp that worked my throat. Everyone around me looked like they'd been doing these dances their entire lives, and I'm sure Kyril was no different. My stomach twisted with nervous energy. "Kyril," I murmured into his ear as he pressed his body against mine and began to move, "I've only had a few dance lessons... I don't wanna embarrass you, and-."

Kyril shushed me, gently cutting me off. "My fire, you could literally shit your pants, and if anyone dared to complain, I'd tell them it was me and to get fucked. That's how little I care for their opinion and speaks only a whisper of how much I care for you and your wellbeing." My anxiety melted, promptly replaced by another emotion. One that I was still breath taken and shocked by.

I chuckled, wrapping my arms around his neck, gazing up into his face. "What did I ever do to deserve you?" Kyril's eyebrows knit together, his face suddenly becoming serious. "Oh Aurelia... You have no idea just how much I don't deserve you. Or how eternally grateful I am to have found you. And for every day you allow me to stand by your side, I'll prove to you how much I cherish you."

My breath caught somewhere in my in my esophagus as it worked on a rough swallow, and my heart that felt like it was exploding into one of the fiery burning suns I could see in the cosmos I always found in Kyril's gaze. My eyes began to water because not only had no one come close to making me feel even an infinitesimal fragment of what I was feeling for this person, but no one had ever shown me that they felt that way for me either. Until Kyril.

Just as I went to bite my lip to keep it from trembling, Kyril pressed his mouth to mine. Our dancing stilled, and as bodies writhed and swayed around us, the depth his our poured from our hearts into one another. He took my head in his hands, mine cupping the back of his neck as his thumbs wiped away the tears that had broken free of my lashes. Our mouths opened in synchronicity, and our tongues met in a tender caress.

After a few moments, the musicians began to play a new song that seemed to sing wordless lyrics that my body and heart intuitively knew. I clasped my hands around his neck, and as though Kyril instinctively knew, we began to dance again. Our lips parted, and I stared up into his eyes awe as he leaned in to kiss away the remaining tears lingering in wet streaks across my cheeks.

As twilight finally gave way to the stars and the moon, the last red, orange, and purple rays of the sun disappearing beyond the horizon, the whole of the palace grounds- hundreds, if not thousands- cheered, and the music began to transform into something heavier and more primal. Many of the musicians exchanged their string and wind instruments for colossal percussive ones.

Some of the more fainthearted immortals began to make their leave and those who remained writhed to the beat. Whatever finery and pomp I'd witnessed from them only minutes before melted away instantly. If it hadn't been for the sheer grandeur, you'd have thought I was back in Pauperes Domos.

Kyril and I undulated in unison, dripping in sweat. The sound of the music pausing and the crowd cheering had my head turning away from Kyril for the first time in I didn't know how many hours. Fire. The massive wooden pyres were being lit consecutively, one after another. I could feel the heat of Kyril's stare as a long, muscled arm curled around me, tucking me into his side as I watched in awe. The touch of a delicate hand on my shoulder had me snapping back to the present. Syan. She was also dripping in sweat and grinning like a fiend. She'd changed from her gown. Her attire now was nothing more than a silk loincloth strapped low on her voluptuous hips by woven strings of silk. Golden metal eels cuffed her arms. Her breasts vaguely concealed by another flap of silk that gave me a full view of her glorious side boob.

. . .

My eyes widened as I arched an eyebrow, meeting her excited grin. "Your loin cloth and side boob are making me feel *things*, Syan." She tipped her head back and howled her laughter at the night sky. I'd never see her so free and happy. I couldn't help but laugh with her. A male, with a dark blue skin tone and similarly webbed appendages, who nearly matched Kyril in height but was even broader in size- no small feat- had his arm draped around her delicate shoulders. His biceps were as big as her head. If there were ever a male that looked her equal, it would be him. They even matched loincloths. He gave me a carnivorous grin and respectfully bowed towards Kyril and me as he reached gently for her hand.

Syan opened her palm and a small sheet of golden chainmail appeared. An eyebrow of mine arched at it. "You're welcome," she said smugly, her words aimed and both me *and* Kyril. She gave me a mischievous grin and placed the dress in my hand, giving me a wink before she disappeared into the lithe crowd with her partner. As I turned to face Kyril again, I noticed that all of the other fae had also changed. Most of the males, and some of the women, weren't even wearing tops, only thin trousers or loin cloths like Syan and her partner.

My jaw literally dropped as I beheld what Kyril wore. He looked more like a Sun God than a vampire. And it made me wonder just what the other half of him was. His lips slowly parted to reveal his perfect, white teeth. Among them those pointy canines that were just slightly longer than everyone else's. An asymmetrical, mid-thigh length loin cloth of a beige gold was draped low, on his hips. His long, bronzed, powerfully built arms were now cuffed in gold at the biceps and wrists. And I'm pretty sure my mouth *watered* at the sight.

· · ·

It was an absolute miracle that I somehow managed to keep my tongue from lolling out of my mouth and falling to the floor. My gaze roamed over his broad, sculpted chest that rose and fell as he watched me with a gaze I could feel burning me to the core. Not that core. *Lower.* A tingling sensation began to radiate from it as my eyes drifted beyond his chest, beyond his abs that looked like they'd been hewn from granite, and all the way down to that long strip of golden cloth and what I knew lay beneath, and his glorious legs, which were heavily corded with muscle. *Sweet Gods.*

"Your turn," he purred. I glanced at the glimmering gold chainmail *napkin* I held in my hand and flitted my eyes back to him. "How do I-." And before I even had to finish my sentence, my hand was empty, and I suddenly felt a breeze along my legs. My bum. My breasts. His eyes widened briefly, his grin becoming wicked. I looked down and saw that while my dress was of a slightly similar design to the silk one, this was... the *hyphenated* version.

The chainmail's cowl began so low, if I dared to lean forward, my nipples would surely pop out. The length of the dress was the equivalent of a t-shirt. The bottom curvature of my rear was exposed, while a glance over my naked shoulder saw a single tendril of gold chainmail that grazed the curve at the top of my bum. The slits along the side of the dress rose to the tops of my hips. I was also now barefoot. Like everyone else.

With the pyres of fire now all lit, the cheering settled, and the music intensified, even more primal than before. I gazed out at the sea of once regal immortals now jumping and writhing like wild, debauched, beautiful beasts. I felt Kyril's gaze upon me, but I couldn't tear my eyes away from the crowd, an entrancing sight. Kyril's lips grazed my ear as he spoke, "If this is too much for you, just say the word, and we can leave."

The feeling of his lips against my jaw sparked something fiery inside me. Electric and burning. I turned to face him and raised a hand to his cheek, caressing it as I pressed the front of my core against him and raised a leg to wrap it around his hips. He emitted a low growl and leaned his head down to gently bite my neck as he wrapped an arm around my waist, the other firmly gripping my hip and palming a fistful of my rear. We began to undulate again to the swell and beat of the drums.

It felt as though time ceased to exist as we danced. And it wasn't until I saw the faintest twilight of dawn beginning to rise that I remembered such a thing existed. That exquisite effervescent wine probably had something to do with it. Kyril seemed to notice the paling of the sky at the same time I did. The music was still in full force as he took my hand in his and began to lead me through the dancing and grinding throng of immortals. As we passed, I caught a glimpse of Nuala and Quetzacoatl. The words nearly flew from my mouth. *Ho-ly. Shit.* Kyril flung his gaze towards me and followed my own. An easy laugh rumbled beside me.

Quetz was dressed in that extraordinary outfit he'd shown us in the dungeons, minus the feathered headdress, which was probably for the better, lest it become damaged by the crowd. As my gaze lingered on him and his tattoos, I felt a small jolt of electricity in my chest and his eyes drew to meet mine. The corner's of his mouth curved upwards, eyes glowing like a crystalline sea.

.   .   .

My gaze wandered to Nuala's breasts which were shielded only by the cupping of two thick straps of darkest blue silk that twisted behind and to the front of her across the waist which finally unfurled itself over her rear and front, but left the entirety of her hips exposed. She bent over in front of him and grabbed her ankles, slowly rising as her hips undulated against his... groin... until her mouth briefly returned to his before sliding down the front of his body all while he ground on her from behind. *Whoa.*

As I turned back towards Kyril and the palace entrance that laid in the distance, I felt the heat of someone's stare, pulling my gaze in the other direction. A tall auburn-haired fae with fair skin stood amongst the crowd, unmoving as he watched me. He wore a long bird's beak mask that covered most of his face, but his bright, pale blue eyes were visible beneath it. Memories of the masked fae flitted through my mind but I couldn't quite recall any of their eyes... I'd been too focused on Nuala and Kyril. And Nuala's poor, young sentry who had clearly bitten off more than he could chew coming to Pauperes Domos that day. I hoped he was ok and had survived. Kyril drew me into his side, and all other thoughts drifted away.

Kyril led me to my bedroom by the hand in silence, save for the thundering of our hearts and faint drumming that could still be heard in the distance. We reached the door, and I found myself gulping as I turned toward him. He laid a gentle but firm hand on the small of my back. "Aurelia," he breathed softly, his lips grazing my forehead.

I realized I'd been holding my breath, and my breasts pressed through the chainmail of my dress into his chest as I finally inhaled.

My hand found the doorknob behind me, and it clicked open. I took a step out of his hands and stalked backwards into the bedroom, holding his gaze, heart pounding. He simply watched me for a moment before entering, the door closing silently behind him on a non-existent breeze. I turned and padded my way to the bathroom, shrugging off my chainmail dress along the way.

A single amber aeternam lantern flickered on as I used my magic to turn the handle of the waterfall shower, steam unfurling in its wake. I could feel Kyril's grin from where he stood by the door. "Show off," he purred, and we both chuckled. I slipped off my panties and stepped beneath the stream of warm water, letting it pour over my hair, my body. Rinsing off the thick layer of sweat from the celebration with it. I poured the floral cleansing oil Syan had given me into my hands as Kyril's own hands closed over my waist.

My heart thumped a heavy beat as he leaned in beneath the thick stream of water to lay a tender kiss on the curve of my neck. I felt the evidence of his desire pressing firmly against my lower back. The towering length and thickness of it. He trailed tender open-mouthed kisses along my neck and shoulders before I turned to face him. His thumbs stroked my cheeks as he looked into my eyes. A sudden bursting sensation poured out of my chest and I felt the tightening of this... tether between us from my heart to his.

As if in response, he stepped forward with his hand on my back to guide me and close the remaining distance between us, pressing me against the wall. My back arched as he stared down at me for a moment before leaning in to kiss my forehead, my eyes, and my cheeks. I already felt like I was going to explode with need for him. I gently grasped his face in my hands and pulled his mouth to mine. Our lips parted, and our tongues met in a passionate caress. He growled into me, and I could feel it in my chest, my heart, all the way down into my core and beyond.

I reached down for the hardness pressing firmly against me but he drew my hand away. "Not yet," he growled gently. "I don't want to do this standing. I want you spread out beneath me for me to feast on at my leisure." I willed the shower off, and I let out a yelp for fear of slipping as he scooped me into his arms with preternatural ease. And the span of a breath, I felt my skin and hair dry before he laid me down on my bed to crawl on top of me.

His perfect, full, cupid's bow lips kissed, licked, and nipped a path down my neck and chest, causing my back to arch at the intense pleasure of it. He cupped my breasts in his hands as his mouth and tongue roamed towards them, the pad of his thumb gently stroking the tip of my nipple back and forth. My core clenched, a soft moan escaping me, and he growled into my chest as he took my other nipple into his mouth before sucking and casually flicking his tongue against it. My toes curled as I cried out in pleasure. My legs parting wider for him, the puddle of my essence pooling between them. My hips writhed, seeking out his massive length and painting it with the wetness of my folds, my core, in back and forth strokes.

Kyril stilled and gripped my hips firmly with his powerful hands. "My fire... if you continue to move like that and make those noises, this is going to be so much shorter than I'd fantasised." I laughed softly, "Trust me when I say I'll be cumming with you." Kyril hummed his approval. "You definitely will be. After I make you come with my mouth." He pulled me to the edge of the bed to stand between my legs, and I couldn't help but admire his beauty, the formidable power that radiated from him.

.　.　.

Kyril took each of my legs in his hands and spread them wide for him to see the wet, glistening entrance to my core, aching with desire. He let out a deep growl that rumbled through me like thunder and had my back arching again in anticipation. In need. He groaned as his fingers finally met the wetness seeping from me, lazily tracing teasing circles against the apex of my core. "*Fuck... Aurelia...* Please tell me this is all for me."

My heart, and pussy, squeezed at his words, and I swore aloud as I could already feel my climax nearing. He sensed it and slowed, letting me cool down. I wanted him, *needed* him inside me. "*Oh fuck... Kyril...* My pussy is all yours. And only yours. *I'm* all yours." Kyril's gaze snapped from my core to my eyes as he growled his approval. "Aurelia, you've always been mine. Before you were given form in this realm, you were mine. Just as I was, and am, yours. Just as we shall remain in this life and the next."

I *shoved* the logic that tried to rear up in my mind far into it's recesses. Logic regarding his nexus mate who had been killed in the war, the fact that we'd only just met days ago... Tears sprung to my eyes just as his mouth dove for my core, and he licked from my entrance to my clit where he hovered to flick his tongue before wrapping his lips around it and *sucked*. Stars burst from behind my eyes, and my back came arching off the bed. I softly cried out his name in a breathy moan as the wave of the most intense pleasure I'd ever known coursed through my body. Sensing the emotion through this tether between us, Kyril's hand found mine and twined our fingers together, squeezing.

My heart swelled to bursting, and I could literally feel this tether between our chests vibrating with the intensity of our... *love.* As ridiculous and unfathomable as it seemed. His tongue firmly lapped up the wetness my body offered him in slow, tender strokes before teasing the apex of my core with the steady flicking of his tongue whilst his thumb began teasing the outside of my entrance. He moaned onto me as his lips wrapped around my bundle of nerves again and firmly sucked while sliding a finger inside me.

My entire body arched, lifting me off the bed, as my pussy firmly spasmed around his finger. The crescendo of my orgasm arriving in a head-to-toe crash of bliss and pleasure so divine and powerful that I could feel every molecule in my body humming with pleasure. I felt fluid between my legs rush out of me as my pussy pulsed. Kyil's lips, tongue, and fingers continuing to make expert work of his ministrations. For a flicker of a moment, I felt mortification at all the... fluid I didn't even know my body could produce but Kyril groaned and reached to pinch my nipple in reprimand. "You are the most delicious thing I've ever tasted, and there is nothing in this world more beautiful and *inspiring* than the sight of you coming undone beneath me."

Kyril licked and sucked up every drop of my juices that dripped from me as I couldn't help but moan loudly, spreading my bent legs even wider. One of his hands found my breast and began caressing whisper soft circles on the peak of my nipple as he rose to stand between my legs. He positioned himself at my entrance as he leaned down to kiss me, and I slowly licked away the wetness of my juices from his lips, his chin. He held my gaze as I did. "*My turn,*" I husked.

I rose and pushed him onto the bed kneeling between his legs as he sat on the edge of the bed. His enormous cock upright before me. I held his gaze as I sucked my cheeks in, gathering the saliva between my lips and allowing it to fall directly onto the broad head of his cock. His eyes burned like the sun as he watched me taking him in my hand and working my saliva his shaft. His fists balled the silk sheets as he hissed and swore his pleasure. His body tensed as I took him in my mouth, sliding him all the way down the back of my throat until I couldn't fit anymore- several inches of him laid bare.

I compensated by utilizing both my hands and mouth to work him slowly. Pausing occasionally to spit and lick the length of him, maintaining eye contact throughout. I relished the taste and feel of every vein and ridge. His breaths became heavy and rapid, his hips beginning to thrust against my own movements in synchronicity. His hands caressed my head and hair tenderly as he watched me through his gorgeous, heavy-lidded gaze. *"Gods, Aurelia...,"* He breathed, his lips parting, a groan escaping before he leaned forward and picked me up, again with that preternatural strength and grace, and smoothly laid me back on the bed.

He set my legs on either side of him- one of which he clutched to his chest, kissing and licking a sensitive spot near the back of my ankle that I didn't even know I had. His eyes remained fixed on mine as he gently eased himself into me in slow, shallow thrusts. My breath caught, and I let out a breathy moan just as he began to gently caress the apex of my core again with his thumb.

The gentle thrusting gradually evolved into longer, harder, deeper strokes as I adjusted to the size of him inside me. And I could already feel my climax approaching again. He leaned down to bring his lips to mine, and after a few moments of the tender and passionate writhing of our tongues, I bit his bottom lip, causing him to let out a low growl, the thrusting of his hips growing harder and wilder.

I rolled and pinned him down beneath me, keeping him still firmly rooted deep inside me. I began a rolling undulation of my hips, his hands firmly gripping fistfuls of my bum in his strong hands, as it bounced and slid around his thick, long cock. I leaned in close and kissed him as I continued the rhythmic vacillation of my hips, my pussy clenching with intense pleasure around him.

I pulled back slightly, bracing myself on the headboard of the bed as he took my breasts in his hands, in his mouth. Breathy moans escaped my lips, and he sat up to wrap his arms around me as I continued to grind on him. "I'm cumming," I moaned softly as my back began arching again, and I ground harder onto him. He held my gaze as he gingerly wrapped one hand around my throat, the other wrapped around my waist.

As the first wave of my orgasm took over me, I heard a groan escape his lips. He braced me firmly and flipped me over onto my back, thrusting himself deep inside of me in a steady, pounding, loving rhythm as he climaxed with a roar. I could feel the steady pulsing streams of his seed spilling inside of me, the realization and feeling of it making my orgasm all the more intense, and my pussy gripped him firmly as if she were trying to draw out every last drop.

I could feel this tether between us pulsing in waves, much like our orgasm, with an overwhelming feeling that made my heart fill to bursting. And I could see by the way his eyes glowed wildly and the expression accompanying his furrowed brow as we stared into one another's eyes that he could feel it too.

Our lips met again as our releases subsided, and he laid down beside me, pulling me in close to him. I rested my face on his chest as our hands gently caressed and explored one another. For several moments we laid there in comfortable silence simply feeling this tether between us. This tether felt distinctly... tangible. Palpable enough you'd think I could touch it. Or at least the tether I felt. I felt a waver of doubt, wondering if I was the only one who felt it. His hand stilled on my back and he brought his hand to my face and tilted it up to meet his gaze. "You needn't ever doubt the what we have is real, Aurelia. I've always felt this tether between us."

My breath hitched. His thumb caressed my cheek as he studied my expression, the corners of his mouth curling upwards. My words were soft, awed. "How long have you known?" A dark shadow fluttered in his eyes, and his smile faded. Before I even consciously had the thought I felt him tugging at that cord, the tether. *The Nexus Bond.* And I felt, sadness and pain. *His* sadness and pain. But I couldn't decipher it. I pushed myself out of his arms, that sadness and pain still leaking into me and I felt tears swelling in my eyes as I sat up. My unease seeped into my words. "What are you not telling me? I can feel your pain bleeding into me." Kyril stared at me with a pained expression as he held his breath. My hands started to shake. "Say it, Kyril. You're scaring me."

Kyril took a deep breath, sitting up beside me, and reached out to touch me. I pulled away, scooting away from him, and my body screamed in protest as the warmth of his naked body was replaced by the cool night air.

"Always."

"Always what? Since we met, you mean?"

His throat worked on a swallow, his pain intensifying. I could feel it all now. Apparently, having sex had solidified and strengthened this 'tether'. Our bond.

"Longer... Much longer."

My heart began to pound.

"How long?" I demanded.

Kyril's jaw feathered and I saw his throat work on a swallow. "Before you were conceived..."

I reared back. "*What?... How?*"

"It's a long story, Aurelia... One that I don't think-."

"Fuck what you think!" I didn't care however he had divined that I was his Nexus. He knew who I was. He knew *where I was from.* My heart cracked, and the air in my lungs fled. "You knew... All these years. You knew I was in Pauperes Domos. This whole time?" I could feel all the pain I saw in his eyes as I waited for him to answer. "Yes." I shook my head as I drew in a shaky breath. "Make it stop." Kyril tried to reach for me, but I snatched my hand away. Another stab of pain. Kyril's face hardened. "There is nothing that I can do to block out the tether between us. Nor would I *ever* do such a thing."

I threw back the covers and climbed out of the bed. My anger, the hurt, roiled inside me- only further exasperating the pain Kyril was experiencing as it streamed into me. "You left me there," I growled through gritted teeth as the tears swelled and swiftly spilt down my cheeks. Kyril stood so quickly that I'd have missed the movement if I'd blinked and reached me in only a few strides. I completely ignored the awe-inspiring beauty of his nudity. Too furious to care. He gently took my face in his hands, forcing me to look up at him. His thumbs caressing my cheeks.

"There is so much you don't know yet, Aurelia... It's not what you think. I swear it. I would never have just left you there."

"*And yet you did,*" I spat furiously. He must have known my mother died at childbirth. Another thing I could some how hate him for when he could have so easily done something to prevent it. And the death of my father in that Gods-forsaken quarry.

"You could have saved them," the words burst from lips with venom and anguish.

Kyril's own eyes pooled with tears, his jaw flexing as he leaned in to kiss my tears away.

"Do not think for one single moment that I did not try," he said with terrifying calm. I huffed a bitter laugh as his lips moved to the other side of my face to kiss away the rest of the tears. "Clearly. They died because you tried *so* hard. I spent the past 31 years as little more than a fucking slave in Pauperes Domos, all because you *tried*."

The words gutted him. And me. I couldn't take looking at him anymore. The tether between us burned like it was on fire. I could feel it tightening, like an anchor being drawn back to it's ship. But I couldn't just ignore this. How he'd permitted me to live for over thirty years in Pauperes Domos. And how my parents had both died because of it. "Leave," I seethed, stepping out of his arms. Kyril tried to pull me back into him, but I shoved him away. "Aurelia, please just let me explain-"

"Did you know that they'd die?"

Pain like I'd never know coursed into me, every bit as intense as physical pain. Tears streaked down Kyril's face, and if it had been anything else... I waited, prayed that he would say 'no', so I could let go of this and let him explain his way out of it.

Kyril shuddered, exhaling a ragged breath. "Yes but-"

"Get out."

"Aurelia."

"You could have saved us. Saved them. They died because of *you* did *nothing* while you lived in luxury, and they *died* in poverty. I grew up motherless because you stood by and did nothing when you could have saved us."

I could feel both of our hearts shattering into a million shards and stabbing both of us. He didn't bother hiding his tears. He only stared at me for a few moments. And then disappeared.

13

After my violent sobbing subsided around midmorning, sleep finally found me. I didn't get out of bed the next day until night had returned. Thankfully, there had been zero sign of the mute, and according to Nualas's allies, no other seals had been stolen. Yet. So for the moment, I was free to wallow.

The nexus between Kyril and I had become so painful that I'd found my hand unwittingly clutching at my chest at times. My body and soul screamed at me for having forsaken him after our union. Even my magic seemed to writhe in protest within me. From what I'd been told during my childhood, the Nexus bond was exceedingly rare for two matched souls, divined as one by The Creators at their making but separated at the beginning of their souls' journeys to the nine realms. It was said that it often took multiple lifetimes, or millennia within one lifetime, for them to evolve enough that they should finally be reunited. A *gift* from The Creators, I'd been told.

.   .   .

Which is why I was so... apprehensive, considering Kyril already had a mate... Maybe they hadn't actually been nexus mates. Maybe they'd been head over heels in love but not actually nexus mates. The fact that Kyril had felt it too... And it explained how he always knew what I was thinking and feeling. And how I could *feel* his pain. And had known about me somehow before I'd even been conceived... My mind reeled at how that was even possible. And I felt like my heart was literally dying. How could he have left me there? Let my parents die? A new wave of sobs wracked me.

Apparently, once The Nexus Bond was consummated by partaking in a *physical* union, it awakened a number of many other gifts, such as sentience that always kept each of them informed about the others well being, telepathic communication even if they didn't naturally possess telepathy, and physically experiencing the emotion of the other when they were intense enough, among numerous other things that I'd long forgotten. Only a few of the elders in Pauperes Domos shared the Nexus bond. Other than that, it had been the stuff of fantasy and folklore to us.

I'd deliberately waited to leave my room until the moon was high for the palace residents to be asleep, or at least not to work and walk through the halls. I stealthily padded my way down the hall to make my way toward the kitchen. The hunger pains in my stomach had become unbearable. Especially after all that sparkling wine the night before.

As I finally reached the staff's entrance into the kitchen and laid my hand on the doorknob, I felt a stillness. A silence. A silence that seemed to devour the typical silence that would fill an empty hall at midnight. The hairs on my skin rose. The gnawing pains of starvation even seemed to pause. Against my will, a flicker of hope that perhaps

Kyril stood behind me, but the pain in the nexus bond in my abdomen told me otherwise.

I whirled around to find that tall, ethereally handsome, fae-like but definitely not fae, heavily tattooed male standing behind me dressed in a pair of silk pyjama bottoms. He didn't flinch. He stared down at me for a moment with that knowingness. That shimmering humour in his eyes. I sighed heavily and leaned against the doorway, grateful for the distraction. "Well, you and *Her Royal Majesty* seem to be getting along swimmingly," I drawled, arching a brow at him.

A smile, lighthearted and warm, graced his handsome otherworldly features. "I see you and your hybrid mate have consummated things," he nodded toward my heart, his gaze lingering as though he could actually see the tether. I clutched at the silk robe as if that would do anything to disguise the Nexus bond that had now indeed become a living, visceral thing since our *union*. Which Quetz seemed to be privy to thanks to not only his gifts but The Creator's Promise that now bound us together.

"Yes, well... It was short-lived," I said briskly, opening the kitchen door. And trying to stifle the well of pained emotion as he followed me into the kitchen. I groaned in relief when I saw piled-high bread, chees, fruit, and cakes. I began stuffing the delicious cheeses and bread into my mouth first. "Care for a snack?... Do you eat... food?" I asked, not bothering to finish chewing first.

Quetz huffed a laugh. "While I occupy my corporeal form, yes. Indeed, I do." A large piece of berry chantilly cake appeared on a plate in his open palm. I glanced to where the previously untouched caked had sat, and sure enough, a slice was now missing. I watched him take a large bite. He did so slowly, savoring every moment of it.

My heart ached for him. I couldn't imagine being trapped in a mirror without being free to experience the physical senses or share anything with anyone for... thirty-one years. I nearly gasped at my realization, like puzzle pieces sliding into place.

Quetzacoatl's knowing gaze coolly slid from his cake to my eyes. "31 years...," he affirmed smoothly as a soft smile curled his lips, his gaze lingering on mine. All the answers to nearly all my other questions clicked into place. Quetz finished his cake, and the plate disappeared. He simply watched me with that penetrative but strangely soothing gaze. The realization hit me like a tidal wave. I felt the tears swelling in my eyes already. "But why... Why didn't he save us then?" I breathed. Quetz sighed thoughtfully. I rubbed at the feeling in the centre of my chest where Quetz's life essence had permeated and rooted itself in my body. It was love that I felt. From him. Not a romantic or lust-driven love. A selfless and unconditional love, like a parent's love for their child.

His smile bloomed, lips parting to reveal his perfect white teeth. "You have a great many things ahead of you, Aurelia. There are many reasons why you had to suffer as you did. Sometimes suffering, despite how painful, is good for us. It gives us perspective. And for the strongest among us, compassion, selflessness, vision, purpose, and inspiration bleed out from our souls and into the lives of others, changing not only your life but theirs as well. You have a great purpose *in* this thread of fate you follow... When Kyril trapped me, it was only because I allowed him to. And then I waited. *For you...*"

My pooling tears breached the dams of my eyelids and cascaded over my cheeks in a steady, unrelenting stream. It took everything within me to keep my face from cracking and not expel the sob clawing in my chest and throat to get out. *"Why?"* The smile he gave me was something purely divine. "... For two reasons: One, because for the first time in the aeons of my existence, I found a creature who dared to seek me not out of their ignorant lust for power or riches or any of the other selfish maladies that plague the creatures of the nine realms and beyond. But for love. Selfless, true, and unending. And two... Well... *I know who you are.*"

And before I even had a chance to think any better of it, I threw myself at him. A little less gracefully than I'd usually have tried but my heart was in it. Arms woven firmly around him, I buried my face in his neck. "Thank you," I whispered on a swallowed sob. Without hesitation, he chuckled, wrapping me up in his arms and giving me a squeeze.

After a few moments, I pulled away, wiping at my cheeks. "Can you take me to him?" Another serene smile and an easy laugh. "He's already here." I leapt toward the kitchen door and swung it open to crash into Kyril's chest. He caught me like an impenetrable wall. The expression on his graceful, seductive features was raw. Pained. But there was something like relief in his reddened, tear-stricken eyes. And worry. "I'm so sorry." The words burst out of me like a small whimpering animal. He simply shook his head gently before wrapping an arm around my waist and sweeping my legs off the ground with the other.

As I wrapped my arms around Kyril's neck, my eyes met Quetz's as he watched us. Studied us, something unreadable in his gaze. The corners of his mouth curved upwards. He gave me a wink just as Kyril folded us into his home. Thankfully, only a wave of minor nausea came and went.

We were in his bedroom. I hadn't paid much attention to it the other day in my lust-addled haze. The wood and stone walls were rich and textured. A massive fireplace crackled across the room in front of the bed adorned in silk and velvet bedding of darkest red. The bed was large enough to accommodate a number of large beasts. A grand piano sat in front of the floor-to-ceiling windows facing the rocky cliffs and sea. Heavy plaits of velvet, thick enough to blot out the sun, were draped at each end of the windows. Intricately woven tapestries of astounding beauty lined the stone wall behind the bed. Handwoven plush wool rugs and furs lined the dark wood floors.

Kyril set me gently on the edge of his bed and kneeled before me. He held my gaze with weary, red eyes. Seeing the pain in his eyes, feeling it through the tether between us, had my eyes burning again. I reached out with a trembling hand as he buried his head in my lap and wrapped his arms around me. He drew a shuddering breath and squeezed me. "You have no idea what it did to me to leave you there." My fingers dove into his hair and picked his head up. "Quetz told me... I'm sorry I didn't let you explain." He studied me for a few moments. "What specifically?"

"Well, that you captured him 31 years ago to find me... And that you couldn't take me from Pauperes Domos because... of some greater purpose, I suppose... that would help me become who I am now... Now that I'm saying it all out loud, I guess there are some blanks you'd have to fill in."

Kyril's throat worked on a swallow as he watched me pensively. I pulled him towards me off the floor, where he was knelt, for him to sit next to me. Kyril exhaled a heavy breath. "During the war, I started having these dreams. Of a couple. Two young fae. A black-haired male with dark eyes and a beautiful dark-haired female with green eyes."

. . .

My breathing stilled. *My parents.* He was describing my parents.

"I had no idea what these dreams meant. I thought maybe I was to meet them in the future... But didn't think much of it. The dreams persisted, and I witnessed snippets of them falling in love. I even saw a brief moment of them *making* love. Years later, towards the end of the war... It was the darkest time in my life. And that's when I started having dreams of... You. It gave me hope. And I honestly don't know that I'd still be here if it weren't for those dreams. I even went to a seer to have them interpret them. She told me you were my nexus.

"Although at the time, I was skeptical. Perhaps she was just saying what I wanted to hear so she could make more money. A century later, the human woman I told you about. I was with her at the time. She had... gifts. She told me what they were, confirming what the seer had said even though I hadn't told her I'd seen one. And then the dreams stopped for the most part, and for many years I would dream of you once or twice a year. They were faint. But then, 31 ago, I started having them again every night. But it was a nightmare. Of your mother... being heavily pregnant... And..." Kyril's voice began to wobble.

Something cracked in my chest, and the burning sensation in my eyes swelled to bursting. A steady stream of tears began to fall. Kyril's throat bobbed, and I noticed his hands were trembling.

"I became desperate... In the visions, it didn't show me whether or not you survived. I always woke up in terror just when I could see that she was..." Kyril hands fisted as he spoke. He didn't need to finish that sentence as he continued. "I had no idea how I could find them if they were even real. That's when I decided to try and trap a vagus...

Or some kind of god, apparently. There'd been sightings in the Western Guard... And several deaths. So I went and lived there for six months, to no avail. So I returned, for the first time since I'd managed to escape after the war, to the only place monsters have to dwell in relative peace... The Sapphire Mountains. I found him and trapped him. To see if you would survive. I was sure I'd die trying to do so, but at that point, I honestly didn't care. Part of me welcomed it.

"By the time I found... Quetz... It was as though he'd already been waiting for me. And he willingly told me everything he could. He told me that you would survive but that there was no way to save your mother... And that I had to leave you in Pauperes Domos. When I told him that I couldn't allow it, he told me that if I interfered with what fate had laid in your path, you would die shortly after. To be reborn in another life, destined to experience that same suffering until you evolved and... fulfilled... your potential. Those years you spent in Pauperes Domos were... Dark for me," he eyed me knowingly, "Although nothing compared to what you experienced, I'm sure. I eventually became desperate to escape the visions I had of you. Suffering. And... also enjoying the company of others with you."

Oh no. He had seen me with the other two males and the handful of women I'd been with. A dark pain encamped his eyes at the memory as he continued. "I was beyond desperate with the longing to rescue you. Free you. To see you. Touch you. But Quetz told me that when you somehow did leave Pauperes Domos, though he didn't bother telling me how that might happen, that we would meet."

My mind was reeling, and my whole body trembled. Listening to his voice was all I could do to keep from shattering completely.

.   .   .

"The night when you tried to escape Pauperes Domos..." Kyril clenched his jaw at the memory. The tremors of my body stilled as the sound of the lykanthir's cry rang in my ears, and the vision appeared in my mind. The tall, broad silhouette of a male ripping the wolf away from me and slamming it into a tree trunk. Its bones snapping like twigs. Of the male ripping its throat out. And towering over the fallen lykanthir's body. That silhouette stepping toward me, picking me up in one graceful swoop with an arm around my waist and the other beneath my legs. *It was him*. He was the guard. Or I'd assumed it was a guard. My breath left me. It was him this whole time.

"It was you...You were the one who... In the woods....," I choked out. His jaw tightened as he nodded. "I was asleep. I'd woken up filled with this terror. Of fear for you. And I could feel the visceral fear you felt through the tether between us. I folded into the forest and followed your scent." I drew my hands to my mouth to stifle the sob I could feel trying to crawl it's way out of my chest as the traumatic memories of that night flooded my mind. Memories I'd tried so hard to push away. And all this time... It had been him who'd rescued me.

"I spoke to Quetz again that night. I was terrified that perhaps I'd intervened too soon. That maybe you'd have survived somehow without me. But he simply told me that *our* time had not come yet. He said that even he could not yet see what the future held for certain. Only potentialities, possible outcomes. And that certain other events had to pass before I could come into your life.

"But I couldn't bear the idea of you returning to Pauperes Domos. To continue living in destitution, slaving away at the quarry. I figured it was already too late if I had intervened too early. So I spoke to Nuala. We'd hardly spoken since the end of the war, outside of whatever meetings were held between the Guards and the Realms. We've... had a tumultuous relationship since...," his throat worked on another rough swallow, "the end of the war... But when I confided to her who you are, she obviously agreed."

He took my quavering hand in his and pressed his lips to my wrist, inhaling my scent. There was still a question that remained to be answered. "Did Quetz ever tell you why? What the point of all this was?" Kyril sighed, shaking his head. "I tried to ask. That night in the dungeon. He only told me that to speak it aloud would alter the future's course. A future that he said needed to happen. For the betterment of the realm and beyond."

Kyril paused, huffing a small laugh. "He did mention that a time would soon come when his will, and your will, would act as one." *The Creator's Promise.* My lips parted in a gobsmacked expression. "I didn't know what he meant at the time, obviously. The ambiguity of his words only further exasperated me. I didn't have the energy to ask what he meant."

I sighed heavily. Kyril leaned toward me and kissed the remaining tears staining my cheeks. His lips, his breath grazed my cheeks as he whispered. "I have waited for you for more than 200 years." Words could not express the overwhelming love and sorrow that filled me. Sorrow for everything he had been through for me. Because of me. Before I'd even been born. I held his gaze as I did, and I saw his eyes glisten. I put all my love, and sorrow for what he'd been through, into the tether between us and leaned into him, pressing my lips to his.

I laid down on my side, on the bed, and pulled him towards me. He brought his mouth to mine again in a gentle caress. I tugged on the hem of his shirt, and it disappeared without him even having to lift a finger to do so. Wrapping a leg around him told me he'd also made his trousers disappear. I pulled the silk sash tying my robe closed, and let it fall open. I was already naked beneath it.

Kyril's hand held my face close to his as the other found my breast and began caressing my nipple, it pebbled beneath his thumb, and a soft moan escaped my lips. The sound of it had him growling, nipping at my bottom lip, and I swear I felt a jolt of electricity reach all the way to my tingling and throbbing clit. I reached down to grab the hardness of him firmly pressed against my stomach and my sopping wet folds. The broad head of him was already wet with pre-cum, and I began to work him in gentle strokes.

He shuddered, groaning before pinning my hands above my head, and drawing himself up to his knees. Still holding me down, he began to kiss and suck my breasts as he slid his free hand between my already parted thighs. *"Fuck... Aurelia,"* he hissed at the wetness that greeted him and nipped at the hardening peaks of my breasts before sucking away the sweet pain. The flick of his tongue on my nipple sent my hips writhing beneath his fingers as he began drawing achingly slow circles around that bundle of nerves. My core throbbed with need for him to fill me. *"Please,"* I begged, tugging on the tether between us while pulling his hips toward mine.

"I need to taste you first." I saw his fangs lengthen slightly, and it only made me crave him more. He kissed, licked, and nipped his way down the inside of my thigh until he reached my core which was literally dripping with need. He growled his desire and began tenderly lapping up all my wetness. His expert tongue flicked back and forth on my clit as he slid a finger inside me, causing my core to clench around him before his lips wrapped around that bundle of nerves and *sucked.*

. . .

As I cried out, my back arched off the bed, my body set alight with tingling, aching euphoria. I moaned in a needy, breathy voice that only he had ever drawn out of me, as I surrendered to his tender ministrations. I found that even the delicate caress of his hands and fingertips lovingly caressing my inner thighs and even outer labia, which I'd never considered to be particularly sensitive or erogenous, as he gingerly sucked and lapped so sweetly and passionately at my clit dramatically intensified the rising build of divine release.

I could feel every ounce of love he felt for me pouring into me from the tether between us. The combination of these heavenly sensations had me moaning and writhing my release in seconds. *"Kyril...,"* I cried softly as my hips undulated beneath his mouth and hands. As the intensity grew overwhelming, my hips bucked off the bed, but he held firm, his ministrations turning soft and slow to draw every last wave of my climax out of me.

As my climax fully receded, he sat back on his heels between my thighs. His voice was filled with love and awe. "The way you taste is more delicious than anything I've ever put to my lips, Aurelia. I'll never be able to go without you again," he husked as he licked my juices from his lips and fingers. His powerful hands grabbed me firmly by the hips, lifting them off the bed to slowly slid himself inside me. My back arched, and I swore in a breathy moan. He licked his lips, still savouring the taste of my release as his gaze met mine whilst thrusting slowly and deeply, letting me adjust to his formidable size.

Not only did he fill me physically, making my pussy clench with that perfect pain, but he filled me emotionally and spiritually- every part of me that had ever felt not enough, or too much, alone, empty, or in pain... He filled. I felt his love enveloping me: mind, body, and soul. On an intuitive urge, I visualised my end of the tether opening fully and pushed every atom of love in my heart towards him. His breath left him in a whoosh, and he groaned, eyes glistening, as he drew me upright into his arms, lifting me off the bed and into his lap, all while keeping himself rooted inside me.

"My fire," he breathed. His hand cradled my head as he licked my lips, the other grasping my breast and caressing my nipple. *"My soul,"* I whispered on a soft moan, holding his gaze as I flicked my hips back and forth on top of his perfect cock, tightening my core's grasp on him, making him growl. I sucked his lip into my mouth before sliding my tongue against his as his hips thrusted to meet mine. After only a few moments of this, I could feel my climax nearing again, which I knew he would be able to feel as well.

He held my gaze as he licked his thumb and reached between us to begin rubbing my clit. That's all it took for my orgasm to burst from me and my core to start fluttering and spasming around that deliciously hard, thick length. As soon as I came down from my climax, I unwrapped my legs around his waist and crawled off of him. "It's my turn to taste you." He seemed to hold his breath as I hungrily took in the sight of him and led him off the bed. He quirked an eyebrow at me.

Kyril let out a low growl of pleasure as I knelt beneath him and stared up into his eyes as I began to work him with both my hands. I sucked on my cheeks to pull as much saliva as I could and spat it onto his huge, gorgeous cock, working it over his head and shaft. Another growl left him, and his voice became tense. "... You're gonna make me cum before you even put me in your mouth." At that, I took in the length of him- as much as I could- into my mouth, my throat, using my hands in synchronicity to work what I couldn't yet fit. And I made a silent vow to one day be able to.

Kyril pulled my hair back from my face, fisting it in one hand. After only a few heartbeats, Kyril stilled, and through the tether, I could feel that he was close to orgasming. And that he didn't want to yet. *"My fire,"* he husked. I worked him languidly, taking my time with him. To help bring him back from the precipice of climax, I pulled him from my mouth to lay full, wet kisses on the head of his cock and every ridge and vein of his shaft, working my way down to his balls that he kept free from hair for me. I gripped him, wrapping one hand around him from the top of his perineum to the base of his cock, licking and sucking on his perfect balls, humming and softly sighing my pleasure.

Kyril's corded muscles tightened and rippled. As soon I drew my other hand down from the head of his cock to its base in one gentle pump, he growled and pulled me to my feet to firmly take my mouth with his own. His arms tightened around me, sliding down my back and bum until his hands guided me down onto the bed with painful gentleness. Before he could settle on top of me, I rolled onto my front, parted my thighs, and arched my back. A growl reverberated in the room, and I turned my head to see Kyril staring hungrily as though he were a starved, feral beast. I gave my hips a little wiggle in invitation, my pussy already *weeping* at his cock's absence.

His hands slid across my bum and hips before giving it a smack that made me hum my pleasure. "My fucking painfully perfect, seductive, insatiable little mate," he purred. He leaned over the bed, bringing his mouth to my core. *"Gods... How is your pussy so sweet..."* he moaned against me before continuing to lick and suck my sanity away. *"Kyril,"*

I whimpered, "I need you inside me." Kyril shifted behind me and aligned his cock to begin massaging my pussy, from clit to entrance, with my juices and his. My pussy clenched as I felt the broad head of his cock slowly stretch me again.

He gradually pushed further in, and I felt the firm, smooth ridge of his cockhead press against my g-spot. I sighed his name on another breathy, needy cry as my hand shot out, reaching behind me to clutch his thigh, holding him still. My pussy fluttered with tingling pleasure as I began to slowly rock back and forth just on the head of him.

Kyril's grip on my hips tightened just as my eyes rolled into the back of my head, back arching. *"Fuuuuuuccckk, Kyril...,"* I cried as he growled behind me, his body tensing. I let go of his thigh to grip the sheets, and Kyril slid the rest of himself inside me until he was seated to the hilt. I gasped at the perfect pain and ground my hips against him. I could feel his muscles shaking with restraint. "My fire... I can't wait any longer," he gritted out. And then began to pump into me with gradually increasing force and speed.

I felt through our tether that the sound of our sweaty bodies, the wet sound of where we were joined, my round ass clapping against his hips, my moans and cries of ecstasy were all an erotic symphony that was driving him closer to a climax he was desperately trying to hold back so that I could cum again.

I loved the sound of *us,* his panting breaths, his growls and groans, his voice and the way he would say my name. He gripped the curve of my backside and took a fistful of my hair in the other. The action sent my toes curling, and my orgasm flooded my veins just as I felt his cock grow impossibly larger inside of me, his thrusts now wild and brutal until I felt his seed pumping into me. He groaned in ecstasy, his strokes slowing, becoming a gentle glide as both of our climaxes gradually subsided.

When his body gave a final shudder, he gently turned me around and laid me back down to crawl on top of me being careful not to bear his full weight on me as he kissed me tenderly along my lips, cheek, and neck; whispering in my ear, "You alone are the heart and soul of me. I am yours, Aurelia. I have *always* been yours and yours alone. *I love you.*"

And although I still couldn't help but wonder about who *she* had been, I pushed away the lingering too-good-to-be-true concern that rose at his breathtaking words. Because I felt the same.

14

I woke to the sensation of strong arms pulling me closer into a muscled chest and warm, full lips trailing kisses along my shoulders. My heart instantly blossomed, overwhelmed with love, joy, and gratitude. I wriggled to turn around and face him, drawing a hand to his heartbreakingly gorgeous face and pressing a kiss to his cupid's bow lips. "I have a gift for you, my love," he whispered against my mouth. My mouth quirked with a grin. I could feel his enormous erection pressed against my thigh and hip. I giggled, pressing myself further against it. "You certainly do," I hummed with pleasure.

Kyril growled and gave a throaty chuckle, gently fisting my hair and murmuring in my ear, "How can something you already own be a gift?" I nearly purred in response. He clutched the back of my head and pulled my neck to his mouth, kissing and laving at my pulse point for a moment before he pulled away and walked to my side of the bed. My pussy was already blossoming with wetness in need.

. . .

"I was going to wait for a special occasion to give this to you but considering everything that's going on, I wanted to give it to you now..." He reached for the end table beside me to pull open a drawer and reveal a large velvet bundle wrapped with a chiffon silk bow. He knelt at my feet as he handed it to me. "It was my mother's."

My lips parted as I stared at the velvet bundle in my hands. Powerful magic radiated from it in waves making my whole body tingle, my own magic rising to meet it. I pulled at the silk ribbon and unfolded the velvet cloth. My breath caught at what lay within. A curved crescent blade black as night with a golden hilt adorned with a line of polished black and white moonstones. "Many a foe has met their end at The Blade of Charon. She named the blade after a God she'd once heard about from a distant realm who was once the ferryman for the souls of the newly deceased."

I stared down at it in complete and utter awe. My heart fluttered at the sight, and my magic swelled inside me as if it recognised the blade. "Kyril...," I breathed, "I... Oh, my Gods... It's unlike anything I've ever seen before. Are you sure? Why don't you use it?" Kyril shook his head. "It's not for me. My mother gave it to me before she passed away. She said it was for my nexus or my wife. Whichever I found, knowing how rare it is for someone to find their nexus." I couldn't help the question spilling from my lips.

"... Did you give it to her too?" Kyril's eyebrows grew tense with emotion as he smiled softly at me. "I have only ever given it to you, my fire. I swear it." A selfish, ridiculous swell of relief filled me. He leaned into me and pressed a kiss to my forehead, whispering, "And I will spend the rest of my life thanking the Gods that I have found both in you." I snapped my gaze to his, tears already filling my eyes. I pulled his mouth to mine. "I can't even begin to express my gratitude, my soul."

Kyril took one of my hands and laid my upturned palm flat on my lap. "Now, allow me to bind it to you. After I do, you'll be able to call upon it no matter where you are, and it will appear in your hand." My jaw dropped. I'd never heard of such a thing, but I suppose I shouldn't have been so surprised considering everything I'd discovered and witnessed as of late. Witnessed and wielded magic I'd only ever dreamed of and heard about growing up in a virtually magic-less quarry, thanks to the palladium collars, and had become little more to me than the stuff of fantasy. Not reality.

"Additionally," Kyril continued, "If you enter a place warded from magic or are bound by magical suppressants while carrying Charon, it will nullify their effects. Only you will be able to wield Charon. And only I know how to transfer its owner. I can teach you if you like." I shook my head in awe. "I'm so honored. I can't even begin to...," I breathed, rendered speechless. Kyril grinned, delighted by my appreciation.

He lifted the blade and murmured a few words I didn't understand in a language I'd never heard before but recognized was definitely not Ancient Fae. He laid his upturned hand flat beside mine and drew the blade across both of our palms in one sweep as he continued to speak in the unfamiliar language. The stones on the dagger began to glow, and Kyril pointed the blade down. He grasped the hilt in one hand and clasped his bleeding hand with mine, raising them above the dagger's hilt just as a small moonstone slid to the side to reveal a hole. Kyril squeezed our bleeding hands as our blood dripped into the receptacle in the handle, speaking in the ancient-sounding language the whole time.

. . .

I felt a strong pull in my chest, and electricity shot down my arm into my bleeding hand. I tried to jerk my hand away to prevent it from hurting Kyril, but he held my hand tight in an unbreakable grip. He shook his head at me and continued chanting the strange words. My eyes widened as I saw a golden energy curling around our blood as it trickled into the receptacle of the hilt. The stones grew so incredibly bright that I had to look away from them. The trickling of our blood slowed, and the hole in the blade's grip clicked shut. The stones dimmed, and Kyril grew silent. My heart was pounding in my chest.

"What language was that?" I breathed.

"Something called Ancient Greek. It was spoken aeons ago in Terrenea."

"How did you learn it?"

"I didn't. I simply memorized the incantation that the male who gave my mother the blade provided."

"How extraordinary... Who gave it to her?"

Kyril shook his head, "He never gave us his name. She found an injured male hiding in an abandoned cave and nursed him back to health. It was only overnight, despite how severe his wounds were. I remember his blood was golden. We thought he would die, and brought him home with us so he could die in peace and not be devoured by one of the beasts of the Sapphires.

"I was only a small boy at the time. He told us stories of Gods that exist in another dimension but who eventually went to visit, or even lived, in Terrenea for some time. That was how my mother came to name the blade. Charon was one of the Gods he told her a story about. As a gift for helping him, he bound the dagger to my mother with this magic. He left before we even woke up and had written the incantation down for us on a piece of parchment. When I was old enough, she made me memorize it in case something ever happened to it."

"Stop closing your eyes!" Kyril laughed. The wild wind whipped through our hair as we stood in the field between Kyril's manor and the cliff after a large lunch, thanks to Kyril's chef, Roah. "I'm trying to visualise where I want to fold!" I shouted back. Kyril smirked with a roll of his eyes. "That's fine as a jumping-off point, but more often than not, closing your eyes to do it could get you killed. You don't need to close your eyes to see in your mind's eye where you want to go." I let out a frustrated groan and stilled myself, trying to focus on my mind's eye. Kyril furrowed his eyebrows and began to chuckle again, watching me. "What?!" I snapped. "I can't focus if you're laughing at me!" It only encouraged his laughter.

"You look like you're struggling to have a bowel movement. And no excuses. Distractions will always be there." I forced myself to stop laughing, taking deep breaths. My patience was wearing thin, and at that moment Kyril's laughter was replaced by empathy. "Look, you don't even have to visualise the place you want to fold into. Just fold into my arms. *Feel* being in my arms already." I scoffed at how easy he made it sound. "I'm going to fold my foot in your ass if you keep distracting me." Focus. More laughter. More soul-warming, core-tingling laughter. *Ugh*. Gods.

Nothing. Not even a wisp of darkness to give me hope that I was even getting close. Kyril grinned with amusement at the frustration in my face. And held his arms wide open for me. *Smug*. He was so *smug*. The image of a fist ramming into his perfectly chiseled stomach filled my mind. So quick and simple, and with no thought, something clicked into place. And Kyril went flying backwards onto his back. He hit the ground with a loud splat in a puddle of mud. He didn't move for two *very* long seconds. "Kyril!" Panic erupted in my chest as I made to run towards him. Just before he coughed and roared with laughter, folding directly in front of me, and threw his arms around me.

"Well done, my fire. Your magic is improving with impressive speed."

I rolled my eyes and swatted at him. "You scared me."

"You knocked the wind out of me."

"Good. That's what you get for being *soooo* smug. Maybe we should be working on self-defense instead of folding." "My soul, sometimes the best form of self-defense *is* folding. Especially now, while you're still honing your skills."

I sighed. He was right. *Again.*

We trained for the rest of the day, alternating from using Thea and The Blade of Charon, among other weapons, hand-to-hand combat, and folding. Until, by the mercy of the Gods, I finally managed to fold directly in front of him. Or onto him, rather. By the end of it, well into the evening, I felt I'd been reduced to a gelatinous puddle. We bathed together but he could tell I had no stamina left for arousal. And thankfully, there hadn't been a whisper of the mute.

"Do you think she doesn't realise where the seal's gone?" I asked as I laid my back on his chest in the bath whilst he scrubbed me down with a luffa. "Who knows... It's possible." The location of each sigillum had become common knowledge over the centuries. The millennia. Perhaps she was looking for it. "The sigilla have a powerful magical signature, though. I imagine, if she doesn't know where it's gone, she will soon..."

. . .

I paused, dread filling me at the thought of the mute. And all that hung in the balance with them. His scrubbing stilled. "Quetz told Nuala that the mute is still in the Southern Guard. She wants to try and take her by surprise. If we can find her. And then we'll have to go to the Eastern Guard. Batlaan is growing impatient with waiting to be reunited with his mate." I twisted around in the tub to look at him.

"Why didn't you tell me all this earlier?"

"Nuala only told me about going to the Southern Guard this morning. I didn't want to ruin your day or training with any... unnecessary anxiety."

"When did you plan on telling me?"

"After you had a chance to relax. In peace."

I gave him a steely stare before turning back around.

"I'd prefer it if you didn't keep me in the dark next time."

"Dually noted," he replied with a kiss on my cheek.

He was right, though. I felt the anxiety beginning to turn my stomach. He massaged my neck, laying tender kisses along the nape of it. "Don't worry. I won't leave your side, not even for a moment." I tried to push the thoughts away. I didn't want to think about it. Any of it. Not right now. Worrying wouldn't do me any good. It would rob me of precious moments that may soon be our last.

"... This morning you mentioned your mother finding the male who gave your mother Charon in the Sapphires... How did she find him? Isn't it dangerous there?" The Sapphire Mountains. The triple-peaked mountains were of legend where few lived, and even fewer returned from. Each mountain hosted a volcano, thusly making it the perfect habitat for cultivating, hence its name, the most prized sapphires in all the nine realms.

· · ·

However, because of the volatile environment, only the most nightmarish and hell-born creatures could survive there. Creatures whose blood simmered with the same heat and flames of that mountain; who bore such an insatiable burning hunger that they were swiftly hunted down should they ever dare to roam beyond the mountain's borders.

He set the luffa aside as I turned around in the bathtub to face him, leaning against the other end. Something painful simmered in his gaze. "As Nuala may have mentioned, my mother was a vampire. I'm actually not sure what my father was. Another hybrid of some kind, perhaps." *Was.* A knot formed in my chest at the word.

"When they met, long before the war, my father was a servant. A stable hand. My mother was a handmaiden. They worked for the same Lord. And after she gave birth to me... she was forced to become his wife's wet nurse." I felt the breath leave my body.

"Vampires, back then, were all indentured servants. But their strength and innate magical abilities were coveted. It was believed that even drinking a vampire mother's breast milk would give your offspring some of that power. When she was forced to feed the Lord's newborn, it left me with very little milk. They managed to escape, but it cost my father his life. My mother fled with me to the Sapphire Mountains. Where other escaped vampires, and numerous other creatures who were either exiled, would be hunted or were too dangerous to live in society had gone, and no others dared to go. That's where I was raised..." The hairs on my arms rose at the idea.

"And it is a place which I pray never to return, but it is the only relatively safe alternative for my kind should anything ever happen.

And despite the current threat... A lot can happen in our lifetimes. If... if we were to ever choose to have children..." No humour or shame traced his earnest, grave expression. "And something was to ever change in the future... Gods forbid."

My heart fluttered at the words, *our children.* I'd never wanted any children. Especially not when I was living in Pauperes Domos. But now... Now that the world had opened up despite what threatened it- and I had met my nexus ... I suddenly found myself wondering. Not that that was something I'd want in the near future, not with The Seven Seals at large... But maybe someday...

I felt his love tug at me. My heart. Through the tether. He held my gaze and drew my hand to his mouth. "Not to mention, I couldn't possibly crave you any more than I already do. I'd surely combust and die by my own flames should I ever be graced with even a drop of your precious blood, my fire." He licked the inside of my wrist, giving it a tender nip, before pressing it to his sensuous lips.

The gesture had me twisting in his arms, and crawling into his lap, in the huge bathtub. He eyed me hungrily, lovingly, and as I straddled his lap, taking his head in my hands, I whispered, "I would rather live in hell with you than in Heaven without you. And whether I hunger for flesh or blood, it makes little difference to me. *You* are what sustains me. You're *mine.*"

The moment the words left my lips, Kyril's lips parted as if in awe. I saw his eyes glisten as his throat worked on a swallow. "Say it again," he whispered breathlessly. I slid my hands through his hair before cradling his jaw as I tilted his head closer to me. *"You're mine,"* I said softly, holding his gaze. His eyes closed, tears purling at his lashes. I leaned in and kissed them away, relishing their salty warmth just before he swiftly lifted me out of the bathtub, legs still wrapped around his waist, with astonishing ease and power.

His fiery gaze met mine, and I caressed my lips against his as he strode into the bedroom, gently laying me on the bed. As soon as he released me, the room's cool air kissing my naked skin sent a shiver over me. The hearth behind us was set alight instantly by some invisible hand, and a whoosh of warm air blanketed me.

"How does it work? If you were to... bite me." I asked as I stared up at him in awe. Kyril lifted my legs to his mouth and began trailing kisses down them, ever nearer to my core. He stilled for a moment, arching an eyebrow at me, the grip on my legs tightening. I reached out to caress his forearms. "Would I become a vampire, too then? A fae-vampire? Or..."

"If I were to simply bite you? No. I would have to... drain you of nearly all your blood until you were on the precipice of death. And then you would have to replenish yourself with mine. You would be given what we call the *fleeting death*. And then you rise again. It is no small feat." He studied me for a moment before resuming his loving ministrations that grew ever nearer to my core.

"And if I offered you my blood... Would you want it?" I whispered, feeling a little sheepish. Kyril's irises heated and flickered, the flames in his eyes undulating like fiery crashing waves as he drew his thumb through the wetness of my entrance and began gently teasing my clit. I moaned softly as my back bowed and my eyes slipped shut. My hips began to slowly writhe against him.

· · ·

Kyril chuckled huskily, "Aurelia... Drinking your blood isn't something I would ever want to do unless you truly desired it. Craved it. And whether or not you eventually do, you are a goddess, and I would die happily so long as it was while worshipping you."

I peaked at him from beneath heavy lids. "Do you though?... Crave it?" I pressed in a voice that sounded unlike my own. Kyril gave a deep growl. "You satiate me regardless, my fire. My fate. But... Yes. Except for my desire to be by your side, I crave it unlike anything else ever before." "Yes," I breathed as he spread my legs, kneeling between them, his stare momentarily lingering at my glistening entrance as he teased my clit and entrance with his thumb. "Don't tease me, Aurelia. I don't have the kind of restraint that good males have."

At that, he firmly gripped my thighs and dragged me forward into his mouth. The first lick pulled a deep moan from my throat. "Tell me again," he murmured in a barely intelligible growl. It took a moment for me to recall what exactly he was referring to, but then I felt it spoken through the tether between us. "You're mine, Kyril... *Mine and mine alone,*" I exhaled softly. His growl reverberated divinely against me as he continued to lave voraciously at my entrance and suck firmly on my aching bead. Within moments, I felt myself nearing the edge of climax, but I needed to feel him inside me.

With a trembling hand, I reached down and gripped him by the hair, pulling his head back. *And Gods, he looked beautiful with me glistening on his mouth.* Without needing to even speak, he knew what I wanted. Needed. "Yes, my queen." He climbed onto the bed, gripping me by the hips and tugged me closer, kneeling with his knees on either side of my hips, and slowly slid himself into me, tenderly filling me inch by inch and giving my core time to adjust to his massive length and girth all while he gazed into my eyes. "And you're *mine.* No other male will ever be blessed with the touch or feel of you ever again. And any who'd dare will meet their final death."

He laid one of my legs to the side and sucked his cheeks in for a brief moment before letting a ball of spit drop with perfect precision directly onto my beautifully aching, tingling, pulsating clit. He drew a thumb to it and began drawing lazy circles around it as he slowly began to thrust deeply inside of me. The act yanked a high-pitched moan from my throat, back arching as I cried his name between a stream of appreciative curses.

Within moments, I could already feel my climax approaching again, and I couldn't hold it back. My eyes began to slip shut as it rose within me like a rapidly swelling tidal wave of euphoria. Kyril used his free hand to tease one of my nipples while the other continued stroking my clit. "Open your eyes for me, my fire. I need to see you as you come undone around my cock." His words were my undoing, and as I obeyed, holding his loving gaze, my core pulsed and gripped him tightly. His name left my lips in a soft, breathy moan.

He groaned, picking up his pace and slamming into me with increasing force, punctuating each declaration with a firm thrust. "*Gods, Aurelia...*" Thrust. "*My fire.*" Thrust. "*My fate.*" Thrust. "*My soul.*" My heart poured all my love and ecstasy into our tether. And in response he gripped my thighs to pull me even harder onto him. "*I love you, Kyril.*" The words came out breathless and desperate as my orgasm reached its zenith.

Kyril lifted my hips off the bed, further deepening the stroke as his thrusts became savage, causing the most delicious type of pain. Within moments, I could feel him tensing further and growing impossibly harder. "*Aurelia...,*" he groaned deeply in a voice that sounded more animal than vampire. "*I need to taste you,*" I rasped between moans. "No," he growled, "I *need* to fill you. *Mark you.* I want every one to smell me on you. In you. So they know who you belong to. As surely as they smell you on me and know exactly to whom I belong."

The words alone sent me hurtling, core first, into my second climax as he pounded mercilessly into me. The electricity of it coiled up my spine and exploded out of every pore as I cried his name. His own climax burst from him, roaring the whole way. He filled me until his *essence* was *seeping* out of me. His thrusts slowed as he lowered himself to me, wrapped me in his arms, and pulled me up against him, positioning us both upright as he sat on his heels. Our lips met in a soft caress of tongues and nipping teeth until I made a trail along his jaw and neck. "Gods, I love you, Kyril. With every ounce of my being." I murmured breathlessly between kisses. "I love you, Aurelia. With every part of my heart. My soul. My body."

I gave a teasing bite to his earlobe before licking away the hurt as my fingers caressed his sides and nipples, eliciting a deep growl from him that I could feel reverberate in my chest. His hands caressed their way back to my hips as I felt him begin to harden again inside me. He kissed my neck and sucked at my pulse point before grazing it with his fangs. Every hair on my body stood on end, and my nipples tightened, aching again with need.

"*Kyril...,*" I moaned breathily as I began to drive my hips harder against his cock. "There was only ever you, my love. My fate," he breathed against me as his lips found their way back to my mouth. "I want you to have it, Kyril. My blood. I want to feed you and sustain you. I want you to carry a part of me inside you." Kyril's grip on me tightened as he stilled for a moment, bringing his hands to cradle my face. He held my gaze for a moment, his chest rising and falling heavily with breaths that grew ragged.

"I want nothing more than to spend the rest of my days proving myself worthy of you and earning the right to stand beside you. To love you. To protect you. And share life with you. I want those things regardless of whether or not, you endow me with the gift, and the honor, of your blood." I pressed a tender kiss to his brow. His lips. Before pulling away. "My blood is yours, Kyril. It was always only ever yours."

He seemed to search my gaze for any hints of reservation, so I reassured him. "There's no part of me that doesn't already belong to you, my soul." The emotion swelling in Kyril's eyes at my words was evident. I swept my hair over my shoulder, tilting my head to the side in invitation, and laid my hands on his chest before sliding my hands up into the soft, dark waves of his black hair, gently tugging him forward.

Kyril's hesitation dissolved as I filled all my desire and longing for this into our tether. His arm firmly wrapped around my waist, bracing me firmly against his body, as he began to thrust in and out of me at a sensual, tender pace whilst bringing his lips to the curve of my neck. He gave gentle kisses, licking and sucking at it until I felt the sharp pressure of his fangs. My body tensed in anticipation. Kyril felt it and froze. "Don't stop," I whispered desperately on an exhale. "It'll only hurt for a heartbeat, my fire," he promised. "I trust you," I whispered. Kyril growled softly as he brought his fangs to my neck again, finally giving their piercing bite.

An animalistic moan poured out of me as I felt a burst of sharp pain, followed a heartbeat later, as promised, by the most exquisite wave of warmth and tingling euphoria that reached all the way down to the core of me, flooding my pussy with a divine sensation that culminated in a full-body climax, unlike anything I'd ever experienced. It felt as if every molecule of my being exploded in a gentle burst that Kyril absorbed with his being, and we truly became one entity, reuniting.

I felt a wave of our love as a soul-bursting pleasure of our union possessing a measure of joy that words could not describe. As our climax eased, the feel of Kyril's grip on me tightened, and something warm and wet dripped onto my ear. *Tears?* Sent me back into my own body. My chest tightened painfully, and I caressed his hair and shoulders as he began to tremble.

I tried to pull away, but he growled, tightening his grip on me. He gulped down another mouth full of blood, growling in between breaths as if overwhelmed by need and emotion. His whole body was trembling. I could feel more tears dripping onto my neck. Just as concern began to rise in me, his body calmed, his grip on me relaxing slightly, and he began to move *inside me* as he drank. *Oh, sweet gods.* The sweetest sensation of ecstasy and full body orgasm filled my body *again*, all without the tension-filled buildup, and instead just filled every molecule of my body, making me go limp. All I could do was surrender to it, a breathy, euphoric moan escaping me.

My eyes slipped shut, and in my mind's eye, my vision was filled with the sight of the golden tether between us, from heart-to-heart, its glow radiating so brightly that it grew to surround the entirety of our bodies, and beyond. A profound surge of emotion poured into me, and I felt an explosion of aching warmth and love in my chest of such soul-shaking depth that my eyes pricked with tears. Seemingly urged by the same force, Kyril's arms tightened around me again as mine too drew tighter around his shoulders, and I cradled his neck whilst he continued to drink from me. Our bodies were pressed so firmly together that there was no space left between us, and thanks to the tingling warmth and euphoria flooding my veins, I couldn't tell where my body ended, and his began.

"Kyril...," I moaned, voice cracking with emotion as he continued to move tenderly inside me and drink from me. He groaned in ecstasy in response. My body felt as though it had been drugged to draw out this unending orgasm that only began to recede when Kyril gently pulled away from my neck. Holding my head in his powerful hands. He stared down at me as we still embraced each other tightly. My blood tinted his fangs and his lips. I could see his eyes glistening. "Aurelia...," he breathed shakily, "I..." His throat worked on a swallow, and I drew my hand to his face. "Tell me," I whispered. He hesitated for a moment before shaking his head and burying his face in my neck and breathing me in. *"My one true nexus. My soul."*

He tenderly licked and kissed the tears spilling onto my cheeks before he drew his wrist to his mouth and pulled it away, blood trickling. "My fire, drink," he whispered. He pressed his wrist to my lips, and I drank. His blood was subtly sweet and velvety, oaky. I felt my senses sharpen, my nerve endings tingled, and the swell of emotion rose in my chest again, encouraging more tears to spill down my cheeks.

Kyril's growl turned into a groan as he shuddered, and his thrusts grew to be harder until they were almost frantic, and I felt his cock pulsing and filling me once more. He withdrew his wrist and laid me down on the bed beneath him, licking and kissing at the healing bite on my neck. I laid tender kisses upon his neck and jaw until our lips met again, and he rested his forehead against mine. I felt him tremble above me, and I opened my eyes to meet his gaze. "Aurelia... Marry me..." I searched his gaze for several moments as tears threatened to spill from mine once more. "Say something, Aurelia. Please..." Kyril implored. I bit my cheek to contain my emotion and nodded. *"Eternally, I am yours, my fire,"* I said into his mind, knowing I would shatter if I tried to speak them aloud.

15

"I don't think we should tell anyone about our engagement yet," I mentioned casually as we walked through the warm, humid air of the Southern Guard that enveloped us like a sticky, wet glove. Kyril and I stalked through the winding alleyways of the coastal village where we were meeting Nuala and Quetz. I could hear the ships' bells being rung in the nearby port. Though the smell of the sea was masked entirely by the stench in our immediate vicinity. The streets smelled of fragrant foods, spices, meats, ale, spirits... and... urine.

Along with the saccharine putrescence of garbage that had been cooking in the sun for gods knew how long. I covered my nose with my cloak. Kyril gripped my hand, keeping me close to him under the gazing camouflage that he'd put around us. His face was tightened in a grimace as we wove through the predominantly drunk crowd.

He flashed me a tense look, "May I ask why, my gorgeous bride?" I let out a deep breath. "I just think the news of it would be a little undermined by everything going on now. Perhaps we should wait until we at least return to the Northern Guard?" Kyril stopped in his tracks and turned me to fully face him. "If anyone asks who you are to me, I will not lie. And nor will you." I nodded my agreement. "No, of course not. I just want our engagement to be unhindered by... ya know... the potential demise of our entire dimension if these entities get their hands on all the seals." His lips quirked, and he pulled my hands to his mouth, kissing them tenderly. "All the more reason not to wait." He winked at me and nipped at my hand with his perfect teeth. My core clenched with desire. "The decision is yours, my fire. I follow where you lead." My heart swelled to bursting. Before I could respond, he pulled me close, kissing my forehead, my lips, and whisked me down the street.

Immortals and mortals of all sizes and shapes were around us. I'd never witnessed such a thing. I'd never even seen a mortal before. There had been none in Pauperes Domos nor at the palace. Some were ruddy looking and ill-kempt in appearance, no doubt due to their painfully slow healing abilities and fleeting life spans. Their skin revealed too much about the years and tribulations they'd experienced. But others were beautiful. Stunningly so. But, regardless of their appearance, there was something so... fragile about them. It made my heart ache just looking at them. I was so lost in thought at taking in all of these new and foreign sights, sounds, and smells that it took me by surprise when Kyril pushed me towards a stone wall—and directly through it.

On the other side, I was surrounded by suffocating darkness. Kyril laid a hand on the small of my back as he stepped through behind me. The energy of the stairwell was oppressive, as was the smell. Dank and mildewy. "What is this place?" I asked in a hoarse whisper. Kyril took a breath as if even he could feel how thin the air was, like that of a cave. "You'll see." A light began to glow... radiating from

Kyril's open palm, drifting out of it to float in front of us. Kyril's eyes darted to mine- wide and glowing above the now bobbing amber orb of fluttering light. Almost like a flame. He offered me a warm smile. "You can do this too, you know."

I smirked. "Add it to the list."

Kyril laced his fingers with mine and silently led me down the stairs. We descended for what seemed like a small eternity. A tangible pressure in the air pushed and crackled against my skin until I felt like I could barely breathe.

"What is that?" I gasped.

Kyril gave my hand a comforting squeeze and a kiss. "A ward. Not much further, my fire. Don't worry."

A few long and suffocating moments later, the pressure began to ease, and we reached the bottom of the staircase to arrive at a dank look-ing, and smelling, landing that led directly into another stone wall. A glowing seam formed in the brick wall shaped like a tall archway. Kyril pressed a hand to it. I inhaled sharply as I watched his hand disappear through it. Kyril removed his hand from the glowing archway and glanced at me, standing wide-eyed beside him. He let out a soft chuckle, studying me for a few moments. "Gods, you're so beautiful it causes me pain." I grinned up at him. "I know the feeling all too well, husband."

Kyril growled his approval- the kind that makes you tingle in all the ultra-sensitive, unseen places. He pulled me towards him, gently laying his hand to my cheek, and pressed his lips to mine. Tenderly at first. "Say it again," he demanded huskily. And all thoughts of the dank stairwell immediately dissolved. "My husband, whose perfec-tion is far beyond what even my imagination would have dared to dream. I can't wait to worship at the alters of your mind, your heart, your soul, and...," I let my hand trail down to the engorged length pressing through his trousers, "... Your cock." Kyril swiftly gripped the backs of my thighs and picked me up. I squealed with delight, throwing my arms around his neck and my legs around his waist.

Sweet Gods, I must have been a fucking saint in a past life for the fates to gift me with you. I love you more than I'll ever be able to even express, Aurelia...," His last words were a seductive growl as he brought his mouth to my neck, grazing me with his euphoria-and-climax-inducing fangs, "But I'm certainly going to fucking try."

Electricity was already flooding my core in waves with his exceedingly impressive dick pressing directly on my core despite the hindrance of our trousers. A soft moan escaped me, inciting another low growl from Kyril. His tongue licked my bottom lip. A silent demand to open for him. A demand I couldn't help but acquiesce to with fervency.

The sound of someone clearing their throat made its way to my ears.

"Fuck off," Kyril snapped at the intruder, only momentarily pulling his lips from mine without even bothering to see who it was. Though we already knew. I peeked open an eyelid and pulled away from him. Nuala now stood on the other side of the glowing brick wall. She was dressed in nothing but her short silk robe, hair slightly mussed. "Hello, *your majesty*," I teased, "Glad to see you're... thoroughly fucked."

Nuala and Kyril both burst into laughter, setting me down on my feet but still keeping his arms wrapped around me. She rolled her eyes and gave me a lopsided grin. "Likewise," she winked, "Although you do realise we have far more suitable accommodation than this musty-ass stairwell...." Nuala disappeared through the brick wall, and I stepped back from Kyril, pulling him along with me.

We stepped through it directly into a jungle. It was dusk. Eerily glowing, nocturnal eyes were watching us. The sounds of wild creatures, seemingly prey and predator alike, that I didn't have the names for filled my ears. Trees that rose above the clouds surrounded us, and what I could only describe as a tree mansion towered overhead. I gasped loudly and looked around in awe. "What... *How*...?" I looked around in awe, completely slack-jawed. A crooked smile graced Kyril's face as he watched me. "It's called a pocket realm. Nuala uses it as a hideout. I haven't been here in ages." I began to make my way toward the *tree mansion,* but Kyril gave my hand a tug and nodded in the direction behind us.

"Sweet Gods..." An ocean with calm crystalline shores beckoned us. While the sea behind Kyril's house offered astounding beauty, there was something dangerous and wild about it. This, however... was something else entirely. A paradise. As he led me towards the water, I glanced back at the tree mansion.

"Aren't they waiting for us?"

"Yes. But not up there."

I looked around a little confused.

"Under there."

Kyril nodded toward the water.

"Who lives in the tree mansion?"

Kyril's expression became thoughtful.

"Hmmm... Less of a who, more of a 'what'."

I quirked an eyebrow. "But it looks so beautiful up there...," I protested.

Kyril shook his head. "It's meant to be. It's a safeguard. If someone unwelcome were to ever find their way here, that's the first place they would go. And it would also be the last. We'd be fine, but I'd rather go with Nuala. She's the only one I imagine she's loyal to." Kyril stepped into the water, pulling me along beside him. The water was the temperature of bathwater. "This place is a dream," I sighed, still looking around in awe. After a few minutes, the water reached our hips.

"Where's Nuala anyway? We entered just behind her."

"As the creator of this pocket realm, she's the only one who can fold into it."

As the water reached our waist, Kyril began to swim and turned to me. "Whatever you do, don't let go of my hand. And keep your eyes open." Before I could say anything more, he disappeared beneath the water, and I gulped down a lungful of air just as he pulled me beneath it.

I opened my eyes to find Kyril beaming a smile at me, his hair floating in waves around his head. "You don't have to hold your breath." The words sounding muffled in the water. I hesitated as every ounce of instinct told me everything about that suggestion was wrong. Kyril demonstrated taking in a lungful of water as though it were air. I dared a tiny sip of air that grew to a full breath. I couldn't help but burst into laughter. Kyril laughed with me before beginning a diving descent towards to ocean floor. In the distance, what I could only describe as a series of interconnected glass bubbles the size of small cottages decorated the sand. "Holy shit." Kyril grinned back at me. "Pretty amazing, I know...," he said with a wink and continued swimming.

We continued to swim forward, I looked around and could make out the faint shapes of fish and other sea creatures peppered in the distance around us. "How real is all of this? The creatures, I mean...

Are they real?" Kyril hummed as though he were trying to determine the answer. "To be honest, I'm not entirely sure. I suppose I would have to ask to what extent. I suppose the answer is both yes and no. It's hard to explain. Will they interact with you, or even fight to survive, or... have a life experience?... Yes. I think so. The ones I've met certainly seem to. However, if you were to try to bring them outside this realm and into ours... I have no idea."

My eyebrows furrowed as I tried to imagine all of the implications of that. "So... Can they have a real effect on us? Here I mean. If one of those fish were to bite me, for instance, would I carry the mark of it into our realm? "

Kyril glanced back at me as we swam at a languid pace and finally arrived at the sea floor. A welcome mat of seaweed laid before a front door to one of the glass bubbles.

"Definitely."

"And what about the one in the tree mansion?"

Kyril huffed a laugh. "She is definitely real. And not a part of this pocket realm."

"And she would hurt us?"

Kyril shrugged nonchalantly. "As Lord of the Northern Guard and close friend and confidant to the queen, I would hope not. But one can never be too sure when it comes to the *edax animae.*" *Soul eaters.* "Their appetites are known to be particularly voracious. You'll meet her now."

I nearly choked on my own saliva. "What?!" I sputtered.

Kyril gave me a flash of white teeth before placing a quick kiss upon my lips and hammered the door knocker, mounted to the right of the door, shaped like a beautiful, naked woman. "*Kyril,*" the door knocker husked. I let out a yelp of surprise. "Severine," Kyril grinned winsomely. She arched an eyebrow at me and gave me a scrutinizing once over before her grin broadened. "I'm trying not to be offended you and your nexus didn't pay me a visit on your way in."

"Well, I'm not entirely sure how well Nuala actually feeds you so...."

Severine looked affronted. "Ya know... I thought you, of all people, would be a little less judgemental," she sniffed.

Kyril's eyebrows leapt up, genuine surprise on his face. "Have you forgotten the last time I was here and we released you from this pocket realm? For an hour."

Severine narrowed her eyes and pursed her lips, speechless for several moments. "... That was a *very* long time ago-." Nuala flung open the door cutting her off. "Are these two harassing you, my love?" Nuala teased with a wink. "Kyril is being most unreasonable," Severine said haughtily. "I'll deal with him, darling," Nuala soothed, "Don't worry... We'll see you in the morning, ok?" Nuala pinched one of the nipples of the door knocker. And Severine beamed, humming her delight.

Nuala clicked the door shut behind us, and yet again, I found myself gaping at the magnificence around us. Sea life swam above the glass dome ceiling, while the dome's interior boasted bone-white marble floors, intricately carved and magnanimously cushioned wooden furniture and floor pillows in the lounge area where Quetz reclined, in his corporeal form, sipping some amber-colored liquid from a carved glass. He offered us a dazzling smile, those turquoise eyes twinkling, and gave me a wink. "You have joyous news," he crooned.

Kyril and I exchanged glances. Kyril gave me a triumphant grin. So much for waiting until we succeeded in preventing the apocalypse. "Indeed we do," Kyril confirmed, smugly. Nuala squealed her excitement. "Shall we have a celebratory drink after you two get settled?" She asked as she joined Quetz on the couch, crawling over his lap to sit beside him on what appeared to be a gigantic chaise longue. Quetz wrapped an arm around her and tucked her into his side. I found myself unsure of who I was more surprised by: Nuala behaving in such a tender and domestic fashion or Quetz.

He kissed her temple and gave her a squeeze. "I imagine it'll be the last opportunity we have to do so for... what I'm hoping will be an insignificant amount of time," she sighed before returning a kiss to Quetz's mouth. Kyril looked down at me in question. I shrugged, "A celebratory drink or two sounds lovely if you're up for it?"

Kyril led me down a glass hallway into another glass dome bedroom boasting a massive four poster bed with white chiffon curtains and a mountain of pillows. A glass partition separated the bathroom and shower behind it. I shook my head, sighing in admiration. Kyril went to turn the shower on as I opened the wardrobe that was already filled with clothing for the both of us, ranging from silk pyjamas to fighting silks and leathers. I thumbed a silk nightie in blue so dark it was almost black.

Strong arms wrapped around me from behind as I felt Kyril's breath on my cheek. "Care to join me in the shower?" Heat and need spiked through my body, followed by that divine tingle between my thighs. I wiggled my bum onto the growing length and girth hidden beneath his clothing, gently grinding my hips. His grip on me tightened, and he let out a soft hum of approval. I turned in his arms and pressed my body against his. "Always," I murmured on his lips.

After our *long* shower, Kyril and I joined Quetz and Nuala in the lounge room for our 'celebratory' drinks, which ended up becoming more of a brainstorming session for a plan of action between Nuala and Kyril while Quetz helped me strengthen my *palisading* abilities lest we come across anyone who would wish to snoop around my mind. Thankfully, the *palisading* proved to be an easier task for my mind to grasp than folding had. Not that I had much to hide so far, thankfully. Quetz also made the delightful suggestion of willing *explicit* memories, as a diversion, to the forefront of my mind should someone try to dismantle the palisades I'd built.

Platters of food, folded from the palace, suddenly began to spread out on the low carved wood coffee table between us as we sat amongst the colorful peppering of floor cushions. Nuala hummed her delight as she opened her palm, and another platter appeared. This one filled with peaches. And based on her excitement, she was either obsessed with peaches, or these were some super special peaches.

"I present to you 'The Peaches of T'ien Shan'," she breathed, eyes wide, "T'ien Shan, also known as 'The Celestial Mountains', are remotely located on Terrenea and were grown by the Celestial Queen Mother. Her peaches provide immortality to her loyal subjects. However, to us, because we are already immortal: youth, instantaneous healing, and rejuvenation...They're also said to be a powerful aphrodisiac," she winked as she extended the platter towards each of us, and her grin became feline, "Lucky for us, The Celestial Queen Mother, Xiwangmu, is a *very* good friend of mine and she always brings me some of her famous peaches whenever she comes to visit Aeternia. I'm thinking of bringing a few peach pits with us to help persuade potential allies across the realms."

"Oh, sweet fuck," I moaned loudly as I took my first bite, blown away by the explosive tangy flavor. My cheeks flushed as the words burst from my lips and everyone's eyes landed on me. Kyril arched an eyebrow as a sultry grin danced across his face, eyes instantly alight with lust. He pulled me into his lap and dipped his head to speak into my ear. "It'll be anything but if you keep talking like that." The feel of his hardness already pressing against the leg of his trousers sent a giddy squeal escaping me. It felt as if all the energy and magic in my body began to tickle and dance beneath my skin in effervescent waves. And I felt... joyous and peaceful. Excited. All at once. I could feel heat traveling to my cheeks, my chest, my... lady flower.

Kyril tilted my head toward him to study my face and let out a laugh. "Oh shit... Your pupils are super dilated." The sight of him literally stole my breath. My heart clenched to the point of the sweetest pain at the very sight of him. And then he laughed, and *oh my gods,* I felt that deep, husky, velvety, soul-warming laughter from the top of my head to the tips of my toes- and everywhere in between- like my clit.

My lips parted as he held my gaze, studying me with amusement for a moment longer before taking a bite into the magically divine peach. The world seemed to narrow, and my gaze instantly fell to the droplets of peach juice that escaped his full lips. He hummed in appreciation. He raised a hand to wipe at the juice, but I stopped him. "Don't you dare," I breathed, drawing my mouth to his. I licked the peach juice from his chin and mouth. Kyril growled his approval and captured my mouth with his in a wet, sensual kiss that was all tongue and lips, sucking and licking. I pulled back to feed him another bite of peach, which he gladly took before feeding me another bite.

And then I *felt* the tinkling of Nuala's laughter like a delicious tingling wave of sensation throughout my body. "I should probably mention that things may get a little... intense," she giggled excitedly. My gaze snapped in her direction just as she licked juices off of her pink, curved lips and a slow, knowing grin blossomed on her face. I couldn't help but beam right back at her, looking at her with an entirely new set of eyes. "Oh my gods... Nuala. You are breathtakingly beautiful." I felt a longing urge to reach out and touch her. Her aura was glowing a radiant gold with shimmering waves of reds and pinks. Nuala's face lit up, and her aura doubled in size. "I think these peaches may be a bit stronger than I remembered...," she said, gazing at me with an awe-like expression, licking her lips as she leaned towards me.

I felt like I was being drawn to her with a gravitational pull. Her slender fingers captured my cheek and kissed my nose, giggling. I hummed with delight, our eyes meeting, almost shyly, before we both leaned in, and she caressed my lips with hers. I sucked on her bottom lip, and her eyes flared wide with desire as she gave me a devilish grin. Her hand drifted from my cheek to my breast, and through my shirt, she seemed to intuitively know exactly where my nipple was and *pinched*. And I swear I felt it, like a jolt of delicious electricity, all the way down to my clit. The gesture had me crawling out of Kyril's lap and on top of her as I gave a gasp of surprise and a high-pitched moan escaped my lips. As soon as my body parted from his, a feeling of deep longing overtook me that had my arm reaching back for him and pulling him towards me.

I felt his hands roam over the curve of my ass as Nuala laid herself beneath me, beaming up at me from beneath heavy-lidded eyes. She reached an arm up to Quetz, watching us with a highly amused, equally desirous look on his face. I also noticed he hadn't taken a bite of his peach yet. I quirked an eyebrow at him, and he brought it to his lips and took a large bite, humming his pleasure before he gave her another bite.

Kyril slowly swiped his fingers across the fabric, covering my wet, aching entrance making my toes instantly curl and my eyes nearly rolled in the back of my head. A needy moan escaped me, louder than I'd ever intended. I gave a yelp as Kyril scooped me up in his arms like the bride I was soon-to-be. Quetz and Nuala watched us knowingly, beaming, as we disappeared around the corner of the hallway. Quetz was already pulling his shirt off. "Did you want to stay with them longer, my fire?" Kyril offered huskily. I chuckled.

"Perhaps another time... I need *you* now." As soon as we reached the bedroom, he deposited me on the bed and began peeling off my trousers. He shook his head at them as though they personally offended him. He had only pulled them off halfway before everything I had been wearing disappeared completely. A small gasp left me, and I looked up from my now naked body to see that his clothes had also disappeared. That massive length of him stood proudly- every vein, ridge, and especially the wetness beading at the tip of the thick, smooth, mouthwatering expanse of his cockhead seemed to beckon me. "I think we need to make a new rule," he husked. Just looking at him had my toes curling, my back arching, and my hands groping their way up my torso until they reached my breasts and began caressing my nipples as if they had their own will to wield. "Tell me, my soul. And I'll happily obey," I sighed, crawling to my knees so I could take him in my mouth.

Kyril tried to push me back down on the bed. His words were almost in disbelief. "I don't think you understand how desperately I need to taste you, my fire." I huffed a laugh, resisting, and tried to push him back down on the bed. "I absolutely do," I purred. Kyril gave me a devilish grin, laid back on the bed, grabbed my hips firmly, and, as though I weighed nothing, angled my core over his face. I nearly wept with ecstasy and relief as his mouth met my clit, my entrance. He groaned against me and pulled me harder against him. I was reduced to whimpering in response.

16

Dressed in our fighting silks and hooded cloaks suitable for the chilly night air, Kyril, Nuala, Quetz, and I spent the entirety of the morning, and afternoon, walking through the capital city of the Southern Guard, Raxanir, going from neighborhood to neighborhood scouring every pub for the female. I'd been checking in with Quetz every so often to see if he could check if the mute had left, and to our luck, she hadn't. My feet were screaming in protest, and my bladder was set to burst, so I finally reduced myself to dampening the progress of our search. "You guys... I need to pee. And my feet are aching from traipsing on those cobblestones all day. Can we maybe take a short break? Quetz said she's still at the same place so..." Kyril tucked me under his arm and kissed the top of my head. "Anyone fancy a pint?"

"You don't have to threaten me with a good time," Nuala sighed, looking around before leading us into a booth by one of the bullion glass windows of the latest pub we'd entered. I promptly handed my cloak over to Kyril and headed for the ladies' toilets. Now that the sun was setting, the pub was warm and cozy, thanks to the amber light cast from the large hearth and candlestick chandeliers. Weaving my way through the crowd, I quickly made my way to the toilet ignoring the stares from drunken male patrons. I finished my business, and as I was washing my hands at one of the sinks, I did a double-take at the young woman who came to wash her hands beside me. I glanced at her in the mirror- black hair, dark eyes...

I perhaps stared a little too long, trying to peer at the collar of her blouse to find the top of a pink scar peeking out above the collar. I felt the heat of her stare in the mirror. I flushed awkwardly. "Sorry. You're just very pretty," I smiled. Awkwardly. Her nostrils flared for a moment, and she turned to face me. My throat worked on a swallow, but I managed to steel myself. She examined me from head to toe, peering at me through narrowed, cat-like eyes. She leaned in to smell me more deeply. "I smell him on you." She stared at my chest, right where the tether linking Quetz and me through the creator's promise was. She reached her hand out and grasped the tether. It suddenly flared to life with illumination, from my chest through the washroom and beyond, all the way to Quetz I would imagine. Her eyes narrowed further. "Who are you to be bound to a deity, I wonder...."

She gave it a tug, and I felt like someone had physically pulled me forward by a rope, and I stumbled into her. She shoved me back into the stall wall behind me roughly and wound the tether around her hand and *squeezed*. I suddenly felt like someone was cutting off a part of my circulation. I winced, grinding my teeth. Electricity crackled at my fingertips and began to coil around the tether as if seeking who was strangling my tether. The mute's features tightened. "You wish to stop me?" She lashed out with her hand, releasing the tether, and grabbed me by my throat, lifting me off the ground. I punched out with my fist, calling upon my magic to blast it into her chest. She flew backwards into the wood wall behind her, it splintering beneath her on impact. The shock registered on her features matched my own before she quickly tamped it down, clenching her jaw. "You got a death wish or something, lady?"

"No. Do you?" I asked incredulously, "Why else in the gods' names would you be trying to open the way between dimensions?" She shook her head bitterly. "You have no idea who or what you're dealing with. Even your deity doesn't stand a chance." I rolled my eyes, rubbing at my now sore throat. "Oh ok, I suppose I should just slit my own throat then. Shall I get some lube and spread my ass cheeks while I'm at it? We're as good as fucked anyway, right?" She stared at me, no longer bothering to mask her shock before she burst into laughter. "Ya know... If it comes down to it. I'll ask them to spare you. Not that I have much say. Gotta go get my lube." She winked at me, moving to leave the bathroom just as Kyril, Quetz, and Nuala appeared behind her. Nuala whacked her over the head with a mostly empty beer mug. The mute hit the ground like a sack of potatoes, beer sloshing.

Nuala burped, and it further endeared me to her. "Whoops," she chirped. Quetz grinned appreciatively. "Classy," Kyril chuckled. "You guys got here just in time," I exhaled, feeling slightly stunned. "We need to take her to your pocket realm so she can't fold out," Quetz said, hoisting the mute over his shoulder. "Before she wakes up and kills us all," Nuala emphasised. "I don't think she wants to kill anyone," I offered. "Pretty sure she will once she realises she's been kidnapped," Kyril murmured as we all clasped hands and folded into an open air, circular loft-like space overlooking the sea. I gazed around at our surroundings. The palace-sized tree house.

. . .

I turned to see Severine dressed in a chiffon bathrobe hugging her remarkably *b*uxom curves. My lips slowly parted in awe of her sensual beauty. She seemed to exude something carnal and seductive so powerfully that it gave me a sneaking suspicion that was how she lured her prey.

Severine opened her palm, and two pairs of golden manacles fell into her hand out of thin air. Quetz laid the mute on a large chaise longue as Severine glided over and quickly secured a set of manacles on the mute's wrists and ankles. She beamed down at the mute as though it were a feast for a king. "My, my, my... You have indeed outdone yourself, your Majesty," Severine crooned joyously. A pale purple tongue peeked out to lick her pillowy lips in anticipation. Severine's skin was a blue so deep it was nearly black- like a post-twilight night sky. Her black irises seemed to absorb the light instead of reflecting it. Nuala stepped forward to stand beside her. "I'm afraid we'll need to pry some information from her before you can glutton yourself. I do apologise, my love."

"You have my utmost gratitude, your majesty," Severine grinned affectionately and bowed her head in gratitude. My nipples pebbled at the sound of her voice. Severine's eyes became hooded, and she licked her lips again. Nuala held her gaze. "Darling, if you keep giving me that look, I might willingly make myself your prey."

Severine's eyes began glowing a shade of vibrant blue that reminded me of twilight as her grin widened. The arousal in the room became palpable, and I found myself squeezing my thighs together. As if it were a cue to Severine, her gaze snapped to mine, briefly flitting between Kyril and me. "The nexus pair. Kyril, would you ever consider sharing your mate with Aurelia and me, if only for a night?"

. . .

Kyril smirked his amusement. "You'll have to ask her. Although, jealousy is not beneath me." Severine threw her head back in laughter. "I always knew you'd be the possessive type." She sauntered over to me and stood only fingers length away from my face. As I stared into her eyes, I suddenly felt the sensation of recognizing something without knowing precisely what it was or how. Her broad nose flared as she breathed softly. "I'm sure she could reassure you, My Lord," Severine purred while holding my gaze, "You do smell divine, Aurelia...."

Her brows slowly drew together, and she tilted her head, studying me, curiosity fluttering across her expression as she chuckled softly. My mouth suddenly became dry. All of its moisture seemed to have descended between legs. Kyril cleared his throat. Quetz stepped beside me. "Severine...," Kyril and Quetz said at the same time. Severine stepped back and offered me a bow. "Do let me know if you'd... like to spend a night with me. I promise to behave myself and return you safely to your charming mate."

I searched Severine's eyes for a few more moments trying to place the familiarity. The jangling of metal sounded, snapping me out of my daze. Nuala was already fisting the front of the mute's dress. The mute merely smirked. "I'll remember it was you who treated me like a beast when I get free. And I will be free," the mute promised. She gazed down at the golden manacles shackling her arms and legs, flopping back down on the couch out of Nuala's grip, and looking thoroughly drained. "What are these? What have you done? I can't breathe properly."

"That would be 'The Bonds of the Sakachi," The Mute's eyes went wide as Nuala continued, "That means you're magically powerless and drastically weakened in every capacity. Not so much because of the manacles themselves, but more so the Sakachi demon they're tethered to. It's draining your life force." The mute's gaze fell, resignation weighing its features. "You won't be able to stop them."

"Who's 'them'?" Nuala asked.

The mute looked up, examining all of us. "I've only met one of them, but I have no idea who actually is. And I would genuinely love to tell you, but it's in my best interest not to."

"And you're 'genuinely' wearing my patience thin," Nuala frowned flatly.

The mute closed its eyes as it spoked. "How long until the Sakachi drains my life force completely?" Nuala shrugged nonchalantly. "That all depends. I was planning on healing you every day so that you remain trapped in this vessel. At least until you decide to cooperate. Otherwise, I'll just give you to my darling Severine over here to give you the final death."

The mute slowly opened its eyes to look at Severine, who was staring rather hungrily at it. A wicked grin curled upon Severine's face, and her black eyes began to sparkle, reminding me of the moon's reflection upon the sea. I had to suppress a shudder, and instantly Kyril's hand enveloped my own. The mute weakly shook it's head. "I have a feeling Severine will be feasting on my soul regardless."

Nuala leaned forward and caressed the mutes cheek with a curled finger. "Why would I ever do such a thing to someone who proves themselves useful?" The mute stared into Nuala's eyes. "You'll never trust me." Nuala straightened and heaved a sigh. "Trust is earned. Now enough banter. Why do you want to open the door between realms?" A mirthless smile fluttered across the mute's face. "It's not me that wants it open. I'd prefer it stay closed."

· · ·

Nuala's jaw flexed, waiting for the mute to elaborate. After a few moments of silence... "Severine, my love," Nuala crooned as she turned on her heel. Severine stepped forward as she grinned in a terrifyingly shark-like manner, and I swore I could see all of her teeth. The mute bolted upright to try and squirm away. "Wait!"

Nuala glanced halfway over her shoulder, her eyes meeting mine and winked, "Do not waste my time, mute."

The mute slumped back into the chaise longue again, looking pale and ill. "I need reassurances."

Nuala hesitated for several moments, "Like?"

"If I tell you what I know... You have to reunite me with my mate. And after I help you, you have to let us go."

My guts churned with empathy at the mention of her having been separated from her mate.

"You will lead us to whoever you're working with?"

The mute's throat worked a swallow as genuine fear seeped into her expression. She took a deep, shuddering breath.

"It's not going to end well. But yes. If you reunite me with my mate and swear to let us go afterwards- and leave us in peace- then yes."

Nuala's face remained unreadable, but Quetz stepped closer and wrapped his arm around her. Severine seemed to be growing impatient.

"Do you have a name? So we can call you something other than mute." Kyril asked.

The mute's eyes flitted between Kyril and me for a moment before speaking, a sad smile falling on her face. "Lisbet."

"And who is your mate?"

Lisbet scowled. "Idra... You will not know him, but he was kidnapped."

Kyril raised an eyebrow. "And you want us to rescue him?"

"Yes."

"And from whom are we supposed to rescue her?"

"... Madame Yiruxat."

Nuala Cursed. Kyril and Quetz both frowned. "He is one of her...."

"Slaves. Yes."

Kyril and Nuala exchanged a knowing glance. Severine looked sorely disappointed.

17

"Who is Madame...-." "Yiruxat," Kyril finished for me as we all folded back into Nuala's underwater haven, "She's a blood demon." My eyebrows drew together in confusion. Kyril answered my question without me even having to ask, as he so often does. "The difference between a blood demon and a vampire is that their hunger is rarely sated. Depending on how long ago I've fed, I can be sated after a glass or two. A blood demon easily requires 5 times that... Meaning two to three donors if they don't want to kill anyone. If they feed without regard for their victim's life, they'd have to drain them completely of blood. And unfortunately, they seem to prefer the latter of the two. In any case, Madame Yiruxat sells sex and blood. Usually, together. Not her own, of course, but that of her slaves. She is extremely dangerous, as are the demons who guard her... facility."

I exhaled heavily, plopping down on the sofa. "Holy shit." Kyril joined me and pulled me onto his lap. Nuala was already pouring glasses of wine, massaging the bridge of her nose between her eyes. "Darling, how difficult do you think it'll be for us to dispose of her and her guards?" Quetz began massaging her shoulders as she gulped at her wine. His eyes glowing brightly for a few moments. "She has a dozen or so, at the moment, surrounding the cave's vicinity. And another thirty inside... So, between all of us... Not terribly. Perhaps an hour or so?"

A smile rose on Nuala's face as her features relaxed as she scanned the group of us. "So grateful for you guys...." Kyril and I grinned. "The feeling's mutual," he said, speaking for both of us. Quetz nuzzled the crook of her neck, making her hum with pleasure. "Indeed it is," he purred. The scent of their arousal filled the air. Quetz wrapped his heavily tattooed, corded arms around her waste. "Finish your wine, female," he growled softly. Nuala's eyes popped open, her mouth twitching happily, and quickly followed his orders. The second she set her glass on the counter, Quetz swept her legs up in his arms and carried her off to their bedroom. "Have lovely dreams tonight, Aurelia... Kyril," Quetz called out to us just before their bedroom door slammed shut behind them.

I couldn't help but grin appreciatively at their display. I felt the heat of Kyril's gaze on me. When I looked up at him, his expression was severe. Which was not what I was expecting. "What's the matter?" He took a deep breath, holding my worried stare for a moment... "Fire of my life...," he began almost wearily. I narrowed my eyes suspiciously. He sighed, bracing himself for the argument.

"I implore you to consider staying behind when we go to Madame Yiruxat's caves."

My jaw dropped. "I beg your pardon."

Kyril leaned into me, wrapped his arms around me, and buried his nose in my neck. "Do you have any idea what lengths Madame Yiruxat would go to to keep you as one of her slaves? Or what her guards would do to you if one of them caught you?" Kyril breathed into my neck. His grip on me tightened firmly, and I could feel the muscles of his jaw flexing against my neck.

I tried to pull away from him, but he only clutched me tighter to his chest. I ran my fingers through his hair and kissed his neck, trailing down to the part of his shoulder exposed from his shirt. He shuddered at the caress of my lips. "I can. And I understand your fear. So surely you will understand why I can't bear the idea of you going without me to help. To protect you and watch your back." Kyril's grip on me loosened, and pulled his head back to stare down at me.

"You have no real experience in combat, much less in battling more than forty blood demons and other hell-spawned creatures... Her caves are warded against folding. I wouldn't even be able to escape with you if you were injured."

"Your concern is valid, but please recognise that my control on my magic has improved exponentially. I have bested you on several occasions when we spar- have I not?"

Kyril took a deep breath, jaw feathering. "You know that's entirely different-."

"Kyril." I placed a firm hand on his chest. "I will not be left behind. If something happened to you...," I shook my head in a feeble attempt to rid my mind of the nightmare, "I'm sorry, but it's not an option."

Kyril's body tensed visibly. "Come with me." Kyril pulled me in the direction of the front door and opened it. "Where are we going?" "To get you another bodyguard." Kyril used Severine's knocker. The miniature bronze sculpture of her head came to life, a smirk curling her face. "Change your mind already, gorgeous?" She asked me in a sultry voice. I opened my mouth to respond, but Kyril quickly cut me off. "How do feel about blood demons, Severine?" Severine's smirk blossomed into a grin. "To fight, fuck, or eat?" A corner of Kyril's mouth began to rise. "Either, darling. Whatever your blackened little heart desires." Severine beamed.

18

"**A**re you insane?" Nuala scolded. Kyril gave a casual shrug. "One could argue it only requires the proper motivation for anyone to be driven to acts of insanity." Nuala's nostrils flared, jaw clenching. "If Severine feeds off however many dozen blood demons, and gods know what else Madame Yiruxat is housing down there, she could grow powerful enough to break the magic binding her to me and this pocket realm!" "She's bound to you?" I tried to ask as casually as possible.

Nuala's scowl deepened, contorting her pretty features. "As charming as Severine may be, she is inconceivably dangerous. I have done her, and our realm, a favour. She gets to live in the lap of luxury and feast off an endless buffet of our enemies instead of the countless innocents that would have surely met an untimely demise otherwise. Not to mention, if she wields her magic near any of us while she's luring her prey- I'm not sure we'd even be able to resist! She might fucking consume us all! And despite all that, she's protected here! Instead of hunted. How do you think I got her to agree to bind herself to me? Hmmm? Before I took her in, she was hiding in a cave in the

Sapphire Mountains with nothing but the tattered clothes on her back."

She lived in The Sapphire Mountains? Had Kyril known her? How had she come to live in Nuala's pocket realm? Kyril cut off my line of thoughts. "You know just as well as I do that she means well. Aside from being a little wanton and lascivious with women," he gave Nuala a pointed look before glancing at me with a warning expression before continuing, "we should have nothing to worry about."

Nuala shook her head in exasperation and palmed her face, "Well, we certainly better fucking hope so."

"She agreed to another binding spell for the occasion," Kyril shrugged. Nuala looked up from her palm. "You've clearly underestimated her. Severine will glut herself on the magic and life-force of dozens of blood demons- breaking those magical binds will be about as challenging as untying a fucking shoelace. We'll have to get a blood oath from her."

Quetz stepped out of the hallway and joined us in the kitchen, grinning relaxedly as though we weren't about to go risk our lives infiltrating Madame Yiruxat's caves. He draped an arm on Nuala's shoulders. "Are you ready, my queen?"

Nuala's mouth curled into a wicked smile as she stood on her toes to kiss him, twining her fingers with his as they reached for our hands, and Nuala folded us into Severine's tree palace, where we appeared a moment later. Severine was lounging on the chaise longue beside

Lisbet, who now appeared to be fighting for consciousness. Her face had grown gaunt overnight, and dark circles were under her eyes. Severine was curling a lock of Lisbet's long black hair around her finger and pulled it beneath her nose to smell it, humming appreciatively.

Nuala stepped forward and gave Severine a sharp look, who only grinned in response as she stood. Nuala took her place beside Lisbet, clasping her hand in her own. Lisbet began to murmur in the Ancient High Fae language as her eyes closed. Lisbet's eyes instantly began to glow brighter, her complexion going from sallow to bright and pink in the cheeks. Lisbet took a deep, rejuvenating breath and sat up, meeting Nuala's gaze only to scowl, but her expression softened as though recalling what exactly we were about to do. Lisbet's throat worked on a swallow, eyes glistening.

"Please... Whatever it is you have to do... to save him. I will bind myself to you eternally if it means you save his life. I have many skills and powers that-." Nuala raised a hand to silence her. Her voice took on a solemn tone as she spoke. "That won't be necessary. I vow to do whatever it is I can to save your mate... We all do." I looked Lisbet in her eyes, taking Kyril's hand, and nodded in confirmation. She seemed to study us all for a moment before nodding to herself. "Thank you...," Libset said softly.

Quetz stepped forward, towering over Lisbet. His eyes glowed brightly. "Describe him to us." "His name is Idra. Dark skin, curly hair... A few inches shorter than you. His skin isn't marked by ink or runes. Handsome. Broad mouth and nose, brilliant smile...." After a few moments, Quetz's eyes dimmed. "I see him... He's... Alive. And not heavily guarded, thankfully."

.   .   .

Lisbet sighed deeply in relief, glancing at Nuala reluctantly as she cleared her throat. "May I... May I bathe? It's been some time since I've seen him." Nuala's steely expression wavered briefly with a look of compassion. "Sure. But the manacles will have to stay, I'm afraid. Down the large hall and four doors to the left." Lisbet gave a small smile of gratitude. "Can someone help me magically remove my clothes? The manacles-" Severine cut her off. "Love to. Go ahead and draw the bath, and I'll be there to assist you shortly." Lowering her gaze, Lisbet nodded and made her way to the bathroom.

After only a few moments, Severine returned, wearing an even more revealing dress of slender swathes of fabric that barely covered her lovely bits before draping *well* below her generously curved hips and pooling around her bare feet. *Battle appropriate, indeed.* All the better to seduce her victims, I supposed. Nuala grinned at the sight of her. Her eyes widened hungrily for a moment before she drew a dagger from her its sheath at her thigh.

Thankfully, Nuala made her swear a very carefully worded blood oath to not betray us all, he took our hands in hers and folded us into the dense forest surrounding The Sapphire Mountains.

The trees were taller than anything I'd ever seen before. Even a few clouds could be seen grazing the tops of them. Thin layers of mist surrounded us. The ground was mostly bare, save for the peppering of ferns and other alien-looking flora. Sunlight trickled in between the branches of the gigantic trees with trunks wider than I was tall. The tree tops were too high and too dense to see any mountains surrounding us, though.

· · ·

My heart swelled in the majesty of the forest. This wasn't at all what I'd imagined the treacherous Sapphire Mountains to look like. "It's so beautiful...," I breathed, looking around in awe. Quetz gazed around with a seemingly wistful and nostalgic look on his face. My breath caught as I recalled the last time he had been here... When Kyril had come here to trap him. His eyes locked with mine as I suddenly felt overwhelmed by emotion.

He gave me a gentle, knowing smile. My eyes became pregnant with tears, but I managed to take a fortifying breath. Kyril was staring at me, and I could feel through the tether that he was experiencing a similar emotion. "I love you... words cannot even begin to express my gratitude, my soul," I murmured against his lips before pressing my mouth firmly against them.

I pulled away to find Quetz turning to follow the others and give Kyril and me a moment of privacy. "Quetzacoatl," I called to his back. He turned to face me, grinning, as always, like a cat with a secret. "Aurelia..." I couldn't help but smile back as I stepped toward him. I flung my arms around his neck and clutched him to me, feeling such an extreme outpouring of gratitude... If he hadn't been willing to let Kyril capture him... He could have killed him. He spent more than thirty years in a dungeon. For me. Everything that Kyril had been through was utterly inconceivable... but he was my mate. My nexus. We were one soul, split into halves at our creation. But Quetz... I couldn't imagine willingly doing anything like that for anyone other than Kyril.

He seemed to somehow know my thoughts, perhaps through our own tether via The Creator's Promise. "It's ok, Aurelia... I would do it all over again without a second thought." The tears I thought I'd successfully managed to stifle now freely poured down my cheeks as

I held him to me. And he held me just as firmly. His arms, his spirit, seemed to envelop me. "Why?" I croaked softly. I felt his chuckle rumble against my chest. "One day, and although that day will not come for some time, I promise all will be made clear. But know that everything I do for you is out of love and gratitude. Who you are. Who you will become. And for all the things you have done, and will do. And trust me when I say it is I who is indebted to you."

I felt his throat work on a swallow against my shoulder. I pulled back to look at him and saw that his eyes had also swelled with tears. I held his gaze, something that seemed to hold unfathomable knowledge: past, present, potentialities... and beyond. My breathing stilled as I saw a flicker of something familiar- a flicker of recognition- but it seemed so impossible and distant that as soon as my mind grasped it, it drifted away, and I became lost in his eyes again, entranced by the alien worlds in the dark and light recesses of his pupils. And something so similar, yet so different from Kyril's... And my heart swelled with love and gratitude for him. I took his face in my hands, standing on my tiptoes, angling him closer to me, and pressed a kiss to his forehead. "Thank you." And then, briefly, to his lips before smiling up at him. I wiped away the tears that had spilt down his cheeks. He gave me a nod, releasing my waist as I stepped back, finding Kyril already standing just behind me.

"I want both of you to know... that if anything-" Kyril silenced me by turning me to him, nodding to Quetz as well as he spoke. "I will protect you both with my life if need be."

Quetz laid his hands on our shoulders. "And mine. But have faith that we *will* walk out of here alive. I see it. There is no circumstance in which we do not...." Kyril nodded to Quetz in gratitude. "Thank you, brother." Quetz flashed Kyril a smile that beheld a brilliance unlike any I'd ever seen just as Kyril took our hands, and we folded to rejoin Nuala and Severine. Nuala peeked briefly back at us, grinning knowingly.

However, within moments, a pang of anxiety and concern slithered into the chestful of love and gratitude I'd been overwhelmed by only moments ago. Kyril, ever the telepath, reassured me. "We're at the edges of The Sapphire Mountains. As long as the sun is out, we'll be fine, but it would be wise to finish our task before the sun sets. Or worse creatures than Madame Yiruxat and her blood demons will come to hunt us."

My hands drifted to Charon and Thea, holstered to my thighs, and my magic reached out, scanning our surroundings for the presence of others. I sensed no one beyond the standard woodland and mountain creatures for the first hour or so of our hike, but as we travelled deeper and deeper into the forest, I gradually recognized a heavy presence in the air. Its weight was tangible. As though it sat upon your shoulders, willing your legs to buckle. In response, my magic was swirling and swelling inside of me, pressing at the barrier of my skin to be let out, and when I looked down, I could see subtle flashes of blue and white light beneath the skin of my arms and hands, reminding of lightening flares behind cumulous clouds.

Eventually, my gaze drifted upwards, and I could finally see the towering mountains above us and the range looming in the distance. It appeared to rise high above the clouds. After only another twenty minutes or so, the build-up of magic was becoming unbearable. My breathing was becoming labored, and I had to clench my jaw to keep from groaning. I felt like a dam ready to burst. Kyril and Quetz both glanced back at me, sensing my mounting distress. Concern filled Kyril's features, but I only found assurity, exhilaration, and pride illuminating Quetz's features as a small smile formed. *"Breathe,"* he whispered within my mind.

I could feel my electricity crackling at my fingertips as Kyril's voice sounded in my mind. *"Your eyes, Aurelia...."* Before I could respond, as if all of our senses detected it in unison, we halted our footsteps, and our gazes snapped to the right of our footpath. I tried to follow Quetz's instructions and control my breathing, but I barely managed to suppress a strangled groan as my magic roared within me to be released like a caged beast at whatever ominous presence lurked in the distance.

Kyril tried to pull me behind him. *"Don't you fucking dare,"* I snarled at him mind-to-mind in a voice I didn't even recognize. His eyes widened slightly in surprise for a fleeting moment, but he quickly shuddered it. *"Do as I say, Aurelia,"* he growled as he brought his hand to the hilt of his sword, eyes scanning the vicinity.

I closed my eyes, readying my magic. Tendrils of energy crackled at my fingertips, and I felt the hairs on my body rise, and a surprising feeling filled my chest. *Excitement. The relief at what I could feel was to come.* I felt a dark, oppressive energy take form behind me, and I whirled around to find several towering creatures. Eight of them. Fae-like in appearance but with dark grey skin, adorned in piercings, tattoos, and fighting leathers. The males and females alike were broad and all over seven feet tall. Their faces carved menacing smiles to reveal their elongated canines. I felt Kyril try to grab me again, but I side-stepped away from him. A white-haired female grinned at me as she stepped forward.

. . .

The well of my magic rose so high that I felt it'd consume me if I didn't release it- like my bones would snap and my muscles would burn off the bone. "The Madame will want to-" Before she could finish her sentence, a loud groan escaped my clenched teeth as my magic poured from me and powerful streams of electricity, the width of tree branches, rained down from above, striking all eight of what I assumed were blood demons. Within seconds, all that was left were eight smoking piles of ash and bone on blackened soil. A heavy sigh escaped me, and I stumbled back into Kyril, who caught me before I could collapse. "Oh sweet fuck," I panted loudly, "I thought I was gonna die if I didn't let that out."

After a few moments of no one speaking and simply staring at me, though no one seemed particularly surprised with the exception of Severine, mildly so. "It seems that it is I who should have asked for your protection," Severin grinned. Nuala's laugh warmed the air. "Well, well, well. And here I thought you two had only been shagging all this time," Nuala chirped. I looked up at Kyril, who was staring down at me, eyes shining with pride. His voice was soft but firm in my mind. *"Trust me when I say, this is only the barest of your potential, Aurelia. Even the most powerful of us can die. Please be careful."* I nodded as my throat worked on a swallow.

As if to prove his point, a bolt flew past my head and buried itself in the tree trunk beside me with a loud *crack*. A plume of splinters showered my face and hair. Kyril pulled me into him and folded us behind a tree. I peeked behind the trunk to find the others had done the same. Kyril turned to look at me. *"Wait here,"* he commanded silently. I scowled and held his stare, but before I could respond, he disappeared. I felt a sharp stab of panic at his absence- fear for his safety- and frantically looked around. A split second later, I heard screams and wails from nearby, accompanied by the sound of flesh and bone submitting to what I assumed was Kyril's blade. Another close scream tore through the air, and I looked up to find Kyril standing on the branch of one of the towering trees just across from me as the body of a blood demon plummeted toward the ground and hit the forest floor with a bone-crunching thwack.

My magic began to well inside me again, causing electricity to crackle and snap around my body. I was about to step out from behind the tree when a streak of darkest blue appeared nearby. Severine stepped into the centre of a clearing and began to shoulder off the strips of cloth covering her breasts. Each breast was large and perfectly rounded to the shape of a voluptuous teardrop. Her dark nipples were tightened into peaks. A wave of her magic poured over me, and I suddenly found my core painfully empty, and I felt breathtakingly desperate with the need to be filled by Kyril's massive cock. Her magic licked at my skin and my own magic, seducing me to give in to her. Severine tugged the rest of her dress down her hips to reveal her perfect, pear-shaped bum and the smooth, hairless pussy nestled between her silken thighs. The crackling of my electricity waned in submission to her. *Holy shit.* Her power was formidable, to say the least.

I shook my head and squeezed my eyes shut to fight against her magic and summon my own again, which, thankfully, came roaring back to me. When I opened my eyes again, I saw at least a dozen blood demon warriors making their way towards her, a trail of weapons surrendered behind them. I stood in awe for a moment, watching as her mesmerized and slack-jawed prey strode toward her.

The first male reached her, already halfway undressed, and I watched as she dug her claws into him and licked up the side of his face before sinking her fangs into his jaw. Despite being seven feet tall, when his body sagged in her arms, she held him upright with ease. He was drained within seconds. All that remained was a withered corpse that fell to the ground beside her, looking like nothing more than a hessian sack of bones- no hint of the formidable blood demon that it once was. *Good gods.* Severine's skin began to shimmer and glow, her power having increased substantially after feeding on the demon. I decided that watching any further would be dangerous, and thanked the Gods she was my bodyguard, *not* my enemy.

When I carefully rounded the massive tree trunk, another bolt flew by. A bolt not intended for me but for Nuala, which she dodged before folding with a large, gleaming sword raised high above her head and reappearing behind the blood demon. She brought her sword down in a high arc, slicing clean through the neck and shoulder of the blood demon, who fell apart in two pieces. No sign of her Chimera form yet. Perhaps there were too few, and too easy, prey to bother shifting for.

I scanned the vicinity for the rest of Madame Yiruxat's guards and for any signs of Quetz and Kyril. I couldn't see or hear them. I made my way towards Nuala, who was also scanning the forest. She sensed me approaching and turned to face me. *"Where's Severine?"* She asked within my mind. I gulped at the image of Severine draining her prey. *"Probably still feasting."* Nuala's brows scrunched together. *"You saw her feeding and were able to resist her magic?"* I nodded. A look of confusion clouded her expression before she seemed to nod in understanding. I took a deep breath again at the memory. *"Barely,"* I conceded.

Nuala led us forward until there was a large crack in the mountain- a cave entrance just wide enough for the body of a giant blood demon to fit through. A few bones littered the ground outside of it. Perhaps the remains of a blood demon's snack. Nuala raised a finger to her lips before she silently stalked into the cave entrance. A sense of dread and panic pressed down on me as claustrophobia set in, and I found my hands unconsciously drifting towards my blades, sheathed at my thighs.

This cave reminded me of the quarry and Pauperes Domos. I steeled myself, willing my plan to fruition, that they would soon be free of Yiruxat. As soon as we stepped into the cave mouth, I felt an enormous weight pressing down on me. My skin began to crawl, and my magic began to pound against my skin like the bars of a cage. I thumbed the hilts of Thea and Charon to comfort myself. Nuala briefly flashed me an edgy look and took my hand in hers. After a few minutes of traveling down the narrow passage, the smell of incense began to fill my nose. And something else I couldn't quite place. It was sweet. So sweet, it was sickly. We heard voices in the distance, but I couldn't make out any words or to whom the voice belonged. Nuala stole another glance back at me, her eyes suddenly wide with fear, just as my vision began to blur. I shook my head willfully to clear it. The sweet scent in the air was cloying and suffocating. I pulled my shirt up to cover my nose and mouth to try and stifle the smell. Nuala did the same. I willed a barrier of magic around us to protect us from the smell, but I was already so dizzy. My heart began to beat wildly in my chest at the realization that there must be some kind of poison lacing the air.

Nuala reached out to balance herself on the cave wall and stumbled forward. I gripped the back of her fighting silks as she fell to one knee. "Nuala!" I whispered frantically, trying to maintain consciousness myself. I pulled her back to her feet from behind and she braced her arms against both sides of the wall before sliding back down again. "Quetz...," Nuala gasped softly. *Quetz!* I cried in my mind as Nuala slumped in my arms. *Kyril, where are you?!* Only silence greeted me. *Kyril, just tell me you're ok!* I gave a tug on our tether but felt nothing on the other side. And then true panic set in. I should have

been able to feel him there. Feel him on the other end of our tether. I
did the same with Quetz, only to find the same emptiness. Like the
shock of weightlessness informing you the anchor snapped free
when you grab its rope.

Thanks to the barrier, the toxic effects began to clear, but my mind
whirled in a fear-driven frenzy. *Where is Severine?* Surely she's
finished feasting and fucking by now? Would she be affected by the
toxic incense? If I dragged Nuala out of the cave to recover while I
continued, she'd be helpless. If I left her in here, she would be
vulnerable. Kyril and Quetz had gone in ahead of us, and they might
already need my help. *Fold.* I needed to fold. I could fold Nuala back
outside to recover with Severine, warn her, and then fold back inside
with the barrier. I only prayed I could manage it without us ending
up Gods knew where.

Despite Kyril's warning, I squeezed my eyes shut and visualized the
forest where I'd last seen Severine devouring the magic, life force,
and souls of her victims. My heart kicked violently in my chest as if it
were trying to escape it's prison within my ribs as thoughts of Kyril
and Quetz being in danger filled my mind. Quetz had reassured us
we would not fail. *But where the fuck were they? Why couldn't
I feel them?*

My body began to tremble with anxiety, not from supporting Nuala's
weight, and I forced myself to focus. *Focus, Aurelia. Forest. Severine.
Withered Husks.* The temperature plummeted briefly, and my eyes
opened to see the dark, clear vastness of the cosmos, causing a spear
of panic to lance me out of fear that I'd accidentally transported
myself to the wrong place. But a fleeting heartbeat later, tendrils of
darkness whorled around me- as if space itself was fleeing the realm
that was now filling my vision- dissipated from my vision as the air

warmed again to reveal Severine clutching a naked female blood demon's body, feeding from her through her breast.

By the time the shroud of darkness completely disappeared, the female's body had been reduced to little more than kindling. Although I was too consumed with terror for Kyril and Quetz's lives to experience any shock at the sight anymore. I scooped Nuala up in my arms and marched over to her just as she released the female. Her gaze snapped to mine. Her eyes were like black, gleaming, crystalline pools shining a feral hunger. Severine was practically glowing like a bright blue lightbulb after her feast. She looked like a Goddess. My footsteps faltered. "Severine?" At the sound of my voice, something in her vision cleared and the haze of her feeding frenzy seemed to dissipate. Her eyes dropped to Nuala, and panic filled her eyes.

"What happened?! Where is Yiruxat?!" Severine cried as she ran naked to capture Nuala in her arms. Nuala, now in the fresh mountain air, was already beginning to revive. "She's laced some kind of magic suppressant and intoxicant with incense. I have to go back. Watch her. And guard the cave entrance." "Wait!" Severine cried too late. I was already folding back into the caves. I couldn't wait a breath longer. My magic was bursting from my skin again, and any moment's hesitation could mean the difference between life or death for Kyril and Quetz.

A second later, I stood in Yiruxat's entrance tunnel again, and I immediately willed my magic to form the barrier again to protect myself from the toxic air. I placed my hands on Thea and Charon as I quickly made my way through the cave. Electricity crackled down my arms and over my hands in anticipation. The tunnel widened to reveal a series of hallways and the toxic incense grew faint.

· · ·

I tried to feel for the tether between Kyril and me, and faintly, I could feel the slightest pull, but I had no idea in which direction I should go. Not wanting to waste another moment, I made a snap decision and went for the one to my right. After several too long moments of rushing down the tunnel, an amber light glowed at the end of it to reveal an opening.

After making my way for what felt like a small eternity, I could hear the sound of stringed and wind instruments being played in the distance. The closer I got, the more voices and laughter I could hear. I slowed, creeping along the wall, gripping the hilt of Charon so hard my bones ached.

Just before I reached the opening, a blood demon, clearly one of Yiruxat's guards, armed with a tremendous sword strapped to his hip, rounded the corner of the tunnel and locked eyes with me. A malevolent grin cut across his face. "Hello, little mouse," he purred in a gravelly and baritone voice. I froze in terror, knowing that if I used my magic, it would attract Gods knew how many other guards. However, I was only newly trained in blades and hand-to-hand combat, and this guy was practically the size of a water buffalo. But taking my chances with one vs potentially more than a dozen was far more favorable. His gaze dropped to my hand on the hilt of my dagger. His grin widened. Considering his size, I knew very well that the only advantages I had over him were speed, and the element of surprise. And the more I hesitated, the less of the latter I had.

"Come now, pretty one. You and I both know that-." I folded directly in front of him, simultaneously drawing Thea, and plunged it directly right of centre in the blood demon's chest- piercing his heart. The velocity of my body ramming against his caused him to stumble backwards into the cave wall.

.   .   .

His eyes, wide with shock, bore into mine as his legs buckled. The two of us slid down the wall, and his mouth moved to speak, but no sound came out. His pupils dilated impossibly wide, and his stricken body finally slackened. I silently drew Thea from his chest, panting heavily with adrenaline and magic electrifying every nerve ending in my body. I crept the rest of the way to the cave wall's edge and snuck a glance around the corner. Patrons and blood slaves were peppered around the room feeding from them, drinking, eating, and watching live music performed by a sextet of various string, percussion, and wind instruments who sat on cushions and animal skins laid on a low dais. I noticed some of the blood slaves were unconscious, and my gut churned at the sight. Thankfully, what I did not see were a ton of guards. *But where are Kyril and Quetz?* This room was completely unscathed, and I saw no other entrances into the room. I swiftly turned and ran back the way I came.

Approaching the central vestibule to the network of hallways, I slowed my pace, stalking silently with Thea gripped tightly in one fist and drawing Charon out with the other. I chose the tunnel directly across from me, straining my ears to hear anyone else who might be approaching before I rushed across the vestibule. I glanced down the cave entrance tunnel hoping that Nuala and Severine were alright. *"Nuala?"* I called out to her in her mind. Icy tendrils of foreboding trickled through my veins as each second passed with no response. Just as I was about to try and call for her again, the hairs on the back of my neck rose. The weight of a dark presence loomed behind me. I whirled, just about ready to burst out of my skin, but no one was there or in the vestibule beyond.

A scream tore through my throat as I turned again and stood face to face with a woman whose greying, wrinkled skin and milky white eyes would suggest that she should no longer stand among the living. Her robe was so old and tattered that the dark, rutty grey-brown color could have been purely from the passage of time. She laughed, seemingly amused by my terror, revealing her few remaining brown and black peg-like teeth. Her laugh was wet and raspy, and immediately, I had the desire to clear the phantom phlegm from my now painfully dry throat.

"Would you like to be reunited with your mates?" My eyebrows furrowed at her plural usage of the word as she clearly confused the Creator's Promise tether between Quetz and me as a duplicate Nexus bond. Now, however, was not the time to correct her. I nodded, and she extended a gnarled hand towards me. I hesitated, dread filling me as warning bells pealed in my mind that this was a trap. But how else would I find Kyril and Quetz? Electricity crackled again on my skin in response. The crone chuckled, clearly enjoying herself. "Are you sure you'd rather try to find your way to them yourself? I can't promise you'd make it in time...," she rasped, sympathetically making me want to clear my throat again. Every instinct in my body screamed in protest as I raised my hand to hers. As though a guillotine would come down on my neck.

My fingers reached hers, and she snatched the whole of my hand with surprising speed, and clutched it with even more shocking strength. I flinched reflexively, but we were already passing through what always reminded me of a tiny window to the cosmos and folded directly into an enormous bedroom adorned with numerous petite alcoves in the cave walls that flickered with candlelight and when I looked around, the crone was nowhere to be seen. I searched my surroundings for her or Yiruxat, dread and panic knotting in my chest, but the room appeared empty. And, worse, there was no door. My breathing stilled.

.   .   .

Where was Kyril? Quetz? Were they trapped in rooms like this? My hands shook, and I breathed, trying to will myself calm. The way out could be right in front of you, but you won't even notice if you're too busy panicking.

I looked around taking in my surroundings, searching for any hint of a way out while trying to master my breathing. The furniture was sparse, but large and varied animal skin rugs decorated the floors. I looked up to find enormous glowing metal braziers hanging from the ceiling, burning what I assumed was whatever that toxic concoction was. My grip on Charon flexed in gratitude that I was still able to use my magic. She must use that incense to subdue her slaves, and I imagined her guards and patrons must be warded against its effects.

In front of me, an enormous four-post bed wrapped with sheer dark red curtains adorned the room. The curtains were drawn so I couldn't see inside it, but I felt a faint pull in that direction. My throat tightened, working on a swallow and threatening to close as yet another near-crippling wave of fear filled me. Approaching the bed, terror speared me through the heart as the dark silhouette of a large body came into view beyond the sheer drapes, dark stains surrounding it. A guttural cry tore from my throat at knowing who lay beyond it.

I ripped open the drapes to discover Kyril unconscious and actively bleeding from several wounds, the worst of which appeared to be a stab wound in his ribs. His face had grown sallow and pale. I extended the barrier to encompass both of us and crawled onto the bed beside him, tears flooding my cheeks in a torrential downpour. "Kyril...," I wept, trying to shake his arm without jostling him too much. His breaths were slow and shallow, but he groaned softly. I reached to caress his cheek and press my forehead to his. "Kyril," I croaked, praying that he would wake up any moment now that my barrier was blocking the toxic air. "*My soul*, please stay with me...." I wept while laying tender kisses on his cheek.

As I drew away to search his face for signs of returning consciousness, a hole in the crook of his neck, about an inch wide, caught my attention. I gently peeled back the fabric of his shirt, revealing three more identical holes, all aligned in a way that indicates bite marks. From fangs on the top and bottom of the predator's mouth. I felt bile rise in my throat as I drew a trembling hand to the wounds before covering them again.

Inwardly, I was cursing myself for not having learned how to heal others with my magic yet. Surely there was a way. Kyril's eyes fluttered open briefly, and dread filled his features. He opened his mouth to say something, but blood came gurgling out instead. Horror and determination, in equal measure, filled my veins. My breaths finally becoming even again. I drew Thea from her sheath as I spoke. "Don't. Save your energy. I'm going to get us-"

Just as I was about to open my wrist to feed Kyril, a husky female voice cut me off. "I must apologize if it seems things got a little out of hand with his... injuries. It wasn't my intention...." My head jerked to the right of the bed to see a tall, curvaceous woman with dark grey skin, seductive features, heavy kohl eyeliner on her large eyes, and straight, shorn hair that grazed her shoulders and had a blunt fringe. *Madame Yiruxat.* She was dressed in a revealing maroon-colored gown from which her curves spilled out of. She offered me a smile with pointed teeth that reminded me of a snake, and I half expected her to have a forked tongue.

. . .

My magic burst from me, and beams of electricity poured into her. Red runes glowed, and the longer volts of my magic poured into her, the more brightly they showed, and her smile only grew wider. A ward of magic was protecting her from my attack. I pulled back on my magic, sweating and panting heavily, feeling weakened from the drain of it. She threw her head back with laughter. "My, my. That was exquisite," she purred, "I haven't tasted magic like that in ages." Her skin, hair, and eyes were now glowing radiantly. It seemed the ward not only protected her from magical attacks but also added to her own power.

I leapt towards her, sweeping Charon and Thea in a downwards arch in front of me to cut her down, but she raised her hand, and I became frozen midair. I tried to scream in fury, but even my vocal cords were incapable of moving. She wore a half smile as she watched me silently battle her magic fruitlessly. Agonizing pain tore through me as I fought her hold on me. "Now, now. None of that, pet. We wouldn't want you getting any scratches. I pride myself on the beauty of my slaves."

I felt like metal spikes were being hammered into my head as I struggled against her. Sweat trickled down my temples, and my neck. Every muscle in my body taught with tension. My heart threw itself against my ribcage like a caged animal in a raucous rhythm as rage swelled deep from within.

She stepped towards me, examining my body and my face. A delicate and soft finger began to caress my cheek. Disgust and fury ignited every cell in my body, and a white-blue glow began to permeate my vision. Her eyes widened, and she shook her head slowly in awe. "You are such a beauty. I do look forward to breaking you. I think I'll keep you for myself for some time... Perhaps you and your mates. Would you like that?" Finally, despite the skull-shattering pain, I felt my grip on Charon and Thea tightening. I could feel her magic's hold over me waining.

Yiruxat narrowed her eyes at me. "Hotep," she called, her voice wavering slightly. The crone reappeared a moment later. "Bring me the manacles. Quickly." "Yes, my lady," Hotep said with a light bow. "And take this one with you," Yiruxat sneered, gesturing towards Kyril's unconscious body, "Put him in my room." Yiruxat grinned at me as Hotep began to shuffle towards Kyril. "Such an interesting hybrid he is, wouldn't you say? Can't say I've ever met another like him, and *gods* is he delicious." She offered me a wink, licking her lips. A wicked smile spread across my face despite the blinding pain erupting from every cell of my body as her magic on me finally began to crack. A look of confusion filled her eyes briefly. Just before electricity erupted from my chest and solar plexus, breaking her hold on me entirely, I folded directly in front of her, my blades burying themselves to the hilt in her chest.

"Don't touch him," I growled at Hotep before jerking the blades in opposite directions- severing flesh and bone and freeing the blades of Yiruxat's body as she dropped to her knees. I willed my barrier to strengthen around Kyril and me as Hotep let out a blood-curdling scream and launched herself at me, again with shocking speed.

With the remaining power I had left after overpowering Yiruxat's magic, I unleashed it in a bolt of lightning that struck her, thanks to Charon's effect, and sent her body slamming into the wall, where she collapsed in a smoking heap. I yanked the blade from Yiruxat's chest. Black blood pumped out of the wound in a steady flow. Her mouth was moving, but only gurgling sounds came out, only one of which I could make out. *"How?"* Ignoring her, I glanced over to Kyril, who was finally beginning to stir on the bed. His wounds had closed, and he had stopped bleeding. The color had returned to his bronze cheeks, causing me to feel an overwhelming flood of relief and gratitude.

Bringing Thea to her chin, I lowered my gaze to hold her eyes. Terror finally darkened her features. I swiftly drew Thea through her neck, cutting through her like butter. Yiruxat's head flew across the room, landing in front of a floor-to-ceiling mirror with spotted, tarnished glass. It rolled until Yiruxat's forehead hit the glass with a soft thud and her black eyes stared back at me. Quetz was rising to his feet on the other side of the glass. "Quetz!" I cried in relief. His voice and demeanor were remarkably calm. "Pierce the mirror with your dagger."

I rushed over to the mirror, grasping the hilt of Charon with both hands and drove it into the mirror. The blade was so sharp the glass didn't even shatter. It simply cut straight through. Glowing runes flared and flickered across the glass for a few brief moments. I stared at the mirror, gripped in anticipation. Finally, a crack formed. And then another. The sound of splintering glass pierced the air before the entire mirror shattered and burst towards me. I instinctively rose my arms, Charon and Thea in hand, to shield my face, but the barrier protected me. I gasped in relief when Quetz's incorporeal form poured out and reformed corporeally again. I winced as I struggled to quickly throw a barrier around him- I was now running on empty. My body was trembling with exhaustion- my magic and adrenaline now wholly depleted. Thankfully, Quetz shook his head. "Her wards went down as soon as you killed her."

I ran back to Kyril, where he still laid, and crawled onto the bed to kneel beside him. He groaned as I accidentally jostled him while tearing his shirt open to see that his wounds, while at least closed, were still red and angry looking. Huge bruises were slowly fading from his ribs, chest, and stomach. I looked back up at Quetz. "Are you able to fold us out of here? I don't think I have the energy." Quetz nodded, and I curled my arms beneath Kyril's shoulders, laying his head in my lap. Kyril's features pinched, and a sigh escaped his lips, but his eyes remained closed. Quetz took hold of my hand, and, just before he folded us into the forest, my gaze fell to the empty spot where Hotep was no longer slumped against the wall.

We arrived in a clearing where in the nearby distance, I could see where Severine had left the remains of her feast. I looked up at Quetz, and without even having to ask, he responded, "They went inside as soon as they felt the wards come down. I'm going to go help gather the slaves. And don't worry, Aurelia, he'll wake soon. Severine and Nuala made quick work of the remaining guards but we do need to leave before dusk." Before I could respond, he disappeared and folded back into Yiruxat's caves. I couldn't help but feel a pang of concern for them, knowing that Hotep was somewhere in there still, alive, but hopefully too busy nursing her wounds.

My gaze fell back to Kyril, whose head still rested in my lap. My stomach churned, and my chest still felt like someone had dropped an anvil on top of it. Seeing him in this injured and weakened state was beyond excruciating. Yet somehow, despite his injuries, he was still the most gorgeous male I'd ever laid eyes on. His beauty made my soul weep. I released a heavy sigh and brushed his hair back off of his face before leaning down to brush a kiss to his lips. The feeling of his lips pressing against mine in response had my heart bursting with relief. Kyril hummed beneath me and captured my face in his hands to hold me in place. Tears pricked my eyes in rejoice. I spoke against his lips.

"Kyril, when I saw you like that... If you-."

"Shhhhh. You saved me. Us. Everything's fine."

I sat back, trying to breathe through the tears, wiping my eyes. "Technically, Charon saved us."

Kyril shook his head. "Without you and your power, Charon wouldn't have been able to do anything. You'll have to fill me in on most of the details, though. I only caught glimpses after that Gods-forsaken incense rendered me unconscious."

19

Quetz returned after a few moments with Idra, Lisbet's lover who slipped in and out of consciousness from being drained of too much blood and was still under the effects of the toxic incense that he'd probably been inhaling since he first had been kidnapped and brought there more than a year ago. Idra, Kyril, and I laid beneath a tree, recuperating, while Quetz, Nuala, and Severine took care of the remaining guards and rescued the slaves.

There had been no sign of Hotep by the time we left. And as it turns out, even after evenly distributing Yiruxat's liquid assets- Aeternam crystals, gold coins, and jewels- between each of the 38 blood and sex slaves Yiruxat had owned and bringing the ones who had no friends or family to return to, to inns, there was still a plethora of her loot left. Including some rather remarkable magical artifacts. After we all decided to store them in Nuala's vaults and go through them once we had more information from Lisbet, Nuala quickly folded them to her palace and returned with several guards and servants to collect and fold them back to the palace with it.

. . .

When we returned to Severine's tree palace in Nuala's pocket realm with Idra, he had recovered considerably and was fully conscious. As soon as he'd woken up and the reality that he'd been rescued settled in, he was reduced to a shaking, sobbing heap. Whatever he had experienced in that year of being Yiruxat's slave and victim to her patrons, it was beyond what I'd dare to fathom. My heart ached for him.

Lisbet was stuck in a towel and hung a bathrobe over her shoulders. She needed our help to magically get dressed while still shackled by the manacles. Although at the sight of Idra, she couldn't have cared less. His weeping only intensified when he saw her; they clung to each other like they'd been born that way. My eyes swelled with tears for them, and I couldn't help but imagine what they had been through.

"I think we should go," I whispered to Kyril as Severine led Lisbet and Idra down the hallway to one of the many superfluous guest chambers. Kyril nodded, a deep frown plastering his features. Nuala and Quetz were also watching them mournfully. "Fine. We'll come back tomorrow," Nuala announced. Kyril took Nuala's hand, and she folded us all back to her underwater home.

We all returned to our rooms, silently walking hand-in-hand. As soon as I shut the door behind us, Kyril turned to me, and I pulled him against me, staring up into his heated gaze. His eyes glistened, mirroring my own. He cupped my cheeks in his hands. "My brave and beautiful Nexus. My soul. Seeing you at the mercy of Yiruxat...," Kyril breathed, his voice cracking with emotion, "I can't put you at risk again. You don't understand, Aurelia...." I shook my head, clutching the collar of his shirt, and pulled his face down to mine.

"Shhhh. I need to replace the horror of nearly losing you," I whispered with trembling lips, failing to stifle my tears. Kyril tenderly kissed them away before capturing my mouth with his. We kissed with a forcefulness that expressed our desperate, suffocating need for one another. The overwhelming relief and gratitude for being safe in each other's arms. Our tongues met in a passionate and desperate caress. Kyril lifted me by my hips in a bruising grip, and I wrapped my legs around his torso. His long, thick erection pressed against my clit as he walked us over to the bed, and before my back even hit the bed, our clothes vanished.

Kyril stood above me at the edge of the bed and stared as though committing every detail of me to memory. And now, more than ever, I was compelled to do the same. "Kyril," I begged, reaching for him. He pressed me back down to the bed and captured my mouth with his. "Don't rush this. I need to savor you," he whispered. He gently collared my throat as he began to kiss my neck and collar bone, nipping and sucking along the way before arriving at my breasts. A breathy moan escaped my lips. I drove my fingers into the soft waves of his hair, pulling him tighter to me. He growled approvingly, making my nipples go taut and tingle in anticipation.

Kyril groaned as he took my left nipple between his teeth, gently biting before sucking at it firmly, and flicking it teasingly with that talented tongue of his as he began to caress my slit, already wet with need. My back arched off the bed, and a needy moan tore from me. He leaned further into me, replacing his gifted finger with his huge, hard dick, resting atop my clit, and I began to thrust my hips against it.

Kyril's whole body tensed, and he growled from around a mouthful breast. His fangs pierced my flesh, and the beginnings of a full body climax surged through me. *"Oh my gods, Kyril...,"* I moaned in a breathy exhale, clutching him harder to me. I thrusted my hips harder and faster against his erection as he drank from me. He reached between us, aligning his throbbing cock with my entrance, and slowly eased into me. My toes curled, and every muscle in my body tensed. He drew back slowly, and I savored the feeling of his every ridge sliding within me. The beauty and intensity of it caused tears to prick the backs of my eyes as he thrust back into me. He withdrew his fangs, but my cry of protest was replaced by one of sheer bliss as he leaned back on his heels, gripped my hips to pull me harder and thrusting slowly and deeply into me between each one. "My goddess... my fire... my soul... my love...," he breathed. "My everything...," I moaned, holding his fiery gaze.

My heart ached at the idea that we had come so close to having all of this taken away from us causing tears to spill down my cheeks. Kyril leaned forward and kissed them from my cheeks. "Nothing will ever separate us, my fire," he swore, driving harder and faster into me. The swell of another orgasm approached, causing my pussy to firmly grip his cock.

I forced the thought from my mind as he pushed his emotions through our tether, and I immediately felt the immense gravity of his love for me. It gripped my heart to bursting, and I pushed my love back to him. Kyril's cock hardened impossibly further before it pulsed inside me with spurt after spurt of his hot cum until it spilled out of me. I reached my climax at the sensation, my pussy spasming around him as I cried out in ecstasy. His strokes became languorous, making my whole body sing in response. Our lips met again as I writhed beneath him, my pussy tingling and pulsing, and his dick began to harden inside me again.

I softly moaned my pleasure at how exquisite he felt, wrapping my arms around his neck and shoulders. Kyril pulled me up against his chest, and I straddled his lap as he sat back on his heels. I took over, working my hips gently in a rocking thrust that had my ass bouncing on top of him. His hands roved down my body before taking my ass in a possessive grip. Lips parting, his eyes widened almost imperceptibly as they tracked the flick of my tongue that laved my fingers.

The corner of my mouth twitch upward in response to my lust-addled delight at his appreciation. He shook his head lightly as he watched me. *"Oh my fucking gods, Aurelia...."* Just before I reached between us to caress his nipples. He groaned, jaw clenching, as his grip on my ass tightened. Every muscle in his body went rigid, and he began thrusting his hips into me in counterpoint to my own.

I brought my lips to his to caress and tease his. Gently licking his bottom lip before biting down on it, making him growl hungrily as I thrust harder against him. I sucked his lower lip into my mouth to kiss away the pain, and he wrapped his arms around me, pressing me harder against him. The pace of his countering thrusts quickened, and I responded in kind. I withdrew one of my hands from caressing his nipples to grip his hair. He collared my throat and pulled my mouth to his in a fierce kiss. My sighs and moans of ecstasy became high-pitched as I felt another orgasm rising within me.

.   .   .

Kyril laid me back down on the bed and flipped me, as though I were weightless, onto my front. His larger body caged mine, placing his weight on one of his forearms on the bed above my shoulder and wrapped the other around my front, taking my breast in his hand. He kissed, sucked, and laved at my shoulder as his thrusts turned languid again. His fangs pierced my flesh, and the ecstasy of it made me boneless. He drank from me in slow, gentle gulps. The hand clutching my breast swept down between my thighs, and the pad of his middle finger began to draw lazy circles around my pulsating bead. Waves of delicious electricity coursed through me, and I moaned into Kyril's mouth as he angled his mouth to mine. The circles he traced on that bundle of nerves became faster as his thrusts quickened. Electricity coiled deep within my core, and my pussy gripped his cock tightly.

Kyril growled and groaned, releasing my mouth and leaning back. I felt his dick harden further, and just when I anticipated his thrusts to become brutal, they slowed, his hands sweetly caressing the curves of my bum. "Your pussy is Heaven, my fire," Kyril husked. "It's your dick that brings me there," I breathed. The coil of energy building deep within my core finally burst, making my pussy spasm and clench around his perfect, massive cock whilst he continued to thrust languidly. Warm liquid spilled from my pussy as his deep, slow strokes made my orgasm soar to new heights. *"Fuck, Aurelia...* Watching you come around my cock is the most beautiful thing I could possibly fathom," he groaned breathlessly, never wavering in his achingly delicious thrusts. His essence spilled inside me, mixing with my own. Kyril draped himself over me and within moments I felt exhaustion overcome me.

Skull-splitting pain coursed through my body as I struggled against invisible binds holding me midair. The groan of a familiar voice sounded behind me, and my eyes burst open to see a naked, voluptuous figure with soft, dark grey skin straddling the large, muscular body of a male whose face I couldn't see. A pool of blood formed a halo around his body. Panic incited a fresh wave of agony as I struggled against the magic holding me. Large, heavily kohl-lined eyes met mine as the female's gaze left the male bleeding out beneath her.

Crimson dripped from her chin as she gave me a broad, terrifying grin. "He tastes even more delicious than he smells, you selfish girl. Hotep is going to bring him back from the precipice of death every night when I fuck him and drain him dry. Perhaps if you behave, I'll let you keep his corpse when I tire of him." I felt my bones cracking as I roared, Yiruxat's magic finally submitting to mine. Like a thousand shards of glass piercing my skin, her magic shattered, and I launched myself at her. Reaching her, I gripped her by the throat, her eyes bulging and slammed her into the wall. She scratched and clawed at my face and body until her eyes rolled back.

Searing fire burst through my back and out of my chest. My blood sprayed across Yiruxat's unconscious face. I released her and clutched at the wound on my chest. I tried to scream in terror, but only a wet gurgling rasp left my lips. I turned, falling to one knee as I felt my life force draining from me with every spurt of blood. I looked up into Hotep's milky gaze as she gave me a blackened grin, but my eyes were quickly drawn to the male lying unconscious on the bed. His empty, lifeless eyes bore straight into mine. The horror of it pierced deeper than the sword impaling me.

A scream tore from my lips as I woke to find Kyril on top of me, cradling my head in his hands. "Aurelia, shhh... My fire. I'm here. You're safe," he cooed soothingly to me.

Dim, watery light filtered in through the sea, enveloping Nuala's home. A soft whimper escaped me as the nightmare fully receded. I wrapped Kyril's large body in my arms and pulled him against me.

My body relaxed at the feel of him, and Kyril shifted to lay back and pulled me onto his chest, holding me in his arms. We laid there for several minutes just holding one another before either of us spoke.

"Do you want to talk about it?" I nuzzled his neck, taking in his scent of balsam and burning embers, making my muscles further relax. I gave my head a small shake. "It was just another version of yesterday's events replaying in my mind." His fingers began to caress my hair, and I sank further onto him. "She's dead. There's nothing she can do from the grave." I exhaled a heavy sigh, relaxing slightly at the memory of Thea's blade parting her head from her neck. I nodded, resolving to not allow her to haunt me. "Are you hungry?"

It was nearly noon when Kyril and I entered the kitchen. Nuala and Quetz were already sitting at the counter eating. Kyril and I hadn't eaten since breakfast the previous day; from the looks of it, neither had they. Quetz frowned and gave me a knowing look but asked anyway. "How'd you sleep?" "Like the dead until that nightmare." I wondered how much he could feel through our tether. Something for a later discussion. Quetz nodded, shoving another strawberry, green stem and all, into his mouth. My mouth quirked watching him. Watching him eat like this reminded me of the fact he didn't eat for thirty years while stuck in that mirror in Nuala's dungeon. I was further intrigued by the fact that he and Nuala seemed so inseparable even though it was her dungeon he'd been trapped in.

"What about you guys?" I asked while popping one of Quetz's strawberries in my mouth. Nuala mumbled something unintelligible to herself. The beginnings of dark circles were under her eyes. Quetz pulled her under his arm, and her body seemed to relax as he pressed a kiss to her head. She finally looked up to respond but ignored my question. "While you guys meet with Lisbet and Idra, I'm leaving briefly to go back to the palace to meet with our best ward-smiths, armourers, and alchemists in the hopes that they can create armours for us that will nullify magic-suppressing wards, among other things."

It wasn't long after we'd arrived at Severine's later that afternoon that Nuala and Quetz joined us, and she healed Lisbet with a few of the healing libations the alchemists from the palace made to rejuvenate her from the Sakachi demon's work via the manacles. Idra seemed to be mostly recovered physically. I couldn't discern what type of immortal he was, I just knew that he was one otherwise, he wouldn't have lasted more than a few hours at Yiruxat's. His face was boyishly handsome and he had a tall, lean form and dark smooth skin.

Despite his stricken expression from Gods-know what kind of trauma, he had a sweet, soft, warm demeanour. He stood as Nuala finished healing Lisbet to face us and held our gazes. "I owe you all my life. In whatever way I may help, I will. I would be proud to serve you, my Queen, and fight beside all of you in whatever we may face. Lisbet has only just told me about everything that has been happening with the seals and what little she knows about those trying to open the portal to the other dimension. I believe I could be of much value to your efforts. I am a draconi."

My jaw dropped. *Draconi? A dragon shifter.* Sweet Gods. "I thought the draconi had gone extinct," I gasped before I could stop myself. He offered a sad smile. "Nearly, but there are a few of us left. We've survived by hiding in our human forms. Mostly in plain sight." "We would certainly be grateful for your help. I can only hope Lisbet is equally willing to be cooperative and loyal," Nuala spoke evenly, giving her a pointed look, "Are you in contact with any of the other draconi?"

. . .

Idra gave a disarmingly charming smile, revealing his brilliant white teeth. "I know where most of them are, but I haven't seen them since that demon female enslaved me... They meet twice a month- a group inconspicuously named 'The Bipeds'- at the Pub where you found Lisbet." I huffed a laugh at the clever name. Draconis are dragons that walk on two feet, unlike other dragons who walk on four. "I can petition on our behalf for them to join our efforts, should we ever need their help. Although, I must ask that you never repeat this information. I'm trusting you because you saved my life and have shown Lisbet mercy. I'm sure I don't have to remind you that if anyone were to ever discover that there were still draconi walking among us, we would be hunted to extinction, as we nearly once were."

Kyril spoke for us. "Whatever is spoken here will not leave this room. I swear it." Nuala nodded gratefully. "Well. I suppose we'll find out, won't we?" Lisbet straightened at the question. "I was working on behalf of a male who calls himself 'Le Mont'. He wears a glamour every time we meet, so I don't actually know what he looks like, and every time we meet, it's somewhere new. The only thing I know for certain is that he's working for someone else. Or perhaps even a group of others. I'm not sure. I get the impression that whoever these seals are for... That they are... God-like beings. It is only a guess... Because even he seems anxious at times." I sniffed the air trying to detect if I could scent any lies, but I found none. Kyril stepped forward and studied her expression. *"Is she speaking the truth?"* She asked within my mind and turned to look back at me. I nodded in affirmation.

"And why did you agree? Surely you could have simply killed 'Le Mont'. You know better than anyone what would happen to this realm if that portal was opened." Lisbet's expression tightened. "Le

Mont told me he would free Idra from Yiruxat. I was planning on killing them after I got Idra back."

Kyril quirked an eyebrow. "Do you think it would have been so easy?"

Lisbet frowned grimly. "It was a risk I was willing to take."

Kyril gave her a sympathetic expression. "I understand," he said without a trace of falsehood. "Have you already given him the first seal?"

"Yes, but it's useless without the others," she sighed.

"And when were you supposed to give him the next seal?" Nuala asked.

Lisbet chewed her cheek. "Tonight."

Nuala and Kyril exchanged a look before she turned back to Lisbet. "Do you think you can still get it in time?"

"If I can get these things off, sure," Lisbet responded, holding up her shackled wrists.

"And where were you supposed to meet him?"

Lisbet shook her head, "As I said, it's different every time. He summons me, and then I appear wherever he wills. I never know ahead of time."

Nuala gave her a sharp look. "Explain."

Lisbet pulled back the sleeve of the bathrobe Severine had let her borrow to reveal the slightly raised skin of a branded symbol in the shape of a lily of the valley flower. "This enables him to fold me to wherever he is. He'll summon me at midnight."

We glanced outside to see it was approximately noon.

Nuala stood. "And how did you manage to steal the first sigillum?"

"I switched bodies with the Lord of the Southern Guard to retrieve it."

Nuala raised her eyebrows. "How did you reach him in the first place?"

"Switched bodies with as many guards as necessary until I reached him."

"And once you leave their bodies, their souls return?"

Lisbet nodded.

"Do they remember anything?"

"No. Only that they suddenly went into a deep sleep. I usually leave them in their beds."

Nuala studied Lisbet and Idra warily for several moments. "Right. Well, you'll come with us now. Do what you need to do. And when Le Mont summons you, you'll give him the Sigillum- with a tracking spell on it so we can hopefully find out who this fucker is, and in case we have to come rescue you. Try to get as much information as you can about whoever it is he's working for, and then we're all gonna take a trip to the other eight other realms."

Lisbet blinked. "And then what?"

"Probably start a war... Who knows. We have to find out who or what it is he's working for."

Lisbet sighed, shaking her head a little miserably. "This is not gonna be good for my anxiety...."

Nuala frowned, laying a hand on her shoulder. "What's the worst that could happen?"

"Ugh... We all die?"

Nuala raised an eyebrow. "And? One end merely means another beginning. You, of all people, know this. Exciting, is it not?"

Lisbet's expression sagged, rolling her eyes in bored annoyance. "No. No, it is not. Pain still fucking hurts. Letting go also sucks massive balls. Losing people you love and getting stuck here alone is also- super fucking soul-crushing. Watching other's suffer- also kinda on my list of 'horrible things that suck festering asshole and would desperately wish to avoid'.

Nuala burst into laughter. "You're delightful," she chirped, caressing Lisbet's cheek before walking away.

20

Kyril folded the whole group of us- an impressive feat- into an alley in the Eastern Guard near the castle wall. We had arrived to finally uphold our end of the bargain in retrieving the Lord of the Eastern Guard's mate, and the male himself was growing rather impatient- understandably so. As with most homes, the castle had been warded from anyone, other than the Lord himself, from folding in. The narrow, dead-end, dirt alleyway was empty between what appeared to be two taverns. The roofs reminded me of the bottom of an enormous wooden ship, with ornately carved wooden spires decorating each end. The sky here was overcast above it. Even though it was only just after midday, it looked like it was near dusk.

The silence had my fingers whispering over the hilts of my blades. Kyril smiled, looking around as if experiencing nostalgia before he glanced down at me. "You know this place?" Kyril studied me for a moment, giving me a melancholy smile. "I do... I have... some cherished memories here. It's been too long." I quirked an eyebrow.

"You'll have to elaborate later...," I said, searching his face, and our tether. A nod was his only response.

Nuala stared at Kyril in a way that made me wonder if they were speaking mind-to-mind, but she quickly turned away, sighing heavily. "I am not looking forward to this." Lisbet, Idra, Quetz, Kyril, and I followed Nuala out of the alley and into the muddy street. The houses were widely separated and appeared to be built primarily from wood. Some had thatched roofs, some had wood shingles that sloped to the ground, while others were built into the sides of hills making the roof an actual grassy knoll. Most of the streets were unpaved except the most central one, which was made of grey cobblestone bricks. I could faintly smell the brine in the air of the nearby sea. The streets weren't nearly as crowded as in The Southern Guard's captial city of Vanaheim. The residents eyed us warily. Most of them dressed in leathers and fur animal skins; their jewellery fashioned out of bone and stone. They looked like a wild people; strong, cunning, and merciless when provoked.

Behind each of the homes, I could see small gardens. Giant statues representing what I assumed were Gods and Goddesses were placed beside most doorways. Cattle and other animals grazed the hills beyond. We passed in front of a small temple; the statue of a female who looked vaguely familiar towered above many of them. At her feet were vines and flowers planted at her base, growing around and up her legs and hips as if clinging to her. Quetz came and stood beside me as I stared up at her. His eyes twinkled as he studied me, and I felt a burst of warmth blossom in my chest, drawing my gaze to his.

Kyril and Quetz exchanged a look. "Who is she?" I asked. Quetz's eyes returned to mine. "The Goddess of Origin." An inscription was carved into the marble at the base beneath her feet, which the vines and flowers seemed to have deliberately grown around and not over. "What does it say?" I asked, staring down at the words written in some ancient runes I didn't understand. The hairs on the back of my neck rose as Quetz read it to me. "The rhythm of my heart beats as one with all that lives and dies. All creation answers to the aether of my being. I am the guardian of all souls, The Goddess of Origin."

After what felt like an eternity of walking beneath the scrutiny of the Eastern Guard's residents, we finally arrived at the castle- if that's what it could be called. There was a stone base, and rising at least half a dozen floors up, were intricately carved, enormous wooden archways and winding balconies. An enormous mote surrounded it and the gates, which were a monstrosity of stone and piked wooden beams, where several watchmen stood atop a high wall encompassing the castle, bowing as Nuala became discernible, the gates parted.

The guards at the gate dropped to one knee, their hands fisted over their hearts as their heads bowed in reverence with palpable sincerity. I scanned all of them: all manner of species, males and females alike- most of whom would never have been allowed to work in such a prestigious position before Nuala's reign. I couldn't help the swell of admiration and pride I felt for Nuala. Seeing the fruit of her efforts. The freedom and respect she'd afforded the 'lesser' classes across the realm.

Half a dozen guards rose, all dressed in fighting leathers and animal furs, and led us through two more gates until we finally reached the towering castle doors made of dark wood carved to depict violent scenes in battle. In the centre of the doors stood a beast of a man wearing a crown and wielding two large swords, surrounded by wolves- the largest of which towering behind him.

The wooden bridge beneath my feet hummed, snapping me out of my reverie at the linenfold relief of Batlaan, the lykanthir Lord of the Eastern Guard, as they opened the left door. The guards escorted us in a v-formation down a cavernous hallway lit with large aeternam lanterns that hung from a central beam in the arched ceiling, casting a warm amber glow over us.

We finally arrived at another large set of doors the guards posted beside and promptly opened. An enormous room with training dummies, swords, malices, bows and arrows, and a whole manner of other weaponry were mounted on the walls. Half a dozen doors on the other side of the room were already open to reveal a vast training field, equipment, and target dummies. In the distance, I could see at least a dozen snow-capped mountain peaks. The loud metal-on-metal clanging hammered my eardrums and pulled my gaze to a small group of males battling one huge one that appeared to border upon seven feet tall, who I assumed could only be Batlaan.

He wore nothing more than fighting leather trousers and boots, revealing muscles that bunched, flexed, and rippled in a rather mesmerizing way as he wielded two swords to fend off the other males. Their grunts and shouts filled the air between the clashing of their swords. The guards beside us led us to the open doors leading out onto the training field. The guards halted and stood silent sentry as we waited for the 'battle' to end.

Batlaan's right sword swept hard to his closest opponent, whose own sword flew through the air and squelched in the mud. Batlaan pressed forward against two tall males baring spears who were charging towards him in unison. Batlaan ran and faked right as he fisted his left sword and launched it through the air. The sword found it's home in muddy grass between the legs of his opponent, halting him in his trajectory, knowing full well that had it been a real battle it'd have been planted in his chest. Within the same breath, Batlaan leapt through the air in a high arc to the left- cutting the left opponent's spear in half before flipping through the air and appearing behind him and forced him to his knees.

Batlaan's gaze flicked to mine, and his lips parted, a tense but indiscernible look shuddering his gaze before it landed on Kyril, who apparently inspired an enormous grin. "Brother!" He shouted joyfully before his gaze shifted to Nuala. A coy grin formed, and he stepped from behind the already kneeling male and dropped to one knee, placing a closed fist over his bare chest, and bowed his head. The males on the field followed suit. "My Queen," Batlaan's voice rang, a gravelly baritone.

I looked over at her just in time to see a slight smirk tilt her lips as she gazed at the males kneeling in front of her, and even I drew satisfaction from it. Moments passed, and I could see a knowing, wicked grin form on Batlaan's face before he slowly rose his gaze to meet Nuala's. Her grin widened. As did Batlaan's, to display his perfectly white broad smile. For all the brutality he exuded, his smile was all masculine beauty and charm. "Is there anything else I may do for you while I'm on my knees, your highness?"

My eyes widened slightly, and I bit my cheek to hide my smile. I squeezed Kyril's hand and glanced over at him to find he seemed to be enjoying this just as much as I was. Quetz stepped forward beaming winsomely, "If you're offering." Batlaan met Quetz's amused gaze and burst into deep, rumbling laughter as he rose to his feet, his men following suit. "Batlaan, this is my new General, Quetzacoatl. He's the one who knows where we can find Eleni." Batlaan's expression grew serious as he stepped towards Quetz, extending a massive hand which Quetz accepted before being pulled into a bear hug. "You have my eternal gratitude," Batlaan said. Quetz returned the hug with equal fervor, my heartwarming at the sight of it.

Batlaan stepped towards Nuala and spread his arms wide, wearing a massive grin, "May I?" Nuala smirked. "Go on then." Batlaan gave another hearty laugh and swooped down to wrap up Nuala in another bear hug that lifted her off her feet. I caught Nuala indulging in a rare, unrestrained smile as her face peaked over a giant shoulder. She waggled her eyebrows, making Kyril and I both chuckle laughter.

Batlaan set her down on her feet, and when he turned to me, his gaze shifted briefly to Kyril for a moment as they communicated something. "My Emissary, Aurelia," Nuala offered. As I braced myself for a bear hug, he instead dropped to one knee, bowed his head and laid an open palm over a large pectoral. "It is an honour." My breath caught in surprise, and my cheeks reddened. I reached out to touch his shoulder and tell him to get up, but he grabbed my hand and touched it to his forehead. Kyril chuckled, and Batlaan's gaze flicked to him once again. Batlaan jumped to his feet and dove for Kyril, who swung his arms around Batlaan and clapped him on the back. "I missed you, you big bastard," Kyril laughed warmly. "And I, you, brother."

I watched as the two of them parted, taking no small amount of pleasure in the exceedingly warm welcome we had been given. Lisbet and Idra stood silently a few feet behind Nuala, who turned halfway towards them. "And these two... Lisbet and her mate, Idra. They'll be assisting us in finding Le Mont," Nuala spoke while holding Lisbet's eyes meaningfully.

Batlaan later led us, guards in tow, down a long hallway illuminated by torches. The watery sunlight shone in through the windows that had the most daedalian muntins I'd ever seen. Each window's wooden muntin had sweeping designs that depicted magnificent things of beauty, such as flowers and other flowing geometric designs. The most notable, however, was that of a beautiful woman with red hair surrounded by various flora and fauna. I couldn't help but gape as I stared up at her, and something about her seemed to stare back.

Batlaan and his guards stopped at a large, round mahogany door. "It would be my absolute pleasure if you all would feast with me this evening," Batlaan said, opening the door for Nuala, "I'll escort everyone to their rooms just down the hall if you'd like to bathe and relax while I get cleaned up. The feast is at dusk." Aurelia gave him a small coy smile as she reached out and pulled Quetz into her bedroom by the shirt collar. Batlaan gave a soul-warming chuckle. "My hero," Batlaan laughed. Even Nuala chuckled, biting her cheek. "See you in a few hours, your Lordship." Nuala shut the door.

Batlaan led Kyril and I, closely followed by Idra and Lisbet, down the hallway and stopped at a door only a few dozen feet beyond Nuala and Quetz's door and directed his words to Idra and Lisbet. "Thank you, Lord Batlaan," Idra offered. Batlaan smiled warmly, "See you at the feast." Batlaan, bearing a perennial and gentle grin, studied him for a moment before his eyes settled on Lisbet. "May I ask where you're from?" Lisbet, much to her credit, seemed entirely unfazed. "Originally?" Batlaan's grin widened. "Of course."

. . .

She studied him for a moment before she seemed to reach a conclusion. "Somewhere we've all been but never remember." Batlaan's perfect white teeth made an appearance as the corners of his mouth rose. "I should like to hear more about this place sometime. Perhaps... My guards are just in the hallway if you need anything at all." Batlaan bowed slightly and strode past Kyril and me, leading us further down the hallway until we reached another door much further than the first two.

Batlaan gave his guards a nod, and with that they turned on their heels, leaving the three of us alone. My gaze lingered on their backs before Kyril tugged me into the room after Batlaan, who shut the door behind us. The room had floors made of wide dark wood panels peppered with furry animal skin rugs that made my heart clench with sympathy for the poor creatures. Pointed ogee archways opened up to a balcony on one side of the room, a separate living area on the other, and what I assumed was the door to the bathroom.

"Thank you for the beautiful room," I said, almost absentmindedly, as I made my way towards the balcony, drawn by its majestic ocean view. "You're most welcome... Lady Aurelia." *That* pulled my attention, huffing a laugh. "I can assure you, I am no 'Lady'. Please, call me Aurelia." Batlaan hummed his approval and clapped his large hand on Kyril's shoulder. "I am truly happy for you, brother. If anyone deserves their mate, it's you... My mother is overjoyed to have you both visit us."

Kyril's eyes bore into me in a way that made me feel naked. "Oh? Will the high priestess be joining us for the feast?" He asked without taking his eyes off me.
Batlaan chuckled. "Now that the two of you are here? Most defi-

nitely." Batlaan turned his attention away from me to Kyril. "Do you remember the last time we saw each other?"

Kyril's soft smile slipped, drawing his eyes to Batlaan's.

"How could I forget."

A deep frown carved Batlaan's ruggedly handsome features, pain flashing in his deep blue eyes. Kyril placed a comforting hand on Batlaan's shoulder. "She'll soon be back at your side, brother." Batlaan grew silent, his eyebrows furrowing. After a moment, Batlaan bowed towards me at the waist. "I'll see you two at the feast."

21

I couldn't help but stare at Kyril's naked form even though I stood in front of a mirror trying to pull my own clothes on. He was eyeing the borrowed clothes of... whom or wherever Batlaan sent them. The clothes, all leather and furs, were the singular choice of fashion in the Eastern Guard. "The feel of your eyes on me is such a sweet caress, my fire," Kyril purred, turning to face me. He walked towards me, fisting a pair of leather trousers in one hand and in the other, a furry animal skin... Cape? Shawl? Whatever the equivalent for a massive battle-hewn male that makes him look like some dark forest dwelling warrior God would be, *it's that.*

He dropped them on the floor at my feet as I pulled the long sleeve of an off-the-shoulder dress over one arm. His heavy dick already swelling with its intent. He grabbed my hand to prevent me from pulling my dress on the rest of the way. "Allow me," he purred as he guided me back to the edge of a table. Kyril bowed his head, holding my gaze, before he took my already aching breasts in his large hands and brought his mouth to one, trailing firm, open-mouthed kisses across it before arriving at its peak, sucking it firmly and flicking his tongue over my hardening nipple. We both groaned simultaneously, and my hands rose to fist the soft waves of his dark hair. Wetness bloomed in my core. Kyril's nostrils flared, followed by a growl. *"Mmmmmm...,"* he sighed from around a soft mouthful of breast, "You have the most divine scent, Aurelia...." Powerless against the bonelessness he induced, my clutch on him loosened as he brought his mouth down on my other breast, flicking and sucking at my nipple. My only response was a whimper.

Kyril slipped one of his hands up beneath the long skirt of my dress, slowly gliding it up, up, up the inside of my thigh until he arrived at my wet slit. He froze at the feel of it and growled viciously, firmly fisting a handful of my skirt with his other hand. *"Gods, Aurelia...,"* he breathed, lifting the skirt of my dress up to stare down at my glistening entrance, "It hurts how breathtakingly beautiful your pussy is in every way. And how quickly she responds to my touch." Kyril lowered himself to one knee and firmly pulled me against his face, breathing in deeply, as he returned one of his hands to my dripping core, lightly caressing my throbbing clit. I lifted one of my legs, and Kyril draped it over his shoulder. *"Gods, Kyril...,"* I moaned breathlessly as he began to firmly tongue and suck at my clit.

After only a few moments, just as I felt as though my legs would surely buckle, he pushed me further back against the edge of the table and spread my legs wide just before he slipped two fingers inside me, curling them upwards, and began to move them in a 'come hither' motion. A breathy, high-pitched whimper rose from my lips, making him growl in male satisfaction from around the tiny bundle of nerves he was sucking between his lips. The flicking of his tongue matched the pace of the quickening movements of his fingers. After only a few moments, the pressure of his fingers became almost overwhelming but then suddenly a wave of energy crested within me-

and *out* of me- as my pussy spasmed around his fingers, and liquid gushed. I cried out softly, my eyes practically rolling in the back of my head as he prolonged my climax until the gushing subsided.

Kyril laid tender kisses and licks along my clit and slit, my eyes fluttering open as I laid boneless beneath him. His ministrations quickly had my arousal picking up again, and just as my hips began to writhe, my pussy yet again aching with need, he surprised me by lifting me off the table and throwing me over his shoulder, making me yelp in surprise. He took a handful of my asscheek in his hand and caressed it before smacking it firmly. I let out another sort of cry. "*Kyril...*" He gave my other ass cheek a firm smack followed by a tender caress. My core spasmed and clenched with the need to be filled by him. "What *are* you doing?" I half moaned, sounding far more pleased than I intended.

He laid me on the bed in front of him. "Spread your legs for me, my fire," he commanded huskily. An eyebrow of mine darted upwards. Kyril raised a challenging eyebrow in response. A coy grin played on my face, and I slowly began to part my legs. I grasped my breasts and arched my back, holding his gaze. A deep rumble sounded from Kyril's chest as his long, thick cock twitched with need.

I trailed my fingertips down from my breasts to my sopping wet core and began to swirl a fingertip over my pert bead. "Am I gonna have to do this myself, or are you actually gonna join me?" The corner of Kyril's mouth quirked upwards as his gaze seemed to penetrate me. His eyes dropped to the floor where my silk gown lay. He reached down to pick it up-

Riiiip.

"Hey!" I shouted indignantly, snapping out of my lust-induced haze. "I loved that gown!"

"I'll have another one made."

Riiiip.

"What the hell are you doing?!"

Kyril pulled a large strip of fabric away from what was left of my poor, beautiful gown and stalked to the side of the bed. He took one of my hands in his and bowed to kiss it gently before he began to tie the silk cloth around one of my wrists. He repeated the action with my other hand. And whilst I felt like I should vocalize some sort of protest at being made submissive to him, I couldn't actually muster the desire to do so. Instead, I watched him raptly as my pussy continued to make a small puddle on the duvet. *Gods help whoever has to clean this room after we leave...*

Kyril tied the remaining fabric around the bedpost before climbing onto the bed in front of me, where my legs had closed again. "Open," he commanded. I bite my cheek, already enjoying this game. I crossed my legs daintily. Kyril gave me a wicked grin as he reached towards the seam of my pussy to caress it teasingly. A soft moan escaped me, and I writhed against his hand, trying to squeeze my legs tighter together. He chuckled as he brushed a kiss against my lips. "Be a good girl, now...," he husked. As if possessing their own will, my legs parted for him. He rewarded me by gently slipping a finger inside me, and just like that, my legs parted further. "Like that?" I asked, holding his gaze through heavy lids.

"Mmhmm. You're such a good girl for me, aren't you?" Kyril purred as his thumb stroked my clit, sliding up and down between it and my entrance. My legs were already beginning to shake with anticipation. Kyril spread my legs further before leaning down to kiss, lick, and nip at my breasts as he aligned his heavy cock with my entrance. A continuous, high-pitched, breathy moan escaped me as he ever-so-slowly slid inside me until he was fully seated. My pussy spasmed at his thickness and length in gratitude. He growled around a mouthful of my breast just as he slowly began to pull out of me. My back arched, and my legs tensed- parting ever wider, toes pointing. *"Kyril... I..."*

My words were cut off as he pressed his lips against mine and a deep seated satisfaction filled me at tasting myself on *his* lips. Just as he withdrew the tip of his cock, he thrust back inside me. The tension in my body grew taught, and I couldn't help but bite down on his bottom lip. Hard. The taste of his blood blossomed on my tongue, and I sucked at it before releasing him, greedily licking his delicious blood on my lips. Kyril beamed at me, but the sight of his blood on his teeth made my stomach instinctively churn.

It had only been a couple days since the incident with Madame Yiruxat... His smile faltered, sensing my pain. "What's wrong, my fire? Are you not enjoying this? We can stop. Just say the word," he said, already reaching for my restraints. I tried to pull my restrained hands away from him. "No, I love it. I just was worried I may have bitten you too hard."

Kyril took my face in his hands and kissed me tenderly, "Never. I love the idea of you taking my blood. I want every part of me inside of you. The idea arouses me tremendously...." The truth of his words were evident in his massive erection, which was seated inside me to the hilt. "As does your tenderness and care." Kyril licked and nipped at my neck, hovering at my pulse point. I could feel his sharp canines elongating and pressing against my skin.

· · ·

He drew a hand to my breasts, caressing one of my peaked nipples. "Are you sure you're ok?" He whispered, starting to move gently inside me again. I felt like I was about to explode with need. My pussy gripped him firmly in answer as I drew my hips up. Kyril's hips jerked, and he groaned in response. "*Gods...* Your pussy is already so tight, but when you do that...." His voice trailed off as he continued to tease my pussy, which was absolutely *weeping* with need, from his achingly slow, deep thrusts.

Just when I thought the teasing couldn't get anymore unbearable, he withdrew entirely and fisted his hard, heavy cock and, in an upwards and downwards motion, began to caress my pussy from my slick entrance to my pulsating clit. A soft cry slipped from my lips as my hips writhed in desperation."*Please...,*" I breathed. I squirmed in my restraints, lifting my hips as I tightened my legs around his waist to force him inside me. Kyril stilled and became as immovable as a stone wall. He gave a dark chuckle. "So impatient." I glared at him but he seemed only endeared by it. "Perhaps, I need to draw more blood," I growled, still writhing my hips against he throbbing cock.

His eyes seemed to glow at my words. He pressed a fang to his bottom lip until blood spilled. My eyes widened briefly at the sight before he leaned forward and brought his mouth down on mine in a savage kiss, his blood trickling across my chest along the way. My back arched again as his blood pooled in my mouth, and I drank. Its honeyed, velvety, smokey flavour was worlds better than even the finest fae wine, and, as I took in more, euphoria filled my body and soul. My entire being tingled, and without him even thrusting, simply feeling his massive cockhead resting within my entrance was enough to have my pussy spasming as an orgasm blossomed within my core.

. . .

Finally, Kyril slid inside me in one long, hard, and deep thrust that tore another cry from my throat as my orgasm crashed over me. His thrusts steadily grew harder and faster with each stroke. My pussy clenched hard around him, and I felt even more wetness spilling from me. I'd have been embarrassed at just how much there was if I hadn't been shaking and quivering at the peak of my orgasm. *"Oh my... Gods... Kyril,"* I wept in ecstasy. Kyril's thrusts became rapid until I felt him grow impossibly harder and thicker inside me, as his seed spilled inside me. He groaned my name before sinking his teeth into the flesh of my breast, causing my orgasm to prolong even further. His arms wrapped around me, tightly holding me to his chest as his thrusts gradually became languid. He reached an arm up, and with one quick jerk, my restraints snapped free from the bedposts. I brought my arms over Kyril's head, resting my forearms on his broad, muscular shoulders. "I love you, Aurelia." "I love you, Kyril. With all my heart and soul." Kyril tucked a stray curl behind my ear and kissed me softly. "With every ounce of my being," he whispered.

A knock on the door sounded. "Fuck off, please," Kyril called out. "Right away, your Lordship. Lord Batlaan sent me to escort you to the feast. I will tell him you'll only be a moment." Kyril trailed kisses along my neck and collarbone. "Thank you so much!" I called out. Kyril took one of my nipples in his mouth again, making me arch in response. But I forced myself to take a fistful of his hair and pulled his head up. "We're never gonna leave this room if you don't stop," I implored, already feeling new wetness beginning to pool between my legs. He arched an incredulous eyebrow at me. "And why exactly would I want to leave this room?"

I chewed my cheek as I sat down in the oversized cushioned chair that Kyril pulled out for me at the gargantuan table in the banquet hall. A large band of musicians played a remarkable variety of wind, string, and percussion instruments. A pang of anxiety knotted itself in my chest as the drums grew to a heavy beat, reminding me of Pauperes Domos. Kyril sat beside me and placed a hand on my thigh, leaning into me to kiss the curve of my neck, hovering for a moment. "You ok, Nexus?" he whispered. His fingertips began to trace soothing circles on the top of my thigh. I took a deep breath, feeling my muscles relax and the tension ease a bit at the simple gesture. "Yeah... Just... This music... Sounds like home." Kyril's fingers stilled. "Pauperes Domos was never your home. I am your home. And you're mine. But I understand..." *"I still have nightmares about living in The Sapphires...,"* he added mind-to-mind. My gaze snapped to his. I couldn't even imagine what it must have been like returning to The Sapphires for Yiruxat... and everything that happened during that. I clutched his hand with both of mine and held his gaze as he spoke within me. *"I will always come for you. You will never be taken from me. In this life, and the next."*

Kyril brought his other hand to cup my cheek. Despite being surrounded by hundreds of people, it felt as though we were the only two people in the room. Everything else had just become white noise. *"And I for you."*

Heavy hands slipped over Kyril's and my shoulders. The two of us looked up to find Batlaan staring down at us, smiling warmly. "Do you think Eleni will be happy I've come for her? Even after all this time?" Kyril laid a comforting hand over Batlaan's, his expression growing anxious. "You're her nexus mate, brother. No amount of time can pass that will change that." Kyril's eyes gleamed with something I couldn't quite place. Batlaan studied Kyril's face, communicating something silently before he gave me an appreciative nod and slipped his hands away to take his seat in the centre of the table.

. . .

Kyril met my gaze as I asked in his mind, "What happened to her?" The muscles in Kyril's jaw feathered, the corners of his mouth tilting downwards. "Eleni was a half Lux Dryadalian shamanness. Her father, Emperor Lussathir, is the ruler of the entire realm... Her mother, however, was a human. Eleni was kidnapped 19 years ago during some off-world conflict between the Lux and Tenebris realms. They are still at war as far as we know... Batlaan went to Lux Dryadalis to seek her father's help, but he refused and nearly killed him. Her father blames Batlaan for kidnapping and keeping her 'insufficiently' protected here on Aeternia. Batlaan even went to the Tenebris Realm to find her, but he only ended up being taken prisoner for 8 months before he escaped, with Morwen's help, and during that time, he was told she was dead."

His words had me feeling like my chest was cracking open. I glanced at Batlaan laughing boisterously with Nuala and Quetz, who sat across from him. When I turned back to look at Kyril, I saw his eyes drawn across the room. He grinned, eyes lighting with amusement. "Care to greet h*is mother?*" I followed his gaze until it landed on a woman who stood around six feet. She had a trim, athletic build, and her long silvery hair fell in a mixture of loose waves and braids down her back. Her skin was significantly fairer than Batlaan's and seemed to have been made a canvas for ink. Unlike her compatriots, she didn't wear the same bone and stone jewellery. Only a feather hung from a plait of hair, and an elaborate silver choker collared her slender throat.

Her very presence seemed to radiate energy. As she stepped further into the room, the guests parted in a wave, all of them bowing as she passed. As soon as she turned toward us, her gaze locked with mine. I could see somewhat of a resemblance in Batlaan, but it made me assume he must share his looks with his father. Where Batlaan's features were defined and hard, they were also warm; his mother's features were all elegant but harsh lines and exuded a cool cunning. However, the way his presence took over a room and the power he projected was definitely a trait from his mother. They were both wildly intimidating. And it was made even more so by the fact that she looked only a handful of years older than me, but the power emanating from her felt ancient.

A grin slowly curled in one corner of her mouth, and she winked at me. "This should be fun," Kyril chuckled. Batlaan stood, his chair screeching across the stone floor, raising a silver chalice. "Mother! Look who's come to join us!" The group of us stood as his mother rounded the table and glided over to Batlaan. She bowed deeply facing Nuala, lowering herself to one knee. "Queen. You honour us." Nuala clicked her tongue, rolling her eyes. "Must you taunt me?" Morwen rose, laughing as she took Nuala in her arms. "What do you expect when you visit us so infrequently?" As they parted, Morwen scanned us all with keen interest, a smile blooming as her eyes landed on Kyril but faltering slightly when it landed on me. Her throat worked on a swallow before rushing toward us. "Oh. My. Goddess," she breathed exuberantly as she strode over to us and wrapped her long arms around me, taking me by surprise before moving on to Kyril and doing the same. She pulled back and shook her head at us, beaming. "Wonderful to see you, Morwen."

"You know I almost didn't believe Batlaan when he told me you were here."Her eyes fell on Quetz, Lisbet, and Idra. ""Your new friends are most fascinating."

Morwen's eyes were a dark silver that seemed to be illuminated from within. They studied me for several moments, and I felt the brush of her magic against my mind. It was a cool caress that seemed to consume all that it touched. I sucked in a sharp breath, and in the same moment, she withdrew it, giving me a soft smile that I guessed meant something. I just wasn't sure what. Her eyes gradually drifted back to Batlaan as he spoke. "Mother, I'd introduce you, but we both know you already know everyone's names, so I'll spare you," Batlaan said, turning towards the rest of us, "But for those of you who haven't yet met my Mother, this is Morwen, High Priestess and General of the Eastern Guard."

22

Kyril gave my thigh a soothing caress as Batlaan stood and thanked his town's residents for joining us, a handful of hours and at least a barrel of fae wine later. Morwen stood and stared down at me from across the table. Another serene smile gracing her face. The touch of her magic caressed my mind again, and I had to steel myself to suppress a shudder, but a small moan escaped my lips. Kyril's head snapped in my direction, arching a haughty eyebrow. He followed my gaze fixed on Morwen and shook his head knowingly. "Morwen... are you trying to steal my mate?" Morwen burst into a short laugh. "Who said anything about stealing?"

Batlaan led the group of us out of the dining hall, guards following, to another palace wing, where he brought us to a large sitting room replete with a six-foot fireplace, more fur rugs, floor cushions, and massive lounge chairs built to accommodate men of Batlaan's stature. Servants entered the room as we sat and poured an amber-coloured liquid into copper mugs. The sound of groaning wood had my head turning from the blazing fire to Batlaan, who was staring at Nuala.

. . .

"In the morning, we will leave for Eleni."

Batlaan posed the question making it sound more like a statement than a question. Nuala nodded.

"Yes, Batlaan. Thank you for your patience...."

"And the Sigillum?"

Nuala held out upturned palms and the air around them began to glow and warp briefly before a hefty, ancient tome appeared in her hands. The tome emanated a heavy power that made it feel like the air was thickening and grew so heavy I felt as though a tremendous weight had been placed on my chest.

Nuala took a deep, steadying breath as though it weighed far more than it appeared. "Clever of you to disguise it," she murmured, her eyes not leaving the tome. As Morwen took the tome from Nuala, the air around the tome shimmered briefly before the tome morphed into a large tree root of hybrid metal and wood that glowed a pale gold and green.

Morwen took a deep breath; a bead of sweat appeared on her brow before she dropped it onto one of the oversized armchairs and stared down at it. Batlaan's brow furrowed with concern as the chair groaned and then collapsed. "Damn it. That was my favorite chair," he frowned to no one in particular before he shifted his attention to Quetz.

"And you're sure she's in Caligo?"

Quetz gave a relaxed nod. "Indeed she is."

Batlaan heaved a sigh, studying him. "And she's ok?"

"I cannot read minds, but her life force is strong... Of that, I am sure."

Batlaan nodded to himself, seemingly lost in thought for a few moments.

"And after? What of this Le Mont?" Wisps of his incorporeal form rose around Quetz'z body, licking at his skin as if in agitation. "I know nothing of him. He has magic that eludes even me. It keeps me from knowing him." My stomach churned, and electricity crackled at my fingertips at his words. Kyril's arm curled around my waist as he pulled me into his side and kissed my temple.

Thankfully, Nuala cut off my escalating train of thought. "I had my alchemists put a tracking spell on it. So when Lisbet gives it to this dickhead 'Le Mont', and hopefully manages to do some kind of reconnaissance before she returns, we know where to find it, and her, should she need us. Then we'll travel to the remaining realms to warn the other Sigillum Guardians to join us in preventing Le Mont and his benefactors from collecting the rest. Best case and most unlikely scenario: they give up. Worst case, and most likely scenario, it starts a war."

Nuala's words hit me like an elephantine push kick to the chest. *A war...* The gravity of it seemed to settle into my bones in that moment. For some reason, I hadn't fathomed such a thing to be an outcome... And that was without the looming confrontation with the newly freed Pauperes Domosians... I took a deep breath that seemed to do nothing to soothe me. *Sweet Gods.*

It became apparent that everyone else in the room was also too busy reeling at this realization to speak. We all stood in stunned silence for several long moments before Nuala sighed heavily and tossed an apathetic hand up.

"On a happier note, at least if the world burns, we'll burn

together, ay?" Lisbet narrowed her eyes at Nuala, "You're detachment from preserving this life is worrisome."

Nuala shrugged, "Darling, I have a feeling you'll do enough worrying for the both of us. Come get me after you return from Le Mont." Nuala gave her a casual pat on the shoulder before making her exit. As though having foreseen this exchange, Quetz was already leaning in the doorway, waiting for her, bowing towards us all before making eye contact with me. "Try to get some rest. You know where to find me." He offered me a slightly strained smile that gave rise to my anxiety. Quetz didn't give strained smiles. His smiles were always warm and easy. Until now.

I sighed heavily, and Kyril's palm rubbed soothing circles in the middle of my back. I looked up at him gratefully. Are you as nervous about all of this as I am? He studied my gaze for a moment. Sometimes. But I know that no matter what happens, nothing will keep us apart. Not even death itself. If something were to happen to me, I would find my way back to you from the next realm. Just as Lisbet found her way here. Kyril's expression grew grim, jaw flexing. And, Gods above and below forbid, if something were to happen to you, I would end it all just to reunite with you. Tears filled my eyes as I stared up at him and leaned into his arms.

The heat of someone's stare had my head turning to find Morwen studying me with a knowing expression that only left me feeling unsettled. She gave me a nod before returning her attention to Batlaan, who was talking to Lisbet and Idra. Lisbet groaned. "I can feel cocksplat's magic tugging on me already, which means he's going to fold me in about 60 seconds. I'll see you all in the morning."

. . .

Morwen quickly turned back towards the Sigillum and removed its 'tome' glamour as she placed it into Lisbet's arms. A whoosh of air was instantly expelled from Lisbet's lungs at the weight and power of the Sigillum. "Fuck *me,* I swear this one's even heavier than the last." Idra pressed a kiss to her lips just before she winked out of thin air a moment later, leaving the rest of us staring at each other wrapped in a blanket of unease.

"Have you ever heard of this 'Le Mont'?" Kyril asked Batlaan. Batlaan shook his head. "No... which is unsettling considering how efficacious my spymasters are. So, either he has more than one alias, or... he's not from our realm."

23

I let the sound of Kyril's soft, rhythmic breaths soothe me as I laid in the dark, staring out through the balcony doors. Just as my eyes finally began to close, I felt the chilling touch of Morwen's magic, snapping them open again as her magic wordlessly beckoned me to her. She stood on the balcony, facing the tumultuous sea. My chest tightened in anticipation, and I held my breath as I attempted to silently climb out of bed.

I reached the door, taking hold of the handle. Before I could open it, she folded in front of me on the other side, reaching through it somehow and pulling me through it to the other side as though I were incorporeal. The breath was stolen from me, and I felt every molecule in my body tingle, lighten, and nearly disappear before reforming again. I fell into her arms as the molecular structure of my body reformed and regained its density and weight, all at once making me feel as though I weighed a ton.

· · ·

"What... in the gods' names... was that?" I whispered. Morwen chuckled softly. "I didn't want you to wake your hyper-vigilant mate." I shook my head, finally standing on my own. "No... What was that? I've only ever seen a wraith do such a thing." Her head quirked to the side. "It's called 'dissolution'. Not very many can do it. It's highly useful for clandestine activities and in places where folding is warded against. You'll soon remember how to do it yourself...."

I couldn't bother to ask her what she meant and instead shuddered at the memory of Yiruxat's caves and Hotep, her phantom-witch-servant-person, whatever she is. Morwen cackled, "There's no need to tremble with fear over that old sack of bones. She's just old and creepy. Nothing more. Don't let your imagination get the best of you; you have more power in a single hair follicle than she has in her entire being." My eyebrows furrowed as I let out an awkward laugh. "That's very generous of you to say, but I think once you get to know me, you'll probably realise you've gravely overestimated my abilities." Morwen rolled her eyes. "Darling, I've known you for far longer than you're remembering. Come with me."

Before I could respond, she firmly took hold of my hand and pulled me behind her as she stepped forward. A wall of energy nearly knocked the breath out of me, and I gasped as we stepped into what I could only describe as a void- a space in which it was black from the absence of light, but I could still see far into the distance, revealing stars, galaxies, and nebulas. And in the span of a blinking eye, she stepped forward again, barreling us through another wall of energy to reveal a labyrinth of stairs made of grass and flowers and clouds where sphynx-like creatures roamed, glancing up at us with an expression that resembled a pleased recognition.

.   .   .

Morwen took another swift step, and we were walking atop a crystalline sea with lilac waters. And in the millisecond it took my brain to process the gargantuan trees standing at a shore in the distance and the airborne ships in the sky, Morwen dragged me forward again. A crushing weight of energy settled on top of me, and freezing winds bit into my skin.

A dark sky of purples, blues, and blacks illuminated the mountains of stone and ice surrounding us as we stepped past a tall, dark, powerful figure with piercing blue eyes and sharp elven features whose gaze flicked from Morwen to me and a glittering smile filled his face as he winked. *At me.* My jaw dropped. She pulled me forward again, and we now stood atop an ice peak. I looked down at my clothes to see I was now wearing furry leathers and boots. I'd have said thank you, but I was at such a loss for words at whatever sort of travelling we'd just done, stunningly similar to how I'd travelled with Quetz and where we could possibly be.

My body, perhaps soul, seemed to be adjusting to the weight of the energy around us. "What are we doing here?" I shouted over the deafening winds, wrapping my arms tighter around myself. *'Here'* being what I assumed was Tenebris Dryadalis. Morwen stepped forward and drew the furry hood tighter around my head. The gesture further endeared me to her.

She studied my eyes intensely for a few moments. I could feel snow beginning to collect on my eyelashes. "... Even I can't see who put this veil over you, but it's time we remove it." My eyebrows furrowed at her words. "Morwen... I'm a little confused... What view? And what exactly are we doing here?" She sighed, shaking her head. "All will be made clear... I'm sorry to force this on you so soon, but you'll thank me later," Morwen shouted over the howling wind and snow.

· · ·

I shook my head, quickly becoming exasperated, just as the dark elf we'd passed earlier winked into being beside her. His handsome features were cold and angular, and he stood at least a foot and a half taller than even Morwen, his form muscular in a lithe, elegant way. His hands alone were longer than my head. He was dressed in clothing that seemed better suited for perhaps a chilly autumn stroll. Not a below-freezing blizzard. His skin a stony blue.

He studied me briefly, grinning, before bowing at the waist. "Your Majesty." I huffed an odd laugh, but before I could respond, Morwen's voice sounded in my head, one voice and a thousand voices all at once as she spoke to the Tenebris Elf. "Nox, anchor me." Nox stepped behind Morwen and grasped her firmly by the shoulders. A tether between them began to glow a brilliant dark gold with swirling purplish hues ranging from lilac to black. *Nexus Mates.* For a heart-beat, I wondered if Morwen and Nox met when she helped Batlaan escape all those years ago after being captured when he'd been searching for his kidnapped mate, Eleni. Perhaps Nox had even helped them.

Those thoughts were cut off as a sword of glimmering black stone appeared in her left hand. Morwen took a fortifying breath and straightened, her eyebrows pulling together. "Sorry about this." My eyes widened in shock. "Mor-." My words were cut off in a wet, guttural groan that gurgled with blood as she plunged the obsidian sword in the centre of my sternum. Before my brain could even process the pain, I looked down at the massive blade protruding from my chest. Only then did the searing pain register. Unlike anything I'd ever known burned through me like fire.

· · ·

My knees buckled and dropped to the snow. Morwen still held tightly onto the handle of the sword, creating an even more excruciating pain. Choking on my own blood, I tried to grip the blade with my hands, but it was slick with my blood, and I only succeeded in cutting open my hands. Lilac and sky blue flames erupted from the blade and travelled down towards me.

I looked up at Morwen in horror to see that she was somehow sweating in the blizzard that seemed to increase its intensity. She was murmuring something in a language I didn't understand, and the tether between her and Nox grew brighter. The flames on the blade drew closer to me. Instinctually, I tried to pull away the closer they got, but I was only met with more soul-shattering pain that held me in place. I tried to scream, but all that came out was a wet choking sound. Morwen's chanting became louder, and Nox joined her.

The flames rushed towards me and engulfed me, but instead of more pain, I felt relief until there was no pain at all. A wall of these painless flames surrounded me, and foreign runes appeared. Morwen swiftly pulled the sword from my chest, and Nox came to stand behind me and laid me down on the snow. The flames still burned brightly around me but did no harm. I felt warm and at ease. But tired... so, so, so tired. I felt a tingling sensation and looked down to see the flames filling the hole in my chest. My vision blurred until all I could see were the darkened silhouettes of Morwen and Nox. I could feel myself fading, yet somehow I didn't care.

My eyes slipped shut, and fleeting images began to play before me. Memories. Memories of battles and wars, lovers and debauchery, suffering- mine and others, thousands died before me, and I reached into their corporeal forms and gently drew out their incorporeal bodies, their spirits, and my spirit led them to the realms beyond.

More memories passed, and I watched as I gave life to plants and creatures of all kinds. I travelled across otherworldly landscapes and architecture of breathtaking beauty until I arrived at a place that looked vaguely familiar... Aeternia. Thousands of memories washed over me until I saw a familiar face. A fae-hybrid male with dark, warm features... *Kyril.*

My mind and my soul became consumed with the memories filling me of Kyril and me together. For years. Nuala, Morwen, Batlaan... They were all my chosen family. We fought in the war together. My heart agonised for them, especially Kyril, that he had to suffer the grief of my death for centuries alone. *I* was the nexus mate he'd had during the war. Who had been killed? A vision, a memory I'd recently lived in a dream returned to me: Kyril's warm body safely curled beside mine. He tugged me into his body, and I fell back asleep. Only to awaken sometime later to the sound of metal singing through the air as a sword arched above my head, and before I could react, the stranger- a powerfully built male with flowing tendrils of white hair despite his youthful appearance- brought his gleaming, golden sword down on my neck.

The image of the white-haired male, a near copy of Kyril, standing in Kyril's office was shown in my mind. *Caelus.* Kyril's uncle... I couldn't fathom it...

The weight of a thousand suns bore down on me, and a strangled cry filled my ears. My eyes burst open to see Morwen and Nox shielding their eyes as they knelt beside me. I sat up, clutching at my chest where Morwen had impaled me, but the hole had already healed and instead found a bright white light radiating from me. My panic lessened, and the light dimmed as I took in more and more life-giving breaths.

.   .   .

Gut-wrenching sadness shook me to my core and aeons of joy, suffering, and experience. Knowledge of things I'd always known filled my mind and overwhelmed me. The sheer insanity of it made me laugh in a way that gradually grew into hysteria. Promptly followed by uncontrollable sobbing at the heartbreak of it all.

Morwen and Nox exchanged glances as she wrapped me in her arms as I wept. "There was no other way," she whispered in my ear. I nodded as I hugged her back, tears still streaming down my face. "I know... It's so good to see you again, Wennie." Morwen pulled back to look into my eyes, and I saw hers, too, filled with tears. I leaned forward and kissed her cheek. "Thank you," I said as I let go of her and stood, dusting off the layers of snow caked to my furry leathers. Nox gave me a knowing look, grinning winsomely before bowing at the waist. "I've heard so much about you. It's truly an honour to meet you, your-" I raised my hand. "Aurelia. Please." Nox studied me, still grinning as he straightened. "As you wish."

The massive blood stain on the front of my coat was already beginning to freeze. And along with it, my tears. Which were now being replaced by rage. Rage for Caelus.

"Do you know of a male named Caelus? He's from another realm... Although, I'm not sure where." Morwen and Nox's brows furrowed. "No?" Morwen spoke for both of them. My jaw clenched at the thought of him. "Kyril's uncle." They seemed even more confused. "And what about him?" "He's my murderer." And undoubtedly the one who put this 'veil' over me to prevent me from remembering myself, him, or anyone else from my life.

24

I held my breath, tempering the newfound energy - and the anger- radiating from me in my attempt not to disturb or worry Kyril as I stood beside the bed deliberating whether or not to wake him and tell him what I'd discovered. "Are you injured, my fire?" Kyril's words were laced with amusement. I could practically feel his gorgeous, smug grin in the darkness. Despite my anxiety and rage, merely the sound of his voice seemed to quell it. And I couldn't help but laugh, finally exhaling my held breath. "How long have you been watching me?" I asked quietly, lowering myself to the edge of the bed. Kyril hummed, pleased with himself, and I felt it in my core. "Long enough to see you creep *in* and *out* of here with Morwen. What you two were sneaking around for, I do wonder."

I shook my head, willing my furry, blood-stained leathers away before I scared him. "You are *such* a turd." I felt Kyril's soft, rumbling laugh. I caressed the aeternam lamp on the end table beside me, bringing it to life in a soft amber glow, revealing my nude form to him. Kyril laid on his side but rose at the sight of me to prop himself up on his elbow, causing the duvet to slip several tantalizing inches down his chest to his waist. His eyes glowed and flickered with hunger, and I could see the thick length of him grow beneath the covers. "My stunningly perfect mate," he husked, "Are you-"

His words cut off as he took me in, nostrils flaring, before abruptly folding to stand beside me. I gave a small yelp, clutching my chest. "*Kyril.*" He grabbed me by the arms and lifted me, drawing my chest to his face and licked between my breasts and growled. "Why is your chest covered in *your* dried blood, Aurelia?" I saw barely tethered rage beginning to radiate from the depths of his eyes. "Who harmed you?"

"Everything is as it should be. Let me reassure you, my soul." Doubt flickered in his gaze, but he leaned forward, and I laid my hands on him, willing soothing, calming energy into his body and spirit. "Aurelia... What..." His grip on me loosened, and his breathing slowed, gazing down at me in confusion.

I willed what I'd worn the night we met, the night of the Summer Solstice celebrations all those years in the Eastern Guard. The crown of whorling silver horns- to represent the true immortality of the soul and protection I offer it- that wove into my hair and over my brow. The collar of snaking silver metal that curved around the base of my neck and spilt over my shoulders, leading the eyes to the brassiere of skeleton hands, one cupping each breast, in honor of the dead, whose souls I undertake. The silvery grey silken skirt, with hip-high slits, draped around my waist, held in place by snaking silver bands, and spilt to the floor. I remained barefoot for practical purposes.

Kyril's lips parted, his breath whooshing out of him, as his eyebrows drew together as if in pain. He shuddered, eyes filling with tears, and shook his head in disbelief. "How?" He breathed. I reached up, caressing his cheeks, and began to pour my memories with Morwen and Nox in Tenebris. His eyes slipped shut, and his breathing quickened. His muscles trembled beneath me as he watched Morwen impale me with her sword. Tears fell down his cheeks, and he clutched me to him. *"My fire,"* Kyril choked out. "I'm never leaving you again, my soul," I whispered as I laid tender, reassuring kisses across his chest.

Anxiety knotted itself in my stomach as I silently deliberated whether or not to tell Kyril just this second about his uncle. We needed to retrieve Eleni... And his uncle probably wasn't even in Aeternia. My mind clamoured, trying to conceive of why his uncle would even want me dead in the first place... Was there some reason he hadn't wanted Naula to win the war? Perhaps he hadn't wanted the 'lower fae' to rise...

Kyril took my head in his hands and pressed a painfully tender kiss to my lips. "Are you ok, fire?" I had to force my throat to not work on a swallow, still holding up the internal wall to keep him from feeling my anxiety and unease that the thoughts of his uncle were inducing. I managed to nod and slid my hands up his firm abdomen until they rested on his broad chest. His eyes were red and still swollen with fresh tears that spilled freely.

Kyril pulled me even tighter to him and buried his face in the curve of my neck. A choked sob escaped him and he shuddered against me as though all the years of mourning my death since I 'd been killed in the war- *by his uncle-* were finally being healed. I determined I didn't want to exasperate the torrent of emotions he was experiencing and pushed thoughts of Calaeus away as I continued to push loving, soothing energy into him, and after a few minutes, his breathing evened out. "Words cannot even begin to express how much I missed you, Aurelia. You don't understand... I felt as though I couldn't breathe- like nothing imbibed would sate my thirst... I felt as though my soul had been torn in half. Had died beside you. I wished for death," he spoke hoarsely, his face still buried in my neck.

"I know, I'm so sorry," I whispered, holding back my own tears. Kyril shook his head, and he finally pulled back. "No. You don't understand... Those dreams. Those premonitions I had after you'd died... That was the only reason I didn't...," Kyril paused. He didn't need to finish his sentence. I already knew what he would say. I took his face in my hands and drew his face to mine. "I'm here now, my fate," I spoke softly. He shook his head. "I have never known such pain...."

Kyril's throat worked on a swallow before taking a deep breath, trying to calm himself. I gingerly pressed my lips to his, wrapping my arms around him. He straightened, and my feet left the ground. He pulled up, and I wrapped my legs around his waist; my warm, wet core pressing against the hardening length of him. We both moaned at the feel of it. "Do you prefer this form or my last?"

Kyril groaned as he inhaled my scent deeply at my neck. "Aurelia... I've had two hundred years to adjust to this new form... I *love* this one just as much as the last, not only because you smell the same, and they bear a striking resemblance, but because it contains the same soul. The soul of my Nexus. The Goddess of Origin I fell in love with from the moment I first laid eyes on you... standing beyond the flames at Morwen's summer solstice celebration all those years ago when she was still the former King's favored seer."

I pressed my forehead to his as the memory filled my mind. *Fae, vampire, human, changelings, and other immortals of all kinds danced beneath the full moon. Bonfires peppered the open field that laid beyond the stone homes with thatched roofs. The Eastern Guard. I stood beside Morwen and Batlaan, sipping fae wine, as we spoke mind-to-mind regarding our desires to bring peace to the realm and end indentured servitude. Warm, tingling energy reached out to me in a gentle caress. My breathing stilled as I felt the pulling of a cord, shifting my attention across the flames of the bonfire to the large silhouette of a man standing on the other side of it watching me with those burning ember eyes, basking me in the depth of their heat. A corner of his mouth quirked up, and we held each other's gaze for a few moments in which the world seemed to still and fall away. Kyril.* He'd been dressed in the same attire as when we'd last gone to Nuala's Summer Solstice celebration.

My heart filled to bursting, eyes watering at the memory. "I could feel you," I whispered. "And I, you," Kyril breathed, "Your soul called to me from The Sapphire Mountains. It woke me from my sleep." I pulled back to look at him. "You never told me that," I laughed dubiously. Kyril grinned. "I wanted you to think I was cool and was trying my best to not seem overly eager." I laughed, kissing him sweetly on his lips and cheeks. "Never," I whispered against his neck between kisses. Kyril hummed his appreciation too soon. "How could I have ever thought you were 'cool'?" I grinned, nipping at him playfully.

Kyril chuckled huskily, burying his face in my neck and biting gently. "We'll see how cool you are when you're writhing with need and coming undone beneath me." Humming excitedly, I licked the shell of his ear. "Mmmmm, I can't wait," I purred before sucking his ear lobe into my mouth. He growled, and it spurred me into grasping him by his hair as I began to hungrily kiss his cheeks, his temples, his nose, his jaw.

· · ·

Kyril turned to lay me on the bed, my clothes vanishing in the process, as he trailed kisses down my neck to my breasts, where he captured one of my nipples in that hot, talented mouth of his, kissing, sucking, and teasing it with his tongue while he slid his huge, gorgeous dick slowly back and forth on top of my clit. A high-pitched moan escaped me as every nerve ending in my body lit up at the dual sensations. *"Nothing has ever felt as glorious as you,"* I breathed, my eyes slipping shut. "Open your eyes, Nexus...."

I did as he bade me, and I felt my soul falling into his fathomless eyes that glowed a dark fiery shade of flames. He leaned back, positioning himself at my entrance that was already throbbing and aching for him to fill me, slowly pushing just the broad head of his cock inside me as he leaned back on his heels. The sensation was so incredible it forced me to suck in a breath. He groaned in ecstasy. *"Sweet Gods, Aurelia..."*

We held each other's gaze as he continued those shallow thrusts that managed to stimulate the inside *and* outside of me in the most exquisite way. He drew my hands to his heartbreakingly beautiful lips, one at a time, to kiss and lick my fingertips. I'd never even considered them an erogenous zone, but somehow the way he did, it made my core clench around his cockhead, as if my pussy were trying to pull him deeper inside me.

The beginnings of an orgasm began to rise, and I found my body tensing in anticipation. Kyril growled with pleasure, his pace picking up slightly. My breath came in shallow, soft pants accompanied by moans that, had I not been on the cusp of orgasm, I might have been embarrassed. "My fire, if you continue to make these beautiful, little noises and grip my cock with that divine pussy of yours, you're going to force me to spill before-."

. . .

I cried out, cutting him off, as the coiling energy burst making my pussy spasm powerfully around him. Kyril grinned, gripping my hips and turned his thrusts long, hard, and deep as he licked his thumb and brought it to my clit to stroke me as he slammed into me. "So soon? And here I was trying to take my time with you," he husked.

A smile curled my lips as I barely managed to speak amidst my now waning orgasm, hips writhing slowly. "It was... a valiant... effort... my soul." He held my gaze, watching me come undone beneath him. His body tensed, and his hard thrusts became languid and deep as something that sounded like the most seductive mixture of a groan, a moan, and a roar all in one burst from him. "*I love you, Aurelia...,*" he breathed as he filled me with his seed, pumping into me. There was so much of it, I could feel it spilling out of me which only further prolonged my climax. "*With all my heart and soul,*" I cried softly.

25

Callused hands slid over my stomach before gently tucking me into a warm, hard body. I sighed my pleasure and draped my arm over the one embracing me as I scooted further into Kyril by snuggling my hips against his hard length. His lips trailed kisses across my shoulder. "Good morning, my fire." Kyril's voice was deep and gravelly from disuse. "My soul," I whispered, still half asleep. The night's events fluttered through my mind, and I found myself taking a deep breath at the weight of it all. And Calaeus' face filled my mind. I needed to tell Kyril...

Just as I was about to tell him, a deep intuitive concern rose for Lisbet. I opened my senses to feel for her in Batlaan's castle, but I couldn't feel her. I immediately searched beyond for her and felt... nothing. Panic filled my veins. Kyril abruptly rose and pulled me onto my back. "Aurelia." My fear contorted his face with worry. My throat worked on a swallow, and I sat up. "Lisbet..." The sun was barely above the horizon. I reached out for her with my senses again. For her spirit. Something. Anything. I should have been able to at least feel her spirit even if Le Mont had somehow discovered she was working with us and killed her. Something was very wrong. "I can't feel her," I breathed.

Batlaan, Nuala, Quetz, Idra, Morwen, and Nox were already in Batlaan's war room when Kyril and I burst through the doors, tailed by two castle guards. Idra was openly weeping. I chewed my cheek. His grief was a palpable thing. Kyril gripped my hand in response. All of them, except Idra, who probably didn't yet realize who I was and was experiencing too much grief to care, bowed at our entrance. I raised a hand to stop them. "What happened to the tracking spell?" I asked tensely. Idra sobbed as he shook his head, "There's something blocking it." My stomach twisted into painful knots. I could only think of one thing that would nullify the tracking spell so thoroughly. Perhaps Le Mont was encasing them in palladium. Or keep me from feeling her spirit. A palladium collar.

Much to my surprise, Nox was the one comforting Idra, his hands on his shoulders murmuring reassurances to him. Idra burst into a violent sob, and Nox pulled him against his chest, wrapping his arms around him. "Shhhhh. We're gonna find her, and you'll be reunited soon enough. I promise...," Nox soothed. Idra sagged in his arms, his eyes slipping shut, and his ragged sobs suddenly cut off. Nox took a deep breath and laid him on a large table with scattered parchment and maps atop it.

"Fuck *me*...," Nox sighed, shaking his head. Morwen rolled her eyes at him. Nox gave her an incredulous look. "What? You should be thanking me. How were we supposed to get anything done with him wailing like that?" "You do realize we're definitely gonna need him to help us, being a draconi and all, right?" Nox leaned a thigh against the table, crossing his arms, making an exaggerated facial expression. His words spoken in a silly, mocking tone. "*You do realise we're* definitely *gonna need him to help us....*" Morwen pursed her lips, trying not to laugh. Nox grinned wickedly, his long, muscled legs closing the distance between them in one step, and took her face in his long hands to kiss her. Morwen melted against him.

Batlaan cleared his throat, shifting his gaze to Kyril and I. "Your majesty-." My face scrunched as I gave him a disbelieving look. "Why? Who are you?" I chuckled in disbelief. The male was like a brother to me. He gave me an appreciative smirk. Quetz's enormous knowing grin caught my eyes. "*I told you it was all within your grasp,*" he cooed within my mind. Tears pricked my eyes. All I could manage was a nod and a sombre smile. "*You did, Quetz. And I have no idea how I'll ever be able to repay you.*"

Quetz chuckled in a way that made everyone turn to give us suspicious looks at having a private conversation. "*Oh, I do. Give it about 200 years or so,*" was Quetz's only, enigmatic, reply. My eyes narrowed dubiously at him, a corner of my mouth quirking upwards. *200 years... Where would we all be in 200 years?* Kyril's arm around me tightened slightly, snapping me out of my thoughts, having felt my overwhelmed emotions through our tether. I felt his mind caress mine in gentle question, and I caressed his in return. I gave a short laugh, shaking my head. "So, all of you knew this *whole* time?"

The group of them eye darted between each other, grinning sheepishly. My eyes slid to Nuala as she folded her arms with displeasure. "Is that all you have to say to me? After all these-." Nuala's words were cut short as I folded in front of her- or rather on top of her- and wrapped her in my arms. The two of us fell to the ground with a heavy thud and the air whooshed out of her lungs. I straddled her and held her face in my hands as I began smothering her face in kisses. "Sorora." *Sister.*

Although we'd been born of different parents, Nuala was more of a sister to me than any of my siblings...My kisses stilled as I realised how still Nuala had become, and when I opened my senses to her, I felt pain. I pulled back to look down at her and saw her eyes swollen with tears. My eyes stung in response, and I leaned down again to hold her in my arms. I squeezed my eyes shut and felt the split-second breathlessness that comes with folding. I opened my eyes when we arrived in mine and Kyril's room in Batlaan's castle. Nuala shook in my arms as she stifled sobs. I rolled to the side and pulled her in close to me, kissing her forehead.

"I swear to the gods if you ever dare to fucking die on me again, I'll fucking kill you," Nuala sobbed into my chest. Tears freely streamed down my cheeks as a laugh bubbled out of me. Images of Calaeus filled my mind again, and I wanted so desperately to tell her. Just as I opened my mouth to say something, Nuala pulled back to look at me incredulously. "You think I'm joking?" I couldn't help but grin through the heartache. And thoughts of Caleaus. Nuala bit her cheek, trying to stifle her own laughter, and failed. "You know I'll never forgive you," she said, laughing through her tears. "I know, my love," I cooed, stroking her hair back. Nuala sighed heavily, relaxing as I pushed soothing, loving energy into her. "Thank you," she said softly.

My worry for Lisbet superseded the rage for Calaeus. As soon as we recovered from our crying a few minutes later, we folded back into the war room. Idra was still unconscious on top of the strategy table. "We have no idea where either Lisbet or the sigillum are?"

Morwen shook her head grimly. "I attempted to divine where he and Lisbet are in the Sentient Waters, but he's done something to prevent us from seeing. Are you able to tell if she's at least alive still?"

I bit my cheek, taking another heavy breath, trying to open my senses up to search for Lisbet, but I only felt emptiness on the other side. Much like when Kyril had been captured by Yiruxat. Unease spread through me like a droplet of poison in a glass of water. "No." I glanced towards Quetz, but he shook his head tensely. *Fuck.* Batlaan continued, "Not even my spymasters have heard of this 'Le Mont', it's strongly indicative that he's probably not even from Aeternia. Perhaps someone on Caligo will know of him."

We folded onto a sandy shore where phosphorescent sea creatures and flora of all shapes and sizes swam, crawled, or drifted in the lazy tide. A row of three moons, each in a different phase, illuminated the black and purple sky. A jungle silhouette and palace stood to our left. Strange music with heavy bass and sensual rhythms blared from beyond the jungle. I hadn't heard this type of music before... Which was highly unsettling considering I was practically as old as time. It sounded vaguely... artificial and unnatural yet tribal with heavy thumping bass. *Peculiar...*

Nuala and Quetz seemed to look around in unified wonder at our surroundings. Nox had an unconscious Idra slung over his shoulder. Nox seemed wholly unburdened by this, as though Idra weighed no more than a handbag. However, he was beginning to 'come to' and gasped awake. I laid a soothing hand on him to prevent any overwhelming emotions from rising. "We're on our way to find her. Stay calm." As clarity returned to him, determination filled his eyes, and he gave me a silent nod as Nox set him on his feet.

As we all turned towards the jungle behind us, the silhouette of dark towering buildings loomed in the distance, and beyond that, the mountains. This place felt different. Far different than I remembered. I opened my senses to feel my surroundings. Batlaan stepped closer to me. "You still feel her here? She's alive?" Searching my face for confirmation of what Quetz had promised. I glanced up to find Batlaan's eyes bright and wild with hope. With soul-deep need. Restless, nervous energy was pouring out of him in waves. I gave him a reassuring nod. "We're going to find her, Batlaan. Don't worry. I feel her too. Her life force is strong." Batlaan's throat worked on a hard swallow. The tense expression on his handsome features softened. Tears pooled in his eyes, his jaw working. My gaze snapped in the direction of the jungle. "We are not alone."

At that, a wall of muscled creatures stepped forward from the shadows. "Your Majesties," the closest one spoke and bowed at the waist. Those beside him followed suit. He held out his hand, and a flame appeared from above, giving us a better look at them. Half a dozen Caligoan Royal Guards dressed in loincloths and silver cuffs stood in front of us. Some had skin as black and shiny as tar, while others had nearly translucent skin. A shimmering gleam flickered around them- a ward. "The Queenes await your presence." The guards flanked us and led us down a garden path of tremendous, glowing flora as petite fairies flitted from plant to plant, tending to them.

The energy here was strange... Massively diminished from the last time I'd been here. My words filled their minds. "Has something catastrophic happened here? Why do I sense such little life?" Nox gave a humorless laugh. "Catastrophic is certainly one word to describe it." Morwen elaborated. "The King you knew a few centuries ago was usurped by his two generals, Ka and Lalaa. They go by one name and work in tandem, Queen KaLalaa...They had a hard time gaining public support, so when they began publicly executing those who opposed them, much of the Caligoan population sought exile elsewhere... That's when the royal alchemists began creating these... shells. Most of the realm has been abandoned." Oh my... "Shells?" Nox shook his head. "You'll see." "And what happened to King Dorcas?" The image of his face's soft, delicate features filled my mind. I could feel his life force energy vaguely. Somewhere in Terrenea... Nox slid his gaze towards me as if reading my mind. "Rumor has it he sought exile in the Terrenean realm."

The human realm. Although numerous gods and goddesses had chosen to make it somewhat of a home, exceedingly few other immortals had dared to live there. The humans from Terrenea were vicious and cunning, violent. Perhaps due to their vulnerability, fragile bodies, and short lifespans it made them most unwelcoming towards most immortals out of fear. The few immortals who had dared to venture there were either slaughtered or lived in hiding. I made a conscious note to myself to try and find King Dorcas after all this was over. He had been a kind and benevolent male, and a just ruler. If he had chosen to seek exile in Terrenea, it was probably out of desperation. Perhaps Nuala would be willing to let him seek exile in Aeternia.

We passed through a peculiar wall of pink neon light and an archway that led through another hall winding around a courtyard. The large glowing, transparent face of a slender woman appeared, hovering in front of us. "Welcome to the Royal Palace of Caligo, where all your dreams can become your reality," the see-through talking head spoke, "Our Majesties KaLalaa are most magnanimous. All the wilds of your imagination are possible here on Caligo when you pledge your eternal allegiance to Queen KaLalaa: The most glorious rulers of all the nine realms...." I couldn't hide my sneer of disgust as I spoke to Nox again, mind-to-mind. "Eternal allegiance? And how exactly are they making everyone's dreams come true?"

Nox's grimace matched my own. *"Depends on what they desire. If it's simply a life of wealth and luxury, they are free to live in the palace for their hedonistic pursuits or through the dreamscape... The majority of the inhabitants here spend most of their lives asleep while KaLalaa's magic works in unison to make their unconscious life more of a reality than waking life. And in return, KaLalaa either feeds off their magic at all times, or they have them serve like this,"* Nox nodded to the guards.

My stomach churned at his words. "And what sort of creature is this? I sense no life force attached to this hologram, past or present." Morwen and Nox exchanged amused looks. "That's because it's one of their shells," Morwen replied, "Something that gives the outward illusion of being alive but in actuality has no life force... Just wait until you encounter the ones given form...." Anxiety clawed at the back of my mind wondering what to anticipate.

The guards led us through a polished stone palace decorated in colours similar, artificial imitations to ones I'd only ever seen in the lands across the seas in Aeternia centuries ago, where the flora was as beautiful and wild as its fauna and its people. Instead of traditional paintings and other artistic mediums, it was decorated with more of the *shells* that were in constant motion- dancing, swimming, walking, and even simply watching with deceptively sentient eyes.

The guards led us through a final set of metal double doors and into a cavernous smokey room where one side was open to the elements via balcony that overlooked the beach we'd just come from. Large pillows and cushions the size of beds peppered the floor beside low tables where groups of three and four drank, smoked, and fucked. I sighed inwardly and exchanged glances with Batlaan, Nox, and Morwen.

Tinkling laughter peeled through the room, drawing my eyes to the dais at the far end of it. I hadn't even noticed a dais because I'd been too entranced by all the hedonism around us. "Truly, this is a blessed day! A Goddess stands before you! Kneel!" The participants of the orgies surrounding us ceased their ministrations, a few doing so with the unmistakably wet 'popping' sound of a mouth abruptly leaving a phallus or vulva, and brought their hands, heads, and knees to the floor. Two women, one highly androgynous, the other more effeminate, stood and bowed as we approached.

The more effeminate of the two, Ka, I sensed, wore a pale lilac skirt with high thigh slits and a silver metal brassiere that enhanced her cleavage. Her skin the color of midnight and painted with delicate silver geometric designs on her arms, neck, and face beneath her eyes. Lalaa was dressed in loose, dark pants gathered at the ankle and had slits through the legs that revealed her muscular legs. A simple silver band wrapped around her chest, covering little more than her nipples. Matching silver cuffed the biceps of her toned arms. She was tall and imposing, with an athletic build. Her hair was shorn close, only the top had any length to it and swooped down near one cat-like, crystalline blue eye. She gave us a crooked smile, a long scar cutting through the left side of it.

She eyed Batlaan. "I know why *you're* here." Batlaan was nearly trembling with restrained rage. "Return her to me," he growled. Lalaa made her way down the dais. Ka remained lounging on her throne. A mask of disinterest on her face. "And what would we get in return?" Lalaa beamed excitedly. Batlaan's face contorted with a scowl. "Your lives," he growled.

Tension stilled the air like a clenched fist around your throat. Lalaa threw her head back in raucous laughter. "It is a great pleasure to finally meet you, Lord Batlaan. I've heard such... spectacular things." Batlaan's hands fisted at his sides as he spoke. "Bring her to me *now,* or I will end you both where you stand." "Depending on

what you're willing to offer, I may have considered it. But she's actu-
àlly not here,"Lalaa smirked.

Batlaan's gaze slammed down on Quetz.

"At the palace, I mean," Lalaa clarified. Batlaan growled loudly.

I stepped forward, growing impatient. "Either you tell us where
she is, or I send your souls to the realms beyond. Separately."

Fear flashed briefly in Ka and Lalaa's steeled expressions. Lalaa
sighed as she swivelled on her heel to stride toward her throne. "If
you do that, I very much doubt you'll ever find her," she shrugged.

I let my energy press itself upon them, and I watched with some
modicum of satisfaction as their bodies tensed, their knuckles turning
white as they gripped the arms of their thrones. "And if you won't tell
us, then what use are you to us anyway?" I countered. Ka and Lalaa both
made a strangled sound as I willed the air from their lungs. Lalaa raised
a hand, grinning smugly despite being suffocated. I released my magic's
hold to let them speak. "I assure you she is well. Her accommodations
are rather luxurious. Sentinals?" Ka sniffed, caressing her throat. Seven-
foot-tall metallic creatures with humanoid bodies and vacant faces
folded in front of us, armed with chunky L-shaped weapons.

"You will never keep her from me." Batlaan spoke in quiet fury as his
body rapidly shifted into its wolf form. In the blink of an eye, bones
cracked and morphed; silken silver, grey, and white fur covered his
skin. His dark blue eyes began to glow an ethereal color that was such
a deep blue it was nearly violet. His leathers, magically enchanted,
disappeared as his wolf form grew, standing nearly seven feet tall on
all fours. It wasn't the first time I'd seen his wolf form, but it was
breathtaking nonetheless. Ka and Lalaa grinned in amusement. "I
should like to keep your fur as a pelt," Lalaa mused.

. . .

Batlaan snarled, leaping into the air, lunging for the queenes. A small explosion came from one of the sentinels' weapons as a deafening bang rent the air. Blood sprayed from Batlaan's wolf's chest. Morwen and I dove for him as she screamed. The wolf was blown back and hit the ground with a loud smack as Nox and Kyril leapt forwards to form a protective barrier around Morwen and me. An unholy growl came from Idra, who stood behind us. A golden light began emanating from him, and as I turned to look at him, his body began rapidly shifting into his draconic form.

My eyes went wide as he grew to be over 20 feet tall and roared a blast of blue and orange flames down at the sentinels reducing them to ash, only to be replaced by dozens more, folding in front of us and firing streams of projectiles. I willed a shield around all of us, forming a tight bubble with the strength of steel. The deadly projectiles crumpled against it and clattered to the ground. "You have to come out of there at some point," Ka chirped.

Batlaan's wolf form began shifting back into his 'human' form. My attention focused on the wound in Batlaan's chest. Blood spilt from his mouth as he tried to speak, clutching his chest. "Shhhhh," I soothed, pouring healing energy into him as I gently pried his hands from the wound. I tore open his leathers to reveal a gaping hole two inches wide in the centre of his chest. *"What have you done?"* I heard Morwen cry out in a furious roar.

Focused solely on Batlaan, I willed whatever projectile had planted itself in him to dissolve and for the wound to close. Kyril bit into his wrist and lifted Batlaan's head to bring his mouth to the blood spilling from it. Batlaan began to drink, doubling my healing efforts. His eyes widened, locking with Kyril's, as he drank.

· · ·

I looked up to Morwen to find her eyes darkening to the point of black, dark veins rising to the surface of her skin. Morwen began to speak in an ancient tongue, making the fine hairs on my body rise. Quetz and I exchanged a knowing look before he shifted into his incorporeal form: whorls of gold and silvery light, twinning with darkness. Only brief flashes of anything discernibly god or fae-like to then disappear within the whorling energy radiating so much power the hairs on my body rose, and my heart began to pound wildly in response, my own magic near bursting in silent answer. And passed through my shield.

Black tears spilled from Morwen's now wholly black eyes as she rose to her feet and continued chanting as she also took an incorporeal form. *"Holy fuck...,"* Nuala breathed as she watched Morwen pass through the shield. "Kill them!" Ka screamed above the chaos.

One of the 'sentinels' raised its weapon, and panic flooded my veins. *"No!"* Nox roared as he leapt up, and ice rapidly formed around the sentinels' metal bodies, freezing them in place. A stray bullet escaped the ice but merely passed directly through Morwen's now diaphanous body.

The sentinels continued to fire their weapons at Quetz and Morwen, bullets passing harmlessly through them. I felt no small swell of satisfaction watching the two queen's eyes widen in fear as they closed in on them. Ka and Lalaa rose to their feet, swords materialising in their hands. Morwen laughed mirthlessly at the sight. Everything in Morwen's path began to blacken before turning to ash.

Lalaa shielded Ka with her body as she screamed. "Enough!" Quetz and Morwen paused on the steps of the dais. Morwen breathed a deadly promise. "You will retrieve my daughter-in-law. And you will assist us in finding the one they call 'Le Mont'. Or I will forbid Quetz from devouring your souls so that I can pry it from your body myself and torture it until I grow bored... *I am easily amused.*"

Batlaan, having now fully recovered, strode up the dais to tower over them. "Where?" Batlaan growled. Ka and Lalaa exchanged a glance before Ka spoke. "She's being kept at King Dorcas's old villa in the mountains." "And who or *what* is guarding her? More of your 'sentinels'?"

Ka shook her head and gave a mirthless laugh. Lalaa spoke for her. "No. No one guards it. It has two wards: The first prevents anyone, other than us or those we permit, from finding her or her location. And the second prohibits her from leaving and limits her use of magic. She won't be able to feel your presence here in Caligo, despite the tether linking the two of you." Batlaan narrowed his eyes at them, offended that they hadn't thought to protect her.

"What do you mean she's not being guarded? So there's no one protecting her in case someone was able to get passed your wards?"

"Have you met your mate?" Ka seethed. "Initially, we tried sending guards to deliver her food and supplies because we thought she might appreciate the company, but they'd never return because apparently, she'd just slaughter them. And to this day, every time I send sentinels in to deliver her food, she destroys them. Not to mention, there's no one here... The only others residing in this realm are those you saw in my throne room, and they have no idea who Eleni even is. We didn't even know who she was until she was brought to us. They're the only ones who survived or remained after Ka and I usurped Dorcas."

. . .

The group of us exchanged wary looks. "And who exactly brought her to you?"

Ka and Lalaa shared a fearful look. "Her father."

Batlaan gave Kyril a meaningful look, to which Kyril gave a firm nod in promise. "Take us to her."

"Wait." Idra had resumed his human form and shifted a single finger into a black talon nearly half the length of my forearm. He knelt in front of the Queen closest to him, Ka, and placed the claw at her throat; a bead of blood trickled down from where the tip of it was pressed. His voice quiet with menace. "Where's Le Mont?"

Ka and Lalaa's eyebrows both furrowed before Ka's eyes sought out Lalaa's, seemingly communicating through their tether. "Speak *aloud,*" Idra growled, applying more pressure to the talon. The blood beading at Ka's neck began trickling, quickly pooling at her collarbones and between her breasts. Lalaa trembled, watching Ka, whose cold features revealed nothing. "I-..." Idra's attention snapped to Lalaa., her throat working on a swallow as she spoke. "We have no idea who he is...," her voice wobbled as the words spilled from her lips, " Idra's eyes narrowed. "And yet you know who we speak of." Lalaa shook her head fearfully. "Only because he stole the Sigillum Lucis from Lux Dryadalis. We overheard Eleni's stepmother telling her about it just the other day...."

I folded the group of us as close to King Dorcas' mountain villa that the wards would allow: about a quarter mile. Batlaan turned to the Queens. "How do we disable the wards so she can leave?" Ka shrugged her narrow shoulders and nodded in my direction. "This one should be able to. Other than that, only her father, I Imagine. He was the one who put them in place."

· · ·

Batlaan didn't bother to respond and took quick sweeping strides before he took off at a run, already sensing which direction his mate was. Morwen didn't hesitate to take off after him, promptly followed by Nox. Kyril and I exchanged a wary look before turning back to look at the remainder of our group. Idra's voice was deceptively calm. "I'll wait here with them." He shifted into his dragon form and curled his tail around them, clutching them so tightly they wheezed. Nuala produced The Bonds of Sakachi and clamped the manacles around their neck, wrists, and ankles. "Just in case."

Kyril and I strode after Batlaan, followed closely by Quetz and Nuala, slowing only when we caught sight of Batlaan's enormous silhouette in the dark, illuminated solely by the ethereal glow of the wild, jungle fauna several yards ahead. Morwen and Nox stood just behind him as she rubbed soothing circles on Batlaan's back. My ears pricked, straining in the cacophony of the jungle. In the distance, I could hear a female's soft, melodious humming. We rounded Batlaan's silhouette to find tears streaming down his cheeks. I peered up at him, his throat working on a swallow.

Kyril laid a supportive hand on his shoulder. Kyril spoke gently. "What are you waiting for, brother?" Batlaan wiped at his cheeks. "Her voice. I haven't heard her beautiful voice in so long... I-," Batlaan's jaw flexed, trying to quell his emotions before continuing. "I don't want her first time seeing me in nearly twenty years to be me in pieces like this. I've always been strong for her... What if Lisbet was right, and she moved on?" Kyril gave me a meaningful look, silently expressing what an impossibility that was. Kyril huffed a laugh. "If Eleni heard you speak such nonsense, she'd break your nose." I couldn't help but give a soft chuckle at this. Morwen proudly hummed her agreement. I didn't even know Eleni, but already I knew I was warming to her. A grin split Batlaan's face as he wiped away the last of his tears, shaking his head, and laughing softly.

. . .

"Hello?" A velvety female voice called out. Presumably, Eleni. Batlaan's breath caught, and he strode forward. The jungle's luminous flora lighitng the way. Eleni's voice took on an annoyed tone, "I swear to the Gods, if you forgot my makolo fruit again, I'm going to smash that metal-." Her voice cut off briefly, followed by a choked cry. Morwen, Kyril, and I rushed forward to catch up with Batlaan to find Eleni clutching onto Batlaan like a baby Koala.

Batlaan clutched her to his chest firmly, dropped to his knees, still holding her tightly, and sat back on his heels. Eleni, looking to be less than half of Batlaan's size, openly sobbed. Batlaan shook with the force of his emotions and his attempt to tamp them down. My heart ached for them, and Kyril's hand quickly found my own and pulled me into his chest. "Promise me that no matter what happens, Kyril, we will *always* find a way back to each other." Kyril took my face in his hands and firmly held my gaze. "Aurelia, not even *death* could keep me from you."

I nodded, remembering his words and how he had dreamt of me and found his way to me even after I'd died in my previous life. "Even if I had to find my way to Lisbet's dimension to reunite with your soul- I would...," he whispered as he pressed my body so firmly against his that it felt as though if he could, he would try to push me inside of him to protect me and always keep me there. Because I was as much a part of him as he was to me. Two halves made whole.

After bringing down the wards, which proved to be only slightly more difficult than I'd anticipated, we trudged our way back to where Idra waited with Ka and Lalaa. The entire time Batlaan clutched Eleni to his huge chest with her legs tightly coiled around his waist.

Her face buried in his neck. When we reached Idra and the queens, she finally slid down his body, and he, reluctantly, set her on her feet. She swiftly withdrew the short sword holstered to Batlaan's thigh and turned, clearly unafraid of the enormous dragon in front of her, and launched herself at Ka and Lalaa, roaring with a fury and power that paralleled even Batlaan's as she swept her arm out.

Ka and Lalaa's eyes widened, lips parting to scream, but before they could, the sword connected with their necks. A red seam bloomed at their throats, like some macabre necklace. They blinked. The group of us held our breath for what felt like the longest second in eternity before Lalaa's head toppled forward, swiftly followed Ka's and rolled to a stop at her feet.

Batlaan stepped forward, pulling her back into his chest and caressed back the wild red curls from her face as she panted heavily. *"Anima mea...,"* he spoke into her ear and slid his hand over hers. *My soul.* The shortsword clattered to the ground. Eleni shaking with her rage, looked down at the heads of Ka and Lalaa and spat. "That was hasty of me. Such a swift death was a mercy they did not deserve." Batlaan nuzzled her neck and hair. "There will be more blood, my queen." She turned to face him to stare into his eyes. "I know. *My father's.*"

26

I folded the group of us into Batlaan's war room. The collective energy heavy with anxiety in anticipation of meeting Lussathir, Eleni's father, The Emperor of Lux Drydalis. Yet *another* seal had already been stolen. Not even 24 hours had passed since Lisbet had disappeared to give Le Mont Batlaan's seal. At this rate, he'd have collected the remaining seals in only a few days time. Batlaan and Eleni were the first to try and leave the room, Idra stepping in front of the door to block their exit. Eleni's expression hardened as she took him in. Idra's voice was empathetic. "I know you are traumatised and exhausted, your highness. But... The one they call 'Le Mont'... he has kidnapped my mate. I cannot rest until I find her."

Eleni's expression softened at this. She took a deep, shaky breath and gently shook her head. "I promise to do everything I can to help you find her but you need to be prepared for the worst outcome..." The unspoken meaning behind her words caused tears to swell in Idra's dark golden eyes. His hands fisted at his sides and blood trickled onto the floor at his side.

· · ·

Eleni laid a hand on his shoulder. "My stepmother... she's a seer. A lot of what she says can seem... like nonsensical ramblings... if you don't piece them together. But we should speak to her. I'm sure she will have some insight." Idra nodded, hope lighting a fire in his eyes. "I am ready." Eleni took a deep breath. "My father keeps her locked in a private wing of his palace. It's heavily guarded. I'm only able to communicate with her via an ensorcelled mirror..." Eleni turned to look at Batlaan. "Do you have my old one?" Batlaan smiled gently at her. "*Dulcis anima mea...* I kept everything of yours."

Morwen folded out of the war room to retrieve the mirror and returned a few breaths later. The mirror was entirely ordinary look- ing- round with a tarnished bronze frame and about a foot and half in diameter, much like a picture frame with a leg that popped out of the back to prop it up on a table. We set it on the same table that Idra's body had rested on only a few hours ago and gathered around it.

Eleni murmured a few ancient words, and instead of reflecting us, the mirror's glass revealed a ceiling painted with the night sky in an ornately decorated bedroom with flowery, gilded decor. From the angle, it seemed as though the mirror was lying on the floor. "*Aelia...,*" Eleni whispered into the mirror.

We waited several seconds but heard nothing. "*Aelia...* I need your help." Eleni's eyebrows furrowed. "That's so weird... Her mirror fits in her pocket, and she carries it with her everywhere...I don't-." Quetz stilled beside me. "Shh." His eyes closed. "Do you hear that?" The group of us collectively strained to listen. Ever so faintly, I could just barely make out the sound of someone breathing softly. "Perhaps she's sleeping?" Nox offered.

. . .

I opened my senses to feel for Aelia. My breath caught as the sensation of a waning life force filled my veins. "Eleni...," I breathed, and I felt Kyril's hand tighten around my waist, "Something's not right... Her life force is fading." Panic filled Eleni's eyes as she quickly leapt to her feet. "I have to go get her. My father-." Batlaan cut her off and pulled her to him, frantic fear in his eyes at the idea of her leaving him again. "We'll go with you." She shook her head. "No, no one can fold into the house except for royal family members. I don't even know if I still can, but I need to try. I'll fold directly into Aelia's room, retrieve her and come right back."

Batlaan's hands shook as he spoke, "No. Eleni, if he catches you there...." She brought her finger to his lips. "He won't. I'll be right back." Batlaan's hold on her tightened around nothing as she disappeared instantly, folding into Aelia's bedroom. Aelia's gasp echoed in the room through the mirror, and a soft cry left her lips. The view from our end of the mirror shifted as though it skidded a few feet across the room. "Eleni!" Batlaan bellowed.

Eleni folded back into the room, carrying in her arms a slender woman with golden hair that was so long it pooled on the floor beneath her. Blood actively dripped onto the floor from a gaping wound on her throat. The group of us rushed to help her lay her body carefully on the floor. "Morwen, grab your healing elixirs!" Aelia's eyes were closed, her fair skin already turning blue. I reached forward, placing my hands over the wound and willed it closed. When I removed my hands, the wound had closed, but I couldn't will the blood back into her body. Aching despair filled my senses, and I looked up to see tears streaming down Eleni's cheeks. Aelia's chest had stilled.

.   .   .

A chill passed over me, and I closed my eyes at the sensation. I could feel her soul leaving her body. "Kyril, give her your blood, *please...*," Eleni begged. My throat worked on a swallow. I couldn't muster the words to tell her it was useless. Kyril's jaw clenched as he took a harrowing breath, knowing as well as I that it was already too late, but did as she asked, opening his wrist for her with his teeth and placing it over Aelia's mouth. His blood dribbled into and over her mouth, some spilling across her cheeks. "*Aelia...*," Eleni cried, "*Please... I need you.*"

Nuala, Quetz, Idra, and I watched in silent horror as Eleni clutched Aelia's lifeless body to hers. Batlaan draped his body over hers as if he could somehow shield her from the pain. Nox and Morwen exchanged a pained look before Morwen touched Kyril's arm and gave him a meaningful look.

Dinner was brought to our respective rooms. Kyril and I sat at a small dining table by the windows. Neither of us had much of an appetite after the day's events, and a foreboding air seemed to press down on us as the inevitable rapidly approached.

I had just slid my robe off to climb into the bath Kyril had drawn for me when a knock on the door sounded. I opened my senses to find Eleni on the other side of it. Pulling my robe back on, I made my way through the room to find Kyril already answering it. Her gaze met mine as I approached. Her eyes were red and swollen, her whole face puffy, red, and splotchy from weeping. My breath caught at the sight of her. "Eleni- come in," I offered. "Thank you," she nodded, stepping inside. Several guards stood in the hallway behind her.

. . .

As soon as the door snicked shut, she turned to me with pleading eyes. Kyril wrapped an arm around my shoulders and pulled me into his side as she spoke. She bowed at the waist briefly as she spoke. "Batlaan and Morwen tell me you're the Goddess of Origin..." I chewed my cheek, taking a deep breath. I already knew where this was leading. As the Goddess of Origin, I could not only sense life and heal, but I could also call upon and exert my will upon the soul. With nothing more than *feeling* my intention, I could reunite a spirit with it's former body. I could also force a spirit to leave its physical body. However, once any amount of time passed and the spirit had already made its way into the next world, the next dimension... More often than not, it had no desire to return to its physical body. Forcing it to return could cause... tremendous anguish.

I drew a heavy breath, sensing for Aelia beyond... "Eleni... I... Aelia has found her peace already in the next dimension...." Eleni shook her head, tears filling her already swollen eyes. I closed my eyes again, opening my senses to feel Aelia's spirit. A powerful and over-whelming sense of love, peace, and rightness poured into me.

"How do you know?"

"Because I can feel her soul."

"She would be happy and at peace here too. Now that I'm free, she could come here to be with Batlaan and me."

My brow dipped in concern.

"But you know that it's not safe here. Not only with our whole dimension at risk because of Le Mont and whoever he works for, but because you know that your father will come for you. For both of you."

Eleni was visibly trembling with fury, speaking through clenched teeth. "And he will *die.*"

I sighed mournfully at her pain and stepped toward her. "Eleni, I'm sorry-."

"Wait. Please. Before you refuse me, please just listen. My father murdered her... She was a seer. She knew something that he was trying to hide. I know that he loved her in his own sick way. He wouldn't have killed her unless there was something big at stake. And no one else would have dared to touch her. And no one had a reason to. She'd been locked in his fucking palace for the last 40 years. Whatever it is that she knows... It might be the key to all of this."

I frowned at the possibility this was our only lead.

"But her body, it's been too long... The brain can't-."

"Morwen used her magic to preserve it the moment she saw her pass."

A sick feeling of unease coiled in my stomach as Kyril, and I followed Eleni into the guest room where she and Batlaan had laid Aelia. She laid on a large bed, similar to the one in the room Kyril and I shared. Her long hair was pooled around her head like a golden halo. The blue hue her skin had taken earlier was no more. Instead, thanks to Morwen's magic, it radiated with a golden light that made her look purely angelic. Thankfully, they'd changed her out of her blood-soaked dress into a white nightgown.

I looked around the room to find Batlaan, Morwen, and Nox already there. Batlaan approached me, laying an enormous hand on my shoulder in gratitude. "Thank you, Aurelia. I know that this is not... Ideal." I sighed, trying my best to offer a sympathetic smile despite knowing how gruesome this experience would be for Aelia's soul. It had been a long time since I'd dared to do such a thing.

The group formed a wall behind my back as I took one of Aelia's hands in both of mine. It was surprisingly warm. Another gift of Morwen's magic. I made a silent note to myself to talk to her about this at a more opportune moment. I took a fortifying breath and

slowly exhaled. I opened my senses to connect with Aelia's spirit...
and gave it a gentle tug.

As I'd suspected I would, I felt resistance. She had found peace. Why
in all the gods names would she want to return to this realm with so
much suffering? Especially in her case, considering she'd been
trapped for the last 40 years in a gilded cage and murdered by her
own husband. I sent a wave of love and reassurance to her spirit and
tried to give her another gentle pull. Fear shot through me from her
spirit, and it recoiled. I opened my eyes and let go of Aelia's hand.
Eleni was literally holding her breath, anxiety gripping lovely her
features. "What's wrong?"

Batlaan tucked her in closer to his side. I chewed my cheek, deciding
against vocalizing any of this to Eleni. She was traumatized enough.
"Perhaps, it would be a good idea for you and Batlaan to get some
fresh air. These things can be stressful and-."

"No," Eleni said firmly, "I understand, but I need to be here for
her when she returns. I'm the only one she trusts. It'll be worse for
her if I'm not here when she returns."

My throat worked on a swallow, and I tried not to grimace.

Morwen and Nox gave me reassuring nods as Kyril rubbed soothing
circles on my back. Kyril's words soothed me as he spoke within my
mind. *"Aurelia, if you aren't comfortable with this, tell me. I'll take care of
it. And we will find another way to get to Le Mont."* I gave a subtle shake
of my head. *"We don't have time to find another way... At this rate, he's
probably already gotten yet* another *seal. We just haven't heard about it
yet."*

.   .   .

I sat down beside Aelia, pressing my hands to her forehead and heart, and closed my eyes. I pushed as much love, healing, and soothing energy into her soul and body that I could muster while reaching out again for Aelia's spirit. This time I didn't bother gently tugging. This needed to happen quickly. Better to rip it off like a bandage than to prolong the torment of slowly dragging her back. As soon as I connected with it, I exerted my will over her and felt a chill pass over me as I, regrettably, forced her ethereal body to return to her physical body. My face contorted in a grimace at the sensation of literally having to slam her soul back into a corporeal cage.

I opened my eyes, feeling the aether energy now residing in her body again. Aelia's eyes moved beneath her lids, and a frown tilted the corners of her mouth. Eleni leapt towards her to take her trembling hand, but they began to roam over her body, settling on the space between her breasts. She began to tug so vigorously at her nightgown that she was clawing at her skin. A pained groan escaped her, and her body began to curl into the fetal position. Eleni settled for placing a hand to her cheek. Aelia hardly seemed to notice. "Aelia, it's Eleni... You're safe now, with Batlaan and me."

Aelia's eyes popped open at this, and as soon as they focused, they darted frantically between us as her voice trembled. "What is this? Why am I here?" Her gaze landed on me, and terror contorted her features. *"You,"* she seethed, revealing the whites of her eyes, *"Why did you bring me back to this place? I don't belong here! This is wrong! Send me back!"* My lips parted as tears pricked my eyes. Kyril pulled me against him. Eleni caressed her hair and tried to soothe her with reassuring words. "Aelia, look at me. Do you remember me?" Aelia's fearful gaze slowly shifted to Eleni's, and her throat worked on a swallow as her face began to crumple. *"Eleni...,"* she wept, shaking her head, "You don't know what you've done." Kyril began to pull me away from Aelia's bedside. Batlaan gave us an apologetic nod as Morwen and Nox walked with us to the door.

Morwen laid a hand on my shoulder. "Thank you... I know that Eleni... Words won't be able to express her gratitude.." I nodded weakly in understanding. Nox gave Kyril a pat on the shoulder. "Try to get some rest. We'll give you an update in the morning."

By the time we returned to the bedroom, I felt the weight of the last couple of days and its events crushing me with exhaustion mentally, emotionally, spiritually, and physically. I couldn't even bring myself to bathe. Kyril sensed this and swept me up in his arms. He walked me to the bed and laid me down with all the tenderness and care fathomable before crawling in bed beside me, pulling the blankets over us as he tucked me against his body. As my eyes shut of their own volition, I felt him caress my hair back and lay tender kisses on my temple and cheeks. *"Sleep, my fire."*

And with that, I fell into a deep sleep. For how long, I had no idea. It could have been thirty seconds or 30 years. It was well known that time, in reality, wasn't at all how we perceived it. Not to mention that traveling into other dimensions meant that the amount of time passing here was very different from the amount of time passing beyond...

The air was warm. Hot even, despite it being dark... wherever this was. The energy here was powerful, so much so that I could feel every molecule of my body vibrating with it. I looked around, somehow able to see in a darkness so deep from the absence of light, yet my vision was crystal clear. A rippling wave of faint light moving across the surface of the water made its way towards me. As it reached me, I looked down to see that my feet were indeed standing on top of a body of water. I hadn't realized because the water's temperature was so warm I couldn't discern where my body ended, and the water began. The light on the ripple of water kissed my skin, and a warm tingle of energy that had my heart swelling with emotion made my breath catch. It made its way up and down my body before continuing into the distance behind me.

I began to tread on the water's surface in the direction of where the light had come from. The further I walked, the more intense the energy in this... place... became. The sound of rushing water could faintly be heard in the distance. My footsteps quickened, the sound of the rushing water intensifying- the sound of a waterfall. I broke into a sprint, feeling a powerful pull in the direction I was heading. I let out a yelp as the water beneath my feet gave way to nothing, and I skidded to a stop just at the edge of the drop-off.

The water I'd been running on spilled over the edge, disappearing into the blackness. I looked up, and in the distance, across a vast expanse of nothingness, I could see bodies of land floating. Illuminated from within, it appeared. Gleaming a vibrant green from the verdant life spilt over the land's edges. Some even had more waterfalls spilling over the edge. I gaped in awe, my eyes gradually being drawn to the many different lands and the stars that twinkled above.

A soft, deep chuckle sounded behind me. I whirled to find a tall, powerfully built, naked male striding leisurely toward me. An impressive set of wings, were flared slightly behind him, as if to prevent them from dragging in the water. The feathers were a dark gold, each feather a varying shade that seemed to glow from within, much like the floating islands in the distance. I tried, and failed, to prevent my eyes drifting down his muscled form to the 'v' between his hips where another remarkably impressive something was hung. Earning me another chuckle.

"I always forget how foreign nudity is to those of the nine realms... so bizarre." His voice was deep and smooth. Each word he spoke felt like a familiar caress, laced with love and affection. A loincloth, nearly the same shade as his golden skin and wings, appeared and wound itself low on his hips. "Is that better?" he asked, a dimple appearing as he gave me a lopsided grin.

"I wasn't complaining," I exhaled, feeling no small amount of disappointment at the appearance of the loincloth. He threw his head back as a deep, warm laugh erupted. His laugh sounded strangely familiar. My mind searched its recesses, but I couldn't recall... anything. I had no sense or knowledge of self. Only that I was. I looked down at my form in wonder before looking up to find him standing only a foot away from me.

"Who are you?" I asked. His head tilted to the side, a soft smile brightening his perfectly formed features. His expression seemed to say I should already know the answer. He hummed thoughtfully. "I am known by many names...." My brows drew together. "This is my realm. I am the God of the Dead...," he said, his voice wrapping itself around me like a blanket of love. I gazed around at his realm, searching inwardly for recognition but found nothing but a pang of disappointment. My heart ached at his frown. "Soon. Soon all will be made clear." I looked up and around us, only just seeing the mouth of the yawning cave we were standing in. "And... what am I?"

His full, cupid's bow lips parted to reveal his perfect white teeth, the most beautiful smile I'd ever seen. Though at this point, it was the only smile I'd ever seen. "You are the one whose heart beats as one with all that lives and dies. All creation answers to the aether of your being. You are the guardian of all souls, The Goddess of Origin." He closed the distance between us and laid his large palm between my breasts, which I also only just realized were bare. As his hand flattened against the centre of my chest, my entire form seemed to dissolve and burst all at once.

The very molecules of my being bloomed and blossomed, flowering around him, filling the space surrounding him. A joy and peace I'd never known filled me, along with another feeling that caused my being to expand exponentially- love. Overwhelming love and unity. I could tangibly feel the droplet of divinity that existed within all creation. And that I was deeply, intrinsically connected to all of it. I could feel the breath of all that lived. I felt the whispers of an infinite number of beings. Another familiar, loving caress. I felt myself, whatever that was, expanding even further... feeling the ends and beginnings of infinite worlds, lives, forms, all shifting. Never dying, only changing. They all seemed to cling to me, reach for me like a flower seeks the sun and rain.

I then found a dark golden energy intertwining with mine, and I felt... whole. In a manner that could only be described as thoughts without words, a knowing filled my being as he spoke. "There is a veil that exists between the verses, the realms, and dimensions...." Before the question, "Why?" even fully formed in my mind, his answer filled me. "The Ones before us willed it into existence to create order and evolution. For aeons, I have been the shepherd of the dead, weighing the virtue of souls who spend millennia in your realms all so that they may evolve and eventually be reunited with The Ones who came before us... This veil must remain. My son has grown disillusioned in his suffering-"

. . .

My being was sucked back into this strange body that suddenly felt terribly unnatural and confining. For a breath of a second, I gazed upon his familiar and awe-inspiring beauty before his gaze snapped to the yawning cave entrance. "We are not alone," he growled. His face contorted into a rictus of rage as he spoke with grave urgency. "Wake, Aurelia."

I felt as though my spirit was slammed back into my body, much as I'd imagined it had felt for Aelia earlier this evening. My eyes burst open to see Kyril launching himself at someone behind me just as the feeling of cool metal slid across my throat, followed by a soft click. Terror filled my *v*eins like a bolt of lightning. Before the scream could even leave my lips, a large hand covered my mouth, and I felt myself being folded.

Through towering floor-to-ceiling windows shone bright golden light that filled a room with vaulted ceilings decorated in golds, greens, and lilacs. *Lux Dryadalis.* The room was unmistakably similar to Aelia's. My kidnapper's hand still smothered my mouth. I thrust an elbow as hard as I could into his gut, pivoted my hips to the side whilst reaching behind me to grip the front of his shirt and sliding one of my legs between his to leg sweep him as I threw him to the ground. I pressed my bare foot to the throat of my attacker and stared down into a familiar face. *Lussathir.* Eleni's father. I hadn't seen him since Nuala, and I had asked for his help during the war. And he had declined.

A choking laugh escaped him. He had a tan, handsome face with sharp features and a beaming white smile that reminded me of a predator flashing its fangs. Long, pale blonde hair pooled around his head from where he was splayed on the floor. "Impressive...," my attacker wheezed. My foot pressed harder onto his throat as I realized he was probably referring to my naked body. I willed fighting silks to cover my form, but nothing happened. My hand went to the collar around my throat as I growled. "If you don't remove this collar, I'm going to fucking kill you. *Now,*" I seethed.

Lussathir folded, leaving my foot stepping on nothing more than the rug covering the polished wood floor, and reappeared standing a few feet away. "Oh, trust me. I plan on it. *After* we come to an understanding." A robe materialized in his hand, and he tossed it to me. I examined it suspiciously before slipping it on.

"The only understanding you need to have is that holding females captive is not the answer to your problems," I ground out, still tugging uselessly at the palladium collar. Lussathir laughed. "Don't I know it." My eyes scanned the room for a weapon but found little more available to me than the lamp on the nightstand beside the bed and the sash tying my robe closed.

My eyes, and breathing, stilled as my gaze landed on the unmoving form of a petite redhead lying unconscious on a chaise longue on the other side of the room. *Lisbet.* Shock barrelled through me at the realisation Lussathir was *Le Mont.* I tried to open my senses, but the palladium collar prevented me from being able to detect if Lisbet was still alive. As I studied her, trying to watch for the rising and falling of her chest, I noticed she also wore a palladium collar. "Don't worry, she's still alive. For now," Lussathir said nonchalantly. My gaze snapped to him. "*You're Le Mont.*"

Lussathir smirked. "I have many names." I narrowed my eyes at him. The bizarre dream I'd had suddenly came to the forefront of my mind at the familiar words. However hazy the dream felt now, nothing about the male in front of me was similar to the one in my dream in any capacity. I shook my head at him. "What could you possibly seek to gain by opening the portal between dimensions?" The male's words in the dream filled my mind, *"... This veil must remain. My son has grown disillusioned in his suffering-..."* This elven sack of excrement couldn't possibly be related to the God of the Dead...

Lussathir sighed wistfully, cutting off my train of thoughts. "My mate." My jaw dropped. "Lussathir... She died more than 300 years ago. You can't be serious. She's probably already reincarnated somewhere else." Lussathir beamed and took a step forward. "Farrah is my Nexus. Wherever she is, in the dimension beyond or reincarnated elsewhere, she will want to be with me." I shook my head in disbelief. "And what if she's been reincarnated? And is a child elsewhere? Or has a family and children?" Lussathir snarled. "Her soul is the same. She belongs with me."

I took a deep breath, trying to decide how to argue with 'crazy'. I also couldn't help but wonder how I would feel in his position. If something had happened to Kyril, what extremes I would go to in order to be reunited with him... I couldn't say I wouldn't do 'crazy' and terrible things. However, potentially ending a child's life and/or tearing apart a family... I could confidently say that was a line I wouldn't cross. To spare myself suffering by forcing it upon others... It was inconceivable.

"And what if her soul is in peace, elsewhere? Have you ever seen what happens to a person when they've been forced back into a body after the soul has left?" Lussathir's face tightened. "Gods, you're as self-righteous and stubborn as you ever were," he sneered. I rolled my eyes in genuine boredom. "Don't even try to pretend like you wouldn't do the same if something happened to Kyril. Perhaps I should have kidnapped him to gain your cooperation?"

I clenched my jaw so hard I was surprised I didn't crack a molar. "If you so much as lay a finger on him, I'll spend the rest of eternity causing you unimaginable suffering. And I'll also make sure that Farrah's soul never enters this dimension again." Lussathir's nostrils flared, jaw ticking. Before he could retort, a soft moan had our attention jerking back to Lisbet. I rushed over to her and dropped to my knees beside her. "Lisbet...," I said, trying my best to keep my voice calm and even. Her eyes remained closed, but she seemed to groan in response. She looked as though she'd been drugged. My gaze slid to Lussathir. "What have you done?" I spat. "Just a little something to calm her down. She was being most unreasonable," Lussathir sniffed.

Lisbet's eyes rolled open, her gaze hazily landing on me and then shifting to Lussathir, at which point horror replaced confusion. Tears filled her eyes.

"Oh Gods, Aurelia...," she shuddered as she tried to sit up but seemed to be weighed down and dizzy. I laid my hands on her shoulders.

"Just lie down, Lisbet. Everything is gonna be ok," I pressed gently.

She shook her head, her bottom lip quivering.

"I tried to resist, but he broke down my palisades and looked into my memories. Or I'd never have told him, I swear."

I shook my head and smoothed her hair from her face. "I believe you, don't worry."

"Is Idra ok?"

"He's worried sick about you but safe as far as I know." Lisbet nodded, tears streaming down her cheeks.

. . .

Lussathir stepped forward to stand beside us, his expression actually resembling something like compassion. "Look, *I'm* trying to be reasonable. All I want is my mate. Nothing more. And the sooner you reunite me with my mate, the sooner you can reunite with yours." I stood to meet his stare. "And what about Lisbet? Are you still going to force her to collect the remaining seals if I help you?" Lussathir's mouth tightened. "Unfortunately for all of us, if she doesn't, then we'll all be killed. The... Entities... I'm dealing with aren't willing to compromise." My stomach churned. Anxiety rose within me, and I could feel the electricity in my body, despite being stifled by the collar, wanting to lash out. "And should I help you, whose body would I be forcing Farrah's soul to reside in?"

Lussathir took a deep breath as if willing himself to have patience. "Well... You see, thanks to the actions of my heedless daughter, I no longer have a body for you to put her soul in." My lips parted in disbelief. "That's why you murdered her?" Lussathir rolled his eyes. "Murder is such a strong word, Aurelia. Aelia was suicidal anyway-" he said with callous nonchalance. I cut him off with a sickened, mirthless laugh. "Oh! I wonder why!" Lussathir ignored my sarcasm and continued. "Ever since I met her, her mind was already half existing in a realm beyond. She was beautiful, remarkably gentle and kind, loving... but utterly insane and mercurial. And wildly demanding. I understand why you think I'm cruel, but if you knew her, I promise you'd wonder if I was actually doing her a favor.

"In any case, after Lisbet returned with the seal last night, it was obvious something had changed, so when I peered into her mind and saw... *you*... I thought all my problems had been solved. All I needed was a body to host my beloved's soul, and you could reunite us. No need to wait for all this sigillum nonsense. I tried to kill her as humanely as possible, and when I left to find you, my daughter had already taken her body by the time I returned. So- this is what's going to happen. Either you put my Nexus' soul in Lisbet's body, or you bring me back the body of my wife. The decision is yours." Lussathir glanced down at Lisbet and examined her, his face tightening again with disappointment. "Although, I do hope you'll choose to bring me back my lovely wife's body."

I was rendered absolutely speechless. I could feel Lisbet's stare burning a hole through me. Her fear was a cloying scent in the air. I knew that he would surely make me swear a blood oath of some kind before he would remove the palladium collar. My mind raced, trying to formulate some kind of plan. An alternative. "What if I bring your soul to hers? If she hasn't reincarnated yet."

Lussathir gave a sad laugh. "You have no idea how often I thought of ending my life with the mere hope that our souls would return to one another in the next realm. But it's a big 'if' if she hasn't been reincarnated elsewhere yet. If I'm not reincarnated, I could be destined to millennia of searching again with no recollection of her. Thankfully, we have other options." A frown carved my face and I felt my chest caving in at the idea of having to go along with this. After a few moments, I managed to close my mouth. "If she hasn't reincarnated yet, and I promise to promptly reunite your souls, will you consider joining her in the next realm as opposed to forcing her to come here?"

Lussathir studied me for a few brief moments, his face neutral. "Who's to say we won't be separated again when we reincarnate?" That I did not have an answer for, and I could only control things so much without upsetting the natural balance of the infinite verses and The Ones. To my surprise, Lussathir seemed saddened by my lack of response. "As I thought." I shook my head, feeling helpless. "Aelia is alive, Lussathir." His jaw clenched, and I could see the stress beneath to surface of his usually calm exterior beginning to rise. "I wonder whose fault that is?" He said in a cool voice that didn't match his tight expression.

"And what if she has been reincarnated? What if I can convince her to come to you?" Lussathir's features relaxed at the idea, but his eyes narrowed. "And what if she's been reincarnated, like you said, and is a child- surely you aren't proposing you kidnap her?" My jaw dropped in horror at the idea, but he continued, becoming increasingly frustrated. "Or she's been reincarnated into some unfortunate circumstance? Or is now male?"

I quirked a brow. "You would turn away your nexus because of her gender?" A broad grin blossomed on Lussathir's handsome but shrewd features. "*Never.* Nor would it be the first time I'd taken a male either," Lussathir said in a seductive tone before his voice grew cold again, "Males make up at least of the harem I've taken since she died... But I know her. I remember her. She will not know me. And perhaps she is wasting away in some primitive civilization where its people are bizarrely concerned with such things, and she may not want me. There are entirely too many 'ifs'."

I glanced down at Lisbet, who remained silent but had calmed, tears no longer streaming down her face, and her fear scent had dissipated somewhat. It fortified my hope. My voice was firm as I met his hopeful gaze. "At least allow me to see. Perhaps she is young and beautiful-."

"My mate will be beautiful no matter her form or age," Lussathir snapped, "She is everything I am not. The love, grace, tenderness, and selflessness that her soul exudes are incomparably beautiful to anything I have ever witnessed. Nothing could hold a candle to her."

I nodded, my heart softening a little towards him at his words. "Even so, perhaps I can find her and introduce the two of you, and you can give her the chance to fall in love with you all over again. Instead of potentially causing her pain and suffering by forcing her into a strange body, away from everything she may have grown to love wherever she is- and all the suffering that would cause her loved ones. These are things she might resent you for...."

Lussathir seemed to be mulling this idea over, but his face revealed nothing. "You realise the odds of this are rather slim?"

I sighed heavily. "Yes."

"And if they are not as favourable as such, then you will put her soul back in my wife's body? Or Lisbet's, should we fail to recover my wife from my daughter."

My jaw worked as a feeling of dread overcame me. What if Farrah was a child? Or happily married? Or in the realm beyond all realms, and at peace... My mind spun at all the possibilities that would lead me to have to end more than one person's life. Lussathir shifted as he waited for me to respond.

"And if I don't?"

Lussathir gave me a sad smile. "How far would you go if you and your Nexus were separated?"

My breathing stilled, and Lussathir's eyes twinkled with dark determination. The threat clear. I growled at it. Rage began to simmer at his implication. But part of me actually wanted to help him, within reason. I couldn't imagine going through what he'd gone through losing his Nexus. Before I could respond, screams arose in the distance beyond the bedroom door. Lussathir's eyes flashed with fury. I looked down at Lisbet, who bolted upright and lunged for Lussathir. "Go get them!" She cried out as she and Lussathir toppled to the ground.

I knew that with her power stifled by the collar, Lisbet would only be able to distract him for seconds, if that. Instead of sprinting for the door, I lept for the nearest heavy object- the bedside lamp- and swung it in an overhead arch towards Lussathir's head. Thankfully, in the fleeting second it took for me to do it, the lamp connected with his temple just as the two of them hit the ground.

Lussathir's body lay limp on the floor, blood forming a dark halo around his head as it seeped into the pale rug. Lisbet locked eyes with me as she leapt to her feet. "Run," I breathed. She didn't hesitate to turn and run for the door. I ran behind her, knowing that even if I tied Lussathir to a chair while he was still unconscious, as soon as he woke up, he would simply fold out of his bindings.

As soon as Lisbet and I made it beyond the door and into the hallway, I realized finding our way in this palace without my ability to fold would be like two rats in a maze. The distant sounds of screaming and fighting were our only hope of reaching who I hoped would be Kyril and the others before Lussathir regained consciousness and reached us. Lisbet and I wound down hallway after hallway until we finally reached a large zigzagging staircase. Relief and hope blossomed in my chest as the sounds of fighting finally grew closer. A roar so loud that it shook the palace rent the air. *Idra.*

A hand fisted my hair at the back of my head, terror striking to replace my hope. A choked cry escaped me as Lussathir slammed my head into a polished wood bannister. A sickening crunch echoed in my head as my nose broke and blood burst from my face. I tried to scramble away, without even bothering to clutch my broken nose, only for Lussathir to grab me by my hair again. I gripped one of the wooden spindles supporting the bannister, and my hope renewed at seeing Lisbet racing down the stairs beneath me.

Lussathir jerked my head backwards, inadvertently helping me to rip the spindle free. I roared as I forced my body to rotate towards him, despite his grip tearing out clumps of hair, and speared the sharp, splintered end into Lussathir's gut. I rose to stand as he clutched the spindle protruding from his stomach and spat a mouthful of blood on the floor. "I wanted to help you," I grit out. Lussathir grimaced as he began to pull the spindle from his stomach, but before he could, I hammer fisted his face, and he dropped to his knees. "I would have helped you freely, you asshole." Blood sprayed from his mouth onto the floor. "Please, Aurelia. All I want is my mate," Lussathir gurgled through the blood in his mouth and throat. "And all you had to do was ask nicely." I leaned against the bannister, finally clutching my nose. *Fuck.* Definitely shattered.

"All of this... For nothing. You're such a cunt, Luss. Always were... At least you're consistent." He spoke as he tried to grip the spindle, but it was slippery, drenched in his blood. "Why? Because I wouldn't help you in your gods-forsaken war?" Lussathir finally managed to grip the spindle, roaring in pain as he pulled it free from his abdomen. I lunged forward, and roundhouse kicked him in the face. The sound of my foot connecting with the side of his face made my stomach clench in empathy. He hit the floor like a sack of potatoes.

"Maybe," I grit out through the throbbing pain in my face, "Yes. Among other things." Lussathir rolled onto his side and spat out blood, and what I was pretty sure was a tooth. His body sagged. "I was still mourning Farrah, Aurelia... And I'm tired of fighting. So... fucking tired... Aren't you?" His eyes watered as he met my gaze. I squatted beside him, trying to keep the thigh-length robe covering all my bits. And failing. Although Lussathir, to his credit, couldn't have cared less. His sad gaze didn't wander from my face. I stared down at him, heart blooming in a morose empathy, seeing him for what he was: a broken male. Powerful but broken.

Lussathir was proof of something I'd always innately believed. That the very root of all evil was due to an absence of love. Love, whether it be the love of a partner, children, friends, parents, life purpose, a connection with the divine, etc. Love is our greatest necessity to feel whole and healthy. Without it, we begin to deteriorate mentally, emotionally, spiritually, and even physically.

"I was...," I said softly, not bothering to finish my sentence. Lussathir knew what went unspoken. *Before I found my Nexus.* Tears streamed through the dried blood on his face. He gave me a sad smile. "You see?" I huffed a breath in exasperation. "Always have." After a few moments, I noticed the sound of silence. The distant sound of battle gone. "Let me remove the collar," Lussathir said weakly. I peered at him a little warily for a brief moment before knelt in front of him. He touched the back of the collar and murmured something in an Elven tongue I couldn't interpret.

As it clattered to the floor, I turned to look down at him, my face pinching with pained empathy. "Do you feel her? In this dimension?" He murmured. I sighed deeply, closing my eyes. Relief swept over me as I opened my senses and felt my power run through and out of me in search of Farrah. I felt another sense of relief when a part of my spirit, my magic, came in contact with hers- far outside these realms. *At least we wouldn't be destroying families.*

I shook my head. "She's in a realm beyond... You realise if we bring her back here... No matter what body we put her in, if this 'entity' gets ahold of all the seals, then we're all at risk. And tearing her from her 'home' could be detrimental to her psyche... I'm speaking from a place of love, Lussathir. I am the guardian of souls. It's my duty to protect them and bring them peace...." Lussathir stared at me for several moments, considering my words. Eventually, his gaze left mine, his head turning to stare in the distance for several moments. "Luss?"

He took a deep breath before he met my stare again. His gaze was calm, peaceful. "Can you please bring my soul to hers?" My face scrunched in confusion. His gut wound was almost completely healed already. "Always so dramatic, Lussathir. Your wound's almost fully healed. It was just a little prick," I teased and reached out to rub his arm in encouragement. Tears streamed down his cheeks. "And please... tell my daughter and wife I said I'm sorry." He gave me a sad smile before he opened his palm and a small blade appeared, made of a dark blood-red stone with flecks of gold. *Mors Lapis. Death Stone.* A stone that would kill an immortal with nothing more than single pass of its blade by severing the harness between body and soul.

My breath caught, and I lunged forward to grab the blade but only managed to dive on top of his bloody abdomen as he drew the blade across his throat. Blood spilt in a gushing waterfall down his front. I groaned in frustration as I tried to fling his blood off me, only further making an even bigger mess. "How typical. You abandon us yet again right when we're on the cusp of another war! You realise I can just force you back into another body to come help us don't you!"

Lussathir gave a gurgled laugh and a smug grin. "Whose body?" I ground my teeth so hard I was shocked they didn't crack, letting out a loud growl as I shouted. "Never in all the millennia I've existed have I ever met such a spectacularly selfish cunt." Lussathir gurgled another laugh. "See you... on the other side." My gaze snapped to him. *"What?"* Lussathir nodded towards the double doors behind us. "He's already here."

I stilled and reached out with my senses, quietening my breaths and straining my ears to listen but was met with silence. My heart rate kicked up in fear. What if this entity had managed to kill Kyril? Quetz? Nuala? Morwen, Batlaan, Nox, and Idra... It seemed impossible to imagine. Terror filled my veins. Electricity crackling at my hands. My senses found them, all life forces intact. Some of my tension loosened.

Perhaps Lussathir hadn't meant here as in the palace but just in the realm... I glanced back at Lussathir to ask just as I felt the slightest drop in temperature to find Lussathir's soul had already left his body. *Of* course, *he's left already. Why in the gods' names would I expect anything else?* I sighed in exasperation and stood.

A door behind me swung open and slammed into the wall. I whirled around to find Kyril, followed by Quetz and Nuala. The moment his eyes landed on me, he folded directly in front of me and took hold of me with excruciating gentleness as he examined my face and body, afraid of where to touch lest he aggravates any wounds. "I'm fine, my love," I breathed as I reached up to grab his face and calm his worry. "Where are the others?" Kyril's brows drew together in concern, feeling my worry. "They're waiting for us... Near the palace entrance.

When Lussathir stopped the guards. They refused to let a dragon into the palace. Or his daughter...." I reached out with my senses again and felt them all there. The remaining guards as well.

"Sweet gods, Aurelia... What'd you do to him," Nuala chuckled, snapping me out of my trance. I scoffed, rolling my eyes at Lussathir's lifeless, inconceivably selfish and inconsiderate dead body. "Nothing...," I spat, failing to keep my annoyance out of my tone, "I just stabbed him with a bannister spindle and knocked out a few of his teeth...." Nuala smirked, hiding no small amount of pride. "And am I supposed to assume he slit his own throat?"

I groaned, bending over to pick up the Mors Lapis blade. I willed a sheath for it and slid it inside. "Yes, actually. Fucking abandoned us. Again." As one, their eyebrows rose in synchronicity. "Eleni's gonna be disappointed," Kyril smirked. "Maybe I'll force his inconsiderate ass back into the body of one of his dead guards just so she can kill him herself." Kyril chuckled, "I bet she'd love you for that."

"Aelia told us he was Le Mont," Nuala said with a roll of her eyes, "I was not surprised... Did he say anything about who it is he's working for? Who wants the seals and why?" I gave a mirthless laugh. "Of course not! That would have been entirely too considerate." I chewed my cheek anxiously. My eyes landed on Quetz, who seemed to be studying Lussathir's body; his ominous last words echoed in my mind... *'He's already here....'* I shook the thought from my head. Quetz would never... Not to mention, he had been trapped inside a mirror for over 30 years...

27

Now that Lussathir was gone, the Lux Dryadalis realm's responsibility fell onto Aelia's shoulders, who was illicitly clear about her interest in ruling the realm. She had none. Aelia stared listlessly into some distant corner of the enormous study we sat in. "I haven't been in this room in 90 years...," she murmured to no one in particular. Eleni and Batlaan exchanged and nervous glance. A knot formed in my gut trying to imagine being trapped in the gilded cage of whatever wing of the palace Lussathir had confined her to. I prayed that perhaps she had at least a private garden to escape to. "Yes... he gave me a garden. And no one was allowed there but the two of us."

A boulder landed in my stomach as I promptly fortified the palisades of my mind. Her gaze gradually left whatever it was she'd been staring at and met mine. "Don't bother." I drew in an uneasy breath and looked over at Eleni, whose sole focus was on her stepmother. She went to sit on her heels at Aelia's feet. Aelia looked down at her. "I was finally at peace, Eleni," she said softly. My heart cracked open at the words. I should have refused Eleni from the beginning.

. . .

Eleni's eyes filled with tears and spilt down her cheeks. Quetz stepped forward and took up the spot beside Aelia whose gaze seemed to pass through Eleni as she spoke distantly. "Quetzacoatl, the lonesome creator god of time and benevelonce... I do wonder where your destiny lies...." Quetzacoatl's mouth quirked upwards in one corner as he studied her. "I stopped asking myself that question worlds ago..." Quetz shifted restlessly on his feet as he continued. "Will you help us find the one looking for the seals? And then Aurelia can send you back home?" Aelia's distant expression remained placid but the air became pregnant with something that I couldn't quite put my finger on. Briefly, Aelia's gaze finally rose to meet Quetz. Just before it slid beyond him and landed on Kyril.

GODDESS OF ORIGIN BOOK TWO
PREVIEW

Quetzacoatl
Anahuac, Terrenea
1,150 A.D. in the 11th Heat Death of the Chiggala Sutta

I twined the long, silken blades of grass between my fingers as I laid, eyes closed, on the ground taking in the glorious heat of the sun. The sounds of distant voices and commotion of day-to-day life in the golden city I'd recently settled in were nothing but white noise beneath the glorious whisper of my beloved zephyr, the winds. Until recently, I'd lived amongst the Toltecs for the last few hundred years joyously and peacefully... until recently. I'd grown restless.

As my mind transcended my body, leaving it behind me momentarily like a beloved coat, it drifted yet again to a not-so-distant-realm and a time in the not-too-distant future... A realm where, unlike Terrenea, mostly immortals dwelled, and few humans survived. As I arrived, unseen by all, I stood before a now familiar spot of land beside a turbulent sea that was home to a male and female couple. Both deities like myself. For some reason, still, unbeknownst to me, I had been drawn to them every time I shut my eyes. I watched silently from their balcony as the deity and her mate swam back to the shore of the nearby sea. They laid down on a blanket in the sand, and I turned my head as I saw them begin to make love. Before I could think any better of it, I found myself again pushing against the blanket of space, time, and gravity. Something that, despite being its eternal guardian, even I was warned against meddling with it. Such a powerful yet delicate thing it was. Like that of a spider's web. Capable of bearing enormous weight yet finer than a human hair.

The world around me shifted and morphed as I willed my being through time. As though diving through the pages of a book. I watched as day shifted to night, seasons changed, and guests came and went. I leapt forward another two hundred years... just to see... the deity now stood only a few feet away from me, leaning against the rail of the balcony. Her mate knelt before her, and nuzzled his face against her swollen, pregnant belly. The male's nostril's flared just as his mate's gaze shifted to mine. My heart took a guilty leap at being caught peering in on such a private, intimate moment. And although I knew they couldn't see me, a knowing grin crossed her face, and she opened her mouth to speak, but before the word's left her mouth, I pressed again into the blanket of space, time, and gravity; this time harder and faster. Why was I being called here?

I willed another quarter of a century to pass in an instant. And then I saw her. Darkest umber hair, light golden skin, bright hazel eyes. She stood on the balcony laughing through a mouthful of strawberry as she shouted back to her father and mother, who were inside their home. My whole being stilled, and even though I didn't have a physical heart in this form, it still stopped and my breath caught at the sight of her. Her smile alone burned a hole straight through my soul.

The sound of someone loudly clearing their throat behind me had me snapping out of my reverie. Time had stilled. I sighed heavily. Already knowing who it was that stood behind me. "Can I help you with something, Moirai?" I took my time, forcefully having to peel my eyes away from the female in front of me, suspended in laughter and the most beautiful thing I'd ever seen, to turn and face Moirai. She had taken on the unified form of the three sisters I knew as Clotho, Lachessis, and Atropos. It was a deliberately intimidating display. Moirai's form oscillated, expanding and condensing almost like that of a folding fan. The three sisters weaving in and out of one another like humanoid tendrils of smoke. Their expressions *never fixed, ever mercurial and chaotic, yo-yo-ing from blissful peace and love to dark and malevolent.*

There weren't many beings that I found intimidating... but she was one of them. I steeled myself, knowing this jarring display was put on purely so they could feed off my reaction. Their voices somehow rang in harmony and discord as they responded in unison. "Do not abuse your gifts, guardian. You wouldn't like the consequences...." The Moirai's eyes, shifting in and out of fractals, and drifted to the woman behind me. Their grins one, and several, grew. I stepped closer to them, blocking their view of her. They threw their heads back and laughed.

The Moirai shifted into their most attractive form: Clotho. Her fair features and golden hair draped over her bare shoulders. She strode toward me in a gossamer night-gown-like garment that, although it was so long it trailed on the ground behind her, I could still see much of the naked body beneath. Her form did nothing but repel me. Because I knew the creature inside.

Despite being in my ethereal body, Her delicate hands swam up the broad panes of my chest. Her palest blue eyes were heavy-lidded as they slid up to mine. Her voice became a seductive purr, but it only reminded me of a snake slithering in the grass. "You wouldn't want anything bad to happen, now would you?" Rage bloomed in my chest at her implication. "I was only visiting," I managed to say coolly, forcing myself to hold her gaze. She hummed as if deciding whether or not to believe me. Though I was, in fact, telling the truth. Most of it.

Her eyes glazed over, becoming brilliant pools of silver.

"So fascinating how the threads of destiny weave themselves...."

I stared down at her, feigning boredom.

"And not even you can manipulate them."

A grin parted her pretty lips to reveal her pointed fangs. "Can't I? Is it not I who weaves the threads of life?"

I couldn't help the small smile sketching one corner of my mouth. "Human life."

Her eyes flashed, returning to their pale blue, her grin broadening even further.

"And oh, the havoc humans can wreak."

THANK YOU

Thank you to my family and friends, who have been so unwaveringly
supportive and believed in me even when I had a hard time
mustering the strength to believe in myself.

Thank you to my readers. Words cannot even begin to express how
grateful I am. The impact you have on the lives of my two boys and
me is truly the stuff of dreams. I wish, from the depths of my heart
and soul, that my writing has had at least a fraction of that positive
impact on you.

Thank you to that source energy, guiding light, inspiration, the
universe, the divine, God/Goddess, or whatever you wish to call it. I
don't dare claim to 'know' what else is out there, simply that I feel
there is something *so* much more beyond what we can even begin to
comprehend or perceive. And that it begins and ends with love.

ABOUT THE AUTHOR

Originally from the US, Chiara Forestieri is a single mother of two [not-do] tiny little love muffins (a 16-year-old and a three-year-old, as of 2022) that spends her days taking care of her small family, practicing Brazilian Jiu-Jitsu and Muay Thai [with the grace of a failing inflatable tube man], pouring her heart and soul into creative and entrepreneurial endeavors, such as this book. All with varying degrees of success , of course. Ranging from 'well, at least no one died!' to 'have you lost your mind?'

Currently, she lives in wonderful London praying desperately for sunshine and warm weather. And while many of her prayers have been answered, this one is most often not.

Some of her favourite things (outside of family and friends) include:

- Hot-warm-and-squishy freshly baked cookies
- Brazilian Jiu-jitsu
- Muay Thai
- All things nature and wilderness
- Animals
- Clean sheets (*drool*)
- Dirty humor
- The sea (her home)
- Sun
- Kindness

- Cuddles
- Oh, and love. Love, love, love. :)